# WOLF'S

# VENDETTA

## CRAIG MACINTOSH

# Wolf's Vendetta

Other books by Craig MacIntosh

*The Fortunate Orphans*
(Beaver's Pond Press, 2009)

*The Last Lightning*
(Beaver's Pond Press, 2013)

*McFadden's War*
(Pugio Books, 2015)

# WOLF'S VENDETTA

ISBN: 978-0-9913611-2-0

Cover design by Kent Mackintosh
Book design by Belldog Media and typeset in Janson Text

Printed in the United States of America
First Printing: 2015

19 18 17 16 15   4 3 2 1 0

Published by Pugio Books
13607 Crosscliffe Place
Rosemount, MN 55068
www.cjmacintosh.com

# ACKNOWLEDGEMENTS

The genesis of this story came from a question I asked a friend about a trip he had taken to Central Asia. He was there to watch a Soyuz launch from Russia's Cosmodome site in the former Soviet republic of Kazakhstan. I was looking for a brief paragraph about his adventure that I might use to reintroduce readers to characters from my previous novel, McFadden's War. The idea was to update my protagonists since their last appearance in print. What began as a few sentences about my friend's tales of the launch and his Moscow stopover resulted in a full-fledged novel. I am indebted to retired Navy SEAL Chuck Wolf for his willingness to share memories of that trip. *Red Mafiya*, a courageous work by the late journalist Robert Friedman exposing the modern scourge of the Russian criminal underworld here at home, also provided major background material for the novel.

My reliable professional crew gave me invaluable support. Editor Cindy Rogers is the lodestar for my novels. All writers should be so blessed. Designer Jeff Wechter provided his skills in getting the book to print and proofreader Molly Miller worked in her usual efficient way to correct any manuscript errors. My brother, Kent Mackintosh, put his design skills to use. My wife, Linda, continues to encourage without complaint.

*"Woe to those who devise wickedness . . ."*
—Micah 2:1

*For the men and women of the CIA, often unappreciated, sometimes maligned, ever dedicated, always vigilant.*

# Chapter 1

*Russia, late winter*

"Napoleon should have flown Air France on his way out of Russia."

From his window seat, Tom Wolf gazed below at a bleak, unbroken landscape stretching to the horizon like a bleached linen burial shroud. The few roads etched in the snow-covered terrain connected towns where buildings huddled together against the cold.

Wolf tapped the glass. "Seriously, I can't imagine the French army, let alone the Germans, fighting and retreating in these conditions, can you?" He elbowed his friend Dan Colter, asleep in the adjacent seat.

Colter did not respond to Wolf's elbow or his comment. Another jab in the ribs and he awoke, irritated. "Huh, what?"

"Dawg," Wolf said, "have you ever seen such an incredible space? There's nothing out there for thousands of miles."

A sleepy-eyed Colter looked past Wolf to the panorama passing beneath them. "Hundreds of thousands of miles, actually."

"Roger that. I was saying how miserable the frogs and krauts must have been slogging through this stuff on their way home."

Colter yawned. "Almost makes you feel sorry for the poor bastards."

"They got what they deserved," said Wolf, grim, his eyes fixed again on the countryside. "Imagine, they had even fewer roads then. Unbelievable."

"With Cossacks kicking ass all the way back to Europe," added Colter, his eyes closing. "How much time we have left in the air?"

"About forty minutes," said Wolf, glancing at his watch.

"Good. Don't disturb me with any more of your 'gee whiz' moments."

Colter went back to sleep and Wolf returned to his window.

Former Navy SEALs who both held commander's rank with ten years in the teams, Wolf and Colter were part of a low-key NASA delegation assigned to keep alive the contact between the two countries' space programs. Flying Aeroflot from Warsaw seven hundred miles to the west, their destination was Sheremetyvo Airport, one of Moscow's three international hubs. The fifteen-member party was en route to witness an American astronaut's ride into space aboard a Soyuz rocket. Scheduled to launch from Kazakhstan in five days, a three-man relief crew was heading to the International Space Station. A three-day Moscow layover was planned for the NASA visitors.

Colter and Wolf carried passports with numerous entry stamps into the U.S. but no imprints from countries they had visited on clandestine missions as SEALs. If questioned about the disparity, the duo had memorized detailed explanations to cover their tracks. As far as the Russians knew, the two were what they appeared to be: retired naval officers accompanying the NASA contingent as guests of the agency. With paperwork scrubbed clean of their time as SEALs, their visas had been issued without a problem.

A closer look at Wolf and Colter might have raised questions. The six-foot, blue-eyed Wolf wore his blond hair longer than his passport photo. Colter, shorter and dark-haired, had shaved his gray-flecked beard, making him appear almost boyish. Career naval officers, yet retired at the relatively young age of forty, both obviously physically fit and not in NASA's employ, why would they be bound for Russia's sprawling version of Cape Canaveral? The question was never asked when their Kazakhstan visit had been approved.

With Moscow's distant lights glittering in his window, Wolf felt the Aeroflot Airbus A330 begin a gradual left-hand turn toward Sheremetyevo International Airport. Colter kept his eyes closed for the final minutes of the flight.

*How can he do that so easily?* wondered Wolf. *Colter could sleep in the middle of a firefight if he wanted to. Definitely an acquired skill few men had.*

Landing in a horizontal burst of snow, they taxied to the terminal.

Bundled in winter parkas, the fifteen Americans were met by a courteous but unsmiling tour liaison officer who shepherded them through immigration and customs. Reclaiming their luggage, the NASA team trailed guide and porters to the Aeroexpress train for the ride to Belorrussky Station near Moscow's heart. When they reached the rail station, their minder commandeered *marshrutkas*—fixed-rate taxis—for the short ride to the Holiday Inn on Lesnaya Street. The minivans delivered them to the hotel where their greeter bid the Americans goodnight. After checking in and having luggage delivered to their rooms, the group reassembled in the lobby and was ushered to the hotel's lounge where a light dinner was served.

From the head of the table, their NASA chaperone, Dr. Fritz Warren, recited the itinerary. "Though it galls me to say it," the bearded engineer said, "we're here because the Russians happen to be running the only game in town these days. You at least deserve the delights of the big city. After all, we're going to Baikonur, not exactly an oasis of comfort and fine dining in the middle of Kazakhstan's desert. But the scale of the rockets and the launch facilities will more than make up for it, I assure you. Good evening."

"Typical NASA geek," scoffed Colter. "Leave it to a rocketeer to care more about hardware than creature comforts or good food."

"He's probably got a career waiting for him in the airline industry when he retires," added Wolf. "And speaking of the devil."

Warren stopped at Wolf and Colter's end of the table. "Your reputations have preceded you, gentlemen. Please try to stay out of trouble. Keep a low profile. I'm sure you can appreciate the situation given the current tensions between our two countries."

"We appreciate the warning," said Wolf. "But you have obviously confused us with someone else. We're retired. That behavior is behind us."

"We're practically ready for assisted living," said Colter.

Warren smiled. "I seriously doubt that, Commander. It's just that I prefer everything run smoothly." Flashing a toothy smile, he left the restaurant with others in the party.

Wolf said, "Well, Dawg, what say we sample this fine hotel's bar."

Colter groaned. "I knew it. I'll go with you on one condition: one nightcap and then I'm heading for the rack."

Wolf grinned. "Don't make promises you can't keep."

# Chapter 2

Morning dawned cold and clear. Up with the sun, Wolf threw off the bedcovers and dropped to the floor for pushups. Scraping frost from the hotel window, he gazed at a Moscow skyline belching steam and smoke. Seen from Wolf's tenth-floor room, bland utilitarian office towers crowded former Tsarist palaces and shops. Shabby Soviet-style apartment buildings squatted next to ostentatious luxury hotels, and omnipresent snow-dusted golden domes crowned with crosses dotted the horizon. *I still can't believe I'm actually in Moscow. Growing up in the Cold War and now*

*I'm actually in the belly of the beast. Ronald Reagan's Evil
Empire. This is incredible, a dream. I'm going to wake up any
moment. Not going to waste the opportunity. I want to see
everything.*

Wolf showered in lukewarm water, shaved and dressed in
layers. Aiming a pillow at the sleeping Colter, he boomed,
"Hit the deck! I'm heading downstairs to get breakfast. Let's
get in some sightseeing. You snooze, you lose."

"I'm awake," mumbled Colter. "Save me a spot downstairs."

"How's your head this morning?"

"Ugh, no thanks to you." Managing a groan, Colter buried
his face in a pillow.

Merciless, Wolf yelled, "Chop chop, sailor! You may have
been through here before, but not me. I'm not likely to get
this chance again."

Wolf went out the door, skipping the elevator to pound
the stairs to the lobby. After flirting with an icy blond
manning the front desk, he took a corner table in the first-
floor lounge and asked for coffee, juice and pastries.

Colter showed twenty minutes later, ordered the same
and pilfered one of Wolf's sweet rolls while he waited.
"What are we doing today?"

Wolf unfolded a large map and studied it. "Got this from
the front desk. This being my first time here I want to see
Red Square, the Kremlin, Lenin's Tomb, St. Basil's..."

"Whoa, whoa, I had to ask."

The server arrived with Colter's order and a carafe,
then withdrew.

Wolf poured coffee for both. "Did I mention Lubyanka?"

"The KGB dungeons? I've heard they give tours.
Don't know if I'm up for that. But don't forget the
subway, Wolfman."

"Outstanding. Their Metro's famous. We can buy a ticket and ride forever. How much trouble can we get into playing tourist?"

Colter arched an eyebrow. "With you along? Don't ask."

While Colter finished his breakfast, Wolf asked the concierge to arrange a taxi to Red Square. After a wasted hour, their ride arrived.

"Lubyanka," said Wolf. Their driver careened into Moscow's traffic with abandon.

"Try to get us there in one piece," added Colter under his breath.

Amazed by the constant stream of newer, expensive cars passing them, the two picked out Audis, Porsches, and Mercedes. Here a Range Rover, there an Escalade. Sleek black Zil limousines, imperious and reluctant to share the road, overtook them, hurrying past. Across the city, sunlight reflected from church cupolas clustered like gold onions amidst monolithic Stalinist towers from another era. Their street-level view of glass-sheathed office buildings and upscale shops was eye opening—New York's Fifth Avenue with the Kremlin as a backdrop.

Skeletal cranes hovered over side streets blockaded by backhoes, cement trucks, and plodding construction crews altering Moscow's face yet again. On the main streets the city's pace was constant. A river of traffic in flood stage surged around islands of Romanov wedding-cake architecture converted to luxury condos or refurbished hotels for wealthy Muscovites and foreigners. The scent of new wealth was in the air—along with an unmistakable whiff of corruption.

Billboards that once trumpeted images of the Soviet Man, tractors, and apple-cheeked Amazons from collective farms now hawked Chanel, furs, and luxury cars. Instead of gigantic dour portraits of Lenin and Marx, passersby now hurried past ads for Rolex watches, Dior, Google, and L'Oreal cosmetics.

Wolf shook his head. "When I was a kid I read something about Khrushchev saying they would bury us. Man, he's gotta be spinning in his grave."

"Capitalism cometh, capitalism triumphs," said Colter.

Having seen enough, Wolf sat back, sighed. "I suppose this is progress."

"Better than the old days of the gulag."

"Oh, that's still out there somewhere."

Colter tapped their driver's shoulder, asked, "Speak English?"

"Nyet," he grunted without looking. He brought the cab to a stop at a snow-packed curb near the plaza's traffic circle and waved to the hulking structure. "Ah, Lubyanka."

The Americans got out. Wolf paid the fare in rubles and added two dollars as a modest tip. He joined Colter on the sidewalk. Struck silent, they gazed at the yellowish stone monstrosity that had outlasted multiple masters.

"Pretty banal. Could be an ugly post office or government patent office," said Colter. "Can you imagine what went on in there?"

From Lenin's Cheka, to Stalin's NKVD, to Andropov's KGB and Putin's FSB, the building had served as secret police headquarters for each in turn. In its basement cells, corridors, and cobbled courtyard, thousands had died at a tyrant's whim or an informer's whispered rumor.

Wolf said, "The scale of this place is overwhelming when you realize what they used it for. Blood ran in the gutters like rainwater. Lenin said it was better to arrest one hundred innocents rather than risk missing one enemy. Man, what an affront to the Russian people this is. I'd raze the place if it was up to me."

The two crossed the street and strolled to a flat, polished granite slab topped with a jutting rock. Wilted bouquets killed by frost lay across engraved letters filled with snow. Colter reverently brushed away the flakes.

"Monument to victims of the Red Terror," read Wolf from a guidebook. "I'm surprised they allowed this reminder to be put here."

"Maybe a guilty conscience or the new Russia," said Colter.

"Hey, Wolfman, on second thought this place bums me out. To hell with a tour or another taxi. How about we hike to Red Square?"

Wolf put away his tourist pamphlet. "Okay by me. There should be a couple of cafés along the way. We can stop and warm up."

"Getting soft?"

"Hey, you want to jog all the way to Lenin's Tomb? Listen to your elders. We'll stop at a café and flirt with the old babushkas who run it."

Wolf consulted the concierge's map then nodded at a street hemmed with parked cars. "That's Nikolskaya. We can follow that all the way to the State Museum on Red Square. That edible blonde at the front desk told me there's a corner café two blocks from the Kremlin. You game?"

"C'mon, let's go. Get the blood moving."

They skipped the café and arrived in Red Square to play tourist.

Linking arms with Lenin and Stalin, Wolf posed with the Kremlin's soaring Spasskaya Tower in the background. The two Bolshevik lookalikes were doing a brisk business at one hundred rubles per photo. Despite the chill, a knot of amused tourists was taking turns with the icons. Changing places with Colter, Wolf snapped a picture of him with the *dvoiniki*—impersonators. A uniformed Czar

Nicolas II wandered over and after paying the fee, Wolf took a selfie with the bearded royal imposter.

"Now that was surreal," he said, emailing the photos to himself.

Though the wide, paved parade grounds had been swept clean of most snow, the base of the Kremlin's imposing red wall wore a skirt of ice. A must-see for a curious Wolf and an indulgent Colter, Lenin's Tomb proved a disappointment. Sandwiched in a constantly moving line of sightseers, they entered the dimly lit memorial, hustled past the waxen corpse, and were grateful to trade the polished stone crypt for sunlight.

"Lenin looked in better shape at Madame Tussauds in Amsterdam."

"Creepy," said Colter. "He looks more like a giant candle these days."

They stayed long enough to watch the mausoleum's changing of the guard. Robotic, jack-booted sentinels wearing greatcoats and over-sized saucer hats goose-stepped with fixed bayonets for camera-toting visitors.

Wolf and Colter tagged along with a tour group across the vast brick cobblestones to the famous GUM Department store with its vaulted glass indoor malls. At a tiny sweet shop the two ordered coffee laced with sugar and crème and gobbled overpriced bite-sized sandwiches. They went outside to shoot St. Basil's Cathedral, a tourist favorite with its iconic Disneyesque domes, then headed for the nearest Metro station.

Belowground, the ornate underground platforms more than lived up to their reputation. The marble columns and frescoes amazed Wolf. More palace and art gallery than subway, the transit stations prompted them to hop on and off to explore each opulent stop. The train cars were clean, but worn.

"Lots of lookers and no hookers," rhymed Wolf. "Not like New York or Chicago where you see spray paint on everything. It would almost be sacrilegious to tag these walls."

Colter was studying the crowd. "If I didn't know better," he said, "I'd say we were being followed."

"Your sixth sense at work?"

"Maybe," said an unsmiling Colter, eyeing the sea of faces. *What is he seeing?* wondered Wolf. *Is he on someone's list?*

Colter nodded at two florid-faced, red-nosed policemen in dark jackets and the familiar saucer hats. The pair hovered in the background, their eyes on the Americans. A subtle reminder of the state's omnipresence, the officers shadowed Wolf and Colter from a discreet distance. Hustling crowds of Muscovites flowed down the stairs, momentarily distracting the policemen. An amused Wolf watched four baffled Japanese tourists stop the cops to ask directions. The inability to understand each other didn't seem to matter. Ushered aboard the next train, the grateful foursome was sent on their way with a smile and a wave. Colter used the distraction to urge Wolf that they make a break for the surface and flag a taxi.

In the cab, Wolf said, "What the hell was that all about?"

"Maybe my overactive imagination," confessed Colter. "Still..."

Wolf momentarily shelved his curiosity about Colter's actions. "In any case," he said, "my money says that Japanese crew will be on the train for at least a week. Plus, we got to screw with the cops' heads."

"Always a plus in my book," said Colter.

He and Colter got back to the hotel without mishap. At dinner with the NASA engineers, the two former SEALs swapped stories about their day. Wolf's tale about the Japanese tourists in the subway—sans Colter's suspicion about the cops—prompted laughter. With dinner out of the way, the city's nightlife beckoned. Colter had an idea but he needed backup. Knowing Wolf's taste for adventure, it was easy to talk him into a walk on Moscow's wild side.

# Chapter 3

Colter's surprise came in the shape of a dull gray, four-door Lada hatchback pulling up to the Holiday Inn's entrance. He called to Wolf. "Our chariot has arrived."

Wolf peered outside. "I dunno about this. Looks like one of those gypsy cabs we were warned about."

"Looks can be deceiving," said Colter, taking Wolf by the elbow. "Trust me. I'll introduce you to the driver."

The man at the Lada's wheel, a barrel-chested fireplug with a gray brush cut and a salt-and-pepper broom mustache, got out and engulfed Colter in an iron bear hug. "Dan, I never see you for such a long time. How are you, my American friend? How you have been all these years?"

"Good, Semyon, now that you are here. Meet my brother in arms."

Released from the Russian's grasp, Colter introduced Wolf. "Meet Semyon Arkadyevich Kozuch, a destroyer man. Semyon Arkadyevich, this is Commander Tom Wolf."

No bear hug, but a crushing handshake for Wolf.

"*Privet*, Tom Wolf. Ah, another warrior like my friend, eh?"

Kozuch gestured to the little car. "Come. We will make a night of it. I have a cousin who has a small club called Zorro. You will like it, I think. Music, girls, the finest vodka. Let us go. You will enjoy yourself. We will tell stories, maybe lie to each other and make toasts, yes? And there is someone special I want you to meet tonight, okay? Did I mention girls?"

Wolf, throwing a leery glance at Colter, squeezed in the rear seat. Colter took the passenger side.

Kozuch barreled down Moscow's streets like a NASCAR dropout as Wolf listened to Colter explain their friendship. "Semyon Arkadyevich was captain third rank—"

The Russian interrupted. "Is equivalent to your navy's lieutenant commander. But I am now retired, a man of leisure as you are, I see."

Colter continued. "He served on the *Admiral Kutsov*, an *Udaloy*-class destroyer."

"My country's answer to your *Arleigh Burke*-class." Kozuch took a hard right, throwing Wolf across the seat. "But not so comfortable, eh."

"True, but you could fuel it with diesel or vodka," said Colter.

"Yes, correct. Very good memory for such an old man." Roaring with laughter at his joke, the Russian tailgated a limo, then swerved past.

Over his shoulder, Colter said, "He was an anti-submarine officer. Served with the Northern Fleet until retirement."

"Ah, retirement. Such a story. Hard times, my friends," said Kozuch. "Little money. I have a navy pension, but is not enough. Now I help my wife's brother. A catering company. I am a capitalist." More laughter. "My wife expects great things from me. Unfortunately, great expensive things."

The three men laughed in unison.

"We met in Malta," Colter explained. "We entertained the *Kutsov*'s captain and officers in our wardroom. The next night they hosted us. Semyon and I became friends and stayed in contact over the years."

Ignoring the street ahead, Kozuch glanced back at Wolf. "Yes, our big bosses wanted us to stay in touch. To spy on each other. To ask each other questions about our jobs, you know? They were such fools to ask this."

Colter laughed. "We never worked very hard at it. But we stayed friends."

"True. I miss those days. Such fun we had, eh? Now I bring cakes to spoiled children and their rich parents. But life is good, yes?"

Another hard turn and Kozuch eased down a narrow street of ornate three-story, nineteenth-century stone buildings. Mid-block, a garish blue neon sign—*Zorro*—pulsed over an arched recessed entry. Kozuch turned into a fenced lot between two buildings across from the nightclub. Filled with expensive cars bathed in the light of a single large bulb on a pole, the lot boasted a guard's shack. Kozuch and the Americans got out. Muted music from the club drifted across the street.

A sullen youth in overalls and a fur cap with drooping earflaps and a face to match sauntered over, his hand out. Surrendering the keys to the Lada, Kozuch playfully punched the attendant's shoulder. Firing Russian at him, he gestured to Wolf and Colter. "My friends, this is Artur, my cousin's boy. He is big man in charge."

Kozuch spoke rapidly in Russian, then turned to Wolf, whispering, "I tell him you are American. Navy men like me. He is impressed. Maybe you give him some dollars when we leave, eh? You know, just a little something for watching the car."

"Of course, Semyon Arkadyevich. My pleasure." Wolf's smile produced a grin from Artur, who got behind the wheel and pulled to the end of the lot.

"Come, my friends," said Kozuch. "Maybe we meet my cousin. He likes Americans." Slapping Wolf on the back, Kozuch laughed as they crossed the street. "He likes the dollar, too. Okay, we go inside."

# Chapter 4

Dressed in leather thug couture, a wrestler type from central casting, complete with knobby ears and flat nose, manned the club's door. Shaking hands and bantering with the big man, Kozuch held the door for Wolf and Colter. A mix of keyboard, sax, guitars, drums, and horns blasted from an entry hall of brick. A hole-in-the-wall cloakroom between two tiny bathrooms took up one side of the hall, lurid movie posters on the opposite wall. A skinny, gum-snapping, orange-haired waif traded the trio's coats for numbered tags.

Bracing against a wall, Wolf and Colter let Kozuch lead the way through the hallway into a world unlike anything they had expected. An ear-splitting raucous, circus-cum-bacchanal. Hard on Kozuch's heels, Wolf and Colter skirted the edge of a dance floor filled beyond capacity—a Moscow fire marshal's nightmare. A long, mirrored bar took up one entire wall opposite a round stage. Gorgeous women, longhaired, long-legged, mini-skirted or poured into miniscule sequined shorts, floated by like perfumed gazelles with glossy lips. On the crowd's margins, vacuous doe-eyed girls wearing plunging halter-tops or sleeveless satin blouses gyrated in glittering platform shoes or shiny thigh-high leather boots. Faun-like males in feathered masks pranced by in leather vests, skimpy loincloths, and neon tennis shoes.

"All very kinky," yelled Colter in Wolf's ear.

"Your kind of crowd, Dawg."

Entwined with their partners—muscular males or sultry girls—a sea of dancers swayed to the hard-working band's hypnotic rhythms. On stage, a voluptuous brunette wearing a red Cossack military great coat saluted and flashed the crowd, revealing breasts and silver G-string to roaring applause.

No stranger to the world's fleshpots in his younger days, Wolf suddenly felt ancient in the midst of the debauchery. "Makes those San Diego titty bars seem kinda tame, doesn't it?"

Colter said, "I think we've stumbled into a porno movie shoot."

Ahead of them, Kozuch bellowed over his shoulder, ordering the two former SEALs to follow him to a private booth on the club's carpeted mezzanine. Overlooking the dance floor, the coveted spots were furnished with soft leather couches patrolled by smiling, scantily clad servers with big hair.

Settling back, the trio caught their breath. A willowy waitress wearing a gauzy robe and little else strolled by. Pulled into Kozuch's lap, she was smothered in kisses and sent on her way with a drink order. Above them, a pair of nude women gyrated on a gilded catwalk suspended over the dancers.

"So, boys, what do you think?" shouted Kozuch.

"I think we're overdressed," said Wolf, prompting a laugh.

When their drinks arrived, Kozuch raised his glass. "*Na zdorovye!*"

The three toasted each other, emptying the fiery vodka in one gulp, then did it again. While Colter and Kozuch traded stories, Wolf signaled a statuesque blonde wearing strategically placed sequins and ordered mineral water to pace himself. Kozuch called for yet another round and Wolf felt obligated to join him. After the third shot, he pretended to drink. For the next half-hour the Russian downed shot after shot of Stolichnaya.

In the midst of yet another flurry of toasts, four unsmiling bouncer types came up the stairs and hovered over Kozuch, interrupting him mid-toast.

Uneasy, Wolf showed a neutral face and eyed the quartet, thinking, *Ex-military, likely Spetsnaz.* The biggest of the four, a brute with massive arms and no neck, bent low, his thick lips to Kozuch's ear. The pensioned sailor listened, nodding, his face pale. Helped from the couch by the burly messenger, Kozuch's eyes signaled Wolf and Colter not to interfere.

"Duty calls, my friends," said Kozuch, his tone less jocular than usual. "I have business with an old acquaintance. Shouldn't be long."

Before he left, Kozuch rattled off a parting drink order in Russian and followed the first two guard dogs down the stairs, the second pair on his heels. Partygoers on the steps read the body language of the men and parted without being told. Kozuch and his escort disappeared in the crowd.

Wolf leaned toward Colter. "What was that all about?"

Colter shook his head. "Didn't look good from where I was sitting. Don't think he wanted to leave, but my guess is he had no choice."

Left on their own, the Americans nursed their drinks, killing time. Wolf waved off a topless trolling server wearing a smile and a thong made of blinking blue LED lights.

"That's gotta hurt," said Colter, eyeing her costume.

They both laughed, Kozuch's dilemma momentarily forgotten. To Wolf's amusement, a disheveled drunken Tatar, egged on by companions in an adjacent alcove, stumbled after the server wearing the lights.

"It's going to be a long night," Wolf yelled to his fellow SEAL.

"Hey, I thought I was jaded," said Colter. "Thought I had seen it all. But this is not the Moscow I knew. Is this what getting old feels like?"

Wolf shrugged, his thoughts returning to Kozuch's dilemma.

Thirty minutes passed. Kozuch had not returned. Wolf turned apologetic. "I really thought we were going to some café to hear balalaika folk music and drink vodka in a quiet corner. I had no idea we'd end up here."

Colter downed what vodka was left in his shot glass. "You are such a bad liar, Wolfman. You're a party animal. Admit it."

"Okay, so I'm a party animal. But this is getting out of hand. When Kozuch shows tell him we can't make a night of it. Maybe we can get a taxi."

"Hell, Wolfman, I don't even know where we are, do you?"

"Not sure. East of the river, maybe. Ask Kozuch when he gets back."

Colter said, "Don't bother. From the look on his face when those gorillas showed, I think my sailor friend is in deep shit. This place has '*mafiya*' written all over it. We're on our own, Wolfman."

Before Wolf could answer, another waitress, tall, long blond hair pinned in thick braids, leaned over the low table, her face inches from his. She made a show of collecting the empty glasses. His conversation with Colter on hold, Wolf shamelessly focused on her décolletage barely concealed by a white diaphanous gown. She spoke in a hurried voice without looking at him.

"You must leave immediately, Commander Wolf."

# Chapter 5

Incredulous at the beautiful woman's warning, Wolf said, "Excuse me. Do I know you?"

She fussed with the glasses, a cloth in her left hand, tray in her right. "They have taken Semyon. They will soon come for you."

Wolf leaned in. "Who are you?"

"I am Yana. No time to explain. Do as I ask. Please. Leave now."

"But how—"

"Do you know Donskoy Monastery? It is not far from Gorky Park."

Colter said, "Yes, I know it."

"Good. My sister Katrina comes to your hotel tomorrow. Go with her. I will meet you. Trust me."

Wolf hesitated. "Look, lady—"

"Artur will take you to hotel," she added. "He is waiting. You must go. NOW!"

The woman balanced the tray on a curvaceous hip and backed from the couch, nervous blue eyes darting around the mezzanine. She made a deliberate show of teasing the drunken Tatars next door. The burly men pawed at her but she laughed at their clumsiness and moved on to the next group before abandoning her tray and going down a back stairway.

Wolf stared after her. 'What the hell...who...what about Kozuch?"

Colter grabbed his friend's elbow. "What about him? Did you hear what the lady said? I'm definitely not liking the vibe, Wolfman. I say we take her advice and get the hell out while we can still walk and talk. Sort it out later."

"You're spooking me, Dawg, but you could be right."

"You could always hold your liquor better than me," said Colter, "but are you okay?"

Wolf said, "I'll be fine. The fresh air will do me good. Better phone Kozuch tomorrow and explain what happened."

"Somehow I don't think he's going to pick up the phone."

"Who were those guys?"

"Gotta go, Wolfman. C'mon!"

The two went down the stairs just as the woman on stage tossed her Cossack coat and whirled, sans G-string, in a spotlight. The mesmerized crowd went wild. Backs to the wall, a sobering Wolf followed Colter around the dance floor toward the entry. The two SEALs demanded their coats, tipped with dollars, and headed for the door, Colter in the lead.

Outside, past the hulking doorkeeper, they found Artur as promised: at the wheel of the warming Lada in the middle of the lot.

"Oh, great, we get the gray pumpkin," shouted Colter.

Given the moment, he and Wolf would have preferred a Mercedes or a Porsche, but the little sedan would have to do. The Americans scrambled in. Accelerating from the slushy lot, Artur drove with his uncle's fatalism. He knew the city well and got them safely to the hotel after a tense forty-minute ride. Stopping mid-block on Lesnaya Street, not far from the inn's entrance, he let them out.

Peeling off five twenties, Wolf closed Artur's fist over the bills. "*Spasiba*, Artur. Appreciate it. More than you know."

"*Da, nezashto. Dosvidanya.*"

"*Dosvidanya*," echoed Wolf.

Colter and Wolf stood in the cold, watching the little car until its taillights disappeared. A sleepy uniformed doorman held the hotel's door for them. The lobby was deserted. Not a night for the stairs, the two opted for the elevator.

While waiting for the lift, Wolf eyed the hotel doorman. "Nice outfit. Whadaya think, Dawg? How does he compare to the Cossack lady?"

"Doesn't even come close," said Colter. "I was ready to marry her."

Saying not another word until they were behind their room's locked door, Colter ran the shower to cover their voices. Fueled by adrenaline, they sat on the tub's edge comparing notes on their bizarre evening and narrow escape.

"Am I paranoid?" said Wolf. "I thought the Cold War was over. Any clue who those players were tonight?"

Colter nodded. "*Vory*. The mob. The club was full of them. Welcome to the new Russia."

"How do you know all this stuff?"

"Instinct."

"Man, you're full of surprises."

They hit the sack. Feeling naked without a weapon, Wolf jammed a chair under the doorknob and slept with a hotel letter opener in hand.

# Chapter 6

In the morning, Colter awakened first to take a call from the front desk—something about an arranged tour of historic Moscow, said the concierge. As requested, the agency had sent a guide. She was waiting for them in the lobby.

"Ah, could this be our savior from last night?" said Wolf as they exited the elevator.

"Hard to tell," whispered Colter. "Too many clothes."

He and Colter crossed the lobby and shook hands with a blonde who bore more than a passing resemblance to the woman they had met on the Zorro's mezzanine. Their visitor wore wool slacks, fur-lined boots, and a heavy coat with a tour badge clipped to the collar. Over her left shoulder she carried a canvas bag of maps and tourist guides.

"I don't believe I got your name last night," said Wolf.

"I am Katrina," she said. "We did not meet last night. You are referring to my sister, Yana. It was she who spoke to you. She is two years older and more beautiful."

Colter shook his head. "I wouldn't go as far as to say that. And may I say your English is excellent."

Their visitor said, "Thank you for your compliment, sir."

An awkward silence followed. Glancing around the lobby uneasily, she said, "Is possible to talk in more private place, yes?"

"The lounge perhaps?" said Wolf.

He and Colter ushered her to an isolated table and ordered three coffees.

When they had been served, Wolf said, "So…Katrina… if that's your real name…"

Taken aback, the woman bristled, "It is, of course. Why do you ask?"

"After last night one has to be careful, wouldn't you agree?"

"I understand. Of course, you must be careful."

"The lighting in the club was not the best," said Wolf. "Forgive us for confusing you with your sister. You could easily pass for her."

She sipped her coffee, looking over the cup's rim at Wolf.

"What happened to Kuzoch?" he said. "And how are you and your sister connected to him?"

"Perhaps we should discuss this in safer place, yes?"

"This suits us fine, but what would you suggest?"

"Did not my sister suggest Donskoy Monastery to you?"

"Yes, she mentioned it," said Colter. "But why there?"

"Because no one would think it odd that you would want to see this place. Even in our winter the grounds are beautiful. We can talk there without being overheard. I have a car outside. Will you come? It is important."

Wolf glanced at Colter, then their visitor. "To be frank, Katrina, you must appreciate our situation. As Americans we are viewed with some suspicion to begin with. What if the same men who took Semyon Arkadyevich decide to come after Dan and me? We would be in danger. Do you agree?"

"Of course. I understand. But you see, Yana is in difficult situation. It was arranged for her to meet you last night, yes? But when she saw Semyon taken away she had to warn you at no small risk to herself."

"Don't think we're ungrateful," said Colter. "But my friend has a point."

"Yes, but you are her only hope, sirs. Please, don't refuse, I beg you."

Flashing a disarming smile, Wolf said, "I have always been a sucker for a beautiful woman asking for help, Katrina. As a result, I have often found myself in trouble. My companion is only looking out for my best interests."

Colter weighed in. "What do you want with us? What is so important that we cannot talk here? Why do we have to go halfway across the city?"

"Is for my sister. She is afraid to come to you. She is in hiding. She risks her life to warn you. Don't let her die at the hand of others before her time."

Wolf rose from the table, his hand on Colter's shoulder. "Will you excuse us, Katrina? I wish to talk to my friend in private."

"Yes, of course. I see. Please, consider my request."

"We will," said Wolf. "In the meantime, perhaps you should spread out a map and your materials to make it look as if we are discussing a tour."

"Excellent idea. Of course, I will do as you ask." In their absence, she set aside the cups and did as Wolf suggested. A server stopped at the table, refilled the cups, and glanced at the maps approvingly before moving on.

In the lobby, speaking in low tones, Wolf and Colter debated the wisdom of accompanying their guest.

"This could be a classic honey trap, Wolfman. You thought of that?"

"You read my mind. Still, I'm curious about what happened to your friend Kozuch. And I'd love to see this Yana for myself. She saved my ass...and yours. We owe her, man."

Colter was skeptical. "You ARE a sucker for a beautiful girl. You don't know for certain that she saved your ass. It may have been set up to look like that. Hell, Wolfman, even those Russki orcs picking up Kozuch may have been an act for all we know. I say we bail on this one. I'm thinking we're too good a target for the bad guys to pass up."

"Rule of thumb, Dawg. Bad ideas are always better when executed with a friend. I know you're that kind of guy. And let's face it...in Russia, friends are few and far between. Look, we could split up when we get to the monastery. You hang back, shadow us just in case it hits the fan."

"And come to your rescue with what? My shoe? We'd be in a bad place, surrounded by bad guys, about to make a bad decision. I vote we skip it."

"I'm going, regardless."

"Damn. You don't give a guy much choice do you? Okay, but don't think I didn't warn you if we step in it."

Throwing an arm around Colter, Wolf smiled. "I like the way you said 'we.' Let's go tell our Girl Scout we're good to go."

# Chapter 7

*Donskoy Monastery*

Circling the monastery's crenellated brick wall with its twelve towers, Katrina parked in a car lot across the street from the main entrance. Wolf and Katrina headed for the gate, discreetly shadowed by Colter thirty meters behind. Despite his uneasiness, Wolf was captivated by the ornate architecture.

The entrance, a massive block of red brick trimmed in white and pierced by a central arch, was topped by a spire of columned sections of baroque masonry dating to 1713. Faced with clocks and an icon, and capped by a bell tower, the building had once been used as a church. The pair entered the arched doorway with its yellow Cyrillic lettering. They passed between heavy doors sheathed with copper plates and emerged on a broad walkway flanked by piles of shoveled snow. Before them was Donskoy's "new" cathedral, built in the late 1600s. Crowned with five black onion-shaped domes, the brick church, its windows trimmed in white, displayed an icon of Mary and the Christ child high above the front steps. Two bundled babushka faithful, their eyes on the ground, shuffled along the shoveled path. An Orthodox priest floated past in flowing black robes and unkempt graying beard. Bells called to each other across the wooded grounds.

Partially hidden by a screen of skeletal trees, more domes belonging to older churches showed, their bell towers capped with snow. "Did you know this place dates to 1591?" asked Katrina. "The great Boris Godunov himself laid the foundation stone of the cathedral. This monastery was built and fortified to protect the southern approach to Moscow. It guarded a road to the Crimea."

"How ironic," muttered Wolf.

"How do you mean ironic?"

He smiled. "The Crimea. It's okay, don't mind me."
Waving his hand at the grounds, he said, "The history of this
place is impressive, Katrina. I read that the walls did not keep
out the French in 1812, however. They trashed the place."

"Trashed?"

Fluttering his hands, he said, "You know, ruin. Make a
mess."

"Oh, yes, I understand."

Wolf and Katrina passed a trio of old people in heavy
dark coats, their gloved hands clasped behind stooped
backs. Wolf avoided eye contact as if studying church
silhouettes beyond the naked trees.

Head bowed, he asked, "Is your sister here?"

"She is here. Among the graves."

"Not a good sign in my book."

"But it is a quiet place."

"No doubt."

"She will find us. We have only to visit the tombs. You
will find the gravestones interesting, I think."

Glancing behind him, Wolf caught Colter lingering at
the base of a tall stone crucifix, his eyes studying Christ's
serene face. Reassured, Wolf resumed his slow pace at
Katrina's side.

She said, "Your friend is not agreeable to this, is he?"

"No. And I can't say I blame him. We are unarmed,
uncomfortable, and unprepared for what might happen
next." Halting to gaze at a headstone, Wolf turned to
Katrina. "And what does happen next?"

"You must ask my sister. She is behind you to your left.
I will leave you alone with her. I shall be in that small
chapel at the end of the walkway. Send your friend
Commander Colter to me. You must tell Yana to come to
me when you are finished with the business, yes?"

# Chapter 8

Wolf, pretending to study a kneeling stone angel, spotted Yana near a granite marker embedded with a small glassed photo of the deceased.

Yana, smiling conspiratorially and dressed identically to Katrina, drifted toward him, hands in her long coat's pockets. Wolf suppressed his surprise. Had he not seen Katrina going up the steps of a domed chapel beyond the graves, he would have taken Yana for her twin.

The statuesque blonde flashed a dazzling, reassuring smile and linked arms with Wolf. She nodded at a small gazebo among the graves.

"Did you know Stalin profaned these consecrated grounds by burying victims of his purges here? The killing went on a long time and not just here."

"I've studied that era. Not a happy time for your people."

"We have a long history of unhappiness. Let's talk, you and I, yes?"

Wolf, hearing footsteps, looked over his shoulder to find Colter walking their way. Passing, he whispered, "So far, so good, Wolfman. Wrap it up as quickly as possible before I have to use my shoe."

Wolf said, "Katrina's waiting for you in the chapel." Colter continued, following Katrina's footsteps toward the domed building.

Yana said, "What does he mean about the shoe?"

"Just his sense of humor. It's nothing." Wolf resumed strolling, content to have this striking Russian woman on his arm.

"Okay, why the mysterious arrangements?" he said. "Why the cloak-and-dagger about meeting here? What's your story?"

"Story?"

"Yes. Why are we here? What is so important, Yana?"

She disarmed him. "Do you know my name means 'God is gracious'?"

Enchanted, Wolf said, "Well, I thought it meant 'God has good taste.'"

"You are not serious enough, Commander."

When they reached the gazebo, Wolf swept snow from the stone bench and sat next to her, grinning. "Did you know my name means 'predator' or 'carnivore'?"

"You mock me, sir."

"Yes, and I apologize," Wolf said. "But tell me, what's an absolutely gorgeous woman like you doing in a place like this?"

"Is this a serious question?"

"Sort of. It's an American saying, meaning, 'What are you doing here?'"

Yana withdrew an four-by-six inch black leather book from her coat and handed it to Wolf. "I want you to do something for me. You must take this back to America for me, please. You must give it to a journalist to read. Please, it is important. It is a valuable record. It has cost seven lives already. I pray that you will not become the next one to die because of this book."

"Appreciate the sentiment, lady."

Wolf scanned the contents. Filled with tidy Cyrillic notes in a crisp hand, each page was followed by sets of dated figures in three columns on opposite pages.

"I don't read much Russian, Yana. I can speak some, but maybe I'm not your man for this."

She leaned close, pleading, her hand over his. "You must take this with you and see it published. Or perhaps you must give it to your friends in the government or police."

"Did Kozuch have something to do with this?"

Tears filled her eyes. "Yes. He was given this book by someone who worked for his cousin. That messenger was the sixth person to die. Semyon Arkadyevich, my uncle, was certainly the seventh."

"Have you word of his death?"

"He was dead the moment those devils came for him. I tell you this, Semyon Arkadyevich was no saint. He catered not only cakes but also drugs from Tajikistan. The drugs come there across the border from Afghanistan. So much money to be had. So little resistance to the lure. My uncle was too weak to resist his cousin and as a result, was trapped."

"Semyon's cousin, the guy who owns the Zorro club? Did he betray Colter's old friend?"

"Yes. It was Gregor who betrayed my uncle. He is *avtorityet*."

"I know the word. In America we call such a man a 'capo' for the mob."

"Of course. Yes. They are all *russkaya mafiya*. The devil's men, doing the devil's work; caring only for themselves and their criminal families."

"How very American, Yana." Wolf flipped through the pages.

She said, "When our country collapsed, the gates of hell were opened."

"Some would say that began in 1917 with your revolution."

"Yes, I understand what you are saying. I do not disagree, Commander Wolf. But perhaps this book can help in some small way with the way things are now."

Wolf balanced the book on his knee. "A very small strike, if that. The *russkaya mafiya* is like a serpent with many heads." He made a chopping motion. "You cut off one head, two or three grow in its place."

"You will see in this book that some of the names do business with the same serpents in America. You have them in your own house."

"Right. East coast and west. We know of these people, Yana."

She gripped his arm tighter. "Will you take this with you for me?"

Wolf said, "My friend can read Russian better than me. I will show this to him and see what he thinks. If he believes it is true...what you say...then I will do what I can to see this gets into the right hands. Good enough?"

Yana buried her head against his shoulder. "You believe me."

"I'll need Commander Colter's help in this decision."

Yana covered her face with her hands. Wolf, not used to comforting crying women, patted her gently on the back, awkwardly trying to show concern. She took Wolf's chin in hand, drawing him to her, and kissed him. He did not pull away.

With the back of her hand, she wiped her tears away. "I am most grateful, Commander. Most grateful."

"I think we can drop the commander title, Yana. Tom will do."

Between sobs, she kissed him again. "Tom, yes. I am grateful."

He slipped the book inside his parka and rose from the bench with her, his arm around her shoulders. "I have to go back to the city."

"Tomorrow you must leave?"

"Afraid so. I'm off to another city. One with no beautiful Russian women such as you, I'm sure."

"I am also grateful for you saying these things to me...Tom."

They stood in the gazebo, Wolf holding her hands. "A woman like you, working in a club like the Zorro, must have a legion of men knocking on your door to bring you flowers and compliments, Yana."

"I don't work at the club," she said, blushing. "I only pretended to be one of the staff. It was my uncle's idea."

"But, the other night—"

"He was to introduce me to you. But his enemies arrived before he had the chance. I only had time enough to warn you before they came back for you."

"Did Commander Colter know this?"

"I don't think so. My uncle said nothing about that."

"But they knew each other."

"A long time ago, yes."

"This is a bit confusing, Yana."

"I understand. But it was all arranged for the book." She raised both his hands, kissing them. "Please believe me. If you change your mind about helping me, I am lost."

"I promised you I'd help."

"And I am grateful. Perhaps we can have time together before you go."

Wolf glanced about him. "It might be dangerous for you. The men who took your uncle will surely be looking for the Americans who were seen with him. Even now they could be searching for us...or you."

"I am willing to take such a chance. I have a small flat near the metro, Tom. I will make a small meal if you agree." Her eyes held promise. "And then later..."

Spotting Colter coming their way, Wolf whispered, "Maybe. Let me see what I can arrange with my friend."

"I know he would agree to do this for you."

"Perhaps," he said. "I would do the same were he in my place. But what about your sister?"

She flashed a coy smile. "She is to care for Mother. Katrina and I trade each week so that one of us can stay with her. She is sick. It keeps our sanity to have time to ourselves, you know. We could have the evening together."

Passing them, Colter muttered, "Time to move, Wolfman. Send Yana to the chapel to trade places with Katrina."

After a quick glance to check if they were being watched, Wolf kissed Yana again. "Until tonight."

"I will have the car. I know your hotel."

"Yes. Come by at six this evening. Wait at the end of the street."

She blew him a kiss. "I come at five. That will give us more time."

Wolf turned. "Five it is. Until then, Yana."

He watched her skip up the steps of the chapel, give a last look, and then go inside. Five seconds passed. Katrina exited to join him in the necropolis. She walked slowly, making a show of pointing out various outbuildings of the monastery to Wolf. She recited more history. He dawdled, playing the perfect tourist, taking pictures of domes, walls, towers, and the soaring gate.

A light snow began. Treetops coated with ice rattled in the wind. Bells rang, the deep sonorous notes trembling in the cold air. Katrina and Wolf retraced their steps through the arch, emerging to a wet street. They got in her car, and while it warmed, Colter crossed the lot and slipped in the backseat.

"Everything on the up and up?"

"I think we're good, Dawg."

Colter rubbed the fogged window. "Drive the speed limit, Katrina. Get us back with no problems."

Snow cloaked the monastery's deserted towers and silent walls. Behind them, trees screened onion domes in the fading light. They rounded a corner and followed a lumbering blue streetcar filled to capacity.

Katrina spoke without looking at Wolf. "So, you and Yana are to have dinner together, eh?"

From the backseat, Colter thundered, "Dinner! No one said anything about dinner to me, Wolfman. Am I invited?"

"How's your Russian?"

"My Russian's fine. What's that got to do with dinner?"

"You've got an assignment. You can call room service."

"The hell with that." Colter leaned over the front seat and tapped Katrina's shoulder. "Dearest, what are you doing for dinner?"

She glanced over her shoulder, then back to the road. "I'm sorry, sir. I have to take care of my mother tonight."

Wolf said, "A very noble task, Katrina."

Colter fumed in the rear seat. "I can't believe you pulled this off, Wolfman. I had your six all that time and you were scheming on me. What the hell?"

"I won't be out late, Dawg. I promise."

"I oughta turn you in to our NASA chaperone."

"Hey, I'll spell you at our next stop."

"Oh, great. I can just imagine the prospects where we're going."

Katrina misread her passengers' give and take. "Have I caused some bad feelings, sirs? If so, I apologize."

"It's not you, darling," said Colter. "It's my horney homie."

"What is this expression? I don't understand."

"If I had time," cooed Colter, "I could explain over a romantic dinner."

"I would like that, sir...but."

"I know. You're already booked with Mother."

# Chapter 9

"You know, Wolfman, if I didn't know better I'd say the earth was flat."

Trying in vain to get comfortable, Colter squared his shoulders against the worn back of seat 26F in the rear of the Aeroflot TU-134. Having bested Wolf in a coin toss for window rights, he viewed a vast featureless desert through smudged glass. Painted in monochromatic brown, Kazakhstan's landscape bored him the moment they entered the former Soviet republic's airspace.

"Flat earth, huh? You and Alexander the Great," said Wolf. "Did you know this was about as far north as he got before turning back? Kind of anti-climactic to conquer a great outdoor nothingness after the Persian Empire. Bet the Mongols loved it, though. Imagine centuries later, hundreds of thousands of them sweeping across this land for days on end with nothing to stop them. Now that would have been something to see."

"Speaking of something to see..."

"Spot something?" Wolf craned his neck toward the window.

"Nada." Shifting again, Colter searched for signs of life on the desert below but failed. "Now I know what an ant on a sheet of plywood must feel like. I'm going to guess there's not much night life where we're going."

"Probably not. Just rocket fuel cocktails, space junk, bad roads, and hookers who look like Bactrian camels. The launch should be fun though."

Colter sulked. "Geez, you're a laugh a minute. You get the girl and I get to order room service so I can study Al Caponeski's diary. What's wrong with this picture?"

"Hey, you got the window seat, Dawg. Can't beat that."

Colter felt the small leather ledger book in the inner pocket of his corduroy jacket. "You wanna hear what I think we have?"

"Not with a lot of strange ears listening in. Loose lips sink ships."

"Roger that. But we'd better have a serious talk when we get some down time. You got your hands on something really special, Wolfman."

"You talking about Yana or the package?"

"Cute. Just had to rub it in, huh? Care to share your memories of the previous evening? It might go a long way to restore our relationship. In the meantime, I can't wait to tell you about my romantic night with the diary."

Wolf smiled. "You did the better thing."

"Bullshit. I would have traded places with you in a heartbeat."

"We'll talk when we have a chance."

"I'm holding you to it, Wolfman."

The twin-engine jet was three-quarters full. In seats behind them a pair of German scientists dozed, their snores like buzz saws. Across the aisle, two pale, humorless French women, their hair tied in buns, bickered over some challenging word puzzle. Ahead of Wolf and Colter sat two of the NASA delegation, one of them reading a paperback, the other one staring zombie-like at Kazakhstan's tabletop geography. Writers and photographers from Time and the Hearst newspaper syndicate spent the flight comparing photos on their smartphones or sharing travel tips. One of the four NASA photographers, Dana, a slim ponytailed brunette Colter had bought a drink for in an airport bar, slept, long legs curled under her. Aside from a group of eight placid Chinese space tourists and a dozen chattering Italians, dour Russians filled the remaining seats.

Circling lower, the TU-134 passed over the Syr Darya, a timeless, shallow serpentine river, sluggish and wide. Below, the city of Baikonur lay locked in a grid of north-south streets laid out in classic 1950s Soviet style—rigid and unimaginative. Home to the Russian space program, the remote metropolis had been shrouded in secrecy—one of the USSR's best-kept secrets until discovered by an American U2 spy plane in 1957.

Here, at the end of the earth, Soviet scientists launched a basketball-sized satellite named *Sputnik*, inaugurating the space race that same year. Here, at the end of the earth, where Silk Road caravans once trod, multiple launch facilities suddenly rose, the builders utilizing the vast desert to take advantage of uninterrupted radio control of ever-larger rockets. Here, at the end of the earth, Krainey Airport, an aging Cold War airfield originally designed solely for Soviet military use, had now become the main entry point for multi-national tours.

Wolf and Colter exited the plane, both underwhelmed by their first glimpse of a bleak, flat tan terrain devoid of life. The two SEALs followed the NASA delegation down the stairs of an obsolete towed ramp parked next to the TU-134. The air was crisp and cold, but at least fifteen degrees warmer than Moscow.

"I feel like I'm entering the Twilight Zone," said Colter.

Descending the stairs, Wolf turned to NASA's Warren behind him. "This place could pass for some remote Texas hub. You sure we're in Kazakhstan?" He laughed, earning a scowl from the engineer.

There was no gate, just a small terminal that had replaced older open hangars once used to process incoming passengers and rocket parts. After sorting their luggage and undergoing a cursory check by uniformed guards, the foreign nationals were herded to four white buses destined for their assigned hotels. Bound for the French-built Sputnik Hotel, the Italians, French, Germans, and Americans shared one vehicle. The buses passed a weathered Mig21 tethered to a pedestal at the airport's entrance and continued four miles to Baikonur's center. Warren pointed out their destination: a two-story, four-wing ochre inn resembling a medium-security prison planted in a lifeless setting.

"Baikonur's newest hotel," he said. "Among the city's finest."

"It looks like the kind of place where they take away your belts and shoelaces when you check in," joked Wolf. Colter and the others in the American party chuckled. Ever serious, Warren was not amused. The Europeans missed Wolf's meaning completely.

"I was told it has a pool, a restaurant, and a bar," volunteered an Italian seated behind Wolf. "The staff is said to be very cordial, very welcoming."

"A bar? Well, then," said Wolf, "what's not to like?" More chuckles rippled through the ranks.

The line of buses passed an old man astride a plodding pony, the rider's heels brushing the ground. Next came a Kazakh teen standing roadside, bridled Bactrian camel in hand. The dusty wooly animal and dull-eyed youth stared at the passing buses filled with strangers. The first bus, carrying Wolf, Colter, and the others, left the main road for the Sputnik Hotel. The remaining buses continued on to the city center.

The Italian was right. The staff was welcoming. Wolf and Colter were assigned a room together. The media drones were spread throughout the same floor, as were NASA's people per Warren's request. The accommodations were plain: two single beds, two sturdy chairs, a small table, wall-mounted TV, and separate tiled bathroom with marble floor.

They put away their luggage and immediately went downstairs to the restaurant and bar.

The hotel's bar was an international watering hole. A dozen languages floated around the room. Wolf was in his element, Colter restless.

"You know what this reminds me of, Dawg?"

"Knowing you," said Colter, "probably your summer camp days as a kid...complete with forbidden alcohol."

Ignoring the dig, Wolf swept an arm around the room. "I was thinking of *Star Wars*. Remember that bar in the first movie? All those goofy aliens bellied up to the bar? Am I right or what?"

Colter grinned. "Yeah, you pegged it. Hey, check out those guys."

Following his friend's gaze, Wolf spotted two hulking Asians the size of refrigerators anchoring the end of the bar. One of the big men stared at both SEALs, lowering his eyes only when Wolf noticed the attention.

After good-natured banter over drinks with Italians and three Brazilian freelance photographers, Wolf and Colter were asked to dine with Warren and his small army of NASA engineers, photographers and guests. After dinner, the two SEALs heard a short recitation of the next day's activities and then excused themselves for a private walk on the hotel's grounds.

Colter pulled his coat tight against evening's chill. "What's Yana's story?"

"Her full name is Yana Alexandra Konev," said Wolf. "She has long legs and incredible blue eyes, is a real blonde, and has a job in a small textile firm. She owns an apartment and a car. Your friend Kozuch is her father's brother."

"Was her father's brother," Colter corrected him.

"Affirmative. *WAS* her father's brother."

"Father's dead, mother's seriously ill. Sounds like congestive heart failure from her description. Yana and Katrina share the apartment and trade off taking care of their mother."

"Yeah, don't I know," Colter said, frowning. "You lucked out getting the week Katrina had the duty."

Wolf laughed. "Sorry, Dawg, that was a last-minute switch Yana made with her sister so she and I could have some time together."

"What? You sonofabitch. You don't play fair. You know that?"

Wolf sounded apologetic. "Hey, it was Yana's idea, not mine."

"Sure it was. Dirty pool, Wolfman. So give it up. What else should we know? What are we getting into?"

"You're the man to answer that. Whatever's in that book you have is the key. She's desperate to get it out of Russia."

Tapping his chest, Colter said, "She has a right to be worried. This book is toxic, Wolfman. Just a cursory read tells me her little black book is full of incriminating stuff. My Russian is passable. But I can tell you this looks like a list of people high in the food chain who have some kind of ties to Ukrainian banks, utilities, provincial officials, you name it."

"You figured out all that? Your Russian is better than you let on."

"That's my gut instinct speaking. Some of it is plain enough but early on the writer lost me for a while. The numbers are real enough but the key is figuring out the pairing between the figures and the names."

"What do you suggest we do with it?"

They stopped at the hotel's fenced limit and retraced their steps. Colter said, "Yana's right to be worried. We should take it to someone whose Russian is flawless. A

skilled linguist would take one-third of the time I would
need to decipher this."

"That's a tall order. Why not our own government
people?"

"I'd give them second crack at it."

"Why?"

Colter stopped, chin in hand. "First, given enough
time, we might be able to figure what the contents
mean. We could check the authenticity of what she's
given us. If it's good as gold, we copy it to someone who
guarantees publication, an exposé. Trouble with the feds
is they might bury it."

"Why would they do that?"

"Wolfman, I'd bet there are probably connections in
here above our pay grade. I mean, even with my so-so
understanding of the language I think it's obvious from
these notes that there are links to Russian movers and
shakers. I don't know how serious the government would
be about pursuing them."

"You don't think the FBI would be interested in what
we have?"

Colter shrugged. "Sure. We could go that route if you
want. All I'm saying is that we should figure this out
before we make a decision. If we're risking our lives for
this, we ought to know what's going down. You hear
what I'm saying?"

"I do. What do you think about turning it over to the
FBI liaison at the embassy when we return to Moscow?
You know, let them take it from there."

Colter smiled. "So young, so naive. Wolfman, my
friend, you're too trusting. Why don't I just give you
this book? You could do with it what you want."

"No, no. If your gut instinct is to hold on to it and get our
own translation, I accept that. We could stop in San Diego on

our way back and talk to my friend Sam McFadden. He's got the kinds of resources you're talking about."

"McFadden, the partner with you in that dive boat business in the Philippines?"

"Yeah. He's good people. He might know some academic in a language department who'd be willing to help."

Colter waved away the suggestion. "Nah, they'd talk. I think we need security. If McFadden has the right connections, set it up."

"Will do. Have to wait until we get back to Moscow. No secure lines here at the hotel."

Colter looked worried. "Question. Do you think Yana's in any kind of danger in our absence?"

"I told her to contact our embassy if she feels threatened. I've got a friend there. Chris Franklin, Marine colonel. Military liaison."

"Maybe he could get her a quickie visa, Wolfman."

"Now that would be a great assignment. Showing the beautiful Russian girl America."

"You'd love that," said Colter. "I'm always getting emails about 'Russian Singles,' you know."

"She's not like that, Dawg. She wasn't working that club if that's what you're thinking. She was only there to meet us. Nah, Yana's special."

"I'll bet she is. Watch out, Wolfman. It's a slippery slope. Next thing you know you'll be taking her home to meet Mom."

"Mom wouldn't approve. Besides, I don't see Yana leaving Moscow as long as her mother and sister need her."

Colter said, "If the people who killed for this book figure out she got it to us, she'll be in the line of fire. Kozuch probably talked before he was killed. You thought of that?"

"It's crossed my mind more than once. When we're done with the launch thing I'll stop on our way out of Moscow. I know where to find her."

"If you know how to find her, so do the boys in the Kremlin."

"I'll just have to get there first, won't I? Okay, can we be done with our strategy session? I'd like to stop in the bar for a nightcap."

Colter patted his jacket. "Don't let me out of sight, Wolfman."

# Chapter 10

The next morning, after a hurried breakfast of tea, bread, and fruit, Wolf and Colter joined the Italians, French, Germans, and Warren's top-heavy NASA group aboard a tour bus bound for the Cosmodome. A stubborn fog gave the ride an unearthly, disconnected feel. They slowed past a dusty city park dominated by a bulky Soyuz7 aimed at a far horizon dotted with aerials, radio towers, and scrub brush. Discarded plastic bags danced across the road like gossamer tumbleweeds. In the center of town a weedy strip lined with skeletal trees poking from the dirt masqueraded as a parkway.

"Where are the babushkas with their little brooms when you need them?" said Wolf.

He and Colter stared at rows of depressing Soviet-style apartment buildings with end walls covered in mosaics of past space glories, the only color for blocks. Dodging potholes, the bus slowed outside a police headquarters draped with an enormous bygone banner showing a square-jawed soldier with AK47 at the ready. Inside the gates stood a bulky statue of Lenin with outstretched arm. Bored uniformed men with little to do watched the bus pass.

"Looks like you-know-who didn't get the memo," said Colter.

Wolf laughed. "Bless the KGB, they're such suckers for nostalgia."

Their unsmiling Russian guide, a taciturn colonel, long in tooth with twenty years at Baikonur, ran his crowd of charges through the usual show-and-tell. Making the first of the obligatory stops, the colonel led the way into the city's space museum, a shrine to Yuri Gagarin, the first man in space, and Sergei Korolev, father of the Soviet rocket program. The busload filled the museum. Wolf and Colter wandered through the exhibits of priceless space memorabilia. Wolf mixed with the Italians.

"They're more fun," he said, ignoring the humorless Warren.

Surrounded by her visitors, the museum's reigning docent explained the artifacts, patiently waiting as her words were translated into English. Back on board the bus, the visitors gawked at crumbling cottages once inhabited by demigods Gagarin and Korolev. They drove past huge scorched pieces of past failures that had cost lives in the race with America. Adding to the forlorn sight of an orphaned, weather-beaten Buran shuttle, discarded rocket litter was a sobering reminder of the risks involved. Everywhere Wolf looked, scraps of twisted metal, abandoned concrete launch pads, and tangled spaghetti-like piping spoke volumes about botched missions.

After a quick series of stops at more heavy-handed propaganda monuments, their bus parked alongside others for a photo op at the Soyuz processing building. Poised on a massive railroad flatcar, the gigantic rocket with its five engine nozzles—seemingly out of scale, too large and heavy to be moved—was bathed in cellphone and camera flashes from an awed crowd. In twos and threes, visitors wandered about the machinery and railcar, taking pictures of themselves or friends, the reclining Soyuz in the background.

Without announcement, the diesel engine started and, under the strain of its burden, its wheels slowly started turning. Picking up speed, the cradled Soyuz inched along tracks leading to the R7 launch site three miles distant. On cue, the fog thinned, revealing cloudless blue skies.

"Feels like we're extras in a movie," said Colter, snapping photos.

Marveling at the massive rocket, Wolf and others were shooed from the empty tracks by soldiers. He said, "Yeah, any moment Bruce Willis is going to roar up in a jeep, fire an RPG at the rocket, and start World War Three."

"Gentlemen, honored guests. Please to board your transport. We will leave for final ceremony prior to launch."

At their next stop, Wolf and Colter hustled from the bus to the front of the crowd. After thirty minutes of milling about, the assembly stirred. The lone American astronaut and his two fellow crewmen emerged to rippling applause. Following the ritual's protocol, the three-man flight crew took position on footprints painted on asphalt. The crowd grew silent. Dressed in bulky pressurized flight suits, the trio came to attention and saluted. A Russian general, gray, gruff, and solemn, returned the salute and shook each man's hand in a touching farewell.

With the official ceremony ended, the space tourists were herded back on board for the trip to viewing stands one mile distant. At the launch pad, the towering gantry had risen, the Soyuz embraced in its muscular arms. The crew arrived and rode an elevator to their waiting capsule. An hour passed. More buses arrived. Chattering groups of Russians, Chinese, Japanese, and westerners filled the viewing stands. Out of habit, Wolf scanned the incoming crowd. A large brooding man drew his attention. One of the heavyweights from the Sputnik's bar was climbing the stands to take up position on the same upper tier. The Tatar eyed the SEALs but averted his gaze when Wolf caught him looking their way.

*A tail? Better mention him to Colter*, thought Wolf. *Could be nothing but curiosity. You never know.* Aside from the stranger's quick glance, Wolf saw nothing else to concern him. He and Colter stood off to one side, near a railing. Below them, Warren and his NASA engineers claimed prominent positions in the first row.

Wolf focused a pair of small binoculars on the bulbous capsule crowning the slender upper stage of the Soyus7. Wolf shifted the glasses, studying the rocket's glistening coat of frost—a result of the liquid oxygen added to the fuel. The support booms and trusses released, dropping away gracefully like petals, leaving a lone support boom steadying the cylindrical second and third stages topped by the spacecraft. Ignition. A distant growl rumbled from the launch site's concrete dock. The first stage's four conical exhausts shook, belching fiery white-hot tongues, enveloping the pad in smoke and fire.

The rocket rose majestically, blasting clear of its support tower and shooting heavenward, trailing volcanic flames. Spontaneous applause broke out among the mesmerized ranks. Within minutes, the four boosters separated, falling away in intersecting vapor trails forming what was called the Korolev cross. The rocket became a glowing torch, then a pinpoint of light arcing high overhead.

"Just another day at the office," said Colter, binoculars locked on the flight. He and Wolf came down the steps and rejoined the NASA engineers milling in the thinning crowd. There were more pictures, congratulations, laughter, and handshakes, then a place in the queue to the buses.

"Did you pick up our tail?" whispered Colter.

"Affirmative. You saw him, too?"

"I did. Hard to fit in at his size. Not a very discreet shadow, is he?"

Wolf said, "If you mean subtle, no. If you mean intimidating, yes. I pegged him for one of those linebackers from the hotel."

"Where's his clone? I didn't see him at the sendoff."

Wolf frowned. "You don't suppose..."

Colter nodded. "I do indeed, Wolfman. We got problems."

# Chapter 11

The two SEALs climbed aboard their tour bus, endured a windy lecture about the Russian space program, and counted the minutes until they returned to their hotel. A final lunch was planned, followed by a ride to the airport for an afternoon flight to Moscow for those leaving. The NASA delegation and the Italians were to stay on a few days. Wolf excused himself and went upstairs. Alone in the hallway, he pressed his ear to the door of his room. Hearing nothing, he entered.

Though things seemed untouched, Wolf wasn't fooled. Someone had been in the room. Maids, turned away by a "Do Not Disturb" sign hanging on the door since breakfast, were not the likely culprits. His luggage and Colter's, black nylon bags with shoulder straps, looked undisturbed. A second look told him otherwise. At Colter's suggestion, the bags' zippers, deliberately left open earlier to satisfy the curious, had been returned to uneven positions along the track.

*An amateur oversight*, thought Wolf. *Cocksure bastards.*

Little things caught Wolf's eye: a lamp off center, the wall-mounted TV now at a slightly different angle as if someone had looked behind it. A faint trace of talcum powder Colter had purposely dusted on the bathroom's threshold that morning, was smudged—the result of a clumsy foot belonging to an uninvited guest. He had seen enough. Locking the door behind him, Wolf went downstairs to warn Colter.

Surrounded by Italians, Colter said, "Hey, Wolfman, pull up a chair."

Wolf nodded politely. "Buongiorno, signori. Per favore exuse noi."

"Naturalmente," said the group's leader.

Colter got up, followed Wolf to a corner table. "I'm impressed. Who knew you spoke Italian?"

"Yeah, all of a dozen words that could get you laid in Naples. Look, Dawg, like you said, we got problems."

"The big boys, right?"

"You got it. Looks like Tatar One stayed behind while Tatar Two went to this morning's launch."

"Probably to keep an eye on us. Okay, what's the problem?"

"Well, Goldilocks, surprise. Someone was in our room while we were gone. My guess is they were looking for our little black book."

Colter glanced around the dining room. "Okay. Our bad boys are probably still checked in. Doubt they're booked on the next flight back to Moscow."

"If they followed us here, they're bound to stick with us until they get what they came for."

"They must know we have the book. Maybe Yana talked."

Wolf stared at the floor, a dozen grisly scenes flashing in his head. "Damn, I should have played hooky and stayed behind."

"I'm not saying that's what happened," said Colter. "I'm only guessing at the probability."

"You could be right. My only hope is that Kozuch gave them our names instead of Yana's. I'm probably grasping at straws, but it's a possibility."

Colter softened. "Sorry, Wolfman. So, what do you want to do about these goons? They seem pretty ham-handed for an assignment like this."

"It's not a very sophisticated operation. Follow us, search our room, find the book, and whack us. Return with said book."

"What if we take them out first?"

"Tempting. But even if we got away with it, how long do you think it would take for the news to get back to Moscow? We'd be picked up as soon as we set foot there. The way things are between the Kremlin and Washington, we'd be hung out to dry."

"More likely we'd disappear," said Colter.

"If we can get back to Moscow intact we have a chance. I like our odds better there than out here in Never-Never Land."

"Yeah, but think about it, Wolfman. These guys will have backup in Moscow. We'd get pulled off the plane or frog-marched out of the airport and taken to some warehouse. The bad guys would have the book and we'd disappear."

"Not exactly how I want to end my first trip to Russia."

Brightening, Colter said, "I have an alternative that might work."

# Chapter 12

"We need to get rid of the book."

At a corner table in the hotel dining room, out of earshot of the nearest group of hotel guests, Wolf and Colter talked over their limited options.

Bewildered by Colter's suggestion, Wolf said, "Get rid of the book? Are you nuts? We're already in deep shit. Why would we get rid of it at this point? No book, no bargaining chip."

"What exactly does that bargaining chip look like?" said Colter. "And how do we go about playing that chip? Once these guys get their hands on it, we're history."

Wolf massaged his temples, trying to shape a response. "As long as we have the book, we stay alive…for now."

Colter lowered his head. "Until they take it from us."

"Exactly. Then we're just so much excess baggage to get rid of. Hold on, Dawg, I see a tactical advantage here."

"I'm all ears."

Wolf spread his hands on the table, his eyes locked on Colter's. "These bozos have overplayed their hand. They turned our room upside down but didn't find anything, right? They don't know we saw their big paw prints all over our stuff. They probably figure we have the book on us, right? That means they'll come after us at some point. If not here, in Moscow."

Colter thrust a hand inside his jacket's breast pocket. "I'm the one out on a limb."

"I appreciate that. So right now our best bet is to stay with a crowd at all times. I don't think they'd try anything in public. Which leads me to think these guys may not be government thugs. If the FSB wanted the book they wouldn't need an excuse to stop and search us."

"That's hardly reassuring. Consider this: the government might be farming this out to some of their own black hats so they can claim plausible deniability if it blows up in their faces."

"Possibly. Volatility is their downside. Kill first, then ask questions."

"How about you babysit the book for a spell."

"You're doing a great job, Dawg. Let's stick with the plan."

"That's it? This is your tactical advantage?"

"Actually, yes. These guys do not know we've made them." Tapping his forehead with an index finger, Wolf said, "We're already one step ahead of them. They think they're invisible right now. That's their weakness."

"I don't disagree, but I still think we should get rid of the book. That's our best option."

"Explain to me how that's supposed to work."

"We photograph every page in the book. Then we embed the image in pictures on our cameras."

The light went on for Wolf. "Of course. Then we wouldn't need the book."

"Affirmative."

"But wait, how do we get the photos out? What if one of these assholes gets their hands on your camera?"

"Won't matter. They won't be able to read what we've got. Once we get the files encrypted on the photos, I'll sweet-talk Dana into using the NASA link to send the data to both our stateside email accounts as backup."

"Would she do that?"

"I'll tell her I want to dump some of the photos because I only have one card. She'll help us send the photos back stateside." Colter grinned like a devious college boy. "That's our ace. They use the link to send launch shots to NASA, CONUS, and all the major media outlets. Hell, we'll be the only ones who will know the initial algorithms used to embed the text. We can decrypt at the other end. Wolfman, it's a slam dunk."

"I like it."

"I have five hundred shots on my camera," said Colter. "Between us we've got more than enough to do the trick. Plus, you sew the card in your coat sleeve as backup. You cool with that?"

"And why am I sewing the card in my coat?"

"Cause it's your turn in the barrel. I've been carrying around this damn book since Moscow."

"Okay, I get it. You sure Dana will go for it?"

"I bought her some drinks the other night. We're tight."

Grinning, Wolf sat back. "Ha, you thought I was the incorrigible one."

Colter punched Wolf's arm. "Lucky for you I'm thinking, sailor."

"I think we should tear out a couple of the pages for safekeeping."

Colter frowned. "Why? If we're caught with them it would just confirm we had the book. I don't think it's worth the risk."

Wolf said, "We may need them down the line at some point. They could be a bargaining chip of some sort."

"Uh, I'm not sure about that. The card ought to be enough."

Putting a hand on Colter's arm, Wolf said, "I'll take the risk. Look, I'll stash a couple of pages in my jacket lining as backup."

A reluctant Colter gave in. "Okay. But we still have the problem with the Tatar twins."

Wolf was focused. "First, step one: copy the pages and have Dana set up the link transfer. Once that's done, step two: we go into town and buy some very sharp Kazakh souvenirs."

"Then, step three."

"Which is?"

"We take out the bad guys."

# Chapter 13

Wolf's role in baiting his trap that night in the hotel's bar proved surprisingly easy. Hamming it up for the eavesdropping Tatars, Wolf played it loud and loose-lipped in the bar after dinner while wearing an outfitter's camping headlamp. He held court at a corner table covered with a large, hand-drawn map of the old Soviet ICBM sites. Wolf pounded the chart for emphasis during a rambling tabletop tour of the long abandoned launch facilities. "There's a lot of Cold War history there," he said. "Tomorrow morning, my friend and I intend to explore it." The western barflies erupted in cheers.

"How are you going to find your way among the ruins?" asked a Brit.

"Good question," said Wolf. "I'm glad you asked."

Wolf mounted a chair and signaled for silence. He and Colter had hired Yorgi, he announced. A local cab driver familiar to western tourists, the wrinkled Kazakh, who claimed descent from a line of khans dating to the great Genghis himself, was instantly the center of attention.

Wolf boomed, "Ladies and gentlemen, may I present tomorrow's guide, the well-known and well-beloved Yorgi!"

Wolf climbed down and threw an arm around the slight and perpetually smiling Kazakh elder. Applause rippled across the room. Wolf bought a round for his audience. Guiding the little man by the elbow, Wolf parted the crowd and leaned over the map, his headlamp darting across the paper. The Kazakh, wearing a faded Soviet Olympic tracksuit and a prized Yankees ball cap, stabbed gnarled fingers at the map.

"I know this place. Very dangerous. Not so good to visit, you know? Plenty trash. Underground is bad. Everything broken there."

Wolf played along. "But it is a very famous place to see, Yorgi. I am not afraid to explore. You will take Colter and me there tomorrow, yes?"

Shaking his head, the chauffeur said, "Yah, yah, I know what you want. There is a big red building, all rust now. By old train depot. I don't think you go there. Too dangerous."

Thumping his chest, Wolf regaled his multinational audience with an anecdote. "Dangerous? Hah! When I was in Gibraltar I spent an entire day exploring tunnels where the big guns used to be. You hear me? An entire day by myself in the dark with a tiny flashlight. You think deserted rocket test pads and crumbling bunkers scare me? Not a chance!"

Between downing shots of vodka and his loud bravado, Wolf lulled the Tatars and everyone else into believing he was drunk. From the corner of his eye, he spotted the big men at the fringe of amused drinkers.

*Listen up, boys. I don't want you to miss a thing.*

"Okay, I take you," sighed the Kazakh. "What time you want to go?"

"Ten o'clock," roared Wolf. "Tomorrow morning. You take us there and come back at three o'clock, okay?" He flashed his diver's watch in the headlamp's glow. Making an exaggerated drunken effort to focus on the dial, he said, "Three o'clock, Yorgi. Go at ten; come back at three. You understand?"

"I know, I know," said the Kazakh. "Three o'clock. Okay. Crazy Amerikanski. Tomorrow." The little man pushed his way through the ring of hooting bystanders.

Colter worked his way to Wolf. "Sir Laurence Olivier couldn't have done it better," he whispered. "How's your sobriety? Had enough?"

"Yeah. I reached my quota two drinks ago. Get me outta here."

Wolf surveyed the crowded room. Reeling in the Tatars, he lifted a shot glass of vodka. "To tomorrow!"

"Tomorrow!" parroted his amused audience, Tatars included.

# Chapter 14

Swirling sand scoured upended blocks of ragged concrete, stinging Wolf's eyes. Kneeling behind a half-buried cement casemate, he turned his backpack to the whirlwind. Colter, his head wrapped in a makeshift turban, lingered at the end of cracked pavement with a water bottle in hand. He gave Yorgi final instructions about the pickup time for the return, then sent him off with a wave. The Kazakh drove away in coiling brown dust.

Colter strode to the ruined bunker where Wolf squatted, sipping from a bottle. "Game's on. Let's set up."

Wolf rose to his feet and pointed at a scorched concrete depression in the distance. "Might be some access belowground over there."

"Lead on."

The two SEALs battled the wind across a landscape littered with crushed piping, burned scraps of fuselage, rusting stripped jeeps and charred girders. More ravaged moonscape than military site, the abandoned ICBM launch pad was a hollow reminder of the catastrophic misfires that had happened there during Russia's nascent rocket age.

Wolf did a three-sixty turn atop a reinforced pad faint with a kerosene scent. "This place makes a Mumbai landfill look good by comparison. Wonder how many acres of Kazakh real estate the Russkis trashed."

"Reminds me of Eastern Europe when the Soviets were in charge," said Colter, disgusted. "Move in, rip a place apart, turn it into a garbage dump, and move on to the next spot."

"The next five generations of Kazakhs are gonna regret letting the Soviets screw up their land."

"Not like they had much choice, Wolfman."

"True. Okay, where do we set up?"

Colter said, "These bunkers ain't deep enough." He nodded at a towering shed. "How about that building? According to Yorgi it's honeycombed with underground passages. That's what we're gonna need for the boys."

"Agreed. My money says they'll collar Yorgi so he can drop them at the same spot he left us."

"That's the plan, Wolfman. He knows what to do."

"We're the only two coming back, Dawg."

"You read my mind. How much time we got?"

"Until fifteen hundred. Don't worry. He'll be on time."

Wolf hunched against the wind. "Okay, let's go prepare a proper Kazakh welcome for the Tatar Twins."

They probed the skeletal entrance to what had been a cavernous rocket assembly building and followed a pair of rusting iron rails leading to a towering doorway. A bony dog watching the two intruders thought better of it and trotted away. As if peeled back by a giant's hand, great sheets of charred, pitted steel riveted to the framework shivered in the gusts. Inside, sheltered from the wind, the two found a ghostly silence. They walked the outer margins of the huge space and found a tangled pile of twisted iron trusses. A section of concrete floor had collapsed; revealing a dark opening roughly rectangular in shape. The access below offered Wolf an idea.

"They'd have to come this way," he said, waving his arm from the building railway tracks to the gaping hole. "Let's see what's down there before we commit."

Both men fit camping headlights over their black balaclavas and donned gloves. Colter went first. He scrambled down a sloping ramp of broken concrete and ended forty feet below the surface, his headlamp a halo of light. He raised an eight-foot length of iron rebar like a staff. "Hey! We can find a use for this." Colter glanced up at the watching Wolf. "The pile is stable enough, but don't take any chances."

"Roger that. Coming down, Dawg."

Wolf dislodged small rocks during his descent and reached Colter's side in a dusty landslide of stone. "Sorry about that."

"No problem. Actually, that's a good thing," said Colter. "No way guys their size could tiptoe without us hearing them coming."

Wolf's voice bounced off the walls. "I don't think these guys give a damn about making noise. And I think they'll be packing when they show." He passed his light over the eroded ceiling. "Might be good to take them when they reach the bottom of this slope. Whadaya think?" His echo died in the dim cavern.

"Let's scout around some more. This spot is too open for me. I'd like to get them in a tight spot where they can't maneuver."

"Oh, great. Mano a mano with blades. Always wanted to do that."

"You have done it, Wolfman. I read your file."

"Not by choice, Dawg. Did you forget the rule about not bringing a knife to a gun fight?"

"No choice."

Colter disappeared behind a row of support girders the size of elephants. Wolf was left to negotiate a towering spaghetti-like tangle of reinforcing rod. With their flashlights throwing cones of light among the ruins, both men explored their surroundings.

"Hard to believe we're rummaging through what's left of the Cold War," boomed Wolf. "Didn't think to ask Yorgi about radioactivity."

Colter's laughter floated from a dark, unseen corner. "Too late."

"Find anything?"

"I got something. Can you see me?"

"Not a thing," said Wolf. "Your light on?"

"Wait one."

A shadow flickered from a narrow opening on Wolf's left. "Got it," he said. "Keep the light going. I'm coming your way."

Bluish light shimmered, outlining a crumbling portal at the bottom of steps piled with rubble. Hearing Colter's voice, Wolf crouched, working his way down a steep, debris-filled hallway. At the threshold, doubled over to gain entrance, he found himself in a low-ceilinged room. The opposite wall was given over to a control panel of long-dead gauges, buttons, switches and levers. Wires snaked everywhere as if ripped from sockets during a botched dismantling. Propped in the room's far corner, an upended chair lay covered in cobwebs. Pulsing with light, Colter's phone lay on a shelf, his disembodied voice spouting nonsense.

Wolf leaned into the room, feeling his way past a partially collapsed wall. Blinded by a flash of light, he cried out.

A hand closed around his throat.

Gasping for breath, he reached for the Kazakh dagger in his belt.

"HOLD IT, WOLFMAN!" Colter's voice boomed in Wolf's right ear.

Still blinded, Wolf sputtered, "What the..."

Colter's ragged laugh filled the cramped room. "Man, you should have seen your face. Actually, I had my eyes closed when the flash popped."

Wolf sagged against a wall, struggling to regain his voice and his vision. "What the...hell was that...all about?"

"If you're one of the Tatars, right about now you're bleeding out."

Wolf rasped, "I was...following...you."

"I know. This is it. This is the spot. If I could fool you..."

Wolf's vision was returning in fuzzy swimming pixels. "You sonofabitch, I could have killed you."

Colter retrieved his blinking phone. "Negative. You were already dead by the time you went for your knife. Let's face it. You lost your night vision and were doubled over coming down that hallway. I had you. Man, you were as dead as Caesar. Admit it."

Wolf nodded. "One for you, Dawg. You're right. Take them here."

"Only we have to get them here, right?"

"Well, I followed you. Saw your light. Heard your voice."

Colter ran his bandana across his face. "That's how we lure them this way. I catch one of them like that, he's toast."

"A big *IF*. If he tangles with you in this space it could get dicey."

"Tell me something I don't know."

"Maybe we should trade places. Knife fighting is in my file, you know."

Colter laughed, shaking his head. "Touché. Nah, I got this, Wolfman. There's a hide just outside the entrance. A perfect blind spot. You lay up there until the ugly twins get down here."

"I like it. Let 'em pass, get stuck in the passageway, then take them out."

"Only one of them is getting out of this dead end alive, Wolfman."

"Right. I'll finish the other guy if he makes a run."

"If he's smart, he will run. Take out his legs with the rebar. Believe me, he'll go down regardless of size."

"Then I gut him."

"Have to move fast. I think they'll come in hot."

Wolf held up his glistening Kazakh blade. "Cold steel."

Colter slashed the air with his knife. "I come at him when he's blinded. Two up, two down. Work for you?"

"Works for me."

"They'll hear voices on the phone and see the light. They'll come down that slope, come this way, and think they've got us cornered."

"Here's hoping we pull it off, Dawg."

"It'll work. They're so hungry for the book they can taste it."

"I'll go topside and keep an eye peeled for our guests."

Colter glanced at his watch. "Good idea. They'll be here soon. Yorgi will see to that."

"You trust him? He could set us up. Could drop a dime on us."

Nodding, Colter said, "Always possible. But we have a leg up."

"How so?"

"We outbid the other guys."

# Chapter 15

The Tatars did come. Delivered by Yorgi as planned, the two large men demanded he wait. Either way, the Kazakh knew he was returning with two.

Picking their way across launch site ruins, the Tatars followed tracks left by Wolf and Colter and headed directly for the deserted plant. Armed with Walther PPKs, they made no attempt to hide their weapons.

Leaving his backpack where the iron rails curved into the abandoned building, Wolf backed away from the entrance. He gained the underground access just before the Tatars reached the gaping doorway. He eyed one of the Tatars rifling the contents of the backpack while the other swept the cavernous shed with his pistol.

Wolf slithered down the rubble on his belly, barely disturbing the rockfall. When he reached the bottom, he signaled Colter by tossing a small pebble in his direction. Light flickered in the burrow's narrow mouth. Colter's voice echoed in the ruins.

*His cellphone. Perfect.*

Wolf retreated to his hidden spot, gripped the heavy iron bar, and waited, his eyes on the yawning hole above.

As expected, Colter's chatter drew the Tatars. For Wolf, the effect on their pursuers was almost comical—like amateurs in a bad spy movie. The armed men tested the slope of rocky debris. One crouched at the jagged cement lip, his Walther covering the debris slope. His partner stumbled down the incline, dislodging small boulders on his way down. He dusted himself off and took up position behind an iron girder, his pistol pointed away from the hidden Wolf. The second Tatar, misjudging his rate of descent, arrived on his backside in a cloud. Both hit men, unsure if the element of surprise had been lost, waited for the dust to settle.

Colter's voice continued its breezy chatter from the bunker. Light from his phone's screen flickered from the narrow doorway. Certain he saw his enemies smile, Wolf's right hand closed around the iron shaft at his side. They passed so close Wolf could smell the fear. The pair whispered short, guttural, angry words in Kazan Tatar, their breath labored. Stones crunched beneath their shoes inches from Wolf in the shadows.

Weapons held out in front, the two queued single-file into the narrow stairway leading to Colter's ambush site.

Coiled to strike, Wolf recited a silent rhyme.

*Come into my parlor, said the spider...*

Wolf pictured the bulky physiques filling the rubble-filled passage and closed his eyes against the expected flash.

A brilliant white flash exploded. A shout. Two shots. Screaming.

Wolf scrambled to his feet, waited, the bar raised high overhead. One of the Tatars, gasping for air, fled the death trap on hands and knees. Blinded, pistol in hand, he pawed at the stones in panic.

Wolf split the prone man's head like a ripe melon. One down. He tossed the bloodied shaft aside, grabbed the Tatar's pistol, and leaped in the stairway. Wolf jammed the weapon against the second man's spine and fired twice.

The struggling stopped.

"DAWG! TALK TO ME!"

A weak response.

"Turn off the fucking phone," screamed Wolf. "I can't hear you!"

Silence.

"You there? Dawg!"

"I'm here. Got nicked."

"Bad?"

"Bad enough." A pause, then, "Get this lard ass off me."

With the Tatar's body wedged in the narrow opening, Colter was trapped. Wolf dropped the pistol and braced his feet against the body. It took him precious minutes to dislodge the corpse. The dead man toppled forward in the rubble. Wolf extended a hand to Colter, hauling him up the steps and propping him by the second body.

Colter eyed the battered corpse. "Geez, what the hell did you do to him?"

"Couldn't help it. He was trying to give himself up when I hit him."

An exhausted Colter clapped Wolf on the shoulder, his grip weak. "Damn. You put the world of hurt on him. Gonna have to add assassination by rebar to your file."

Wolf didn't laugh. He lifted Colter's shirt, examining a deep gash. "He cut you, Dawg."

Colter said, "He did. I lit him up with the flash. Hit him with the blade just under the jaw. Sucker was an ox. Got off a shot. We fought for the knife. Got his hands on it and cut me. I took his gun and fired but you finished him."

"You're bleeding bad. We need to stop it."

"No shit."

Wolf took off his jacket, tore a sweatshirt over his head, and ripped his T-shirt into strips. He made a thick compress and pressed it into Colter's wound. "Hold it there. Keep the pressure on."

"Can do."

"Good. You might be going into shock. Got to elevate your feet."

"I know the drill."

Wolf covered Colter with his parka and propped his feet on a chunk of concrete. He glanced at his watch. "Yorgi should be sitting out there. Can you hold on?"

"No choice. I'm walking out."

"We'll see about that. Got to haul this asshole into the bunker."

He wrestled his Tatar down the narrow steps. Twice, the dead man's body lodged itself in the confined space, frustrating Wolf's efforts. "Next time," he bellowed from the bunker, "let's pick on smaller targets."

Colter laughed despite his pain.

Wolf used a fireman's carry to surface with Colter on his back. They made their way to the pickup point and found Yorgi's car. The Kazakh asked no questions. He took Colter's right arm. Wolf, the left. Colter collapsed in the backseat, his hand planted on his side.

"My friend fell," deadpanned Wolf. "He's hurt bad, I think."

The Kazakh played along. "I tell you before. Dangerous. You don't listen so good. See what happens?"

Wolf accepted the Kazakh's rebuke. "You were right, Yorgi. We were wrong. Won't do that again."

"Good. We go back to hotel?"

"Yeah. When we get there, keep him in the car until I come back for him, okay?"

Yorgi nodded, his eyes in the rearview mirror. He had no love for the Tatars. Besides, Americans always paid better.

# Chapter 16

The wait before returning to Moscow proved to be among the longest forty-eight hours of Wolf's life. He summoned Paolo, the Italian team's doctor, whom Colter had

befriended. The ex-navy physician, voicing solidarity with the Americans, went to work immediately, cleaning and stitching the knife wound. He pumped the former SEAL full of antibiotics and pledged his silence. Colter, an iron man, endured the emergency operation without complaint.

With Wolf covering for him, Colter begged off attending the next programmed event—a European satellite launch. He took meals in their room, assuring Wolf the crisis was past. Though the Americans worried, no one seemed to notice the missing Tatars, despite their size.

The day they left, Colter moved slowly, blaming a stubborn cold and fatigue. Along with the Italians and NASA's contingent, he and Wolf boarded Perm Airline's three o'clock afternoon Moscow flight. Colter seemed to be healing well. Wolf spent the entire two-hour-and-forty-five minute trip in the midst of the Italians, laughing, regaling them with tales, playing cards, and trading reviews of American films.

They landed at Domodedovo, Russia's largest airport—a gleaming modern showcase twenty-six miles southeast of Moscow. Wolf and Colter immediately noticed the two watchdogs waiting patiently for the Baikanour flight. To frustrate their new trackers, Wolf split the pair by initially staying with Warren and his fifteen-member NASA group. He made a phone call from the safety of their numbers.

Colter went in another direction. The Italians surrounded him and escorted him en masse to a nearby restroom. In a locked stall, Paolo hurriedly changed Colter's dressing and pronounced the SEAL well enough to continue his travel with a warning. "Do not delay seeing a physician when you return to America."

The Italians and Americans milled about, saying their goodbyes. A second pair of spotters showed, cut from the same cloth as thugs one and two. When he saw his chance, Wolf signaled Colter.

Wolf knew he had five hours to make his part of the plan work and used Domodedovo's sea of foot traffic to disappear. He slipped away in the buzzing hive that was the main terminal, doubled back, and headed for the AeroExpress train platform. Once he was confident he had been undetected, he bought round-trip business class passage from one of the line's red-suited mobile ticket sellers. The next train, she cautioned, was due to leave in five minutes.

With only a small carry-on bag over one shoulder, Wolf picked up a discarded newspaper for camouflage and hurried to the sleek red coach with only minutes to spare. He settled into a reserved plush blue seat and buried his nose in newsprint as late arrivals filled the coach. One of the last to board, a plump, fur-wearing matron with rubbery jowls, sank down next to him in a cloud of cheap perfume. Wolf's polite smile was rebuffed with a disapproving frown. No matter; he was grateful for the cover. A soothing recorded voice announced the departure for Moscow's Pavelestsky Station. The doors hissed shut and the train began to move.

In Wolf's absence, Colter, accompanied by Paolo, used the same tactic to shake his shadows. A tail and his backup quickly lost contact with Colter in the milling crowd. Using the ensuing confusion, the SEAL and the doctor rendezvoused with the remaining Italians who were waiting at a café for their flight to be called. Colter ordered a coffee, killing time for the next two hours. When the Italians eventually rose to leave, Colter shook hands with each. His newly arrived tails loitered several tables away, pretending disinterest. Walking Paolo and friends to a security checkpoint, Colter bade them farewell with promises to stay in touch.

Colter checked his watch. He had four hours to kill before the Japan Airlines connection. He wandered to a crowded gift shop, one eye on the trinkets, one on his hovering trackers. Staying in the open where the shadows could see him but not betray themselves by rushing him was his best option until Wolf returned.

# Chapter 17

The Domodedovo commuter train glided to a stop at its terminus: a wide, open-air platform where seven tracks ended beneath a neon sign spelling Moscow in tall Cyrillic letters. Seeking anonymity among the rushing throng, Wolf stepped from the car. Two policemen led by a harnessed dog parted the wave of incoming passengers. Stepping aside, Wolf smiled, nodded, and kept walking. In the main terminal, as instructed by phone, he walked to the third entrance where Yana, wrapped in fur, waited.

"You are as beautiful as I remembered," he said, embracing her.

Muffled in his hug, she said, "I like this plan you have for us."

Walking arm in arm, Wolf said, "I had to see you. I was worried about you."

"As I was for you. And yet you risk your life to have just hours together. You have taken a great chance, Tom."

Exiting the station to the outdoor plaza, he said, "Perhaps we both have taken a risk. Colter read some of the book you gave us. Disturbing things."

"But you will see it published, yes?"

"We'll try, Yana. First, we have to get out of Russia with it."

"Do you have it with you?"

Wolf smiled. "It's in good hands." He read his watch. "I have four hours before I leave for Tokyo."

"Come, I have a quiet place not far from here."

"Another amazing hideaway, huh? I suppose a cousin."

"A friend. She trusts me. Is just a few blocks on Novokuznetskaya."

*I must be nuts to be doing this*, Wolf thought. *There are genuine bad guys out there looking for both of us and I'm acting*

*like a lovesick kid. I am nuts. Why this particular woman?*
*What is it about her?*

Their refuge was an apartment on the second floor of a
four-story yellow stone building with windows trimmed in
white stone. Narrow-barred ground-floor windows flanked
a heavy carved archway, like an entrance to a cave. A skirt
of dirty snow hid most of a broken sidewalk lined with the
usual black- and-white curbstones. Two sets of streetcar
tracks divided the middle of the aging pavement. Naked
trees lined the street behind iron fences.

She led him inside, up a curving staircase to the
second floor.

"I feel like Dr. Zhivago," said Wolf. "Which means
you must be—"

She unlocked the door. "Lara, the temptress."

"Yes, Lara," he whispered. "Zhivago was a risk-taker,
you know."

"They come to a sad end, yes? So very Russian, don't
you think?"

Shedding his parka, he threw his arms around her.
"We could write our own ending if we wanted to."

They kissed again. She broke away, leading him to a bed
covered in quilts and soft pillows. They undressed and
slipped beneath the covers.

Later, Wolf laughed, arms around her. "I'm sure I felt
the earth move. How about you?"

Yana giggled. "It was only a streetcar," she said, waving
at the arched window. Barefooted and wrapped in a quilt,
she tiptoed into the tiny kitchen, put a tea kettle on the
stove, and crawled back in bed beside him.

They made love again.

Tea water boiled, hissing softly. Another streetcar
rumbled below.

"Have you ever dreamed of perhaps coming to America?"

Yana shook her head. "How could I abandon my mother and sister?"

"I know." Stroking her hair, he said, "I understand. I admire you for it."

They wrapped quilts around themselves and sat at a small, scarred wooden table next to a curtained window, sipping tea as if they had been lovers forever.

Breaking the spell, Wolf lowered his voice. "Do the men who killed your uncle know he gave you the book?"

"No. He would never betray me."

"But he would point the finger at Colter and me?"

Yana locked her blue eyes with his. "He knew you were...how to say this...able to defend yourselves. Please, if you can find it in your hearts, forgive his weakness."

Wolf sat back. "Every man has his breaking point, Yana. Neither of us would hold that against your uncle." He smiled. "Better us than you."

Her quilt fell away. She put a hand on his arm. "But you face evil men and the odds are not so good for you, yes?"

"True. But Colter and I are not Boy Scouts, Yana."

"Yes. But you are angels, are you not?"

"We've been called many things, but angels is not one of them."

An ancient clock crowning an even older glass-lined cabinet rang the hour. Next to the timepiece, Wolf's cellphone hummed. He plucked it from the top shelf and glanced at an incoming text from Colter.

*Feeling like Custer. Assistance appreciated whenever.*

"I have to go. Colter needs me."

Yana stood, one hand clutching the quilt low on her hips. Letting it fall to the floor, she leaned across the table and kissed him, her blonde hair falling over him, her eyes wet with tears. Wolf groaned, wanting the moment to last forever, but she broke away and began dressing. He did the same.

They walked along Novokuznetskaya Street to the station. A trolley rattled past. Looking at each other simultaneously, they burst out laughing. At the station, Yana buried her face against his chest, sobbing. She wiped away her tears, kissed Wolf one last time and sent him on his way without looking back.

Wolf boarded the now familiar red AeroExpress to Domodedovo. Other airport-bound passengers dragging wheeled luggage filled the seats around him. A hostess wearing the line's scarlet livery came by, offering hot or cold drinks. Wolf declined, his mind on Yana.

Colter's words in the club came back to him.

*Is this what it means to feel old?*

The train began to move, picking up speed as it fled through Moscow's shabby depressing outskirts. The remainder of the trip passed in silence, save for the low murmur of fellow passengers. Wolf thought of Colter. The trackers who had lost him would be on a short leash and foultempered once they found him again. These new men would likely not be the bumblers he and Colter had outfoxed in Baikonur. These reinforcements would be angry at being outwitted on their home turf and thus, dangerous.

If Yana was right about her uncle's pointing at Colter and him she might be safe. Leaving her behind was among the hardest things he had done. Why? There had been other women. *Why should she be any different?* In these few short days, Yana had become more than just a lover. Or had she? *I hope you know what you're doing*, he told himself. *Think. Gotta focus, focus.*

# Chapter 18

*Domodedovo Airport*

Wolf found Colter at a small coffee bar in the overseas terminal. The perspiring SEAL was pale and agitated, his back against a pillar giving him a clear view of the foot traffic. "Never thought I'd say I was glad to see your ugly mug."

Wolf pulled up a chair. "Likewise, Dawg. How long you been holed up here?"

"Two hours plus. I stayed with the Italians as long as I could."

"Maybe I shouldn't have left you out in the open."

"No big deal, Wolfman. I was with you in spirit. Hope it was worth it."

Smiling, Wolf said, "Appreciate the sentiment. We played chess."

"I'll bet you did."

Colter shrugged. "Given our situation I think we can kiss our luggage goodbye. It's a given these low-lifes have the baggage handlers in their pocket. They've probably already sliced and diced it looking for the book. Likely tossed our belongings when they couldn't find it. No big deal. They're welcome to my dirty laundry."

"How you holding up?"

"Been better. Been worse. Fucking Tatars. I took one for the team back there but I'm not falling over until we get to the States if that's what you're asking."

"What's the pain level?"

"Manageable."

"You have a fever?"

"Mild one."

"Paolo leave you with enough medicine?"

"I'm good."

"Our flight's not for another hour," said Wolf. "The crowd is starting to thin. These assholes will probably make a run at us soon."

Defiant, Colter shot a scowl at Wolf. "Let 'em try it. I've been screwing with these pea-brains ever since you went off to see Cinderella. By the way, how was the lady? Did you get lucky again?"

Wolf grinned.

Colter groaned. "I knew it. And you call yourself a gentleman. Shit, I'll be the one wearing a shirt that reads, 'Visited Russia and all I got was this scar and a lousy T-shirt.' You, on the other hand, will have a T-shirt reading—"

"Don't say it. Don't even think it." Wolf beamed, his eyes closed. "I am in your debt. There's no way I can make this up to you. Not in a thousand years. I think I'm in love."

"You're sick, Wolfman. Damn. Here I was arranging the chairs at the Alamo while you were off chasing tail. I hope it was worth it."

"Hey, you were having tail chase you. What's to complain about? The way I see it, we're practically even."

"Not by a long shot. You're right, you owe me big time."

Aside from the carry-ons both had, and the card and three pages sewn in his jacket's sleeve, Wolf and Colter were clear of the one thing that could prove incriminating: the actual book. But Colter had attracted the full quartet of bloodhounds in the middle of Russia's busiest airport.

Wolf nodded at two of the surly thugs on couches screened by plants. "How long they been here?"

"Two hours at least. They must have bladders of iron."

"How about you? We could change your dressing."

Colter grimaced. "Paolo took care of that. But if I don't make a pit stop soon I'm going to end up using one of those potted shrubs. My guess is cops here frown on that kind of behavior."

"Okay, there's a head just around the corner. We could trade off to be safe. You game?"

"They've been waiting for something like this. They'll take the opportunity. You know they will."

Rolling a magazine into a baton, Wolf said, "I'll cover the door."

"They might be carrying, Wolfman."

"It's a risk. If they come after me, I'll make a scene. Loud."

"Okay, sounds like a plan...sort of. Just so you know, in training we never covered how to defend yourself in a head."

"Just think of high school. Improvise."

"Better yet," said Wolf, "I'll round up some airport cops to interfere."

"I like that idea. Evens the odds."

Fifteen minutes passed before a pair of policemen came strolling their way. Timing was critical. Wolf nodded, sending Colter for the bathroom. Rolled magazine in hand, he played rear guard. On cue, four watchdogs followed. An unfortunate Chinese businessman exited to find himself between the American and the gangsters. Pushing the bewildered Chinese aside, two thugs rushed Wolf, who shouted in Russian.

*"POLITSYE! POLITSYE!"*

One goon threw a wild punch at Wolf. Ducking, Wolf jammed the rolled magazine in the man's throat, stunning him. He seized the attacker's wrist, snapping it and sending the gagging man to his knees in pain. The second heavy leaped his disabled mate to lunge at Wolf but missed Colter bolting from the bathroom. The wounded SEAL took a kick in the side from Wolf's fallen assailant who refused to yield.

Colter flicked his fingers in the second man's eyes, blinding him, and followed with a knee to the groin of the attacker, dropping him. Clearly surprised at the resistance they had witnessed, the two backups melted into the background when cops, drawn by the shouting, rushed in.

Despite the officers' arrival, Wolf would not release the wrist of his downed assailant until ordered to do so. The second attacker was on his hands and knees, gasping for breath. Another set of blue-shirted police arrived to assist. Gawkers gathered but were shooed away by additional officers summoned to the scene.

Propped against the wall, his right side slick with blood, Colter babbled in Russian that he and Wolf, thinking they were about to be robbed, had yelled for help. Wolf showed the Tokyo tickets and protested their innocence.

"They attacked us!" he yelled, pointing at the fallen pair.

"*Amerikanski?*" asked the lead cop.

Wolf and Colter nodded. The officer demanded to see passports. Reluctant to surrender them, the SEALs had no choice given the circumstances. Wolf took one look at Colter's bloodied shirt and crouched beside him.

"Oh, shit, Dawg. You opened up again. We gotta get you to a doc."

"Ain't gonna happen, Wolfman. I'm losing it...don't feel so good. I told them we were defending ourselves, didn't mean to cause a distraction."

"He knows," said Wolf. "I doubt we can pass for ordinary tourists after what we did to those two. That and your wound."

"Tell them...one of the guys had a knife...and tossed it."

Wolf applied pressure to Colter's side and pleaded for a medic.

Colter drifted. "Take my keys. Check my...computer. Don't let..."

A team appeared in minutes with a wheeled stretcher. Colter's eyes closed as he was rolled away to an elevator commandeered by police. Wolf tried to follow but was held back. A policeman said, "He is going to hospital."

After conferring with a newly arrived superior, the policemen called for electric carts. Wolf rode in one, glowering handcuffed thugs in another. It was the last he saw of his attackers. Wolf and three cops rode an elevator to the airport's lower level where he was hustled into the backseat of a van, a policeman on either side. Wolf resigned himself to the worst when he arrived at a nearby police station. A portly senior policeman processing him only shrugged upon hearing about the airport scuffle. Wolf was left alone in a spartan room furnished with a table and six chairs. If the setting was designed to disorient, it had the effect. Chipped whitewashed concrete walls met scarred beige tile and a single bare bulb dangled overhead.

Wolf paced, calming himself for whatever was next. To his surprise a silent orderly arrived with a tray containing a pot of coffee, crème, two sugared rolls, and a tumbler of vodka. Wolf opted for the vodka, then nibbled at the rolls. The coffee was strong, hot. He downed it to kill his sudden hunger.

The door opened and a uniformed, hatchet-faced FSB major joined him. Wolf's passport in one hand, the carry-on bag in the other, he placed both on the table and removed his military greatcoat.

Taking a chair opposite Wolf, the Russian said, "Good evening, Commander Wolf. On behalf of my government allow me to extend my sympathies to you and Commander Colter. I can assure you such crimes against visitors are rare here and dealt with accordingly."

"I certainly hope so, Major. How is my friend?"

"In most serious condition at this hour. He apparently suffered a knife wound though both assailants claim they did not attack like that."

"The wound speaks for itself."

"Ah, yes it does. Our physicians will do their best to restore Commander Colter's well-being. That said, I have questions. Strictly routine, of course."

"Of course." Wolf put down the cup of coffee and waited.

For the next ten minutes, Wolf was probed about the incident.

"Did you know these men who attacked you?"

"No. We were waiting for our Tokyo flight. I was exiting the toilet facilities when those two attacked me. My friend came to my rescue when he heard me shouting for the police."

"You defended yourselves quite admirably, though I regret that your companion was grievously wounded by one of your attackers."

"Only the arrival of your police officers saved us."

"Do you wish to file charges to your attackers?"

"Would that require us to remain?"

Shrugging, the major said, "Sometimes this is necessary to see justice in cases like this. It would take time, yes."

"Once my friend is able to travel we would prefer to continue on our way. Is that possible?"

"Hmm, I believe that is possible, yes. The men who attacked you are of the criminal element that sometimes targets unsuspecting visitors. And perhaps you can appreciate the fact that Westerners, and Americans in particular, are not so popular these days. Such is the way of our world today."

"Of course. We were indebted to your officers. They likely saved our lives. Despite our nations' current differences we will not forget the actions of your police."

"Yes, gratitude takes many forms, does it not?"

Wolf recognized the veiled solicitation. He leaned forward, his eyes meeting the major's gaze. "I am, of course, most grateful. Perhaps you might use your authority to assign a policeman to accompany me to the hospital where my friend is being cared for, sir. You can understand my concern, yes?"

The FSB man rubbed his hands together and smiled. "I think this is able to be arranged."

A smiling Wolf rose to shake hands with the major while palming a thick wad of dollars and rubles. Pocketing the money, the FSB man picked up his coat.

Wolf said, "I take it I am free to go, sir."

"Of course. In due time." The FSB officer donned his coat and left Wolf alone in the depressing interview room.

*Damn, now what? Another shakedown. What's happening with Colter?*

Despite Wolf's entreaties, two hours passed with no word.

Three hours after being delivered to the station, the corpulent duty officer appeared in the door, behind him a serious-looking younger man in a dark suit and trench coat, briefcase in hand. The officer ushered Wolf's visitor into the room.

"Ah, one of your countrymen," said the policeman.

Wolf, sensing a trap, studied the newcomer who extended a hand.

"Chase Taylor, American Embassy. Sorry to hear about the altercation, Commander. I'm here to help."

Wolf said, "I've always been told to watch out when someone says, 'I'm from the government and I'm here to help you.'"

A nervous laugh and Taylor glanced at the policeman. "Might I have a moment with my fellow citizen?"

The Russian turned to Taylor. "Of course. I hope this unfortunate episode does not reflect on our citizens. Perhaps the commander might return someday. I take my leave, gentlemen."

The embassy man tossed his coat on an empty chair and smoothed his dark hair. "Officious bastard," he said, pulling a yellow legal pad and pen from his briefcase. "He's probably sniffing for rubles."

"He's got mouths to feed," said Wolf, thinking of the greedy FSB major. "They all do it. They don't pay their cops enough."

"They'll get nothing from me on my watch." Flashing an earnest smile, Taylor said, "We'll get you out of here. I have a few questions, Commander."

Wolf interrupted Taylor. "Where's Dan Colter?"

"He's been taken to the hospital. One of our people is with him. We'll keep an eye on him until he's well enough to travel."

"We were to fly out to Tokyo tonight."

"Yes, so I'm told." Taylor glanced at his watch. "Sorry, that's a moot point now. Your flight to Japan boarded twenty minutes ago. Not to worry. We've rebooked you on an embassy red-eye to Dulles tonight. I've been authorized to send two staff with you as a precaution."

Up from his chair, Wolf paced, hands in pockets. "Precaution? What do you think is going to happen?"

"Commander, that's just the point. After what's occurred we want to make sure you return home safely. These are rather awkward times between our two countries. Surely, as a military man you can appreciate the situation."

"Feels like overkill to me. Taxpayers' money and all."

Taylor hovered over the legal pad, avoiding Wolf's eyes. "Never mind the cost. It's my job to make sure you are returned home without further incident. We've got to get you out of Russia for your own good."

"We were attacked. We didn't do anything to provoke those guys."

Taylor fiddled with his pen. "Understood. I just have a few questions you might help me with, please. The ambassador is anxious to know the details of this outrage. We'll want to file a diplomatic protest, of course."

"As if that will do any good." Pushing from the table, Wolf wandered the room. "Let's see your credentials."

"Excuse me?"

"Your credentials, Mr. Taylor. You obviously know who I am. I want to see who you are. No ID, no answers."

Wolf's flustered visitor produced a flat wallet and handed it to him.

"Looks in order," said Wolf, handing back the wallet. "The Russkis have always been good at this kind of thing, but I'm willing to give it a shot. Okay, let's get this over with. Then I want to see Colter."

Taylor regained his composure and read his questions.

"How do you know Dan Colter?"

"We're both navy. Served together. Crossed paths like everyone else. Ever served, Mr. Taylor?"

"Never had the privilege."

"It is that."

"So I'm told," said Taylor, arching an eyebrow. "What exactly were you two doing in Russia?"

Wolf hid his anger at the younger man's implied disdain. "We were invited to Baikonur to watch a fellow officer, astronaut Roger Keller, ride a Soyuz to the International Space Station. Check with the folks at NASA. They offered the invite."

"These men who attacked you—"

"*Mafiya* goons. Thought we were easy pickings."

"I see. Could they have been government agents?"

*An odd question*, thought Wolf. *Why ask that?*

"Didn't occur to me. I figured they were doing a smash and grab. Maybe we looked vulnerable."

"Well, you certainly disabused them of that notion. Anything else?"

Wolf shook his head.

"Well, I think that does it for now, Commander. I regret having to rush you out of the country at such a late hour, but as I said, it's for your own good. We are trying to keep a low profile despite provocations like this."

"I'd like to check on Commander Colter before I go."

"Not possible. We've been told he's in surgery. I can assure you we will look after him. I will personally guarantee his return to the states as soon as he's able to travel. Oh, and we have your luggage. I must tell you it has been treated rather badly. I suppose the powers that be thought it worth going through. Not to be unexpected these days. I'll have that put aboard your flight as well. And the embassy will hold Commander Colter's belongings until he's ready to return."

"Why the rush? I'd prefer to stick around until Dan's good to go."

Taylor's brow narrowed. "Not an option, Commander. We intervened to make sure you were being treated well, but it's not possible to prolong your stay. The Russians want you on your way. We're determined that they not change their minds and hold you in some sort of detention facilities to embarrass us."

"Hey, let's not forget we were the ones who were attacked."

"I didn't mean to minimize the unpleasantness, but frankly, we don't know what the Russian mindset is these days. We can't take the chance they'd put a different spin on what happened and detain you further."

"You play hardball when you have to, don't you, Taylor?"

He smirked. "I abhor pulling rank, Commander, but as an American government representative, my instructions are to see you safely home."

On his feet, Taylor put away his legal pad, snapped shut his briefcase and held the door for a skeptical Wolf. Outside the police station, the two got into a black Escalade with a driver and two unsmiling passengers who sandwiched Wolf in the backseat.

"Commander Wolf, this is Mr. Charter and Mr. Gentz. Their job is to get you home in one piece. Your luggage is in the back. We're going back to Domodedovo. This time you'll be in good hands."

Sizing up the two as contractors, Wolf pretended to doze. He thought of Colter. *Not my choice*, Dawg. *I'm outnumbered, outflanked, and outplayed this round. Stay strong.*

## Chapter 19

*Alexandria, Virginia*

Weary from failed attempts to sleep on the way home, a haggard Wolf was dropped at his condo in pre-dawn darkness. His two escorts were all business right up until they saw him to his door. They left him with his luggage but with no update on Colter's condition. Wolf's earlier attempts to get them to talk during the flight had been fruitless. Somewhere over the North Atlantic, he had abandoned the effort for fitful sleep.

Colter and Yana filled Wolf's head. The whole business, so promising at the start, had ended so badly. Excitement about his Russian adventure had been tempered by Kozuch's abduction. His dalliance with Yana couldn't overcome Baikonur's depressing remoteness. Even the thrill of the Soyuz launch had been overshadowed by the bloody business with the Tatars.

And Colter's wounding. *That was a freakish thing. Should have been me in that bunker,* he thought. *Could have been me. Too confining a space. Only one man was coming out alive.*

*Maybe we should have taken them in the open. No. Think about it. That would have been bringing knives to a gunfight. Never a good idea. Still...Got to check on Dawg first thing.*

The airport debacle. Colter's coming to his rescue despite the risk. The interrogations that followed. Valuable time wasted going over the obvious. His impotency in the face of bureaucracy—*theirs and ours.* Things out of his control. Not a feeling Wolf had experienced before.

Wolf left a trail of clothes on the bedroom floor and headed for the shower, his first in days. The hot water pummeled his muscles as Wolf leaned against the tiles, feeling ancient. His body cried out. Every ache accumulated in the last two weeks surfaced, reminding him of his limits. Wolf stood under the showerhead until the hot water ran out, then wrapped himself in a towel and shuffled to his den. He thought of checking his computer but opted for sleep.

*Tomorrow,* he told himself. *In the morning I'll check my emails, then drive to Colter's condo. Got to rest.*

Wolf pulled back the covers, grateful for the familiar feeling of his bed. He slept for ten hours, Colter's words haunting him.

*Is this what it's like to get old?*

An incessant ringing rudely shook him from his slumber. A groggy Wolf groped for his alarm and hit the snooze button twice without success. The irritating sound would not cease. Cellphone. An unfamiliar number on the tiny screen. Clearing his throat he rasped, "Yeah?"

"Commander Tom Wolf?"

"What?"

"Good morning, this is Robert Nells from the State Department."

In no mood to talk, Wolf propped himself on an elbow. "And?"

"I'd like to talk to you about your recent overseas trip."

"What the hell? I already did the drill with your embassy man, uh..." He had forgotten the name.

"Chase Taylor."

"Yeah, that's him. Been there, done that."

The voice dropped. "Well, we have a complication."

Wolf sat up, his feet planted on the floor. "Say again."

"A complication."

Wolf dreaded the words he knew were coming.

"It's Commander Colter."

"What? What's happened?"

"I'm sorry to report that he has expired."

"Expired? Hell, use real words! You mean Dan is dead?"

"Exactly. Commander Dan Colter has ex...has died."

Rubbing a hand across his face, Wolf asked, "In a Russian hospital?"

"Yes. We received confirmation earlier this morning."

"Details?"

"Not much to add."

"You have to do better than that."

"Sorry. Our information is a bit incomplete. Our people over there are doing what they can to find out."

"Taylor was supposed to keep tabs on this. What happened?"

"We'll have more answers in due time."

Wolf sagged, barely hearing his caller's follow-up.

"Perhaps if you're willing," said Nells, "we'd like to do some follow-up with you about this matter. Would it be possible to schedule an interview at State? At your earliest convenience, of course."

"What? You want me to come down there?"

"That would be preferable."

"Give me a number. I'll call you back when I'm upright."

"Of course. I understand. The sooner the better, of course. You know, while events are still fresh in your mind."

"Yeah, yeah. The number, dammit." Wolf scribbled on a pad, repeated the number, and ended the call.

*Dan Colter dead? In a Russian hospital? Who do I call? Family? Somebody in Nebraska. Wasn't that where Colter was from? What was the name of that town? Geez, I should know that. I'll call someone from the teams. These people at State better have details.*

Wolf fell back against the pillows, hands over his eyes. *What did State want from me? What can I tell them?*

# Chapter 20

When Wolf had shaved and dressed he called the number on the notepad and arranged a time to meet. He took the Metro to the Foggy Bottom Station near George Washington University and stopped at a café to refuel with coffee and a bagel. He hailed a cab and had the driver drop him at the State Department. Ten minutes late, but still angry about Colter's death, he didn't care about making some bureaucrat wait. He passed through security, signed

in, and was collected by a frowning female functionary wearing an androgynous pantsuit. The two rode an elevator in silence to a lower level. She showed him to a pale green, windowless room with muted lighting, a table, and three chairs. Wolf thought of the police station in Moscow and his mood darkened.

"Your appointment was fifteen minutes past the hour," scolded the woman gently. "It is now thirty minutes past. If I might...a word to the wise. Punctuality is something Mr.

Nells expects in others. He will be with you as soon as he finishes his current appointment—"

Wolf interrupted the reproach by running a hand over the table's polished surface. He pretended to study the inlay. "Huh, mahogany isn't it? Good workmanship. Did you know most mahogany comes from Africa these days?"

The aide reddened, flustered by Wolf's non sequitur. "An appointment he was forced to move up in light of this morning's...delay."

"Kinda makes me nostalgic for the South American stock. Course, that's endangered, I believe." Wearing an innocent expression, Wolf looked up. "Sorry...you were saying...?"

"Mr. Nells will be with you shortly." Turning on her heel, the frustrated woman marched from the room.

*Score one for us, Dawg.* Wolf dragged a chair to the corner and settled in, a benign look on his face. Ten minutes passed. He thought of leaving.

A knock. A round-shouldered, ascetic Brahmin in tidy tweeds and red bowtie entered the room. Wolf guessed Ivy League, likely student body politics, Phi Beta Kappa or Skull and Bones. Certainly chess. In his late forties, with thinning reddish hair, the officious bureaucrat extended a delicate hand.

"Robert Nells, Commander. Don't know how you managed it, but you rendered my usually unflappable assistant speechless." Wolf shook hands.

"Did she send you to the corner?" he asked, nodding at the chair Wolf had been sitting in.

Wolf dragged it to the table. "I was just practicing a little mind control."

"Ah, wit and sarcasm. Another of your talents, I suppose." Sitting opposite Wolf, Nells arranged manila folders in front of him. "Actually, I am one who appreciates a quick wit. In my job I see so little of it. You're a man of many talents, Commander. I must say your file impressed me. And I am not easily impressed."

"And you appreciate punctuality, according to your apparatchik."

Smiling, Nells smoothed the papers in front of him. "Now there's a word I haven't heard in a long, long time. Takes me back to the old days."

"From my recent experience in Russia, I'd say the old days have returned in a big way, Mr. Nells."

"Oh, I shouldn't be surprised if you're right, Commander. The whole Crimea adventure showed their hand. And of course, Ukraine. Hopefully the Baltic states are not next. Now, to the purpose of our meeting."

Stealing the initiative, Wolf crossed arms, leaned forward, eyes locked on Nells. "That was a rather disturbing wake-up call."

"Yes," admitted Nells, "suppose it was. Sorry about that. I wanted to let you know about Dan Colter's death. Seems the doctors were unable to save him, poor fellow. Our man Taylor asked if I might contact you to pass the news. Our office extends our condolences."

"I should have been with him."

Nells softened. "Don't be too hard on yourself. It wasn't possible for you to stay given the circumstances. I'm glad we got you out of there as soon as we did. Downside, of course, was leaving Commander Colter behind."

Wolf stared at the table, silent. Across from him, Nells rustled papers and uncapped a gold pen. Propping reading glasses on his nose, he flipped through a report. "The airport brawl, Commander. Might we start with that?"

Wolf threw a curve. "What are the burial arrangements for my friend?"

"His body will be shipped back home. My office can contact you as soon as relatives are notified if you wish. Did you know his family?"

Wolf shook his head. "Funny, I couldn't remember his hometown. Some place in Nebraska. Not sure. We roomed together during BUD/S; graduated in the same class. Did more training together, then were assigned to different platoons, different teams."

"An admirable career, Commander. Both your records show it."

Wolf sighed. "Dan Colter outdid me in a lot of ways."

Nells read from the papers in his hands. "Were you aware he specialized in the Russian language? Graduated top in his class at Monterrey's Defense Language Institute."

"Yes, but he didn't brag about that kind of thing. Ran into him in San Diego after that. Said he was into a more sophisticated line of work."

"How about you, Commander? What were you doing at the time?"

Wolf laughed. "I was more of a crash 'em and bash 'em kind of guy. You know, huff and puff; blow the door down. Shoot bad guys in the face. My job was to make people fall over."

Nells smiled condescendingly at the bravado and continued reading from the paperwork. "Your records show you were cited numerous times for your bravery. Again, most admirable." Pausing a beat, he said, "Was your friend part of the Iraq and Afghanistan years?"

Wolf pointed at the folder in Nells's hands. "We all were. Read the paper trail and you'll find the answer."

"Hmm, he worked with the International Security Assistance Force—ISAF. What does that mean to you? Did he ever explain what that entailed?"

Wolf shrugged. "Not really. You must have that. Matter of fact, you seem to know a lot about both of us. And why is State so interested?"

"Our curiosity stems from that episode in Russia, Commander Wolf. We believe you and Commander Colter were targeted, not by *mafiya* as you supposed, but by the government."

"Why would they do that? Makes no sense. Why risk an international incident like that in front of hundreds at the country's biggest airport?"

Nells steepled his hands, looked at Wolf. "True. That's the missing piece of the puzzle. We haven't figured that out yet. That's the reason for our little chat today. If you're willing, let's start with you and Colter first being contacted by NASA to be part of the launch group."

"It's a long story."

"I have time," said Nells.

Wolf couldn't resist. "Not according to your assistant."

Nells huffed, "Leave her out of this. She's suffered enough at your hands for one day."

A stenographer was summoned to take down Wolf's every word. Careful to leave out incriminating points he wanted to keep to himself, Wolf talked for an hour. Nells probed skillfully. Knowing how interrogations worked, sometimes Wolf answered truthfully; sometimes he parried.

After sixty minutes of cordial fencing, he left with his secrets intact.

# Chapter 21

*New York City*

Just two hundred twenty-five miles distant, Brooklyn's Brighton Beach and Washington DC might as well be continents apart. Beginning in the seventies, an incoming tide of immigrants from the Soviet Union flooded the seaside neighborhood and changed it forever. Heavily salted with criminals, the new arrivals turned their refuge into an incubator for the Russian mafia.

Slow to recognize the threat, federal and local law enforcement left the newcomers alone. Studying at the knee of fourth-generation Sicilian mafia, Russian gangsters grew exponentially like tenement cockroaches. In some cases, they joined forces with the Italians. They adapted to the New York families' loan-sharking, prostitution, narcotics, money laundering, and murder. The fall of the Soviet Union only exacerbated the problem. Inevitable internecine warfare followed, culling the ranks. Among the survivors was the wily Brighton Beach godfather, Ukranian Boris Levich. An agnostic Jew, Levich was a cunning, grim-faced veteran of the gulag who had outlived most of his peers by murdering them.

Levich held court in a heavily fortified penthouse done in gilded Czarist-bordello style, ruling with a hand the Romanovs would have recognized. Balding, cadaverous, and pale, he studied the contents of a sheet of paper in his palsied hands. Levich eyed the letter, hand-delivered that morning by a courier from Moscow. "This is most important. Do you understand what you are to do?"

Two *Boyevik*—soldiers, men who formed the backbone of the gangs— nodded solemnly, their eyes following the trembling paper. Summoned along with their lieutenant, Sasha Mikoyan, to the boss's apartment, the pair hung on the old man's every word. "You have been instructed?" he rasped.

The two nodded in unison, showing eagerness for the assignment, hoping their obligatory enthusiasm would win Levich's favor. The godfather frowned, his face a wrinkled map. "Do not fail me. Those who serve me must not disappoint me. You know this?"

The price paid by those who had failed Levich in even the smallest task was well known. The pair bobbed heads, modern-day serfs kowtowing to the master of the estate. Levich dismissed his hunting dogs away with a wave.

Alone with his thoughts, he read the letter again, then tossed it in his fireplace. Levich sank into a favorite velvet chair. *So much is being asked of me*, he lamented. *So much at risk. Fools! Why had they allowed records to be kept in the first place? Things like this are never to be put to paper. Written words talk. In the wrong hands they can destroy. Those two had better return with success in their pockets. Heads have rolled for much lesser mistakes. Mine will not be one of them.*

Levich picked up a cordless phone and called Dimitri Ivanov, his much younger second-in-command. "I have just dispatched Sasha's two wolves. Yes, yes, Dimitri, I know you wished to go in their stead. Is not possible. I need you here. Sasha will stay in contact with them and report to you."

Levich held the receiver against his good left ear, enduring Ivanov's protest for a brief moment. "Listen to me, my boy. You must cultivate fear in your subordinates. Do you understand? Once they fear you they will do what you want. And you must delegate. It is your duty to learn this. If you do not understand what I am telling you I may end up outliving you, eh? Yah, I know, you are loyal. Like a son, Dimitri Ivanov. And like a son I must teach you discipline. It is a meal that must be eaten in small bites from time to time. You understand? Good."

Levich shuffled into his library, the phone to his ear. "I have a task for you. Do not think this beneath you. I must be satisfied. My honor demands it. There is an old acquaintance of mine who owes me money. Is not much. The sum is not important. But I cannot suffer this impertinence. Come see me tomorrow and I entrust you with this task, eh? Good. I will see you then."

His housekeeper appeared in the doorway as Levich ended the call. The plump, gray-haired woman folded her hands in front of her like a timid schoolgirl. "What is it, Lydia?" he said.

"A small lunch for you. You must be hungry, yes?"

"Da. I will eat here, in the library."

Bowing, the little woman turned on her heel, reappearing moments later with a steaming bowl, soft bread, and hot tea. Levich dismissed her and let the soup cool. His thoughts turned to old comrades, better times. He ate half of what she had put before him and nodded off, his chin dropping to his chest, his eyes fluttering and closing.

Tomorrow. Dimitri Ivanov will come. I will have my satisfaction.

# Chapter 22

Wolf returned on the Metro, reaching home in early afternoon. He brooded about Colter's death and the exchange with the State Department's Nells. He changed into jeans and sweatshirt, then made himself a sandwich and a promise to check his email. As Wolf ate, he culled accumulated snail mail; tossing the junk, separating the bills, trashing solicitations. Between bites he cleared phone messages and opened a beer to wash down the last of the sandwich. He went into his den to power up his computer and tackle emails. Wolf typed his password and leaned back as the screen came alive. His eyes studied the sliding glass door to his patio.

*Something not quite right.* His old tradecraft trick, easy to miss by someone in a hurry. Down on one knee, Wolf found two crushed beads in the door's track. Small enough to be overlooked, the clay beads had been left as a primitive warning should the door be opened in his absence. The townhome's front door, visible to neighbors, had been undisturbed. Curious, Wolf slid back the door, stepped on his ground-floor patio and walked the length of it. Possible footprints in the sodden patch of grass where a stubborn remnant of snow had melted.

*Maybe, maybe not. Don't see things that aren't there.*

Large ceramic pots stuffed with dead blossoms were where they were supposed to be. What few pieces of patio furniture he had were exactly as he had left them.

*Still...*

He went back inside, uneasy. His monitor showed a white box asking for another password to his search engine. He typed it in, got his desktop with its scattered icons. A try at opening his email failed. A message: *You are not connected to the Internet.*

"Yes I am," he barked at the machine. Another attempt. Same rebuff.

Wolf pushed the monitor aside, found a loose cable, fixed it, and tried again. This time the search engine came up. He logged in for email and got a laundry list. Scanning the incoming mail puzzled him. There was no encrypted mail sent via NASA's link. He quit the search engine, did a restart, and hit another dead end. He and Colter had both sent the same message with its attachments. He had seen the NASA photographer do it. It had to be there.

*Don't jump to conclusions. Colter's computer. He'd have it.*

Wolf glanced at his watch. Four o'clock. He thought about Colter's last words. *Take my keys. Check my home computer.*

Colter's home was three hours away—a condo in Virginia Beach, close to the sea. Traffic this time of day would be a problem. But he had no choice. Having some backup would be a good idea. He and Colter had a mutual friend living there. If luck held, the retiree was still around. A Marine Recon gunnery sergeant who had washed ashore after a long career, Keith Lindgren was a bit of a "gray man" himself. The kind of man who might come in handy. Someone who could be trusted to keep his mouth shut.

Wolf dusted off his contacts and called, getting Lindgren's wife on the third ring. "Hello, Carol, it's Tom Wolf. Is Keith there?"

"Oh, Lord help us," she said on hearing Wolf's name. "A voice from the past. Yes, he's here. Did you know he's happily retired?"

Hearing suspicion in the woman's voice, Wolf said, "Word gets around, Carol. I'm enjoying the fruits of retirement myself these days."

She wasn't convinced. "Do tell. I've heard some of the stories."

"Don't believe everything he tells you. Can you put him on?"

A yelling in the background and Lindgren came on the line.

"Keith, how the hell are you?"

A rasping laugh. "I'm not sure I'm allowed to talk to you, Wolfman."

"Who's in charge down there?"

"That's what I ask myself all the time. If you were to ask Carol…"

"Well, I'm not asking Carol. I'm asking you. Good to hear your voice, Keith. Seriously, how you doing?"

"I'm high and dry, fluffed and buffed, even-keeled, and content."

"A poet. Glad to hear it." Wolf got to the point. "I need your help."

"Stand by. Let me take your call in the other room."

Wolf waited, heard TV's *Jeopardy* in the background, then a click.

"Okay. I'm here," said Lindgren. "What's the problem? Please tell me you're not up to something dicey."

"It's Dan Colter."

A groan like someone deflating in Wolf's ear. "Were you involved in that?"

Puzzled, Wolf said, "Involved? What are you referring to?"

"That thing in Moscow?"

"How...how did you know about that?"

Lindgren babbled. "It's been all over CNN and Fox. Don't you watch the news? Didn't you see the video?"

"I haven't watched television or read a paper since I got back two days ago. Enlighten me."

Lindgren said, "CNN had cellphone videos of a robbery in Domodedovo airport. A YouTube video. It's been all over the news."

"Been out of touch, Keith. What did it have to do with Colter?"

"Some traveler posted it on YouTube. Couple of guys mixing it up. They showed Dan Colter's picture; said an American tourist died in a robbery attempt by some skinheads or something. I don't know all the details. But they showed Colter's picture. Said he was stabbed to death. The thing's gone viral. I can't believe you haven't seen it. You must live under a rock."

Wolf, speechless, sank down on the couch in his den. *Television? The State Department guy hadn't mentioned a video. Had he known? How did the Russians let that video get past them?*

Wolf said, "I've been out of touch, Keith. Haven't had a chance to catch up with things."

"The news people are reporting it as a robbery gone bad. Apologies all around. The Russians have to be embarrassed. Geez, Wolfman, are you telling me you were mixed up in that? They never mentioned a second American."

"I was there, Keith. It's a long story. Look, I have to come down to Dan's place. He asked me to go there when I got back. He knew something."

"Are you going to ask me to go with you?"

"Yeah. Just in case I need some backup."

Lindgren paused. "I don't know. It sounds kinda loosey-goosey to me."

"He asked me, Keith. Gave me his keys just before they took him away to the hospital. I gave him my word."

"Says you."

"C'mon, you know me better than that. Dan and I were tight. I owe him."

"Okay, let's do this. There's a Mexican restaurant on Highway 60, Shore Drive. You know it?"

"Guadalajara. I vaguely remember it. I'll find it."

"Good. I can meet you there. What's your ETA?"

Wolf read his watch, said, "I figure twenty-hundred hours if traffic plays nice."

Lindgren said, "Make it twenty-thirty to be sure."

"Got it. Give me your cell number. I'll call you when I cross the Lesner Bridge." Scribbling the number Lindgren gave him, Wolf said, "I'm leaving in ten minutes. Appreciate your being willing to meet me."

"No harm in listening to what you're up to. I figure this will square us."

"You got it, Gunny," Wolf said, relieved. "I have some questions about what Dan was up to these last few years. I have my suspicions but I need to hear it from someone who knew him better than me."

"I'll tell you what I can," said Lindgren, "nothing more. I'm betting you haven't slowed down a bit. Russia, huh? Geez. I want to know what you two were doing over there."

"It's a long story. I'll buy. Thanks, Keith. See you at the restaurant. Tell Carol goodbye for me."

"She keeps a list, Wolfman. And you're still on it, you know."

"Then maybe it's best you don't mention my being in Russia."

# Chapter 23

Wolf stopped on Alexandria's outskirts to fill his BMW's tank for the two-hundred-mile drive. Fighting his way south with the other sheep, he took I-95 toward Richmond. Racing a dying sun, he pushed south through Virginia's dark and bloody ground—crossing the Rapahannock above Fredricksburg, where Burnside blundered. Somewhere in the twilight, west of the highway, were Spotsylvania and The Wilderness, each with their ghosts.

North of Richmond, he circled southeast on the 295 bypass to I-64. Traffic thinned beyond the capitol and Wolf gained on the clock. With the York River on his left, the James on his right, he pushed down the peninsula. Passing between pre-colonial Williamsburg in the west and Yorktown's hallowed ground east along the York, Wolf

joined a stream of cars and trucks flowing through
Newport News. To him, it seemed every vehicle on the
eastern seaboard was sharing his road. He aimed at
Hampton, and beyond the tip of the peninsula: Norfolk.

With the sun a dying sliver of gold on the horizon, Wolf
tagged behind a bus and a string of vans across the dark
waters of Hampton Roads. Fireflies—lights of cars on Fort
Monroe's tumorous littoral—marked Chesapeake Bay.
Swallowed by darkness, the broad body of water had
disappeared, leaving behind a shimmering necklace of car
lights crawling east and west across the distant Bay Bridge
to Wolf's left. Keeping one eye on his GPS, Wolf split
from I-64 and took Highway 13 north. He snagged his
cellphone and called Lindgren.

"Okay," growled the Marine. "I'm leaving for the
restaurant. By the time you cross Lesner Bridge, I'll be
finishing my first margarita."

"I need you sober, Gunny."

"Just messing with you, Wolfman. I gave that up two
years ago."

Wolf laughed. "Maybe you're right—I might not be able
to recognize you after all."

"I'll be waiting."

"On my way. Give me ten minutes and order for me."

"Aye, aye, sir. Whadaya like?"

"Surprise me."

"Oh, I certainly will."

# Chapter 24

*Virginia Beach*

Wolf found the restaurant on Shore Drive and parked. Inside,
a white-bearded Falstaffian figure signaled from a corner

booth. The retired Marine rose to embrace Wolf. "Well, well, the Wolfman, in the flesh."

"Look at you, Keith. You're right about not recognizing you. You have changed. Gone is the perpetual scowl and the ever-present cigar stub. Retirement must agree with you."

The two sat opposite each other, Lindgren saying, "I ate at home. But I ordered for you. Hope you like enchiladas. No margaritas, though."

The server arrived with Wolf's steaming plate and refilled Lindgren's coffee. Hungrier than he realized, Wolf attacked his food while answering questions.

"I drove by Dan Colter's place on the way over here," said Lindgren.

Wolf asked, "Anything out of the ordinary?"

"Looked calm. No cars in the driveway. One upstairs light on. Porch light as well. On timers, I'd guess. Otherwise, pretty routine. It's a three-story condo. Nice place. Big bucks being that close to the beach. Expensive, but packed in tight and a little cookie-cutter for my tastes."

Working on his meal, Wolf said, "You have much contact with Dan?"

Lindgren sipped his coffee. "I retired here first. When he called out of the blue four years ago to ask about houses, I was surprised. I knew Colter had divorced while serving with the teams but I never thought of him as the nesting kind."

Wolf kept eating. In between bites, he asked. "What about you? What keeps you busy? And what's with the whiskers?"

Stroking his luxuriant white beard, Lindgren smiled. "I gave up the fast lane to play jolly St. Nick."

"You serious?"

Lindgren arched an eyebrow as if offended. "Absolutely. Carol and I do a nice side business with the Santa Claus thing. Parties, charities, special appearances, hospital visits, that sort of thing. Kids love it. And the parents book us six months in advance. Started as a hobby but it took off. We stick around until Christmas wraps up. Then we head south with our fifth-wheeler."

"I can't reconcile your image—which I have to admit is damn near perfect—with your past." Wolf smiled. "Do these little people and their parents know who's behind that beard? Do they have any idea about your 'other' skills?"

"Aw, c'mon, Wolfman. That was in another lifetime. Hell, even Mrs. Claus doesn't know what I was involved in after I got out of the Marines."

"She know anything about your unofficial tours in Iraq and Afghanistan?"

"No."

"Still do some work for our friends at Langley?"

Lindgren shrugged. "Maybe a little consulting now and then."

"In for a penny, in for a pound, Keith."

Lindgren growled. "It's not like that, Wolfman."

"Oh really? Carol know about Central America? Africa?"

Shaking his head, Lindgren said, "No. And I'm counting on you to keep your mouth shut while you're here. No need to stir the pot."

"Wouldn't think of it. Does she know you and Colter go back?"

"Not a clue. She only met him at a housewarming when he moved here."

Wolf threw up his hands. "Then she won't hear it from me."

"Good." Lindgren tapped his temple. "What Dan and I did after we both left the service is locked away forever in here. The man was fearless. A patriot. God bless his memory...and yours."

"Appreciate the sentiment, Santa. Seriously, none of us did anything to be ashamed of."

Lindgren finished his coffee. "Speak for yourself. Desperate times sometimes call for desperate measures."

Wolf shrugged in agreement. "That they do. Let's leave it at that."

He pushed away his plate. "Any idea what Dan was doing these last few years?"

"You asking as a friend or officially?"

"C'mon, Keith, I'm off the grid myself. I came down here because he asked me to. Said he wanted me to check something on his computer. It was the last thing he said."

"Yeah, Dan was involved in some pretty heavy stuff."

"How do you know that?"

"He was working on threat finance the last time we talked."

Wolf leaned forward, arms crossed. "Threat finance, as in terrorism banking, money laundering, that sort of thing?"

"Yeah. State runs a program to follow the money. Dan was hooked up with them. My guess is he was spending a lot of time overseas trying to untangle some of the threads between banking, terrorists, and rogue governments."

A waitress made the rounds collecting plates and pouring more coffee.

Lindgren glanced at his watch. "How much time do you need to check Dan's place?"

"I figure we could be in and out in under an hour, maybe less."

"What exactly are you looking for?"

"Dan and I sent emails from Kazakhstan. We routed them through NASA's uplink. Something happened to mine. I want to see if his came through okay."

Lindgren was cautious. "That's it? You came all the way down here to look at emails? There's gotta be more to it than that."

"That's what he asked me to do."

Lindgren signaled for the check. "Why would you need me for backup just to check Dan's emails? What else is involved? What's in those messages?"

Wolf dropped a twenty on the table and the two abandoned the booth. "We stumbled on some interesting info while we were in Moscow. Dan said it was important. That's why we sent it stateside."

The two walked outside to Wolf's car. Lindgren said, "Did it have anything to do with his death?"

Wolf hesitated. "Huh, at first I didn't think so. Now I'm not so sure. The jury's still out on that as a motive."

"Might be murder made to look like a robbery."

"I've thought about that these last few days."

"Okay, I said I'd help you, Wolfman. I will. But if you're not telling me everything I need to know it won't go well with you."

"What? You'll scratch me off your Christmas list?"

"For starters I'll force feed you lumps of coal and turn Mrs. Claus loose on you."

"Now you've got my attention."

Wolf got in his car. "Ride with me, Keith. No reason to take two cars."

"Okay, but I'll drive. I know his place. It's on Riptide Court, a little dead end off of Ocean Shore Drive. Nice neighborhood. Some foliage for cover. We'll park on the street to avoid attracting attention."

"Good idea, Gunny. Lead on."

"It's what I usually do with officers...even retired ones."

# Chapter 25

A stone's throw from the beach, Colter's condo sat at the end of a short street of paving blocks. The street's three-story townhouses each wore white vinyl clapboard and high, peaked roofs. A pair of garage doors and a quaint, arched garden gate fronted each unit's concrete pad, which was wide enough to park two cars. Having donned latex gloves, Wolf went through the garden gate and let himself in the front door using the keys Colter had given him. Lindgren followed, closing the door behind them.

Inside, Wolf disarmed a silent, blinking alarm by tapping a security code Colter had given him. Pointing a penlight at railings, he took the stairs to the second floor, Lindgren on his heels.

Wolf turned right at the top of the landing, where Colter had kept an office. Lindgren drew the drapes and shut the door. Finding a desk light, Wolf flicked it on and stood back, staring at a family of orphaned cables. No computer.

"What the hell?"

"Don't look at me," said Lindgren. "This is the first time I've been here since the housewarming."

"We're too late."

"Obviously. I suggest we vacate the premises pronto."

Wolf glanced around the room. "Maybe Colter was in the habit of disconnecting his computer when he wasn't home."

Lindgren scoffed. "Then why would he ask you to check on it? No computer, no emails."

"It was just a thought," said Wolf. "Okay, we're out of here."

Wolf killed the light and the two crept downstairs, retracing their steps to the entry where Wolf keyed the alarm and locked the front door. He and Lindgren returned to Wolf's parked car.

"What's next?" asked Lindgren.

"This is getting crazy," said Wolf, staring across the street at Colter's townhouse. "First me, now this."

"What does 'first me, now this' mean?"

Facing Lindgren, Wolf said, "When I checked my computer, the email we sent from Kazakhstan wasn't there. Had never arrived."

"That happens sometimes."

"Sure. It's possible. But I have my suspicions someone made themselves at home before I got back." Wolf explained finding clues of an entry through his patio door. "And now, with Colter's computer missing, it adds up."

Lindgren said, "Adds up to what? And who is 'they'? Why would they take his computer? Why not just trash the email? Or scrub the hard disc? Doesn't make sense to arouse suspicion by walking away with his hardware."

"Exactly," said Wolf. "Could be whoever did this got here just before we did. Or they didn't give a damn about showing their hand. Arrogant."

Lindgren said, "Probably not a burglar. Nothing else was disturbed. Didn't see any drawers open. Flat-screen TV in the living room was still there. Definitely after whatever was on that computer."

"Well, that was a wasted trip," sighed Wolf.

"Maybe not. It helps you focus on the fact somebody didn't want either of you to download those emails you sent. What was so damn important that they would do that? What were you guys into?"

Wolf said, "That's the problem, Gunny. Colter used some technique to combine pictures he took with other pictures of pages in a book we were given in Russia."

Lindgren said, "You're talking about steganography."

"If you say so."

"Yeah. We used that process when I was doing contract work. It's an old idea updated to work with image files.

Colter would have been familiar with it. Why not go back to the original source?"

"It doesn't exist. We burned the book after taking photos of the pages."

"Well, that's a helluva fix, Wolfman. What now?"

About to answer, Wolf looked past Lindgren's shaggy profile. "We have company, Keith."

# Chapter 26

An unmarked sedan rolled toward them, its headlights dark. At the mouth of Riptide Court, the car stopped, blocking the street. The driver and his passenger got out of the car and headed for Colter's townhouse. Despite the distance, Wolf could tell the pair was armed with handguns.

"Those don't look like cops," whispered Lindgren.

"Hard to tell," said Wolf.

"Trust me, Wolfman. Those are not the local cops."

"Government people? Contractors?"

"Could be. Write this down." Lindgren read the plate to Wolf, who scribbled the numerals and letters.

Wolf tapped Lindgren on the shoulder. "Let's get the hell out of here before they figure out they're not the only ones making a house call tonight."

"Your first good idea tonight. But I have a better one."

Lindgren started the engine and left the car in park, its headlights off. He turned off the dome light. With his eyes on the other car, he gestured at the glove compartment. "Check, I should have an icepick in there."

Wolf rummaged among the paperwork and tools. "Got it. Do I want to ask why you carry this?"

Lindgren waved him off, held out his hand without looking at Wolf. "No, you do not want to ask me why I carry this."

"Seriously, Gunny."

"Comes in handy."

"What are you thinking?"

"Wait here." Heaving himself from the front seat, Lindgren scanned the street in both directions and then jogged across the pavement to the parked car. As Wolf watched, the retired Marine punched front and back tires on the driver's side. His sabotage accomplished, Lindgren hurried back to Wolf's car and got in. Without speaking, he drove to the end of the block, did a U-turn, and parked in shadows fifty yards behind the wounded vehicle.

Wolf stared at the listing car. "What were you thinking?"

Lindgren didn't answer. His beard glowing in the light from his cellphone, he tapped in a number and held the phone to his ear. Finger to his lips to silence Wolf, he said, "Hey, it's Gunny Lindgren. Yeah, I'm good. You got any cars cruising on Shore Drive? Good. Look, I got something for you. I'm sitting on Ocean Shore Drive, parked behind a suspicious-looking car. Was driving by Riptide Court and saw two guys up to no good. No, didn't recognize them. But I think they're making an unauthorized house call."

Shaking his head and smiling, Wolf covered his eyes.

"Hey, no problem," said Lindgren. "Just doing my citizen thing."

Wolf looked ahead to Colter's townhouse and nudged Lindgren's shoulder. He nodded at figures slipping through the shadows.

"Okay, thanks," said Lindgren, his eyes following Wolf's gaze. "I don't think these guys are going anywhere soon. See ya."

Lindgren pocketed the phone and grinned. "This will be fun."

Back in their car, the two intruders started the engine and drove from the curb, both left tires wobbling. Stopping mid-block, the driver got out to inspect his front left wheel. A hurried conference with his passenger followed. The second man got out, came around the back and discovered the flattened rear tire. The pair paced, the driver on his phone. Back in the car, the two drove ahead, limping slowly on the rims. A patrol car rounded the corner at the end of the block, its lights off.

Imagining the driver's surprise, Lindgren chuckled, infecting Wolf as well. Both men began laughing. The police car hit its lights and parked diagonally across the street. Braking to a stop, the strangers were stymied by flat tires and an unyielding cop, gun in hand.

"Didn't I tell you this would be fun?" Lindgren roared, punching Wolf's arm. "Look at these idiots. Trying to act nonchalant as if nothing was wrong."

"You're sick. Don't ever go over to the dark side."

Lindgren chuckled. "I already have."

Another patrol car roared past them, its lights flashing. Blocking any retreat, the second cop parked behind the hobbled car, got out, and mirrored his partner's stance.

Told to exit the car with hands held high, two cornered men in dark tracksuits stood, arms raised, the driver glaring at the sagging tires. Ordered to assume the stance, the men were frisked and cuffed. Both were placed in the backseat of separate squad cars. Standing in the middle of Ocean Shore Drive, the two cops talked. One cop kept an eye on the manacled prisoners while the other searched the getaway car.

The squads' pulsing strobe lights finally awakened the neighborhood. Robed residents congregated on front steps or balconies. The more timid watched the night's drama from upper-story windows.

A third patrol car arrived, driven by the shift commander. A barrel-chested sergeant, made even larger by his vest, got out of his car. "What do we have here?" he drawled.

"Couple of stalkers sitting in a car, Sarge." Holding up two confiscated handguns, the patrolman added, "We checked their ride. Not your ordinary perps."

The sergeant focused his flashlight on the rear bumper. "Huh, Maryland. You call in the plates?

"Already done."

"Tow truck?"

"On the way."

"Good." The sergeant aimed his light at a morose suspect slumped in the closest squad's backseat, said, "What's their story?"

"They don't seem to have one."

He walked to the next car and focused his blinding beam at the second glum suspect. He frowned at the squinting man. "ID? Names?"

"They're not talking, Sarge."

"Just out house hunting," volunteered the second cop.

"Okay," sighed their superior. "Get 'em out of here."

The squads went down Ocean Shore and on to Shore Drive, their unwilling passengers locked in handcuffs and silence. The sergeant went back to his car to check in. When the tow truck arrived, he and the driver talked. Trailing the impounded car, the patrol supervisor abandoned the scene to the watching Wolf and Lindgren.

The two returned to the restaurant's deserted lot. Lindgren parked and got out. "Had my old ticker moving pretty fast back there," he said. "Just like being back in the game. Whoa, I don't need to be doing that at my age."

"Keep this for future reference," said Wolf, handing Lindgren a copy of the license plate number. "Run it by your cop friends when you have time." At the wheel of his idling car, he said, "Suddenly, everything gets a little sticky. I'll do some checking of my own when I get back. Thanks for going with me, Gunny. Sorry to get you involved in this...whatever this is."

"You gotta admit watching that bust was a helluva lot of fun tonight."

Wolf nodded. "Man, that was something."

"My lips are sealed," said Lindgren. "I'll hear the details from the cop I called. He'll want to know how I happened to be driving by when this went down."

"Keep me out of it if you can."

"Shouldn't be a problem on the first pass. I like living here so I try not to lie to John Law if I don't have to. My advice to you—"

"Which I didn't ask for," interrupted Wolf.

"Affirmative...which the gentleman did not ask for...is not to get in too deep, Wolfman. Depending who tonight's miscreants are, this could get real ugly, real quick. I have a sixth sense about this kinda thing. When the pucker factor gets high it's time to look for a friendly landing zone."

"I'll figure this out," promised Wolf. "Don't tell Carol I put you in harm's way tonight."

"She'll pester me," said Lindgren. "Pillow talk is not my strong suit. What can I tell you? She has a nose for this kind of thing."

They shook hands. Promising to stay in touch, Wolf got back on the road.

# Chapter 27

As promised, two days later, Lindgren called Wolf on his cellphone. "Hey, it's Keith. You make it back without any problems?"

"Came through rain outside Richmond. Roads were slick. Traffic was light until I got closer to the District."

"That's to be expected. We're getting the tail end of that two-day front."

"I don't suppose you called to chat about the weather, Gunny."

"No, I did not. We've got trouble, Wolfman."

"I figured as much. Give it to me straight."

Taking a deep breath, Lindgren said, "I've got good news and bad news. Two questions: Are you sitting down? And which do you want to hear first?"

Troubled by the call, Wolf said, "I'm sitting. The good news?"

"Our cops ran the plates. Car was stolen in Baltimore a week ago."

"No surprise there. What were those guys doing?"

"That's the bad news."

"Just tell me Colter wasn't involved."

A pause. "I'd have to qualify that."

"Okay. I'll bite. Qualify it. Is the glass half-full?"

"Hard to tell at this point. Last chance to tell me what you guys were doing in Russia."

Irritated, Wolf sighed. "The launch in Kazakhstan, remember?"

"I remember you telling me that. Was that all there was to it?"

"Skip to the bad news, Gunny."

"Our boys were Russian."

"Define Russian."

"Russian as in gangster. Russian as in *mafiya. Vory*."

"Are we talking about our own home-grown dirt bags or black hats from the motherland?"

"We're looking at our own crooked family tree. Made in the USA."

Intrigued, Wolf said, "All that from these two guys?"

"Didn't hear it from them. Of the two, one is a naturalized citizen biting the hand that welcomed him, the other is a *boyevik*—a warrior."

"Like a street soldier in the mafia."

"Correct. Turns out this *boyevik* is an illegal. He's got a rap sheet and it makes me wonder how come he hasn't been sent home before this."

Wolf thought out loud. "Must have a good lawyer or been on the run until now."

"You should be a cop, Wolfman. You are correct. My guess is that he's going to be a guest of the feds for a while. I'd be happy to see him shipped back home but that may take some time. The other guy was spawned here, unfortunately. They have a slick New York lawyer working their case as of yesterday afternoon. The guy's expensive."

"New York, huh? Interesting. Brighton Beach again, I suppose. Where are these bad boys now?"

"Sitting in jail. I gotta tell you, Wolfman, the case against them is good but not waterproof. They have the weapons charge, of course. Maybe the immigration charge for the one, but this mob lawyer is working overtime to spring both. They claim they bought the car from a dealer. Didn't know it was stolen."

"Who's going to buy that story? And why were they snooping around Colter's place?"

"That's where you come in."

"You didn't mention me, did you?"

Indignation in his voice, Lindgren roared back, "Not a word! You know me better than that. No one puts us together at the scene, before or after. These punks are the ones in the spotlight, not us."

"So...the Russians were likely after what we were looking for."

"Not 'we,' you."

"Roger that. Me."

"Those emails you were looking for must be hot. If you didn't find them, and the Russians didn't find them, then whoever took the computer must have stopped by Colter's place right after he died or just before."

Wolf thought about the card sewn in his jacket but remained silent.

Lindgren cleared his throat. "Another thing. According to my sources, these guys do lay their ugly heads at Brighton Beach in Brooklyn."

"That figures. Little Odessa," said Wolf. "Why am I not surprised? Are you talking to local sources for this information or your friends at Langley? You seem to know a lot for Santa."

"A little bit here, a little bit there. Just because I'm retired doesn't mean I spend my days playing pinochle or checkers, you know."

"That figures. Anyway, I haven't made much headway at my end."

"Can't you recreate the emails you need?"

"Not a chance," said Wolf. "If I could get my hand on Colter's camera I could download his photos. But where is his camera? Where is his luggage? The embassy people said they were going to send it back with him."

Lindgren said, "What about his family? What are the funeral plans? If you could get to them, they might let you look at his camera."

"I was told they would let me know the arrangements after his family was contacted. Frankly, I don't know their whereabouts. Can't even recall where his wife was from."

"Try someone who knew him from his days with the teams."

"What can you tell me?"

"I know about as much as you."

"Well, I've already made a few calls. Waiting to hear back."

"I'm thinking maybe you ought to think seriously about disappearing for a while until this Russian mob thing is sorted out."

Wolf sounded a defiant note. "I'm not running from my own territory."

"Hey, don't underestimate these guys. They're in a league of their own. They don't play well with others. If they had Colter on their radar you'd be next. Even a blind man could see your connection to him is obvious."

"I don't know if these are the same people who trashed my emails."

"Don't take a chance. Find a hole to hide in for a spell."

"Not likely. But thanks for the sit-rep. I'll check in with you in a day or so to see if you have more news. Meantime, stay out of trouble."

Lindgren laughed. "That's rich, coming from you."

# Chapter 28

*Brighton Beach, Brooklyn*

Impatience was one of Dimitri Ivanov's faults. His other flaw was a cruel delight in carrying out killings assigned to his crew. Not one to delegate, Ivanov was "hands on" when it came to eliminating enemies. An *avtorityet*—akin to a mafia capo—Ivanov ran a crew of *boyeviks*, street soldiers. Wielding such authority, he could have assigned the bloody side of business to any one of his underlings but he had a perverse desire to get his hands dirty.

Rescued from a life of obscurity in a New York City sweatshop, Ivanov owed his position to one of Little Odessa's most powerful godfathers, Ukrainian Jew Boris Levich. In gratitude for being taken in and eventually anointed a "made man," Ivanov served Levich well. A surrogate son to the older man, he had risen through the ranks, earning his reputation the hard way—often over the bodies of enemies and peers. Looking more angelic seminarian than gangster, the slight, blond Ivanov was no bull-necked, slow-witted rival like those he had dispatched in any number of gruesome ways. Ivanov's reputation was that of an executioner, a man to be feared. Like other battling crabs in the bucket that was Brighton Beach, he lived on borrowed time in a seaside city swarming with *russkaya mafiya*.

Today, much to Ivanov's disappointment, he and an associate would be delivering a message—not a fatal shot to the head—to Mikhail Drogenev, a pensioner and gambler who owed an unpaid sum to Ivanov's boss.

Levich called his avenging angel to his fifth-floor fortress in a brick apartment building in the heart of Little Odessa. Hands clasped behind his back, the gulag veteran cautioned his mercurial aide about tactics in private.

"It is important Mikhail Drogenev is put on notice. You are to tell him that this slight pains me. He will repay me within a fortnight. But hear me, Dimitri Ivanov, I say to you what God said about Job to Satan. Do you know the story?"

A blank face. "I do not."

Throwing up his hands, Levich said, "Ach, I suspected as much. You forget your roots, Dimitri. Ah, your generation. Very well. So, God says to Satan, 'Job is in your hands, but you must spare his life.' You understand?"

"I understand, Boss."

"What are you to do?"

"I am to spare Drogenev's life."

"Good," rasped Levich. "Go. Pay your visit but remember my words."

Leaving the apartment building, Ivanov collected Sergei Helinski, his brooding backup. They drove to Brighton Beach Avenue, a bustling strip of shops and crowded tenements filled with their countrymen.

Mikhail Drogenev was easy to find. Fond of red borscht, Levich's debtor was a regular at the Poltava Café, a crowded, old-world eatery favored by immigrants but frowned at by the city's department of health. The narrow, high-tin-ceilinged café had once been a saloon, a beauty shop, a failed hardware store, a barbershop, and bakery in turn. Here, in a front room crowded with eight tables and floor-to-ceiling windows in desperate need of cleaning, wrinkled gossiping *babushkas*, laborers, low-ranking *Vory*, and homesick immigrants sought anonymity in bottomless bowls of red borscht, black bread, and vodka.

A turn-of-the-century throwback, the Poltava might have been lifted straight from the pages of a tsarist picture album. English was a foreign language among the staff and clientele. Presided over by a shriveled dwarf-crone, the café's open kitchen was manned by her scowling nephew and a surly pair of waiters for whom hygiene was an alien concept. A long counter lined with anchored stools faced an antiquated gas stove crowded with boiling pots and fryers beneath a blackened exhaust hood. A sagging back hallway led from the dining room past a single cramped bathroom and storeroom. Beyond that was an addition—once a bathhouse, now a gathering spot off-limits to all but intimates who entered from the alley. Filled with cigarette smoke and ruled by toothless backgammon-playing pensioners barking oaths at each other, the space was a refuge for Mikhail Drogenev. Until today.

For Ivanov, finding his prey was child's play. Either an idiot or supremely confident that the size of his debt was not worth the godfather's attention, the unshaven Drogenev was at his usual corner table. With three games under his belt, the last one a gammon, Drogenev was taunting his luckless opponent by offering him the doubling cube midway through the fourth game. About to risk the challenge, his rival looked past Drogenev and paled. Certain he had seen a *dybbuk* wearing Ivanov's skin, he hurriedly excused himself. Ivanov took the retreating man's place, settling opposite the debtor. Leaning across the scarred table, he plucked two red checkers from the playing board, his hard eyes on the unkempt Drogenev.

"So, Mikhail Drogenev, you pass your time here when you could be working to pay off your obligations, eh?"

Unbowed, Drogenev met Ivanov's gaze. "I know why you are here, Dimitri Ivanov. I tell Boris I pay him this summer, no sooner."

"You presume too much," said Ivanov. "True, you and my boss shared hard times in the gulag, but that is no excuse for your insult to his charity." Ivanov rolled a wooden piece between his fingers and lowered his voice. "Promises, promises. First it was last fall, then mid-winter. It's obvious you have no intention of honoring your word, you son of a whore."

Drogenev attempted to rise but felt the iron clamp of Sergei Helinski's hand on his shoulder, forcing him to stay seated. The trembling debtor wet himself in anticipation of Ivanov's cruelty. He eyed his fellow gamers but found no help there. Cowed backgammon players gathered their draughts and put away their boards. Tails between their legs, they abandoned the tables, exiting the Poltava's annex. Ivanov's muscle stepped back, a wooden bat resting on his shoulder.

"What's this?" Ivanov said. "All your friends have fled the building. You alone are left. Why is that, Mikhail Drogenev?"

Ivanov swept the playing board from the table, scattering the die and wooden checkers across the room. "They don't have the stomach to play alongside a man who cannot even control his bladder! Such a man who doesn't pay his debts is a THIEF!"

Holding out his hand for the wooden bat, Ivanov caught it in mid-air. Yanked backwards from his chair, Drogenev was dragged from the room, his bony legs kicking at the yellowed linoleum in a macabre dance, losing a shoe in the process. Seeing nothing, hearing nothing, diners in the adjacent room stared holes in their meat dumplings or spooned borscht in silence. Not one patron bolted outside to call police from the sidewalk. No one intervened in Drogenev's fate.

No match for the muscled Helinski, Drogenev's eyes bulged. Animal-like squeals echoed down the narrow hallway. The crone's nephew shut the rear door behind the three men and went back to his boiling pots.

In the alley, Helinski forced Drogenev to kneel. His pleading words were cut short by a noose of twisted shirt around his neck. Forced on his back, his mouth stuffed with garbage, Drogenev lay defenseless.

A grinning Ivanov went to work with the bat. Striking his victim's knees repeatedly, he shattered both kneecaps, then splintered the man's lower bones. Drogenev screamed in muffled agony. Ivanov taunted him. "You don't pay your debts, you don't get to walk like a man. Crawl like the insect you are, Mikhail Drogenev!"

To add to his prey's misery, an amused Ivanov doused the bat with lighter fluid, set it on fire, and tossed it between Drogenev's useless legs. Shrieking like a wounded animal, he dragged himself on elbows through garbage to avoid the flames.

Inches from his victim's face, Ivanov spit a final warning. "You owe your life to the benevolence of Boris Levich. See that your debt does not remain unpaid."

# Chapter 29

That evening, Gunny Lindgren's warning about the Russians played over and over in Wolf's head. *If they had Colter on their radar you'd be next. Even a blind man could see your connection to him is obvious.*

Wolf knew the Marine's advice was sound. One of the worst plagues to hit America, the Russian Mafia had metastasized from a handful of parasitic immigrants to an inoperable cancer. Targeted on two continents for the contents of the mysterious book, Wolf had one option: go through with his original plan to ask former Green Beret Sam McFadden for help. Following Lindgren's advice, Wolf decided to disappear in the morning. He called his friend on a second cell phone, one of six prepaid phones he had kept for purposes like this. He got McFadden's answering machine.

"Sam, Wolfman. Heading west. No emails. Need cover. Will explain."

Packing light, he alerted a neighbor he would be away for a while.

"You don't even stay long enough for me to invite you to dinner," complained the older woman. A seventy-plus widow who cared for two grandchildren weekday afternoons, she often watched Wolf's townhome when he was out of town. Hard of hearing, she had obviously failed him during his recent trip to Russia. But having considered the professionalism of those who had tampered with his computer, he forgave her lapse. Avoiding the hassle of reporting, Wolf had not alerted her or the cops. He would do his own investigating.

"It's business," said Wolf. "Heading for Europe. Doing some consulting."

"Well, be careful," she chided. "Can't trust foreigners, you know."

He dismissed her bigotry with a benign smile. "Sometimes it's the people closer to home that should worry us more. Think about that." Before she could trap him in more conversation, he crossed her patch of lawn to his front steps.

Unsure whether his computer had been mined, he called a trusted friend, asking her to go online and book him the cheapest one-way, non-stop ticket to San Diego. Sworn to silence, she offered a ride to Dulles—her fee a future steak dinner and bottle of wine. At dawn, the car was waiting in a light drizzle. She dropped him at the check-in level. He kissed her goodbye and made a vague promise to call. Once through security, he was on his way, Colter and Yana on his mind.

Four hours and thirty-one minutes later, his plane began its descent over brown hills covered in serpentine roads lined with housing. Runway 27 at San Diego's Lindbergh Field beckoned in the distance. From his window seat, Wolf took in the southern half of the city and beyond that, Tijuana's hazy skyline—all reassuringly familiar. After descending deceptively close to glittering downtown high-rises and condos, Wolf spotted the moored USS *Midway*. The decommissioned carrier crawled with ant-like tourists inspecting the collection of vintage aircraft parked on the angled flight deck. The sprawling naval shipyard at 32nd Street was lined with cranes, dry docks, and ships in various stages of repair. He felt the power adjustments as the captain jockeyed into perfect position to touch down in the first five hundred to one thousand feet of runway.

# Chapter 30

*San Diego*

In no particular hurry and shouldering a carry-on, Wolf joined the stream of travelers marching through Terminal 2, and took an escalator to the lower-level sidewalk. He strolled to a pickup zone dotted with towering palms and travelers guarding suitcases in the sun. Wolf's eyes wandered over a line of idling cars. His cellphone buzzed.

"Wolf."

A sultry voice. "Welcome to San Diego. I'm looking right at you."

Scanning the length of the pickup zone, Wolf smiled. "Regina? Don't see you."

"Losing your touch? See the silver SUV? Behind the minivan?"

Wolf made his way to the waiting car, tossed his bag in the backseat, and got in beside Regina McFadden. Rewarded with a kiss on the cheek, he settled back as she pulled from the curb.

"Where's Sam?"

"Last-minute glitch at work. Sent me. Hope that's okay."

Wolf laughed. "Perfect. It's always been a goal of mine to be picked up by a beautiful woman."

Glancing at him with a raised eyebrow, Regina said, "Apparently, you haven't changed much since our wedding. Same old Tom Wolf." She laughed, perfect white teeth setting off her tan; shiny black tresses tied back, her hair even longer than he remembered. The pale blue linen blouse and baggy khaki shorts did little to hide her curves. Wolf was struck again by how attractive she was. McFadden had been right all along to fall in love with this Filipino-American beauty.

She drove east along Harbor Drive, the marinas filled with sleek white hulls and a forest of aluminum masts. Wolf felt himself relax, the sun warm on his face and arms. Across the bay was the graceful arch of the Coronado Bay Bridge connecting North Island's Naval Air Station, which dominated the upper end of the Coronado peninsula. In the distance, the long gray silhouette of the USS *Ronald Reagan*, CVN 76, broke the horizon, a line of smaller warships moored astern of the carrier. Wolf's attention was drawn by a pair of RIBs— rigid inflatable boats—churning high-speed wakes in a training exercise in the bay. He imagined SEALs going airborne over chop, salty spray like buckshot in their faces.

Following his eyes, Regina said, "Do you miss it? Being in the service, I mean. Sam says you do."

"He should talk." Wolf fixed his eyes on the water. "Yeah, sometimes. Then I remember how much fun Hell Week was. Wading in the surf; rolling in the sand; turning into a sugar cookie; back in the surf. Hauling logs, boats, the cold, the fog." Turning back to her, Wolf said, "Then I come to my senses. Sure, I miss some of it. Sam probably does too."

She jockeyed to loop north, away from the airport and the city without taking her eyes off the merging traffic. Wolf said, "Last year Sam told me he was expanding the gun range and the classrooms because of demand."

"True. He and his partners are also adding a paintball maze. Big boys and their toys, I guess. He says we have to spend money to make money."

"True enough. You both deserve a piece of the pie."

"It's mostly Sam's doing. Mother's invested some money as well. He'll want to give you the tour. He's proud of the facility."

"I appreciate the welcome on such short notice." He heard a protesting horn behind them. "You pick up your driving skills from watching Manila taxis?"

She laughed. "California drivers are not very forgiving."

They stayed on State Route 163, heading north and eventually intersecting with I-15 just south of the Miramar Marine Corps Air Station. On cue, two MV-22 Ospreys dipped above the interstate in their final approach. Wolf stared at the aircraft. Regina ignored them, instead saying, "Do I dare ask what you two are cooking up this time?"

"Just thought it was time to see you and Sam."

"Still the keeper of secrets, huh? The two of you act like brothers with some sort of agreed-upon, unwritten code."

Wolf sighed. "Some things are better left unsaid."

"Well, maybe it's your turn to drag Sam into something. He certainly owes you for what happened in Zamboanga."

"That was a lifetime ago, Regina. Lot of water has gone under the bridge since our little adventure. Hey, he got you out of the deal. Can't be all bad."

"Flatterer." She joined a queue on the interstate's Mira Mesa exit. "We'll have time to talk over dinner. We have a pool house suite with its own office and kitchen. Stay as long as you like."

"Thanks, Regina. I think I got out of Dodge just in time."

She turned to him, concern on her face. "So much for your vow of silence. I hope you're not in some kind of trouble."

Waving away her concern, he said, "Nothing I can't handle."

"That's just what Sam would say."

She left the highway, went right two blocks, and turned left on Scripps Ranch Boulevard at the base of a rocky, near-vertical hillside with clinging eucalyptus trees and a wall of gray townhouses above. Shaking her head, she said, "What am I going to do with the two of you?"

Wolf stared out his window at the curving road bisecting rising hills crowned with red-tiled homes. "My dad always used to say, 'This too shall pass.'" He changed the subject. "Looks dry. Still not getting enough rain?"

She followed his eyes to the hillsides. "Never enough rain when we need it, too much when we don't. Not as green as the Philippines."

A wistful Wolf said, "Nothing's as green as the islands, Regina."

Flashing him a mischievous glance, she said, "By the way, Sam changed my name. He calls me Reggie now. At first, I didn't care for it. But it's grown on me. My American half, I guess."

"Reggie, huh? I like it. It fits you. How's your mom and your sister?"

She grinned, spoke about her younger sister. "Ivy is a mother for the second time."

"Congratulations, Aunt Reggie."

A mock frown. "That makes me sound old," she said. "Auntie will do."

"And your mom?"

"Still in Santa Barbara. She's a great support."

"She like having a Green Beret for a son-in-law?"

"She's delighted with Sam. Thinks the world of him."

"So do I, Reggie."

"Then don't do anything foolish. Life is too perfect now."

"Wouldn't think of it. Just here to ask Sam's advice."

"Uh-huh." She nodded right, at a momentary patch of blue above the sea of tiled roofs. "Miramar Lake."

"Nice," Wolf said. "I miss being by water. I'm landlocked where I am."

"Pack up and move here. The beach is not far away."

"I'd need a good woman to share it with."

"I could introduce you to a dozen friends who would find you fascinating."

"Well...actually, I did meet a woman recently."

"Oh? Not another word. I want Sam to hear this over dinner."

"Okay, my lips are sealed. Until dinner."

# Chapter 31

Sam McFadden arrived like a good host—with a case of chilled San Miguel, fresh bread, and an apology. He embraced Wolf by the pool. "Sorry for the delay, Wolfman. Work, you know."

"Not a problem. Regina…Reggie…filled in. Got me here in one piece despite her being behind the wheel."

"Yeah, she's a terror on the roads. Gotta say, you're looking good, man. Life agrees with you." McFadden took out two beers and excused himself to greet his wife. "Be right back. You have to bring me up to speed. Your phone call was sketchy but I gather you have a problem."

McFadden returned and hoisted a sweating bottle of San Miguel. "Mabuhay."

Wolf toasted his friend. "Mabuhay. To you and Reggie, Sam. Like her moniker, like the welcome, and especially like your choice of beer."

"Reggie's idea. Glad you're here. How did we let so much time get away from us?"

Wolf said, "Beats me. I've been halfway around the world in the last month. Seen a lot of things; had a lot of close calls. Glad to be here."

McFadden turned serious. "Okay, what's the skinny? Your message hinted at trouble."

Wolf said, "You heard about Colter."

"Saw the news," said a subdued McFadden. "I remember you saying something about the two of you going to Kazakhstan for a launch. That part of this business?"

For the next half-hour, leaving out Yana, he recited the Moscow misadventure, the Kazakhstan debacle, and the Domodedovo ambush.

McFadden said, "Let's get this straight. You're on the run from the Russian mafia?"

"And maybe some of our own people," interrupted Wolf.

"Our own people?" said McFadden. "That's heavy, Wolfman. But these Russian guys have a long reach. Good news is I've got some folks who might help. Can't make any promises, but it's a start. I'll make some calls to get the ball rolling. Meanwhile, you stay with us, out of sight."

Wolf gestured to the pool and surrounding hillsides. "That I can handle, Sam." Below them a shimmering Miramar Lake, beyond it, I-15, the lake's namesake air station, and the city. An easterly wind had chased the marine layer offshore, leaving them with a crystal-clear San Diego day. Wolf strolled to the edge of the pool's concrete apron and looked across the hills. He smiled. "You've got yourself good high ground."

"Glad you approve." McFadden said, joining him. "I knew this was it when I first saw the spot. You're welcome as long as you need our hospitality. Let's brainstorm after dinner."

Regina posed in the sliding glass doors, signaling both men. "Put aside any top-secret talk and come to dinner. Tom has a lot of explaining to do. I want to hear all about this mysterious woman."

McFadden shot a puzzled look at Wolf. "Woman? Did you leave something out of the telling?"

Wolf shrugged. "A fringe benefit to the Moscow trip. Reggie made me promise I wouldn't say a word until dinner."

Regina settled next to the former SEAL and rubbed her hands in anticipation.

"You're on deck," warned McFadden. "No way you're getting excused until the missus is satisfied. Answer honestly and she may let you off easy."

Wolf smiled at Reggie. "I can handle this. Remember when we first met at your hotel in Zamboanga? This should be a piece of cake compared to that. Say grace and then ask away, lady."

She did just that. They talked through dinner about the Philippines, Wolf's Russian trip, Kazakhstan, Regina's family, McFadden's new business venture, and lastly—mostly—about Yana.

# Chapter 32

After dinner, McFadden retreated to his home office and made several calls while Wolf sat on a leather couch, listening. When McFadden finished he reported the conversations.

"That first call went to Steve Schmit, former army. He's our office prankster and resident geek. He's agreed to decode your camera chip. Second call was Gary Kurskov, a Russian expert. Third generation. Teaches at the local college. Both these guys do part-time contract work for us. Trustworthy. Good people. You heard me sketch your problem to them. They're interested. Reggie has no need to know. Let's keep it that way."

"Roger that. My thoughts exactly."

"At least no one knows where you are right now. That's a good thing."

Wolf held up a camera card. "I've been carrying this sewn in my jacket for a long time. If your guys are able to make sense of the files, my job is half done."

"I hear you. We'll meet them at our site tomorrow. By the way, anything in your emails yet?"

"Nothing since this evening." He swiped his cellphone screen. A quick check showed scant traffic since his previous look. His inquiries to former team members concerning Colter had yet to bear fruit. There was a message from the State Department's Nells requesting another interview.

"Not gonna happen this week or the next," he said aloud.

"That the guy from State?" asked McFadden.

Nodding, Wolf asked, "What do you know about Threat Finance, Sam?"

"Was that what Colter was into?"

"I believe so. I know a guy Colter worked with. This guy's a retired Marine gunny in Virginia Beach. He's done some freelancing for The Company. He hinted that Colter was tied up with SOCOM—Special Operations Command South, ISAF—International Security Assistance Force, Afghanistan; and EUCOM—European Command."

Hands behind his head, McFadden said, "Lot of alphabet soup there. What the hell did you and Colter get yourselves into?"

Wolf passed the camera card to McFadden. "Dunno, Sam. I'm counting on your guys to unpack what's in this. My future's in their hands."

# Chapter 33

*Brighton Beach, Brooklyn*

To disappoint Boris Levich is to sign one's own death sentence. As *pakhan*—godfather—he demanded blind obedience. From his inner circle to the lowliest *shestyorka*—recruits not yet sworn members of the criminal fraternity—Levich's word was law. No one knew the rule better than Dimitri Ivanov. His latest assignment, the brutal beating of Mikhail Drogenev, had been carried out within hours of being given the task. Summoned to a meeting with the boss, Ivanov had no reason to suspect anything other than a pat on the back or an intimate lunch with Levich.

Instead, after entering the towering seaside condominium's ground floor restaurant, Ivanov was met by two bull-necked *byki*—bodyguards—belonging to Anton Sheveski, a Levich ally and notorious drug and arms dealer. Halting Ivanov, the pair gruffly asked him to surrender any weapons he carried before entering the dining room. Instantly wary, Ivanov was surprised to see another Levich familiar, the bearded Sasha Mikoyan, pacing in the inner sanctum's hallway just beyond the guards.

Given no choice, Ivanov gave up his weapons, a 9mm Glock and a Spetsnaz tactical knife. Ivanov was told to join a visibly nervous Mikoyan and wait until Levich called both. Mikoyan was exhibiting all the symptoms of a man on a wire.

"You've heard about my boys in Virginia Beach, I take it."

"Yes. I thought it foolish to send them, Sasha. They're in trouble."

"I'm in bigger trouble," whispered Mikoyan. "What should I do?"

"Hear what the boss has to say. Then promise him anything he wants. But make sure you deliver. You won't get a second chance."

Hushed by one of the sentinels, the two followed the hulking bodyguard down a paneled hallway lined with dimmed sconces. They stopped at a set of curtained French doors. A rap on the glass and the two were shown into a smaller side room set for a private party. A dozen linen-covered tables sat beneath glittering chandeliers floating in a bluish layer of cigarette smoke. Heavy damask drapes had been drawn across tall windows, blocking the view of the sea. Glasses, carafes of water, over-flowing ashtrays, and half-full bottles of vodka clustered in the center of a table with a half-dozen chairs.

Mikoyan and Ivanov were facing three men. The first two were nameless *byki*—automatons wearing the ubiquitous jogging suit. The frowning pair stood behind Konstantin Verlov, a recent arrival from Donetsk. Like a dangerous scarred bull, Verlov had stormed Levich's inner circle with a mixture of charm and menace. Bulky and pocked-faced, the mercurial Ukrainian was unfailingly

polite and threatening in turn. For the past month he had
been glued to the godfather's elbow, gaining influence at
the expense of others. It was the man's hold over Levich
that disturbed his lieutenants most. Ivanov in particular
thought the interloper bore watching.

At today's meeting it was the little things the newcomer
did that troubled him. When Levich drained his vodka,
Verlov refilled it. When Levich paused, groping for the
right word, Verlov filled in the blank. And when Levich
hesitated, Verlov picked up the godfather's unraveling
threads to finish the thought.

Levich began. "So, Sasha, do you know what has become
of those two idiots you sent to Virginia Beach?" Downing
his vodka, the old man slammed the empty shot glass on
the table.

*Sasha has a right to be nervous*, thought Ivanov.

As Mikoyan fumbled for an answer, the Ukranian,
Verlov, filled Levich's glass and said, "I'll tell you what
has happened, Boss. Both of Sasha's boys now sit in jail
awaiting rescue in the wake of their failure." Like a
frowning Buddha, Verlov sat back, a malevolent hint of a
grin beginning to show. Levich drummed his fingers on
the linen, awaiting a reply.

Knowing Mikoyan's predicament was one of his own
making, Ivanov ignored his fellow gang member's
unease. Silence his wisest course, he stared at a spot on a
tapestry behind Levich. The assignment in Virginia
Beach had been too vague to suit Ivanov. Something
about a computer. Something about a particular man.
Something about damaging information and precious
little else. Risking the godfather's ire, he had counseled
Levich against sending men to Virginia Beach. Not to be
denied, a furious Levich had dismissed Ivanov, turning
instead to one of the more ambitious crabs in the

bucket. Eager to best Ivanov, Mikoyan had volunteered two of his crew. Having curried Levich's favor to win the assignment and then failing, Mikoyan was on the spot.

The manipulative Verlov badgered Mikoyan. "Not only have your men failed, they were caught in the act." Putting on a long face, he shook his head. "Tsk, tsk, embarrassing."

"Yes. Inexcusable," Levich growled. "This will not do. We find ourselves in an untenable position." Turning to his other young acolyte, he said, "What do you suggest, Dimitri?"

Verlov interrupted, playing Levich like an instrument. "How could you have known these two would act the clumsy fool and be caught? You have not been well served in this matter, Boris Levich." Sipping his vodka, Verlov said, "You have sent the lawyer to Virginia. What does he think our chances are to get Sasha's men back?"

Ivanov caught Levich's eye and spoke up, naming the jailed men. "Not good. Of the two, Markov will undoubtedly be handed over to the feds for immigration problems. He and Suskin will have to answer a weapons charge. Both will face burglary and auto theft charges. They will be of no use to us now."

Throwing up his hands, Verlov sighed. "My thoughts exactly. What are we to do with such men?"

Levich took the bait. "Dimitri, my boy, wait outside."

Ivanov got up from the table and left without looking at the defeated Mikoyan. He stood in the hallway with his back to the wall, waiting to be summoned again. Hearing loud, accusatory voices, chairs toppling, muffled cries, and then feet kicking at carpet, he turned his thoughts elsewhere until the sounds of scuffling ended.

The doors opened and one of the drones in shirtsleeves beckoned him. The room showed evidence of the brief struggle. The other guard dog was righting upended chairs, kicking away bits of broken glass, and straightening the linen tablecloth. Though hardened by his own work on Levich's behalf, Ivanov fought to hide his surprise. A large blue tarp had been placed on the floor in the middle of the room. Overlapping the tarp was a sheet of clear plastic. In the middle knelt a hooded Sasha Mikoyan, hands tied behind his back, ankles bound. Stifled sobs earned him a backhand, nearly toppling him. Watching the drama, a flushed Boris Levich remained seated, his bony fingers gripping a half-filled vodka shot glass. Verlov stood over Mikoyan, suppressed Marakov pistol in his hand. Arms folded, the two impassive byki retreated to the background.

Levich said, "Ah, Dimitri. Our Sasha made a rather serious mistake, don't you agree? We cannot afford such lapses. Poor boy. He's become an object lesson, I'm afraid."

Verlov circled Mikoyan, the pistol prodding the nape of Mikoyan's neck. The smiling Ukranian looked at Levich, expectant.

His anger palpable, the godfather held up a hand. "Wait."

Smiling paternally, he turned to Ivanov. "You do it, Dimitri."

Shrugging, Verlov offered the pistol to Ivanov.

Grasping the weapon, Ivanov stepped on the plastic. Arm's length behind Mikoyan, he pressed the gun's muzzle against Sasha's skull and fired.

# Chapter 34

Wolf watched the petite redhead in lane four empty her handgun at a paper target forty feet away. On either side of her, other women fired at hanging paper targets, shredding black silhouettes with precision. The muffled sound of firing died away. The women lay down their handguns, stepped back, and raised their right hands. A male instructor wearing khakis and a blue short-sleeved shirt went down the line, checking each handgun and empty magazine. Satisfied, he removed his earmuffs and gathered the shooters in a circle for what looked like an animated exchange.

"He's getting their feedback," said McFadden. He and Wolf watched from a hallway, separated from the range by thick, bulletproof and soundproof windows. "What do you think?" asked McFadden, his eyes on the range instructor and the shooters.

"I think you've got some damn fine gunslingers in the making."

McFadden laughed. "Well, we try. It's Ladies' Night."

"Impressive. When do the boys come out to play?"

McFadden glanced at his watch. "Another half hour and the big dogs will be doing their thing. Then at eight, we'll have open range til ten."

"Get a lot of couples?"

"Surprisingly, yes. Seems like folks want to feel a little more secure these days, Wolfman. We're tough on safety and background checks."

"Don't want any crazies, huh?"

"Exactly. No self-respecting range needs that kind of publicity."

Wolf rubbed his hands together. "Okay, what else you have going on?"

"C'mon, I'll show you around. Schmit and Kurskov will be here soon. We've got leadership lectures going on. Self-defense seminars and fitness classes. Kinda like a one-stop shop for self-protection and awareness."

"What about a drumming class for men?"

"Same old skeptical Wolfman, huh?"

"I'm just checking to make sure you haven't gone all New Age on me."

"Not a chance."

McFadden led Wolf on a tour of classrooms and the fitness studio. He showed him an indoor mock-up of a cityscape complete with faux stores, schoolrooms, and a parking lot. The former SEAL approved. "You've got a great thing going here, Sam."

"We think so." Pointing to an unfinished portion of the warehouse space, McFadden said, "We've got plans for an urban paintball setup and a virtual range using laser Glocks and Berettas. Our clients can choose to shoot at spring-loaded targets or real-life scenarios in one of our 270-degree screen rooms."

"What about law enforcement? They tight with you?"

"Absolutely. They're welcome anytime. Challenges them."

Raising his arms, Wolf said, "Well, I have to admit, Sam, you've put together a nice facility. You're prospering, my son."

"I've got two partners, both Special Ops guys."

"SEALs?"

"Couldn't operate in San Diego without them, Wolfman."

"Good. Just checking. Like to know the brothers are getting a piece of the pie. How's Reggie feel about this empire? She cool with it?"

"We're starting to make money on the investment. She's got some change in this operation. So does her mom."

"So she said. Nice to keep it in the family."

McFadden took a call. Nodding at Wolf he said, "The guys are here."

"Good," said Wolf. "Let's get this show on the road."

# Chapter 35

Wolf shook hands with Schmit and Kurskov. He studied both men as McFadden bantered during introductions. Kurskov, stocky, reserved, showed faint hints of Central Asia in his eyes and cheekbones. Schmit was the opposite. Lanky, bearded, and bespectacled, the Midwest transplant wore a perpetual impish grin, a red plaid shirt, and jeans.

Beginning with Schmit, McFadden sketched a brief description for Wolf. "Some of this I told you. Steve's our resident wild child and IT guy. Around here we break things, he fixes things. Top in his class in Fort Huachuca. Did most of his time stateside with one tour in the sandbox. As apt to plant a whoopee cushion on my chair as he is to get us back up and running when disaster strikes. We like to say, 'Schmit happens.' Handy guy to have around and our top resident geek."

Waving at McFadden's description, Schmit stroked his beard. "Guilty as charged and proud of it."

McFadden turned to the placid Kurskov. "Gary is an interesting case. Our academic brain trust. He's a hopeless TV game show addict. Fluent in three languages: English, Russian, and German."

"Four...if you count pidgin," added Schmit.

"How could I forget? Gary was born in Hawaii. Grew up there."

Wolf was intrigued by the Hawaiian connection. "Sam told me you're a third-generation Russian-American. Where does Hawaii fit in?"

"My grandfather was Russian, my grandma Uzbek. Not sure how that happened. They were just teens when they fled to Austria right after the war."

"The original odd couple," volunteered Schmit. "Gary's a United Nations poster child."

"Yeah, I am that. My grandparents settled in Cleveland, where my dad was born. The youngest of five, he joined the Air Force out of high school, ended up at Hickam, and met my mom. She's Chinese-Hawaiian. I was born in Honolulu."

"We affectionately call him 'Poi Dog' behind his back," said Schmit.

Kurskov playfully slapped the back of the tech's head.

Wolf leaned forward. "Sam says your Russian's excellent."

"My grandparents used to speak it at home. My ancestry interested me in college. Seemed to come naturally."

"His Russian is good as gold," interrupted McFadden. "He'll handle the decoding. Anything you want to add, Wolfman?"

"Only that I appreciate what you're doing." Wolf passed the camera's memory card and a note with a scribbled algorithm to Schmit. "The info on this cost a good friend his life. Seven other people died because of it. I'd like to think this is the end of the line."

Planting both hands on his desk, McFadden stood. "This is a 'your eyes only' situation, guys. I've signed on as well. Work on this in the evening for starters. If you need daylight hours let me know and I'll okay your time. Anything we learn stays here. Got it?"

The solemnity of the moment settled in the office. McFadden broke the spell. "Okay, let's get on it." He and Wolf shook hands with Schmit and Kurskov.

When the two had left, McFadden read his watch. "Hey, Wolfman. If you're up to it, how about some target work? Whadaya say we find ourselves some open lanes?"

"Now you're talking my language, Sam."

# Chapter 36

"So, what are you going to do about Verlov?"

Ivanov took a long pull of vodka and passed the chilled bottle to his left without answering. Helinski tried again, adding a warning. "I know you well enough to know you're thinking about Verlov. The longer he goes unchallenged the harder it will be to take him down."

Ivanov stirred. "Who said anything about taking him down?"

Emboldened by alcohol, a swaying Ivor Sergov said, "Sergei's right. It's only a matter of time, Dimitri."

Ivanov took another long swallow. "You speak like jealous schoolgirls. So Verlov has the boss's ear. I serve the boss, nothing else matters."

"He killed Sasha," said Helinski. "Or had his bodyguards do it."

"You know nothing. Sasha made his own bed."

Helinski, fueled by vodka, grew bolder. "Wake up, Dimitri. Your turn may come tomorrow or the week after. We won't be around to help you. Verlov will eliminate us one by one, leaving the boss surrounded by new faces. He worms his way into Levich's heart right under your nose."

"Yah, and who needs heartworm," hissed Sergov.

The two giggled at the play on words. The pair, young ruthless boyeviks from Ivanov's crew, had joined him for a night of drinking on the nearly deserted boardwalk. Ivanov turned up his collar against the night chill and stared at the dark sea. The two loudmouths were doing his thinking out loud.

*Reckless to talk like this*, he thought. *They are right, but Levich has ears everywhere.* He stepped off the boardwalk and plodded across the abandoned beach.

Sergov tossed the empty bottle toward the water in a high arc. He and Helinski followed Ivanov. The two drunken soldiers caught up with him and fell silent. Light from windows in the high-rises lining the boardwalk cast the trio's shadows on the sand. A solitary dog walker hurried along, throwing a suspicious glance at the three.

Ivanov stood facing the sea. A stupefied Sergov fell to his knees, mesmerized by the waves. The briny air cleared Ivanov's head. He spoke without looking at either man. "It would have to be done so discreetly that no one would point a finger at us."

Helinski cocked his head toward Ivanov. "Those two byki will be a problem. Verlov never goes anywhere without them."

Ivanov's eyes remained locked on the breakers. "They have to sleep sometime. Verlov has to be taken when he's isolated."

Sergov fell back on the sand, his arms outstretched, eyes closed. "Maybe at one of the clubs. He likes to go out to play, you know. We could catch him at Caspian Nights."

Ivanov dismissed the idea. "No good. That's Levich's club. He'd never forgive that. Plus, there would be too many witnesses. Too crowded. Too many innocents."

"Since when do you worry about innocents, Dimitri?"

"Sergei, do you even know what the word 'discreet' means?"

"It means…whatever you want it to mean…I guess."

Ivanov tapped his temple. "It means 'to think.' We need to know Verlov's routine. He appears each day at the boss's apartment with his two bulls. I don't know where he stays. Neither do you."

A voice from the sand. "He sleeps at Dagmar Danilev's place."

Ivanov leaned over the sprawled Sergov. "How do you know this?"

"Her nephew Yuri is friends with my cousin. They are studying together for their Bar Mitzvahs."

"She's young enough to be his daughter," snarled Helinski.

"So? Maybe she has a thing for older men."

Kneeling, Ivanov gripped Sergov's jaw. "You know this for a fact?"

"Yes. He likes her. Yuri told my cousin Verlov brings her gifts."

"How long has this been going on?"

Sergov shrugged.

"Who's at the home during the day?"

"Huh, no one, I guess. Yuri's in school and Dagmar works."

"When do the bodyguards come for Verlov?"

"Don't know."

"We need to know that," said Ivanov. Wheels turned in his head. To Helinski, "This week you and Sergov make a visit during the day. Go on foot through the alley. Draw up a floor plan of the house. I want to know which bedroom is hers."

"Then what?"

"Then we find out where his guys stay. What time they pick him up each day. Maybe where they go for breakfast before they come to Levich's apartment. The boss is never up before nine."

Helinski said, "That would give us plenty of time."

Ivanov pulled Sergov to his feet with an assist from Helinski.

"Speak to no one about this," warned Ivanov. "None of the others must know what was said tonight. If I hear one word..."

"Nothing," swore both men in unison. "We say nothing."

"See that you keep your word. This is the kind of thing that can get you killed."

# Chapter 37

Downloading Wolf's memory card took two days of Schmit's time. Working nights, he isolated the embedded images from the originals on his office computer. Behind locked doors, the tech made backup copies of the originals and prepared his presentation for Wolf, McFadden, and Kurskov. Cornering Schmit in the company break room, McFadden asked for an update.

Schmit finished off a can of Coke. "Wrapped up two hours ago."

"Okay, sorry to hound you. It's just that Wolf is antsy to find out."

"Join the club. I know how to work with steganography but my Russian is zip. I'll get the files over to Kurskov ASAP."

"Do that. I'll call Wolf and have him come by at five. Good enough?"

"Fine with me. I'll brief you guys in your office."

"See you at five," said McFadden.

That evening, after leaving the range in good hands, McFadden cleared his desk for Schmit to work his magic. With Kurskov busy with the files from the Russian ledger, Schmit was to explain his end of the operation to Wolf and McFadden.

Wolf arrived with a cooler of beer and a fresh pizza. Taking over McFadden's desk, Schmit popped a beer and snagged two pieces of hot pizza. The three ate in silence while Schmit's fingers danced across the keyboard of his boss's computer.

"Where's Kurskov," said Wolf. "Shouldn't he be here?"

"He knows better," whispered McFadden. "Give it a few minutes and you'll see what I mean."

Opening a window displaying photos from the Russian trip—including the launch at Baikonur—Schmit led his two-man audience through his sleuthing steps: a Steganography 101 tutorial.

"I dumped everything on your card. Three hundred-fifty photos. Some nice shots, lots of mediocre ones. You are apparently fond of redundancy."

Wolf and McFadden chuckled between bites of pizza.

"Humor me," said Schmit. "A brief outline of steganography. Ancient Greek word meaning 'covered writing.' They used to write secret messages on wood tablets and cover them with wax. New message gets scratched in wax and nobody's the wiser. Guy sends off tablet. Recipient gets tablet, melts the wax and voila—secret message appears. You with me so far?"

McFadden groaned. "Don't dumb it down. We know the basics. Give us the *Reader's Digest* version of the science."

Warming to his task, Schmit took a slice of pizza and said, "Patience. How often do I get a captive audience?"

He hit a key and a picture of Moscow's Red Square appeared. "So, using your innocent-looking tourist picture, let's say we want to add another file to it. The original picture becomes a 'carrier' for our secret file. Normally, that would significantly increase the overall size of the file and call attention to a possible hidden message."

Wolf said, "Someone who knows the process might be able to pick up on that, right?"

"Correct. If they had access to the original file they'd detect the hidden data by looking at the size."

Rolling his eyes, McFadden turned to Wolf. "This is why we never ask Schmitty for the time. He'll tell you how the watch works, where it was made, and maybe the history of time as well."

Schmit frowned. "You're stealing my thunder, Boss."

"I'm listening," said Wolf.

"Thank you. As I was saying...So, we replace bits of the original picture with new bits from our secret message. A digital image is made up of thousands of pixels. Those could be eight bit or twenty-four bit. With the eight bit you get 256 colors to create an image. For the twenty-four bit you get more color. Do the math. Each pixel is worth three bytes. The bigger number of bits, the more we have to play with when it comes to hiding a message."

"You're making my head hurt," complained McFadden.

Schmit kept going. "When we convert the available bits into a binary code, we can simply replace the right side of that lineup—what we call 'Least Significant Bits'—with the secret bits. That way the left side, which is the 'Most Significant Bits,' remains intact. So does the image. To the naked eye the picture is not altered significantly. You tracking with me?"

"Sort of," said Wolf. "One byte contains eight bits, and each byte is a color combination of red, green, and blue. RGB, correct?"

"You paid attention."

McFadden frowned. "Cut to the chase, Schmitty. With all due respect, we don't want to be here all night."

Schmit kept on, oblivious to his own chatter. Eventually, he wrapped up his presentation with the news Wolf wanted to hear. Using the algorithm Wolf had provided, he had discovered hidden files totaling 135 pages of notes, names, figures, and dates—all in tidy Russian script. Kurskov had the files and, according to Schmit, was already at home, hard at work.

McFadden boxed up pizza scraps while Wolf chatted with Schmit about the tech's Fort Huachuca days and Iraq sojourn. With the camera card back in hand, Wolf thanked him for his work.

"Anytime," said Schmit. "Hope we can make them pay for Commander Colter's death."

# Chapter 38

Kurskov spent the better part of ten days decoding and transcribing the messages hidden in the camera images from Russian to English. Working mostly at night at home or in his locked office, he would not be rushed.

Wolf used the interval to visit the SEAL training facility on Coronado, made contact with friends from his days in the teams. Later, at the naval base officer's club, he reminisced with two of Dan Colter's fellow SEALs. Nothing the pair said to Wolf shed light on the dead man's background. Follow-ups to earlier phone calls he had made before coming west met a similar fate.

During the week, after-dinner conversations ended in dead ends. Quizzed by McFadden about his Russian trip, Wolf could only remember generalities Colter had served up during their hours together. The blanks only added to his frustration. At the time, he told McFadden, he had not thought the gaps in Colter's background important. Recalling their camaraderie during SEALs training, Wolf said, "We focused on surviving during that time. We were just glad to make it from one day to the next. I mean, we'd do a bit of small talk but who remembers it years later?"

Sympathetic, McFadden said, "I know what you mean. Your mind gets fuzzy after a while. You concentrate on tactics and daily routine."

"Exactly. When you're freezing your ass off in the ocean, even words take too much energy at that point. Then, training's over and we go our separate ways. Different teams. Different platoons. Different coasts."

"And you're getting nothing from your old contacts?"

"Spooky, huh?" said Wolf. "Somewhere out there is an ex-wife."

"Good luck with that, Wolfman. Best to let that one alone."

"Could be a clue."

McFadden snorted. "Could also make you sorry you asked."

Near the end of Week Two, after an afternoon workout in the pool, Wolf complained to McFadden. Resting in the shallow end, his crossed arms on the tiles, he said, "Hard to believe the guys in the teams know less about Colter than me."

"Check his service record. He's got to have one. Or it could be his file's been scrubbed clean. He could be a ghost, an invisible man."

"It's possible. I'll have to contact State when I get back."

"Wouldn't put a lot of stock in getting answers from that quarter."

"I'm going nuts thinking about this, Sam. We were in some deep shit over there. Colter had my back and I had his. He didn't return and I want to know why. I mean, he was hurt bad but someone has to know what happened to him once he left my sight."

"Give it a rest for now, Wolfman. I just talked to Kurskov. We're meeting with him tonight."

"Finally. Did he give you a heads up on what he's found?"

"He'll only say he found something fascinating. With Kurskov that qualifies as an understatement."

"It better be worth it."

McFadden tossed Wolf a towel. "Put it this way. I've never heard him sound more mysterious. Kurskov's not exactly an excitable guy, but for once he was champing at the bit."

"Okay, if you were trying to get my attention, you got it."

Wrapping the towel around his shoulders, Wolf headed to his guest quarters, McFadden to the house.

# Chapter 39

"I've got bad news...and bad news. Which do you want first?" Kurskov, his normally placid expression replaced by a worried frown, stared at Wolf and McFadden.

"What gives?" said McFadden.

"This is way beyond my pay grade. This kind of information can topple governments and get people killed."

Kurskov dimmed the lights and took a seat at the end of the table, his laptop connected to the projector.

"Okay," McFadden said, "give us the bad news."

"It's all bad."

Impatient, Wolf said, "Start with the least bad news."

Kurskov tapped the keyboard. A vertical ledger page appeared, its tidy Cyrillic script and numerals familiar to Wolf. "Schmit found 135 pages with notes like this. The person who wrote these accounts was very specific, very detailed about the who, what, where, and when."

Kurskov aimed a penlight's laser at the screen. "This is page one—just an example of what we're dealing with. It took longer than I would have liked to get everything lined up. It's hard to believe none of this was in code."

Wolf studied the image. "But you were able to figure out what this means, right?"

"Yes. I did some cross-checking on the names. Just wanted to make sure what I was seeing. It added a couple days to the job."

"Impressive," said McFadden. "Show us what the translations look like."

A tap on the keyboard and a second slide appeared showing side-by-side Russian and English versions. Running the laser's red arrow over the figures in right-hand columns, Kurskov said, "I've converted rubles to dollars to make it easier to understand."

Wolf and McFadden stared at the listed amounts. "Someone's moving a lot of money around," said Wolf. "I'm reading bank names in English, but they don't match with the Russian names on the same line. What's that about?"

Kurskov beamed. "It's a primitive cypher. You see just names on the Russian version, but I was curious. I went down some rabbit trails before it dawned on me these fictitious names were being substituted for the banks. Some of the later stuff didn't compute. That's when I figured out the writer had switched to some kind of code for the banks. It took some doing but I was able to marry up most of these names using the bank numbers."

"Why do all that?" said Wolf.

"You'd have to ask the writer. Maybe he got spooked and decided to hide what he was doing."

"Or took his secret to the grave," said McFadden. Turning to Wolf he said, "You mentioned seven people had died because of this book, right?"

Wolf shrugged. "That's what Colter and I were told. Not sure if it's true or not."

"But you had people trailing you," said Kurskov. "Colter died as a result of having the book...or the information...in his possession."

"True. We assumed our attackers were after the book."

"Okay," said McFadden, "what does this mean? All these names, some of them codes for banks. What's going on?"

"Let me show you another dozen pages so you can get a feel for the entire book." Kurskov ran through more slides, pointed out more of the same names, explained which sums belonged to which name. Leaving another split image of a Russian page and its English version on the screen, he planted his hands on the table.

"The book is divided into three parts. The first two-thirds deal with money coming in and going out. Pretty straightforward. There are some footnotes on weights and margin comments about what I suspect are drug deals. Also found numerous notations about weapon shipments."

McFadden asked, "So we've got drugs and arms deals going on?"

"I wouldn't be surprised," said Wolf, gesturing at the screen. "You think this is a record of state doings? Or *mafiya* doings?"

"Both. These days what Moscow bank isn't mobbed up?"

"They're all dirty," fumed Wolf. "One big rotten family, including the Kremlin."

"I recognize some of the oligarchs on these lists," said Kurskov. "It's impossible for anyone to do business in Russia today without rubbing shoulders with the Brotherhood—the Russian Mafia. Way too much money changing hands. Look at the amounts on these pages. That's probably just the tip of the iceberg. One writer's take on things."

Wolf caught Kurskov's eye. "What about State's involvement? You said this was the kind of information that could topple governments and get people killed. How does what we're seeing play into that?"

Kurskov called up another image. "Example. The eight banks listed on this page are major Ukranian ones. The Central Bank and seven private ones. Lot of money being poured in. Question: who's doing the banking? Look at the outflow on the next page. It dates back five years. The last three look like a dam breaking. Out goes the money, leaving insolvent banks. No capital to work with. There are several major banks on these pages. Big players. Most of them in Kiev. Several in the eastern part of the country."

"Russian pressure squeezing the government in Ukraine?"

"Absolutely," said Kurskov. "It's been going on for a while."

McFadden stared at the screen. "Where does the money go?"

"My guess is that it ends up in Moscow banks."

"And we know who controls the Russian banks," groused Wolf.

"Are you saying this is a paper trail of an orchestrated effort by Moscow to collapse Ukraine's economy?" McFadden asked.

"That's always been suspected. This just confirms it," replied Kurskov. "I want to do more digging to cross-reference these names. We know the ones involved with the banks...both Russian and Ukrainian."

"And the others?" said Wolf.

"Probably mob figures or Kremlin inner circle."

Wolf grumbled. "Hard to tell the difference."

"True," Kurskov agreed. "But it's the Ukranian names that prove interesting. Just a guess, but I think it's insiders selling out their country."

Wolf slammed a fist on the table. "All things are possible when you're talking this kind of money."

"Always follow the money," said McFadden.

Holding up a hand, Kurskov cautioned. "Do that and you will likely find this money going through Moscow and then overseas. It's not a pretty picture, Sam." He fast-forwarded to a new pair of pages listing prominent western banks. His viewers scanned the names.

"London," sneered Wolf. "Switzerland. No surprise there. Vienna."

McFadden drummed his fingers on the table. "Barbados. The Caymans."

Kurskov tapped his keyboard, pausing his show. "New York."

Staring at the ceiling, McFadden leaned back, let go a low whistle, arms behind his head. "If you take enough money out of a national economy, hollow out the banking system, and stimulate a little panic, you can collapse any government...or country."

"That's what we're seeing here," said Wolf.

"That's the bad news," answered Kurskov. "The least bad news."

In unison, Wolf and McFadden said, "The least bad news?"

Bringing the screen back to life, Kurskov scrolled through four slides, again showing side-by-side Russian and English translations complete with footnotes.

"Holy shit," exclaimed Wolf. "You sure about this?"

"It's a word-for-word translation," Kurskov assured him. "If you compare the money amounts and see what it's being used for, you have to acknowledge what's happening."

"This is where it gets dicey," said McFadden. "If what you're showing us is genuine..."

"It's a faithful translation. You can vet it with another source. I wouldn't be offended, Sam."

"No need to," said McFadden. "I trust your work." He pointed in turn to the money figures and the written explanation beneath. "This is history repeating itself. This is a recipe for disaster."

# Chapter 40

Fog settled like cotton over the coast, softening the distant lights of San Diego, and crept inland. Wolf and McFadden finished dinner and came outside to talk poolside. Reggie had joined them briefly before being driven indoors by the hilltop's chilly night air. Nursing two San Miguels, their faces glowing from the pool's underwater light, the two friends sipped in silence.

Wolf broke the quiet with his usual bluntness. "Kurskov's notes tell me we're looking at a blueprint for a proxy war, Sam. You know I'm right. Look at those funds going for secret militias."

McFadden shrugged. "Maybe. For the sake of argument, let's say that what Kurskov showed us last night is true. That would mean these plans were already in the works. If that's the case, then things over there are going to get a lot worse."

"It has all the right signs. I know I'm on to something."

"You're like a broken record."

"They don't make records any more, Sam."

A short laugh and McFadden turned glum. "You know what I mean. I'm skeptical but I'm open to your arguments. I need to say this: is it possible that Colter brought you in on this as a straw man? You know, wanted to have you be part of this to provide some sort of cover for what he was involved in?"

"No way," said Wolf. "Colter never would have done that. We were tight, Sam. I'm frankly surprised you asked that question."

"Had to ask. Just seems odd that you and Colter hadn't seen each other for a while and then he shows up for this trip to Russia. I wanted to get that out on the table in case someone else asks the same question. Okay, what about a course of action? I'd like us to be on the same page when we're done talking." Wolf nodded in agreement.

"All this might explain why somebody in Washington is interested in what you and Colter found. It could prove embarrassing."

"It's potentially embarrassing because somebody's off the reservation and doing this on their own. Maybe some half-assed idea that started out as a drawing on a cocktail napkin...or, it goes even higher up the food chain, maybe the White House."

"Whoa," said McFadden, "I don't think we're there yet."

"Point taken. But let's think about the Russians," said Wolf. "My guess is both the Kremlin and the mob would like to see those names, find out who's screwing them out of their money and who's involved with setting up anti-Russian militias. It's not only about money...which is considerable."

"It's obvious, isn't it?" answered McFadden. "This lays bare what's been going on for years. How can Kiev counter this kind of campaign? Hell, they were broke to begin with. The Kremlin yanks the energy chain whenever they want just to keep them in line. Kiev's been outflanked from the get-go." He added, "It doesn't help when some of your own people are in bed with the enemy."

"Must pay well," said Wolf. "These Ukrainian guys feather their nests and no one's the wiser."

McFadden took a long pull on his bottle. "The facts speak for themselves. Follow that money and you'll embarrass a lot of people, maybe some of them still in government over there. It's a list of people on the take. Any words of wisdom?"

"Always. First, my money says most of these scum are probably connected to the mob. Second, they're likely skimming whatever cash there is and coughing up the rest to their *mafiya* buddies."

"And what about our own people?" said McFadden. "Let's say you're right. If word got out the White House was setting up a proxy war using confiscated mob money, they'd be on the hot seat."

"Nobody does this kind of thing without putting up a lot of firewalls."

"If the media gets hold of this, we're gonna see a lot of unhappy people in high places," said Wolf. "Here and in Russia. Though I can't imagine the Russkis being as embarrassed about it as the West. Plenty to go around when it hits the fan." He got up to stretch. "Don't forget, Sam, the person who gave us this book wanted the facts to see the light of day."

"Define 'light of day,'" said McFadden.

"The media. The idea was to get this out in the open."

McFadden straddled his chair, facing Wolf. "You still think that's wise? You realize what this would do if the public finds out? Kurskov's right. This kind of news could topple a government...or get people killed."

"You think I don't know that? Colter already paid the price."

"You're right. But did he agree with you about airing this?"

"That was our plan."

"You sure about that? Why would he want to do that? I mean, he was working for our side. Blowing this wide open would make the old red, white, and blue look bad."

Wolf sat down, McFadden's words in his ears. "Colter said not all proxy wars are created equal. He felt passionate about the prospect of Ukraine being left on its own. He thought it was a lousy idea; thought the West couldn't be trusted to back Ukraine if their role in this 'Splendid Little War' went public. They've been hung out to dry before. He thought it was bound to happen again. Colter said the best way to sabotage this was to make sure the public had a right to know."

"You're talking whistleblower, Wolfman. I can't see Colter playing that card. He was a patriot. Wouldn't this be betraying the country?"

"Betrayal, hell. Aren't you paying attention? He thought the whole scenario was fucked up after he read the book's notes about funding guerillas in the eastern part of Ukraine. We've all had friends killed in the line of duty, Sam. You of all people know what that's like. Maybe it was some desk jockey in the West Wing deciding the boys in the Kremlin should pay a price for their land grab. What better way than to fund a campaign in their own backyard? Tapping the Kremlin's overseas accounts before they figure out what's happening had a certain appeal to someone with the balls to try it."

"Kinda far-fetched," said McFadden. "What kind of resistance could you buy to go up against the Russian steamroller? Ukraine is split along fault lines as it is. Any resistance would be crushed by pro-Russian militias working with Russian troops."

Wolf scoffed. "Don't sell short the potential of little men in the woods. Remember how that worked out for Moscow in Chechnya?"

McFadden shot back. "Aside from a few Black Widows blowing themselves up now and then Chechnya's been pretty quiet."

"Granted," said Wolf. "But we weren't in the business of rerouting mob money to fund jihadi nutcases were we? Ukraine is different. Maybe it's all about our side keeping the Russians busy. Colter was thinking ahead. Maybe it's about Ukraine today, Latvia and Estonia tomorrow. Hell, Sam, I don't know what these pointy heads in Washington are up to and neither do you." Throwing up his hands, he said, "The one thing I do know is that proxy wars always find a way to come back and bite you in the ass. Getting someone else to fight a war for you is a cheap way of doing things. And using Russian mob money to do it is immoral."

"The money's neutral," said McFadden.

"The hell it is, Sam. It's dirty cash. And somebody walked off with it."

"I was thinking more about the problem of all that money floating around out there," said McFadden. "Let's say the White House authorized seizing laundered mob funds before they went back to Russia. Where are those dollars? Who's holding them?"

"Colter was convinced they were being set up to fund a proxy war and someone intercepted them along the line. If it was done on this end, maybe it was the Russian mob operating out of Little Odessa—Brighton Beach."

"But we don't know who was orchestrating the siphoning of the cash."

"The usual suspects. Take your pick. White House, CIA, the Pentagon."

"We're talking about tens of millions," said McFadden. "Can't be Congress. That place leaks like a sieve. Couldn't happen without the media knowing."

"That means it's probably coming from the top, Sam."

"That's your paranoia talking again."

Wolf downed his beer. "That's why I'd put it out there. Smoke 'em out. Let the people know what the government's up to. It might bring the whole scheme to a stop."

McFadden scoffed. "As if the public gives a rip."

"But it's mob money, Sam. It's the principle."

"You think the public cares? As long as their sons and daughters aren't asked to do the fighting they'd be content to let other parties go at it."

"Hey," said Wolf, "don't go all preachy on me."

"Sorry. I'm just not sure going public is the way to handle this."

"It's what Colter wanted."

"So you say."

"If he was here, he'd back me up, Sam."

"So, who gets to tell the story?"

"That's where you come in. I thought you might know someone we could trust to give this the treatment it deserves."

"You determined to do it this way?"

"I owe Colter, Sam."

"Okay, I'll help. But if it goes south you're on your own."

"I think it's the right thing to do. It may not change the outcome, but it will throw some sand in the machinery for a while. Maybe give some people pause about what they're doing."

"You always were an optimist, Wolfman."

"So…you have someone in mind? Who do you know?"

McFadden said, "There's this guy, used to be a reporter for the *LA Times*. Won a Pulitzer chasing dirty cops there but moved on. Met him in the sandbox. Mosul. He humped with us on a couple missions. Kept pace. No whining. Told it straight. Earned the team's respect."

"This isn't about Special Ops, Sam. This is about people's deep shit and dirty laundry. Politics. Moving money."

"He'd fit right in. Used to write for the Times when he lived out east. Bonus for you is he's written a lot about the Russian mob, a lot more than he should have. If you're determined to do this, he's your man."

"Damn. You been holding out on me, Sam? You mingling with the literati? Hanging with the beautiful people in my absence?"

"Not likely. Remember, he only tagged along with me once."

"What's this guy doing now?"

"Freelancing. Did some time in Syria. If you're serious…"

Leaning close to McFadden, Wolf said, "I'm determined."

"He's back and forth on both coasts. Has a place near Santa Barbara, I think. I'll make some calls, track him down."

"Appreciate it."

"The White House could make your life miserable."

"They're amateurs, Sam. A fresh set every four years."

"And the *mafiya* plays for keeps, Wolfman."

"So do I."

# Chapter 41

Clubbing for Dimitri Ivanov was a means to an end. It had not always been that way. Blinded by Brighton Beach's nightlife as a young man, Ivanov had plunged into the fleshpots, a different woman—sometimes two—every night. A case of too much, too soon earned Boris Levich's disapproval. What would have been a fatal misstep for others in Levich's employ turned out to be a learning experience for Ivanov. The old Russian mobster had apparently seen something in Ivanov worth salvaging. A short-lived, unhappy exile from Levich's court to the streets and a verbal scourging taught the jaded Ivanov a hard lesson. Though not a monk, he adopted moderation in his vices.

Ivanov's humbling pleased his patron. Once back in Levich's good graces, he resumed his career as the godfather's chosen one. With Ivanov in tow, the old man gave up the club scene for all but the highest level sit-downs. He now trusted his anointed to act in his place. Power was as much about fear and perception as it was about visiting that savagery on enemies or doubters. Violence had its place.

The clubs were now more about being seen. Content to sit back and watch others make fools of themselves, Ivanov paced himself with both the alcohol and the women. As Levich's feared enforcer, Ivanov was guaranteed the same choice corner booth where he and his crew could watch that particular club's dance floor. Courted in turn by those seeking a favor or flattered by low-ranking gangsters hoping to be noticed, Ivanov reigned with a nod, a smile, a wink, or a handshake. Having learned the subtle signs at Levich's elbow, he now acted as the godfather's eyes and ears. No one's coming or going escaped his eye. As much an object of curiosity to the club's glittering crowd as he was feared, Ivanov was young, handsome, and at the top of his game. Only the recently arrived Konstatin Verlov had similar access to Levich's ear, a nagging mystery to Ivanov.

The Caspian Nights, a nightclub in which Boris Levich owned a controlling interest for his money laundering, drew a mixed crowd—weekend moths drawn to the same flame. Beautiful women, over-sexed male poseurs for whom the word "no" does not exist, ear-pounding music, and bottomless vats of chilled vodka in one hundred flavors. Manhattan millennials seeking cheap thrills rubbed shoulders with real and imagined gangsters. Around this circus mix predatory Russian thugs circled like reef sharks.

Ivanov exited his Escalade curbside with two of his crew. While Andrei Helinski ran interference in front, Ivor Sergov did his best to part a waiting line of hopefuls clogging the club's entrance. A bouncer, a beefy, bearded Baku bear named Anton, left his post and approached Ivanov. Helinski, hand on his concealed Glock, stood in the big man's way.

Anton rolled his eyes, pretending the smaller man didn't exist. Speaking to Ivanov, he said, "Dimitri, perhaps you don't want to go inside tonight, eh?"

Ivanov brushed past Helinski and reached for the bouncer's hand. "Anton, how are things? And why shouldn't I visit the club tonight?"

The hulking man whispered, "Verlov. He and his two dogs came in twenty minutes ago. He is sitting in your booth. We don't need the trouble, Dimitri. Perhaps you think about not being here, okay?"

Ivanov asked what the club's manager had done about the usurper. "So, your boss lets this stranger take my place? Does he forget Boris Levich? Does he forget who I am? I come to enjoy the evening with my boys. Why this insult?"

The Azerbaijani pleaded, "Please, no trouble, eh? I think Verlov wants to make trouble. To make a statement. Don't give him the pleasure, Dimitri. You know my boss don't stand up to a man like Verlov."

"If I turn around and leave there will be more trouble in the end," Ivanov said. "Anton, my friend, I know you want to keep the peace. You are a good man. Boris Levich knows you keep trouble from his door. I know this. This is not a problem. Believe me, you will see."

Sergov held the door. Ivanov stopped on the threshold, his eyes fixed on two curvaceous, heavily painted blondes at the head of the line. "Your names?" he snapped.

Flattered by the attention, the taller of the two women batted long lashes dusted with glitter. "I'm Katy and she's Marina."

Ivanov grasped the lapels of the woman's fur coat, opened it, and eyed her form-fitting beaded top, décolletage, skimpy silver lamé skirt, and platform shoes. "Perfect. You'll do." Offering his arms to both, Ivanov smiled. "Why wait in the cold. Come with me, eh? I'm meeting a friend. I know he will be happy to see you."

Winking at a puzzled Sergov, Ivanov headed inside, the giggling pair clinging to him. Behind him, Anton resumed his post at the club's door, shaking his head. Helinski and Sergov followed in Ivanov's wake, both primed for, but dreading, the expected showdown with Verlov.

Leonid, the club's manager, a doughy nephew of one of Levich's gulag comrades, intercepted Ivanov. Visibly nervous, the overwrought man ignored the blondes on Ivanov's arms. "Did Anton not warn you?" he said.

"He did."

"It's not my fault, Dimitri. Before I could seat Verlov at another booth he headed straight for yours. What could I do?" Ignorant of the meaning of the exchange between Ivanov and the club's boss, the women blinked at each other. "So, now you're here. What am I to do?"

"Do not give it a second thought, Leonid. Watch and learn."

Ivanov handed the women's coats to Sergov. "Tell Andrei to call for backup. Then both of you find a piece of wall and stay there. Keep an eye on Verlov's bulldogs."

Patting his weapon, Sergov said, "If there's trouble..."

"There won't be trouble."

Ivanov nodded at the women. "Now, let's meet my friend, shall we?" He headed straight for the seated Verlov.

The Ukranian gangster baited him. "I was told this is where you sit, Dimitri. I told that little mouse of a manager that I liked this spot. It suits me. One can see everything."

Ivanov looked around the club. "What? All alone. Where are your two chimpanzees?" Verlov reddened but Ivanov ignored it. "I told these two lovely ladies I was meeting a friend. Girls, this is the well-known Konstantin Verlov." With a hand at the small of each woman's back, Ivanov pushed the women toward the booth and slid in behind them. "Say hello to Katy and Marina." Reading Verlov's expression, Ivanov knew he had gained the upper hand. He signaled a server. "A round for us. Champagne or vodka, ladies?"

The blonde named Katy shot a tentative look at Verlov and forced a smile. "Champagne. Why not?"

"Why not indeed," said Ivanov. "Marina, what about you?"

The second woman nodded eagerly. Ivanov leaned toward Verlov and raised his glass in salute. "More vodka? Nothing's too good for my guest." Verlov forced a grin.

"Ah, vodka it is," said Ivanov. He ordered champagne for the women and vodka for Verlov and himself. When the server returned, Ivanov took the opportunity to scan the mass of club-goers. Sergov and Helinski were in good position to head off any trouble. Verlov's pouting bodyguards sat by themselves, ignored by the partiers around them. Music boomed across the club, dancers crowded the floor, and servers hurried the bartenders.

At his end of the booth, outfoxed and knowing it, Verlov drained his glass and took refill after refill. Laughing a bit too loudly at inane comments the blonde Katy made, he eventually tired of the game he had started. Short of ordering one of his *byki* to shoot Ivanov, the contest had ended in a stalemate. The women emptied the bottle much too fast. Both were slurring their words. Ivanov took Marina to the dance floor twice.

On Ivanov's second go-around, Verlov broke the impasse by taking the opportunity to decamp, leaving the stupefied Katy slumped in the booth. Enjoying his win, Ivanov sent the two pouting women home in a cab. The reinforcements Helinski had called in were released to the dance floor. Later, in a private room upstairs in the club, Ivanov and his lieutenants talked about the confrontation.

"I underestimated you," said an admiring Helinski.

"So did Verlov," said Ivanov.

"You used the Blonde Option," said Sergov. "Very clever."

Ivanov laughed. "The longer it went the older those girls looked."

"Still, not a bad way to outfox an enemy," said Helinski.

Ivanov, grim, propped his chin in his hand. "Next time won't be so easy. Verlov wants me out of the way. I think he's already planning how to do it. I won't see it coming next time. That worries me."

"It should," said Helinski. "He wants to take over sooner than you think. You're in his way. With you gone he can take his time with Levich. Grab the top spot."

"I ain't worried," snarled Sergov. "Fuck Verlov. He's *beshenaya sobaka*—a mad dog. You know what I say is true."

Ivanov dismissed the bravado. "You speak like a *durak*— a fool. Verlov is made of iron. He's ruthless. How do you think a man like him survives?"

Helinski said, "You're more ruthless. You have no heart... hey, no disrespect...I mean this in a good way, you know?"

"Enough about Verlov," said Ivanov. "What happened tonight tells me we have to move faster than I thought. We have to catch him when he's at Dagmar Danilev's place. I need that layout of her house you promised me."

"We'll do it," swore Helinski. "By the end of the week."

Ivanov ended the meeting. "We're done. Drop me at my place."

# Chapter 42

Within two days McFadden kept his promise to contact the journalist. "It took some doing to track this guy down," he told Wolf at breakfast.

Wolf pushed aside an empty plate. "So what's the verdict?"

"He sounded wary but interested. He wants to talk to you first."

"Outstanding. Who is he and where is he?"

"Name's Nash. Naturalized Irishman. Has a condo in Santa Barbara." McFadden handed Wolf a card with the contact's name, phone and address. "Reggie can drive you up there if you'd like. She could drop in on her mom and let you have the car for the day."

"Works for me, Sam."

"I didn't give away a lot other than you're a friend from the service. Take along one of the CDs Kurskov made for us."

"Good idea. This guy Nash speak Russian?"

"I assume so. I do know he's persona non grata with the Russian mob. That makes two of you. You'll probably get along just fine."

"Appreciate it, Sam. I'll give him a call before lunch."

"Do that. He's expecting to hear from you."

Reggie wandered past the table, gave her husband a kiss and propped a hand on her hip, her eyes on Wolf. "I hear we might be making a trip to Santa Barbara."

"Hope you don't mind being seen with me," said Wolf.

She arched an eyebrow. "You can ride in the back under a scrap of carpet. And we can stay overnight at Mother's."

McFadden said, "Not a bad idea, Wolfman. Could give you a lot more time with Nash. You two will have a lot to talk about. You game?"

"I like it, Sam." Wolf glanced at Reggie.

"Mother would enjoy seeing you again. That would give me more time with her."

"Then it's settled," said McFadden.

Wolf made his call. Nash agreed to meet the following morning at a small café near his gated condo development. If they found common ground, he told Wolf, they could return to his home to continue the discussion. Alerting Reggie that they would leave within the hour, Wolf sought out McFadden, who was supervising a pool cleaning crew. Out of earshot of the maintenance duo, he said, "You were right. Nash sounded cautious."

"Given what he's been through, he has a right to be. You should know he lost his wife over his reporting on the Russian mob. Bastards rigged a bomb in their car."

"That's a helluva note. I hope he's willing to talk."

McFadden snorted. "He's doing it as a favor to me. Maybe this guy can set you straight about mob money being used to fund a proxy war."

"Or confirm what I think is going on."

His eyes on the pool crew wrestling with a hose, McFadden spoke without looking at Wolf. "Well, either way you're going to get an education. Like I told you, I've read this guy's stuff. He's good. Tells it like it is. If he thinks you're wrong about your theory, he'll probably say so."

"I could handle that."

McFadden looked at Wolf. "I hope this works out for you. Just do me a favor. Don't let Reggie anywhere near this. Don't let her know any details."

"What does she know?"

"Only that you're going to meet this journalist. She doesn't know a lot about him other than he's a writer who tagged along with me over there. She'll ask what you're up to, of course."

"Yeah, I would expect that. She doesn't miss much."

"True. But she's better off being in the dark."

# Chapter 43

Not sure what Verlov's next move would be, Ivanov broke his routine. As a precaution he slept in different beds, some belonging to old girlfriends, some newly won. Other nights he stayed in homes where members of his crew lived. A couch here, a bed there—all in an effort to throw Verlov off his trail.

The business of loan-sharking, collecting protection payoffs, below-the-radar drug dealing, and shaking down new immigrants continued with occasional glances over the shoulder. Cordial to Ivanov in Boris Levich's presence, Verlov bided his time, acting the perfect team player in the old man's court. Ivanov knew better, his instincts in a heightened state.

The contents of a second letter—like a previous missive, hand-delivered to Levich by a recent arrival from Moscow —caught Ivanov off guard. Called to the godfather's fifth-floor penthouse fortress, Ivanov and Helinski stepped off the elevator. Greeted by two unsmiling bodyguards, the pair surrendered weapons and endured the usual pat-down. Neither Verlov nor his byki were to be seen.

*A good sign*, thought Ivanov.

Passed to the inner sanctum alone, he approached the seated Levich, who waved him to a gilded chair. "Ah, Dimitri, good of you to come."

Ivanov knew to hold his tongue.

Levich leaned forward. "You remember when I sent two of Sasha's boys on that errand? The one that ended badly?"

"Virginia Beach?"

"Yes. You had asked to go but I gave you a task instead."

"I did as asked."

Like a grinning skull, Levich nodded at the memory. "Ah, yes, faithful Dimitri. Trustworthy, my boy. I will not make a mistake like that again. I should have sent you. Poor Sasha, a fool."

Waving the letter in his hand, Levich said, "The Brotherhood is insistent we try again. Sasha's men were to find a ledger...a book of secrets." Levich paused for breath, grasping for words just out of reach.

"A book? This is what Sasha's crew was looking for?"

Levich said, "Yes. This accursed book has become a stumbling block. We must have it. All I know is that it contains information that should never have been committed to paper. So, we must simply get it back. You understand?"

"I'm sure my men will not fail you."

Fire blazed in the old man's eyes. "NO. You must return this book to me personally, Dimitri. You alone are capable."

Sensing a trap, Ivanov said, "Surely Verlov would be an excellent choice to handle this. He is more experienced than me, Boss."

Levich waved both hands, dismissing the suggestion. "You must go, Dimitri. I know you will not fail me. I don't need to suffer more of the same aggravation this damned book has already caused me."

"Where to begin? Surely, I can't return to Virginia Beach."

"Of course not. That is a dead end. I would not risk you there. No, you will go to Los Angeles. We have friends there. They are to assist you in whatever you need."

"Los Angeles? Perhaps I can take some of my boys with me."

"No. They stay here. I may need to call on them. You will have all the help you want on the coast. All you need do is ask."

"And we are certain this book is now in California?"

Shaking the letter, Levich growled, "It seems the man who has this book has traveled there to seek help in understanding its contents. It is your job to get this book before it ends up in the wrong hands."

"It seems as if it has already reached the wrong hands."

"True, but your job is to get it back. Do what you need to do to make sure that it goes no further. Do you understand, Dimitri?"

"I will do my best."

"Of course you will." Handing his instrument of wrath a thick envelope, Levich said, "You leave tonight. What you need to know is in this envelope. Tickets, contacts, and money. Verlov assured me you would be the perfect one to succeed where others had failed. I agreed."

The audience over, Levich rose to usher Ivanov from the study. On the threshold the frail Levich enveloped the younger man in a hug. Aware now that Verlov's hand was involved and resigned to what he considered an impossible assignment, Ivanov felt as if death himself was embracing him.

# Chapter 44

Driving north on I-5, Wolf was a captive audience to Reggie's chatter from San Diego to San Clemente. The woman could talk. At San Juan Capistrano he traded seats. With him behind the wheel, she poured out her hope to visit the Philippines again with McFadden.

"Probably not a trip he wants to make, Reggie."

"If you said it was a good idea, Sam would do it. He'll listen to you."

"Ain't gonna happen. You'd have to do some serious convincing to get him back there. Don't forget, Sam and I are not exactly welcome there after what we did."

"Enough time has passed. I'm sure you've been forgiven."

"I doubt it. Save your breath. Sam will never go for it."

She backed off, changing subjects for the moment. They passed the time talking of other things: Sam's growing business, her mother. Coming full-circle, she again tried out her idea of visiting the Philippines. Staying neutral, Wolf played sounding board to his best friend's wife.

South of Mission Viejo they took Highway 73 toward Newport Beach, the first in a crowded coastal corridor of like towns filled with hordes of surfers and over-priced real estate. After that came Huntington Beach with its iconic pier and surfers scrapping over choppy waist-high waves. Picking up U.S. 405, they skirted Garden Grove and Anaheim to their north, gritty Long Beach to their south. Under a sun veiled in smog, they fled the contiguous sprawl that was Los Angeles and joined the swollen river of traffic flowing along the coast. At Reggie's insistence, they stopped for lunch at an Asian place near Santa Monica.

Digging into a bowl of shrimp and noodles, she flashed a coy smile. "Care to share what you and Sam are up to?"

Wolf averted his eyes and worked on a heaping plate of fried rice with chopsticks. "Why do you always think we're up to something?"

"And why do you always answer my question with a question?"

Acting surprised, he said, "Really, I do that?"

"Don't patronize me. You and Sam have this amazing ability to pick up where you left off regardless of how much time has passed."

"It's a male art. We're sworn not to reveal it to women."

"I can keep a secret."

"I don't think so." Wolf laughed. "Nice try, Reggie, but you'll have to wait until we get back to San Diego. As for knowing what I'm doing...I haven't got a clue at this point."

"You're a terrible liar," she said.

"It's for your own good."

"I don't believe you."

"Ask your mother."

"I will."

"She'll back me up, Reggie. You'll see."

"We're eating with Mother tonight. She'll get you to talk."

"That's what a dinner guest said to Calvin Coolidge once."

"Who?"

"President Coolidge. Silent Cal. A woman sitting next to him said she had bet a friend she could get him to say at least three words."

"Did she succeed?"

"Coolidge turned to her and said, 'You lose.'"

The pout returned.

After lunch, they topped off the tank and traded places again. Uncharacteristically quiet, Reggie got them back in line on the freeway. Aiming north, she picked up Route 101, the Ventura Freeway. Near Encino they finally dropped to the coast and flanked Oxnard by hugging the coast. Only thirty-five miles from their destination, the constant traffic, not the hours or the distance, caught up with Reggie and she surrendered the wheel to Wolf.

A day of travel had worked on Wolf as well. Gazing out the windshield at the drab landscape unsettled him. Studying the Santa Monica Mountains, he saw undulating parched brown hills thirsting for water. Teasing clouds drifted, offering no relief. To his left, the view was more to his liking: a vast blue Pacific with rows of swells marching toward the coast. He imagined paddling into those long lines, dropping into a sweeping turn, feet planted firmly on his board.

*Not to be*, he thought. *Not this trip. You're on a mission. Focus. The waves will wait. Think of Colter. . . and Yana.*

# Chapter 45

*Santa Barbara*

The next morning, Wolf slouched behind the wheel of Reggie's car, keeping an eye on those coming and going from a small café. Sean Nash had agreed to meet him at seven. Forty minutes early, Wolf had parked in the corner of the lot along with empty cars belonging to early risers and restaurant staff. One of the habits left over from his old life, Wolf's early-bird tactic was a safeguard against being surprised.

Eight minutes later, and much to Wolf's surprise, a dark-haired, stocky bespectacled figure in denim exited an aged Mercedes sedan parked directly behind. Strolling past, the writer tapped the car's hood and indicated with a toss of his head that Wolf should follow him to the café. Chagrined, Wolf got out of his car, locked it, and followed.

Nash led the way to a corner booth and sat with his back against the wall. Wolf flopped down opposite.

Armed with menus and a pot of steaming coffee, a thirty-something brunette with tattooed arms and pierced eyebrows, approached. "Coffee for starters?" Wolf nodded, as did Nash. "Who's your friend, Sean?" she said. Filling their mugs without looking, the woman fixed dark eyes on Wolf.

The writer smiled, took his mug and dumped in sugar. "Some drifter."

The waitress flashed a crooked grin. "Well, hello, Drifter. See anything you like or do you need a menu?" Without waiting for an answer she pushed one across the table. Turning to Nash, she said, "The usual?"

"What's the usual?" said Wolf.

She said, "Two cakes, side of sausage, OJ and hash browns."

"I'll have the usual. Skip the hash browns."

"They're to die for," she cooed. "Fresh as a newly coined insult."

Wolf was speechless, the effect she wanted. He found his voice. "So be it. Hash browns."

"Don't go anywhere," she said in parting. "By the way, I'm Edie."

The two stared after her exaggerated saunter to the kitchen pass-through and heard her rattle off the order in flawless Spanish. Another pair of morning people came in the door and she turned her attention there.

Nash squinted across the booth, thick eyebrows forming a shallow V over rimless glasses. "Edie's a trip. An out-of-work actor. Legend has it she slept with all seven dwarfs... and Snow White. So you're Wolf."

"And you're Nash."

"Guilty. I got here early," said the writer. "Curious to see if you would."

"Could have fooled me," said Wolf. "Thought I'd catch you coming in. Didn't see you back there."

"I was low in the seat. Show early to take your measure of me?"

"Something like that. I take it you're a cautious man, Mr. Nash."

He laughed. "Call me Sean. And yes, I'm a cautious man. Have to be these days. Wasn't always this way. Learned the hard way, Mr. Wolf."

"As did I. Call me Tom."

"Okay. Tom. Sam McFadden says you're a Navy SEAL."

"Retired. I'm just your average civilian these days."

"Bullshit. I can tell by looking that you're no average white dude. Were you a lifer?"

Wolf sipped his coffee. "Twenty years."

"That's a lifer in anyone's book. What you doing now?"

Shrugging, Wolf said, "Travel. Some consulting, you know."

"Defense work?"

"Consulting, you might say."

About to challenge Wolf's comment, Nash paused as their food arrived. "Anything else...I can get you," purred their server.

"Edie, please don't frighten my guest," scolded Nash.

The waitress folded her arms, her eyes fastened on Wolf. "You're not in the least bit frightened are you?"

"Flattered," said Wolf, "not frightened."

"You should be."

"Flattered or frightened?"

"Both. I get off at two."

"That makes for a long day," he said.

"I go to bed early...and often."

"Edie the actress," said Nash, rolling his eyes. "Does wonders for an old man's ego, though. Thank you, sweetheart. You may go now."

She giggled in leaving.

Turning to the business at hand, Wolf wasted no more time. "Sam McFadden thinks you might be able to help me."

"Maybe. Don't know about you, Tom, but I can talk and eat at the same time." He shoveled in a wedge of pancake and sausage. "Give me an idea of what you're looking for—why a guy like you might need my help."

"Fair enough. I'll start with a trip I recently took to Kazakhstan to see a man about a launch."

In between bites of breakfast, Wolf outlined his dilemma. By the time both cleaned their plates and were on their second cup of coffee, he had earned an invitation to Nash's beachside condo two miles away. Insisting on paying for breakfast, he included a generous tip for Edie and followed Nash to his gated community just up the coast.

# Chapter 46

Dimitri Ivanov issued terse last-minute instructions to his crew. At La Guardia's ticketing level he delivered an impassioned curbside warning about Verlov's perfidy.

"He'll come at you the moment I'm gone. Count on it."

To a man, his soldiers voiced their loathing for the Ukrainian usurper. Despite their bravado, Ivanov saw through their declaration of solidarity. "Stick together," he cautioned. "He'll try to split you up any way he can. Don't cozy up to him when he comes around. Don't travel alone. Don't go to clubs while I'm gone. Never go anywhere with him. Vary your routines like I was doing. Don't be predictable."

"Maybe we take him down while you're gone," boasted Sergov.

"Don't try it alone, Ivor. Wait."

On the sidewalk outside the terminal, Ivanov repeated his warning. "Do not underestimate Verlov. He will eat you alive, one by one. Do not trust him. Do not tell him what you're doing or where you're going. Do not initiate contact with him. Stay away from him. Stick together. I will return within a week."

"How do you know this will only take a week?" said Helinski.

"Because that's all I'm planning to spend on this wild goose chase. This whole thing may have been Verlov's idea in the first place for all I know."

"But Levich is sending you, Dimitri."

"Yeah, the boss may be sending me, but Verlov put him up to it."

The light went on in Sergov's eyes. "That's why he wants you out of town, huh? He's separating you from us. The sonofabitch."

"Were you listening, Ivor?" He threw an arm around Helinski. "Keep an eye on Sergov for me. He's a bit slow on understanding what's happening here."

# Chapter 47

*Los Angeles*

Ivanov found a bullet-headed, uniformed limo driver waiting for him beyond the checkpoint in the airport's domestic terminal.

In a low voice, the big man asked, "Dimitri Yegor Ivanov?"

"Possibly."

"You are Dimitri Ivanov?"

"Yes. And you are?"

"Alexi."

"Who sent you?"

"Shurkov."

The name matched the one Ivanov had been given by Levich. Reaching for Ivanov's carry-on, the stocky man said, "This is all? You have more luggage, yes?"

"This is it. I had to travel on short notice."

"I understand. My car is outside. You follow, okay?"

Forty-five minutes later, Ivanov was pacing a shabby two-room motel suite on Sepulveda Boulevard in Van Nuys with no idea where he was. Unarmed and alone in a room with peeling wallpaper, sixty-watt bulbs, leaky toilet, and the kitchenette's dripping faucet, Ivanov felt disoriented.

*A lesson in humility? Verlov's hand at work here as well?* He glanced at the cellphone he'd been given by the taciturn driver.

Though told to stay put until called, Ivanov went downstairs to the postage stamp-sized lobby. The counter was manned by a pasty, overweight matron with mousy brown hair and facial moles the size of quarters. The cow knew little English. She flashed a "deer in the headlights" look when Ivanov switched to Russian. Asking for a restaurant where he could get pizza, he pantomimed eating. She waddled from behind the counter and shooed him outside. Using sign language she directed him down the trash-strewn street, pointing to a stuccoed shed-like structure.

Ten minutes later, Ivanov peered into a narrow carryout window. He ordered a small pizza. A pair of cement tables crowned with tilting aluminum umbrellas sat next to an asphalt parking lot. Hopping about, small nervous birds picked at scraps. Ivanov bought a soda and gobbled half of the cardboard pizza. He tossed the remnants. Disconsolate, he returned to his monk's cell on the motel's second level and locked the door.

*Yes, this was Verlov's doing. Boris Levich will hear of this.*

At 8:10, Ivanov vomited his supper. At 8:15, Shurkov called on the cellphone the chauffeur had left behind.

# Chapter 48

At Nash's condo, the journalist interrupted a tour to take a phone call. Wolf wandered out to a sheltered deck overlooking a curving stretch of sand hemmed with rocks on both ends. Leaning on the railing, he studied a couple walking a dog, a jogger, and a small knot of surfers waiting for a set two hundred yards offshore. Pocketing his phone, Nash came outside. He stood beside Wolf, looked at the bobbing shapes.

"That was Sam McFadden, making sure we had been able to meet."

"He's keeping tabs on me. I drove up here with his wife and dropped her at her mother's in Santa Barbara."

"Sam says you're originally from California."

"Born and raised in Santa Cruz."

Nodding at the figures in the sea, Nash said, "Do any surfing as a kid?"

"Only came out of the water to sleep."

"Never tried it myself," said Nash. "I'm really just a transplanted midwesterner. And the water's too cold. Like Lake Michigan."

"Maybe colder," said Wolf. "So, whereabouts in the Midwest?"

"Illinois. Little town. I doubt you've heard of it."

"Try me."

Nash smiled at some memory. "Watseka."

Wolf faced the writer. "South of Chicago, close to the Indiana border."

"Damn. You're the first person I've met out here who actually knows where the hell Watseka is. Consider me duly impressed."

"Classic small-town Americana. Too land-locked for me, of course."

Nash shrugged. "Me as well. My dad had a successful car dealership. His plan was for me to take over the business but I was antsy. Small-town living has its charms, but it's hard to keep 'em down on the farm once they've seen New York."

"Or Chicago."

"Yeah, or Chicago...and its lake."

"Or Los Angeles."

Nash snorted. "Different animal entirely. Home to nomads, myself included. Smog and quakes, Hollywood and Vine. Charlie Manson and Watts. Been there, done that."

"Feeling jaded after all these years?"

"Maybe." Rubbing his hands together, Nash said, "I guess your pinpointing Watseka is a sign I'm obligated to help you."

"Karma, huh?"

"How very California of you, Mr. Wolf. On that note, perhaps we should go inside and take a look at your very considerable problem."

Nash settled behind a computer and Wolf handed him the duplicate CD Kurskov had given him. Nash copied the contents to his hard drive. "Help yourself to more coffee or make some tea," said Nash. "This might take a while."

"I'll check out your artwork and bookcases while I'm waiting."

"Suit yourself."

Soon engrossed in Nash's collection of history books, travel volumes, and heavy coffee table books of Russian art, Wolf easily filled an hour without a word exchanged between the two. Nash's occasional "Ah, interesting" or "What the...?" broke the silence. Finally, a profanity followed by, "You've got to be kidding me!" drew Wolf's attention.

He looked up from the couch where he sat, glossy art book in his lap. "Find something interesting?"

Nash didn't bite. Instead, he continued staring at the computer screen filled with Kurskov's paired pages from the suspect ledger. Wolf went into the kitchen to make tea. The hissing teapot got Nash's attention. He joined Wolf in the kitchen, accepted a hot mug, and confessed his amazement at what he was seeing on the screen.

"This is heavy stuff. Very scary. If you thought you were in trouble before, you ain't seen nothing yet."

"It cost a friend of mine his life."

"That would be Colter, right?"

Nodding, Wolf tested his tea. "Dan Colter. He seemed to know what he got his hands on. Said it was toxic. Governments could fall, people could die."

Mug in hand, Nash went back to work, saying over his shoulder, "He was right. This is the tip of a very big, very ugly iceberg." Gesturing at the images, he said, "And this is just one slice of what's been going on. Think of it as one man's take on what he was seeing."

Wolf stirred his tea and watched the journalist work.

"Your earlier guess about the author being dead is probably correct." Ejecting the disc, Nash handed it back to Wolf. "Tell me again what you want to do with this. What do you hope to accomplish?"

Wolf sipped his tea. "Colter wanted this to see the light of day; thought we should get it to a journalist...someone like yourself."

Nash said to Wolf, "There are stories here that would knock a lot of people on their collective asses. Hell, look at this, for example." Gesturing to a notebook filled in his hurried cursive hand, he flipped the pages. "I've been making notes. You've got drug trafficking, arms dealing, money laundering, and what looks like skimming of government and *mafiya* bank accounts."

"Lot of wheeling and dealing going on, huh? Colter thought so."

His back to Wolf, Nash tapped away. "Somebody's got a lot of 'splaining to do about some very nasty people named in these notes."

Wolf peered over Nash's shoulder. "Dangerous people who are probably not used to being screwed over."

"Exactly. If there's any screwing to be done, they want to be the ones doing it. Then we have this Ukrainian angle. This is a treasure trove, friend."

"So, Sean...you interested in running with this information?"

"It's not that I'm ungrateful to have this dropped in my lap. It's the stuff a journalist's wet dream is made of."

"I hear a 'but' coming."

Nash swiveled in his chair to face Wolf, who had dropped back on the couch. "The last time I opened a Pandora's box like this it didn't turn out so well for me."

"I'm listening."

Glancing at his half-empty mug, Nash turned reflective. "The telling of this particular tale requires something stronger than tea."

# Chapter 49

Nash rooted in the cupboard and returned from the kitchen with an opened bottle of Jameson Irish whiskey. He topped off his mug and filled Wolf's. Hoisting his mug, he said, "As we Irish like to say, 'Here's a toast to your enemies' enemies.'"

"I'll drink to that," answered Wolf.

"Not saying I'm your man, but I'm tempted. Knowledge is power and this information is powerful stuff."

"Hell, I know that. McFadden and I differ about what's on that disc, but we agree on honoring Dan Colter's request."

Nash poured another round, his nose reddening but his thoughts clear. "You do know that I've done my share of stories about the Russian mob, right?"

"Sam said you were the one to ask. That's why I'm here on your doorstep. That and your availability, right?"

"Maybe. I'm between assignments right now." Nash stared into his mug, musing. "I've followed this particular trail since the beginning. I was a stringer back East in the early eighties. Just a kid out of journalism school when I first stumbled across these lowlifes."

"Sam says you were the first reporter to write about the Russian immigrants flooding Brighton Beach. How did that happen?"

"I wasn't actually the first to write about the influx of Russians. I was working for the *Daily News* in 1982, just doing my wide-eyed, newly minted reporter thing. I was sent to cover my first homicide in a nightclub there. Two Russian Jews shot execution style while sitting in a booth with girlfriends."

"Were they mobbed up?"

"Just like the Sicilians. Made men, but from Ukraine—*Vory*. Local cops thought they were seeing the old Murder Incorporated at work again. I wrote it that way, but it took me a year of nosing around in Little Odessa to find out these guys were soldiers in the Russian *Mafiya*. Nobody was taking it seriously back then."

"What about the FBI? They must have been tracking these guys."

Nash snorted. "You kidding? They were behind the curve from the beginning. They're better at it now but they're still playing catch-up."

"What happened to your stories about the immigrants?"

"I got the ball rolling. Started looking into the Russians. It was like lifting up the corner of a rug and finding a swarm of cockroaches. They were killing each other left and right. No finesse. Right out in the open. Like they didn't care who knew it. They came over here, took a page from the Sicilians, and went them one better with the violence thing."

"Kurskov says this book shows their fingers in our banking system."

"They're in deep. These days Russian mob money is everywhere. There's too much cash being made to shut off the spigot. Our banks and theirs look the other way. There are two parallel governments running Russia: the Kremlin and the mob."

Wolf held out his mug. Nash refilled it with the blended Jameson. "Want to hear my theory about some of that confiscated mob money being used to fund a proxy war in Ukraine?"

Nash emptied the bottle in his mug. "I know what you're getting at. You might be on to something. But I'd have to talk to a lot of the right people to get a fix on it. Wouldn't be easy to do given the situation."

"Could you do it?"

"No question."

"But would you do it?"

"Ah, there's the rub." Nash took the empty into the kitchen, came back with another bottle. He dropped on the couch, opened the bottle, and topped off his mug. "Good question. Not sure. The last time I broke a story on these animals it cost me."

"McFadden told me," said Wolf, "about your wife's murder."

No tears, only resignation on Nash's face. "These guys have a certain primitive way of doing business." He dropped a handful of ice cubes in his mug. "New York. I was an up-and-comer. Full of myself. Kept dancing closer to the flame. Couldn't stop." Turning to Wolf, he said, "There were warning shots fired across my bow but I didn't feel a thing. Was so wrapped up in pursuing the story I left Danae—my wife—vulnerable."

His eyes following Nash, Wolf didn't answer, just listened.

"One night on Long Island someone wired a bomb to my car. There had been threats, notes. I was thinking, 'What could go wrong?' This was the land of the free and the home of the brave, you know."

Wolf held up a hand. "You don't have to talk about it."

"No, it's okay. I've thought about it every day since then. Danae took my car that morning. Hers wouldn't start. They must have tampered with it. One moment she's there, the next moment, gone. Poof. Turned to ash."

"No suspects?"

"No arrests. Lots of condolences. Flowers from one of the Russian bastards in Little Odessa I had been writing about. Imagine. This mob boss had the balls...the chutzpah to send flowers for my wife's funeral."

"Did that prompt you to write your book?"

"My exposé about the Russian mob? Yeah, I poured my heart into it."

"Must have shaken something loose."

"Hit the *New York Times* bestseller list for five weeks. Made the rounds on the weekend talk shows but nothing happened. Television. What a joke. Talk about short attention spans. The morning shows were no better. I'd get five minutes between the cooking segment and hemorrhoid commercials. Only the feds had shorter attention spans in those days."

"Is that when you moved out here?"

"Yeah. The *LA Times* offered me a job. I got out of town. Was grateful. Then I ran into a shit storm after doing investigative pieces on the Rampart cop scandals. Sure, I won some prizes for my reporting but suddenly I was persona non grata all over again, this time with the cops. A pariah."

Wolf asked, "So you left the Times. What then?"

Nash sighed. "I'd been doing long investigative pieces for *Vanity Fair*, the *Atlantic*, occasional profiles for *Playboy*, freelance pieces for *Time*. It paid the bills. Did a turn in Iraq."

"That's where you met McFadden."

"Correct. Good guy. A patriot. And I don't mean that lightly. Ran a tight ship...for an army guy. I came back. Drifted. Wrote screenplays. They're gathering dust in my files—mob stuff, of course. Intelligent if I do say so myself. Not that infantile shoot-'em-up crap like you see on network TV."

"McFadden showed me that series of articles you did for *Sports Illustrated* on the Russian mob's fingers in the NHL and the NBA. Solid reporting. Impressive. You nailed it."

"Thanks. But it didn't move people, did it? We're asleep at the wheel in this country. Sorry to say this, but the Russian *Mafiya* is here to stay."

"Hey, you're preaching to the choir."

"Well, it's a very small choir. One day we're gonna wake up and find they've taken over the whole church."

"That's why I was hoping this little book Colter and I brought back from Russia would open some eyes. I don't think it's too late to blow the lid off this. And I think we might be getting our ass in a sling if I'm right about this proxy war in Ukraine."

"Kinda like the 'Contra' war in Nicaragua, huh?"

"And tweaking the Russian bear in Afghanistan in the eighties. Ancient history but yeah, something like that."

Nash flopped down in the chair at the computer. "I'll think about it."

"I hope you do. This could save us a lot of trouble if we can head off this cluster fuck before it gets out of hand."

"Not...promising anything. Not saying...I won't...help..." Nash drifted away without finishing. Nash laid back, in a leather recliner, his head resting on his chest, his breathing steady, his eyes closed.

With their conversation over, Wolf abandoned the couch for the kitchen. He capped the remaining Jameson and made a pot of strong coffee. His day was running out of hours and he had to think about Reggie at her mother's house nearby. They expected him for dinner. The last thing he needed was a DUI on his way back to Santa Barbara. Coffee and a run would cure that.

Wolf downed a fresh cup of coffee, doffed his shirt, and slipped out the glass doors to the deck. He took the stairs to the beach and went for a bare-chested, barefooted, sobering jog. The wind had turned onshore, ruining the surf and scouring the sand with a sudden chill. He did one mile up, then retraced his own footprints, stopping to chat with the surfers who had abandoned the sloppy break and come ashore.

By the time Wolf returned to the condo with a clear head, Nash was fast asleep. He scribbled his phone number and a brief note of encouragement for the writer, then let himself out the front door, locking it behind him. He would call tomorrow and hopefully get a decision to expose the secrets Colter had died to bring to light. If Nash agreed to sign on, all well and good. If not, Wolf would start his search anew, racing the clock to find someone willing to agree the gamble worth it.

The next morning, during breakfast, Reggie took a call from Sam and after ten minutes of chatting, turned the phone over to Wolf. He excused himself from the table and went outside to talk.

"Hey, Sam. What's up?"

"Two of your fan club came by the shop yesterday. FBI. Seems you're a popular guy. The folks at State asked them to make a courtesy call. Guess your contacts in Washington would like to continue their conversation with you. You knew they'd track you down eventually."

"Well, at least we got in some quality time before they figured it out."

"I didn't lie. I said you'd be back. That you were off making some contacts with people you knew."

"They buy it?"

"Seemed to. And why not? It's true. They left their cards. I told them you'd call when you checked in with me."

"Okay. I'm just waiting for Nash to make a decision about whether or not he'll take on the story."

"Give me a heads up. Does he agree with you about the proxy war angle?"

"He's interested. Said he'd think about it."

"Reggie on to you?"

"Not a peep. She did her best, Sam, but I didn't give you up, man."

"Good. So, what's the plan?"

Wolf circled the pool, glancing in the kitchen window and catching Reggie's eye. He waved. "I'll check with Nash today. If he needs me I'll stay on for a day or so if that's okay with you."

"Do what you need to, Wolfman. No reason to hurry back."

"Appreciate it. And thanks for the news about those feds."

"You know they'll be back," said McFadden.

"I'll throw 'em a bone. Maybe call them when Nash signs on."

"And if he doesn't?"

"There is no Plan B."

# Chapter 50

With Dimitri Ivanov not yet gone thirty-six hours, Verlov struck. His first victim: the swaggering, slow-witted Ivor Sergov. Netted outside the Crimean Nights by Verlov's two drones, a tipsy Sergov was easily disarmed and bundled into the cargo space of a black van.

Hooded and bound, the terrified Sergov pleaded for his life. To silence the babbling man, Verlov clubbed Sergov with a steel pipe. Later, Verlov tossed him from the van at the foot of a landfill, Sergov's hands tied behind his back. Verlov drew a blade across Sergov's throat and sent the dying Sergov stumbling down a slope of rotting garbage. In the morning, crews would find the bound corpse and call the cops. Sergov was not missed until twenty-four hours passed. It would take three days to ID the victim.

In the meantime, Verlov made himself even more indispensable in Dmitri Ivanov's absence. He was the picture of solicitous counsel to Boris Levich once news of Sergov's death reached the mob boss.

The old man gripped Verlov's arm and whispered in his ear. "I want whoever is responsible for his death to know they will not escape punishment. Such a thing is an insult to me personally. To execute one of my men without permission must not stand. Do you understand me?"

"Of course. You are correct. Such an affront will be seen as weakness unless we find those responsible and make an example of them."

Levich relaxed his iron grip and shuffled to an armchair. Waving Verlov to sit as well, he railed against enemies known and unknown. Nodding, Verlov encouraged Levich's paranoia, planting seeds where he could. Stroking his chin as if thinking, he said, "Can you trust Anton Sheveski these days?"

"Sheveski? Why would I not trust him? We have accommodated each other for years without a problem. No, I don't think he would do such things."

Verlov shrugged. "You know best, of course. With your permission, Boss, I'm just thinking out loud. I know Sheveski courts your good will but I sometimes wonder if his words are genuine."

"You doubt the man's sincerity?"

"I doubt everyone's sincerity where your well-being is concerned."

The sentiment brought a faint smile to Levich's lips. With Ivanov gone, he was susceptible to such subtlety and Verlov played the concerned, loyal retainer to perfection.

Levich pursed his lips. "There is Vasili Kirov. But we go back so far."

"Bonds sometimes outlive their usefulness despite their origins."

"Ah, Verlov. You may be right. Perhaps you hear things I don't. Sometimes a man says things in the presence of others he would not dare to say to another's face. You have heard such things, I suppose."

"I wouldn't presume to question the loyalty of those you know so well. Still...I have overheard comments from time to time."

Levich thrust his head forward. "What things? What have you heard?"

"It's probably nothing. Idle talk. Forgive me for mentioning it. I don't wish to upset you."

Digging his fingers into the armrests, Levich bristled. "Well, you have succeeded in doing just that. I want to know what you have heard."

"Some say that perhaps your...age has softened your awareness of what goes on around you these days."

Levich bolted from the chair and stabbed a bony finger in Verlov's chest. "Who says such things? I'm soft, eh? I will make them regret such talk."

Verlov cast his eyes at the floor, feigning reluctance to surrender the offenders' names. "Kirov and Sheveski among others," he stammered.

"Who else?"

"Sergei Helinski thinks you've lost your touch."

"Dimitri Ivanov's top man? Impossible. He's loyal to a fault."

Verlov threw a dart. "Loyal, yes, but to Ivanov, not you. It pains me to say that."

Hands clasped behind his back, Levich paced, his head bowed. "It pains me more to hear it."

"Perhaps those I've mentioned were indiscreet, nothing more."

Whirling on Verlov, the old man barely contained his rage at the hints of disloyalty he was hearing. "Indiscreet, you say? In my position indiscretion is sometimes the handmaiden of disloyalty."

"True. It cannot be tolerated," agreed Verlov. "But what's to be done?"

Silence. Levich wandered to a tall window, grasping the heavy drapes to steady himself. Moments passed. Unsure if he had overreached with his denunciations, Verlov kept silent. A gilded Romanov clock sounded the hour from a fireplace mantel.

"Start with Helinski," said Levich in a flat voice.

"Start? What do you mean?"

"You know very well what I mean, Verlov."

"As you wish, Boss. Am I to understand I have your—"

Levich interrupted, his voice detached, robotic. "Yes. You have my permission to cut out this cancer before it spreads."

"And the others? Sheveski. Kirov."

"Must I do your thinking for you, Verlov?"

"Of course not. Forgive me, Boss. I didn't want to overstep myself."

"You may have saved me a great deal of trouble. How could I be so blind to such treasonous behavior behind my back?"

Verlov oiled his blade. "How could you have known? Don't doubt yourself, Boss."

"I never have, Verlov. And I won't begin now."

# Chapter 51

Wolf's phone hummed on the nightstand next to his pillow. He groped for the vibrating phone, picked it up, and glanced at the time.

*6:15. Who the hell?* Wolf propped himself on an elbow. "Yeah?"

Nash's voice. "I'm in. Made up my mind last night. I've already made some calls to get more background on what's in your little book."

Wolf felt a weight lift from his shoulders. "That's good news, Sean. I know Colter would be pleased."

"I'll want to talk to this Gary Kurskov to compare notes."

"That can be arranged."

"Good. I'll pitch the idea to editors at *Vanity Fair* and the *Atlantic* for starters. If they like it we may find ourselves in a bidding war."

"Not 'we,' just you," said Wolf. "This is your baby. Run with it."

"But you brought this to me, dropped it in my lap. You've got skin in this game."

"I'm just the messenger. You're the wordsmith."

A pause, then, "Okay, have it your way. I appreciate the shot at it."

"I hope this hits the fan big time."

Nash laughed. "There's enough to cover everyone involved."

"I'll get on the horn to Kurskov to grease the wheels. And I'll call Sam to let him know what we're doing. Anything else I can do?"

"No. I'll take it from here," said Nash. "I'll try to keep your role in this as anonymous as possible unless you want credit."

"Any credit given should go to Dan Colter. He died to get this in the hands of the public."

"Okay. Shoot me that email with Kurskov's contact info."

"Good. Oh, there is one thing you can do for me, Sean."

"Ask and ye shall receive."

"Tell Edie the waitress hello for me the next time you see her."

A laugh and then Nash was gone. Grinning, Wolf pounded the pillow. *Gotta call Sam ASAP. He'll want to know. Reggie and I can head back to San Diego. Mission accomplished.*

Wolf showered, shaved, and dressed. He made coffee in the bungalow and sat by a window watching for lights to come on in the main house. An hour later, he crossed the lanai by the pool to join Reggie and her mom for breakfast. It was all he could do to keep the news about Nash a secret. Wolf played the perfect guest throughout the meal. He returned to the pool cottage and called McFadden at his office.

"Good news, Sam. Nash's taking on the story. He wants to talk to Kurskov to compare notes."

"That is good news, Wolfman. Gary's out of town until tomorrow but I'll tell him when he comes in. He'll be anxious to help out."

Wolf said, "Thanks again for the intro to Nash. I think he's going to do Colter proud. I owe you."

"No problem. When you get back let's do some more range time."

"Outstanding. Maybe you can introduce me to that little redhead I saw in lane four the other night."

"Be careful what you wish for, Wolfman. She can put a tight group dead center at fifteen yards."

"Sounds like my kind of woman."

Wolf hung up, opened his laptop, and checked his emails. Still no answers from former team members about Colter's background.

*What's with the mystery?*

There were four new messages from Nells at the State Department. He read them and trashed them all, then remembered McFadden's warning about the visit the FBI agents had made earlier that week.

*I'll call the feds when I get to Sam's.*

# Chapter 52

*Van Nuys*

Finally summoned by Leonid Shurkov, his mysterious host, Ivanov was told to be ready in five minutes. Alexi, the same taciturn chauffeur who had picked him up at the airport, was waiting outside the motel's shabby office. The hulking driver crushed a cigarette under a heel and opened the town car's door for Ivanov. "I am to take you to Shurkov."

Ivanov slipped in the backseat without speaking. After two days of bad food and ugly lodgings, the soft leather felt luxurious, the town car's interior like a royal coach. A minibar held unopened bottles of soda water but no vodka. Russian language newspapers and magazines peeked from pockets behind the driver's seat. Ivanov studied his surroundings for the next forty-five minutes. A hazy veil of smog hovered above the city. Toward the end of the drive the monotonous scenery changed. Storefronts and used car lots side by side with the occasional one-story, flat-roofed bungalows gave way to anorexic palms and office buildings plastered with "For Lease" signs.

Ivanov's driver pulled to the curb outside a print shop, got out, and held the door. Alexi lumbered ahead to the shop, Ivanov following. The pair went past a deserted service counter and down a hall, passing a room crammed with six large copiers. Two thin harried-looking women were harvesting sheets of text spitting from the machines amidst the ear-shattering din. At the end of the hall the bulky chauffeur rapped twice on a door and ushered Ivanov into a back office paneled in cheap faux cedar.

Mysterious puppet master Leonid Shurkov proved a disappointment. After all the cloak-and-dagger business Ivanov had expected a glowering, menacing figure dressed in an expensive suit and wreathed in smoke. Instead, he got a squat, rotund, shirt-sleeved *apparatchik* with a bad comb-over. The wreath of smoke was there—the result of two chewed cigars smoldering in a mound of ashes in a glass ashtray. Shurkov, his ear glued to the phone, acknowledged his visitor with a quick wave while barking thick, Russian-accented English in his phone. Ivanov assumed the person on the other end of the conversation had displeased Shurkov by failing to complete an assignment. The call continued as if Ivanov and his minder did not exist.

Alexi shifted piles of paperwork from two weathered vinyl yard chairs to a corner of Shurkov's groaning desk. The driver offered Ivanov one of the chairs and took the other. Ivanov sat, his eyes taking in the rodent's nest.

Shurkov slammed the phone, concluding the call. He snagged one of the cigar stubs and puffed it back to life. "So, you are Dimitri Ivanov, one of Boris Levich's young sharks, eh?"

"And finally I meet you, the renowned Leonid Shurkov. My boss sends his greetings."

Shurkov leaned back, blowing smoke rings at a yellowed ceiling panel above his desk. "Good. And how is the old bandit? Is he well? Do not lie."

"He is well."

"Still feared and respected."

"As always."

"Do you know why you are here, Dimitri Ivanov?"

"I don't need to know. I only need to serve Boris Levich in whatever way I can."

Shurkov chuckled. "So young, so diplomatic."

Ivanov kept his emotions in check, his eyes neutral, a hint of a polite smile showing.

His eyes on his visitor, Shurkov said, "What do you think, Alexi? Will Dimitri Ivanov carry out the mission the brothers in Moscow have burdened him with?"

The bull-necked man squirmed sideways to appraise Ivanov. "Perhaps. Surely Levich would not have sent a child to do a man's work."

Ivanov smiled, the driver's insult ignored.

"Ah, he has a sense of humor," said Shurkov. "He may need it, eh?"

Shurkov planted his elbows on the desk, propped hands under his ample chin, and narrowed his eyes. "So, Dimitri Ivanov, tell us what you know of your mission. Why does my friend Boris Levich send you all the way out here to California?"

Ivanov recited the briefing Levich had given him in Brighton Beach. "To find a certain book belonging to a certain man. My boss said you have sources that have traced the whereabouts of this book. He said the Brotherhood in the motherland wants it back. It belongs to them."

"Good," said Shurkov. "Do you know why it is important, this book?"

Ivanov shrugged. "No. I know only that my boss has been given the job of finding it and returning it to its rightful owners. This assignment he, in turn, has given to me. Why I have to come all the way out here is a mystery to me. And why you put me up in some shit hole is also a mystery to me."

The sounds of the machines in the front room died down. A ceiling fan slowed. Ivanov heard Shurkov's voice drop lower, taking on a more menacing tone.

"Arrogant pup. You know nothing. Listen carefully to me, Dimitri Ivanov. I tell you why this book is so important. And I tell you about a man who now has this book that does not belong to him. I will tell you who he is and where he can be found. And when you take the book from him you bring it to me. As for your accommodations...your shit hole, as you call it...do you know nothing of how to disappear among the people? Do you think you are some big New York man who can come in here without being noticed? No, you don't think of these things. Your job is not to be seen, fool. Now, you listen to me. I explain to you how things are and what you are to do."

For the next thirty minutes, Shurkov unraveled the mystery of the book for Ivanov. When he finished, he paused dramatically and asked a final question. "And when you have the book, what do you do to this man?"

Without hesitating, Ivanov said, "I will most certainly kill him."

"Exactly!" Shurkov thundered, clapping his hands. "And for that you need a weapon, which you do not now have. Alexi will furnish this. You cannot fail, Dimitri Ivanov. Failure, as Americans so often say, is not an option."

Shurkov pointed to his driver. "Alexi will be with you to see this is accomplished."

On his feet, Ivanov returned Shurkov's stare. "I prefer to work alone."

Shurkov waved away the objection. "You have no say in this. Alexi is my eyes and ears. Remember, I have a stake in this as well. And thus Boris Levich has a stake also. You succeed, I succeed. Your boss succeeds. You fail, I fail...and Levich fails."

Ivanov relented. "Of course. I know this. I only thought—"

"Ah, mistake number one. Do not try to think, just do. Alexi will be with you every step of the way. You can rely on him. You work for Levich, Alexi works for me. We all work for the Brotherhood, do we not? When you finish, hand over the book to Alexi. He will give you a return ticket and a token of my gratitude for your success."

Shurkov came from behind his desk. Though not quite six feet, Ivanov loomed over the smaller man. Wagging a stubby finger in the air, Shurkov said, "We will not meet again. If you do your job right, I may not even read about it. Go with Alexi. Find this man who has the book, take it from him, and see that you give it to Alexi."

Ivanov felt his patience fray. "And where do we find this man?"

"Did Boris Levich not tell you?"

"He only said to me that you had sources who knew about this book now being in California and that is why I had to come all this way."

"Ah, only because your people missed their chance in Virginia Beach. There would have been no need for you to come this far if they had done their job correctly the first time."

Ivanov bristled. "Those were not my people."

"Nonetheless, they missed their chance."

"I still don't understand why your man Alexi here cannot find this book without my help. Surely you have others with ah, certain skills."

"This is a favor I do for my old friend Boris Levich. He wishes to correct the mistake his people made. He must think highly of you to send you this way. Understand, Dimitri Ivanov, I don't do this strictly for friendship, you see. It is in my interest to do this."

"So, where do we find this man?"

"San Diego."

# Chapter 53

On the opposite coast, Verlov was thinning the ranks of potential rivals with grim efficiency. A week following Sergov's execution, he caught two of Ivanov's crew off-balance in a twenty-four hour Laundromat. The pair were lured by a phony drug deal too good to pass up and trapped by Verlov's hired guns. Vasily Philipenko and Yuri Borkov, forced to kneel alongside a terrified patron at the rear of the business, were executed with a single shot at the nape of the neck. The witness bolted through a back door only to be brought down in the alley. Alerted by an anonymous caller, police arrived one hour later to find the unlucky customer sprawled by a Dumpster at the back of the business. A search of the Laundromat turned up two corpses—Philipenko and Borkov—stuffed like pretzels in industrial-sized dryers.

That night a panicked Sergei Helinski called Ivanov.

"Dimitri, bad news. Terrible."

"Levich is dead?"

"No. Worse. Sergov's dead. And Philipenko and Borkov. All dead."

Ivanov groaned. Three of his crew wiped out. "Verlov?"

"Has to be."

Fighting to recover, Ivanov said, "Does the boss know?"

"I can't get to him. Nobody can get to him. He's locked up tight."

"No way to send word to him?"

"How? I can't risk trying to see him. Verlov's byki are now with the boss most days. They trade off with the old regulars. Anyone wanting to talk to Levich now has to go through Verlov."

"I knew it. I told you not to let your guard down. I said Verlov would be making a run at you. I just didn't think it would happen this quick."

A whine in Helinski's voice. "When do you come back?"

"I leave tomorrow to wrap up a job here before I can return. It may take me two days, perhaps three at the most."

"Three days! That's a lifetime, Dimitri. So what am I to do? There's only me, Yuri, and Petor left."

"You find a place to hide. Get out of town for a while. Disappear."

Ivanov heard despair in Helinski's voice. "If we do what you say, Verlov will tell Levich we've run out on him. You know how paranoid the old man can be."

"I know. But you have no choice. I'll fix things with the boss when I get back. It's important that you not take on Verlov without me."

"Maybe me and Yuri can take him when he's over at Dagmar Danilev's like you planned. It could work."

"Don't try it. You need me there, Andrei."

An accusation. "And you ain't here, are you?"

"Not by choice. You think I want to be here?"

"I don't know what to do, Dimitri. I didn't figure on this."

"Do what I tell you. Get the guys and go to ground somewhere."

"Yeah, but Verlov—"

"Fuck Verlov! You want to survive to fight another day, then you disappear now! You listening to me, Andrei?"

A pause. "Yeah, yeah. I hear you. Okay, I do it. Only you got to come back or we're not gonna make it out alive, Dimitri."

"I'm coming back. Don't you forget. Wait until you're somewhere safe before you call this number again. You talk to nobody but me, got it?"

"Just don't take too long or there won't be nothing to come back to."

"I'm trying, Andrei. Just remember, leave Verlov to me."

# Chapter 54

After a prolonged breakfast at Reggie's mom's insistence, and promises to visit again soon, Wolf and Reggie got back on the highway. She drove, her usual chatter subdued after the tearful mother-daughter goodbye. Leaving Santa Barbara behind, they joined a serpentine stream of traffic battling coastal fog for an hour. Finally thinned by offshore winds, the clouds yielded, revealing a sparkling Pacific. The view brought back memories for Wolf. As a youth, he had driven this very road, exploring the coast for surf in a van filled with boards and adolescent tribal mates. All that behind him now, he still longed for the occasional reunion with graying acquaintances—longboarders like himself. Lost in his reminiscing he didn't hear Reggie's questions.

"Tom, have you heard anything I've said?"

"Thankfully, no. Just kidding. What were you saying?"

"Shame on you. I was asking about your visit with the writer. You never shared much with Mother and me."

Wolf faced her. "Not much to say, really. I think he's agreed to look into some of the information I furnished him. He's going to check the validity of what I gave him."

"You're being evasive. That doesn't answer my question."

"That's all I can say at this point, really."

"But it's a non-answer."

"It's the best I can do, Reggie."

"You and Sam are so frustrating at times."

"Reggie, you'll have to ask Sam about all this when we get home. He knows more about what we're doing than I do."

"And what exactly are you two doing?"

"Fair enough. Without going into too many details, we're trying to make sure Dan Colter didn't die in vain."

"Oh, I didn't realize that was the purpose of your visit."

"It was Sam's idea." A solemn Wolf stared at the road ahead. "That's all I'm going to say about it for now. Good enough?"

Chastened, she nodded, her green eyes sympathetic.

After an hour fighting the sluggish LA pace, Reggie surrendered the wheel. Wolf drove the remaining miles to San Diego. Nearing home, Reggie took a call from McFadden.

"Hi, Sam. We're twenty minutes out. Mother insisted we stay for a long breakfast. You know her. She hates to say goodbye. Were you worried?" A change in Reggie's tone caught Wolf's attention. "Oh, I see." He took his eyes off the road to read her troubled expression. She handed the cellphone to him. "Sam wants to talk to you."

Left hand on the wheel, Wolf pressed the phone to his right ear. "I'm here. Go ahead, Sam."

It was Reggie's turn to study Wolf's face. Betraying nothing, he nodded, saying, "I understand. Yes. Roger that. Fill me in later." He gave back the phone. "Sam wants to say goodbye."

"Honey, anything wrong? Please tell me what's going on."

Wolf's eyes darted from the road to Reggie and back again. He kept his expression neutral. *No sense in panicking her*, he thought. *That's Sam's problem. Plenty of time for that later.*

Reggie finished the call and turned to Wolf, her eyes pleading. "All Sam will tell me is that we have some sort of situation. He wants us to go straight home and meet him there. Why would he say that? What's this about?"

Wolf tossed her a half-truth. "Seems those FBI agents want to come by the house and do a sit-down with me, maybe Sam as well."

"Is this about Dan Colter? What's your involvement?"

"When Dan and I were in Russia, we were assaulted in the airport while waiting for our connection to Tokyo. We think it was gang members who came after us. One of them had a knife and seriously wounded Dan. He ended up being taken to a Russian hospital where he died."

"We saw the news reports," she said. "And we saw that horrible phone video one of the passengers took. It was all over Fox and CNN."

"Well, the whole episode left me with a lot of unanswered questions. I made something of a nuisance of myself with the State Department."

"Sam said that. I'm sorry, Tom. Those details...I didn't realize—"

"Don't worry about it, Reggie. My guess is the feds want to interview me again. I'm hoping they have some news about why this went down."

"That's it?"

"That's enough, isn't it? I mean, it's not every day I sit down with the FBI. I hope their coming by the house hasn't upset you. I suppose we could ask them to move the interview to Sam's office."

"No. That's fine. We'll get through this. I'll stay out of sight."

"Don't worry. You're not part of this, Reggie."

"Good. The whole idea makes me nervous."

Certain she had bought the story, Wolf switched subjects. Avoiding her eyes, he said, "We're almost there, Reggie. I don't know about you but I've had enough time on the road to last for a while."

# Chapter 55

"Why are San Diego Police Department cars in front of our house?"

A uniformed officer spotted Wolf at the wheel of the approaching SUV and broke off a conversation with a colleague in a second squad car. The bareheaded cop strolled to the middle of the street and blocked

McFadden's driveway. Wolf eased to a stop and lowered the window.

"What's this all about, officer?"

"Are you Mr. Wolf?"

"I am. And this is Ms. McFadden. Her husband is expecting us."

The policeman said, "May I see some ID, please?"

Reggie stiffened. "That's my house, Officer."

Polite but firm, the cop held up a hand. "Just a precaution, ma'am."

Wolf showed his license and waited as Reggie dug in her purse. After scanning both, the deputy waved them into the driveway.

"Probably just an escort for the FBI team," said Wolf. "A professional courtesy."

"You're such a bad liar, Tom. There's more to it than that."

Wolf didn't have an answer. He eased into the driveway next to an unmarked car. Reggie got out of the SUV. "That's got government issue written all over it," she said.

"I'll get the luggage," he said.

Once inside with the bags, he found Sam and Reggie locked in an embrace. McFadden broke away. "We've got company, Wolfman."

Wolf set Reggie's bags on the floor. "So I see. Where are the Hoover suits?"

"Poolside. I asked them to wait on the lanai. They're here to see you. I'll join you in a few minutes." Arm around his wife, McFadden said, "Let me get Reggie settled."

"Do that."

"Will someone please tell me what's going on?" she wailed.

Wolf didn't wait to hear Sam's answer. He went through the kitchen, grabbed a San Miguel, and went out to the pool. Two suited agents got to their feet, removed their sunglasses, and straightened their ties. The heavier of the two, a balding white male, thrust out a hand. "Agent Tom Smathers." They shook hands. "My associate, Agent Larry Kutzler." The second man, athletic, square-jawed, and serious, nodded at Wolf.

Wolf pulled up a chair in the umbrella's shade. "Gentlemen. What can I do for you?" He took a long pull on the bottle.

Smathers said, "We're helping out the State Department, Commander. Seems you're a popular man back east. They say they've had a hard time getting hold of you."

Another sip, the icy beer refreshing. "Judging from my emails, I'd agree. I've been away, busy. What exactly are we talking about here?"

"The incident in Moscow…and now this unfortunate turn of events here in San Diego."

"You mean the Kurskov thing?"

"How did you find out about that?" said Kutzler.

"Sam called me on the road. Gave me the basics."

"That's not why we're here, of course," said Smathers. "I'm sure the locals will want to hear your take on that at some point. We'd like to know if it's somehow connected."

"Have you talked to Sam McFadden about this?"

"Just briefly, sir. We had hoped to interview you prior to this recent development—the Kurskov case—but you were unavailable."

"Well, I'm here now."

"Okay, what can you tell us about rumors of some sort of ledger or notebook that may or may not have had something to do with Dan Colter's death during your trip to Moscow?"

Wolf danced around the subject, careful with his words. "We didn't bring back any book, Agent Smathers. There seems to be a misunderstanding about that. Criminals, who may have mistaken us for another party, attacked us in

Domodovo Airport. Commander Colter paid for their mistake with his life."

"Yes, we're aware of that. A tragedy, of course."

"Part of the tragedy is the inability of State to furnish me with any details about his eventual death or the follow-up. Family, funeral arrangements. I've been left completely in the dark."

"We're aware you've made some inquiries, Commander."

"Oh, really? Such as?"

"I'm not at liberty to say."

"I didn't know I was on the Bureau's radar. Are you interested in this because of the possible terrorism angle?"

Agent Kutzler ignored Wolf's question and moved his chair closer. "Could you tell us the purpose of your trip here to San Diego?"

Another long draw on the beer. "Came out here to see my old friend, Sam McFadden. It's a great spot to clear your head. He's a sympathetic ear."

Smathers again. "I think it would make our job a lot easier if you'd touch base with Robert Nells at State. He's most concerned that the two of you finish the conversation you started."

"I can certainly manage that...on my timetable, though."

"Will you be returning to the east coast in the near future?"

"Don't see why not. I've done what I needed to do out here."

McFadden came across the lanai. "Got room for another?" Without waiting for an answer he sat down next to Wolf. "You fellas getting what you need?"

"Not exactly," said Smathers. "We now have this situation with Mr. Kurskov. It's a complication. Either of you have any idea if this ties into our investigation into Commander Colter's death?"

Wolf said, "Which I assume includes my role."

"Beyond your role as a witness to his stabbing in the airport, I'm not sure what part you play in this new scenario. Unless, of course, there is something that may have escaped your recollection of events."

"I think it's a bit of a stretch, but I'll be sure to let the Bureau know if something turns up."

As a fencing match it was becoming a draw. As a hint, McFadden rose to his feet and parked his chair at the table. "Will you be following the Kurskov case, Agent Smathers?"

"As of right now it's a local case. If the San Diego PD asks, we're ready to assist. If we find some link—"

Challenging Smathers, Wolf said, "A link to what?"

The agent shrugged. "One can never tell. Odd things happen in cases like this. There's always a loose thread that ties in somehow. We'll be in touch."

The FBI agents handed business cards to both men. Kutzler said to Wolf in parting, "Good luck with your conversation with State."

Wolf ignored the remark and stayed behind as McFadden walked the feds to their car.

When McFadden returned he motioned for Wolf to abandon the umbrella table for the fire pit at the far end of the lanai, away from the house.

"Where's Reggie?" said Wolf.

"Sleeping. Major headache. She's not taking this latest chapter in the Sam and Wolfman saga very well."

"Hey, if I'm a hindrance I can be gone before dinner."

"You're not going anywhere, Wolfman. This too shall pass."

"That's what they say about kidney stones."

McFadden laughed. "I've thought of you as many things but never a kidney stone. Don't even think about leaving."

"Okay, Sam, give me more details about the Kurskov thing. What's the skinny? What the hell happened?"

"I didn't give you the gory details because I didn't want you to drive off the road. And I didn't want Reggie to eavesdrop. We got big problems, man."

"Lay it out for me. You said Kurskov fucked up bad."

McFadden squeezed his eyes shut as if in pain. "The cops are calling it a home invasion, but I know better. Turns out Kurskov did a little freelance research on that book of yours."

"Explain freelance research."

"I told him explicitly NOT to go outside his own expertise to translate those pages."

"I got a bad feeling," said Wolf, a catch in his throat.

"Yeah. He took the disc to a former language professor of his."

"Don't tell me...the guy's Russian."

"Bingo. Kurskov got this guy to look at the stuff to corroborate what he found. Shouldn't have bothered. The prof confirmed Kurskov's translation."

"How do you know this?"

"His wife, Suzanne, told me."

"Oh, great. Another leak. So what happened?"

"Turns out this retired professor plays chess every Friday night with a certain friend from the Old Country."

"Shit. I can guess where this is going."

Nodding, McFadden said, "Bingo again. The old saying: loose lips sink ships. So, the old guy gets in his cups. Vodka, of course. Next thing you know the news is out about this amazing little book and all its interesting secrets."

"Suzanne told me once Kurskov realized what he had done he panicked; told her what had happened. The next night they got three phone calls. Each one worse than the last. The caller wanted the book, said if Kurskov didn't give it up, they would kill his family...in front of him."

"These animals don't play around."

McFadden pinched the bridge of his nose. "Suzanne wanted to call the cops, but Kurskov said he'd make a duplicate of the disc and give them that. Said he'd tell them the book no longer existed."

"I can't see those numb-nuts swallowing that."

"They didn't. They made a house call, caught Kurskov packing."

"What about his family?"

"They had been staying with relatives after the first phone call."

"So, these guys caught Kurskov?"

"Gorillas, man. They took their time with him. Got the disc and two copies he had made. Trashed the house. Beat the shit out of him. Destroyed his computers. Sons of bitches cut off two of his fingers before they were done. I'm surprised he wasn't killed. He crawled to a neighbor's house."

"But he survived."

"Barely. He's lost sight in one eye, has brain damage, and is not out of the woods yet. At this point it's not a given he'll make it."

"And the cops call this a home invasion?"

"That's what they told me," said McFadden. "They've already been to the office twice and talked to everyone on staff who worked with Kurskov. We looked through our records to see if any clients had a problem with him. Came up empty. Even his community college students were squeaky clean."

McFadden said, "That's how the police are playing it for now. They don't know what else to call it, and they don't know about the discs or the book, Wolfman."

"But his wife knows. Why hasn't she told the cops?"

"She's scared what these animals will do next."

"They've done their worst."

"Maybe. Hell, how would you even know who these people are? Where would you start?"

"I'd start with the professor."

"And then what?"

"Work up the ladder. Kick ass and take names."

"Maybe you should let the cops do their job."

"You do realize that whoever wanted that book bad enough to hurt Kurskov is not going to be satisfied with those discs." Wolf got up to pace around the fire pit, his mind racing. "Sam, these assholes are going to open that disc and see scanned pages. They're going to think the book still exists. They're bound to figure out Kurskov worked for you. He may have even told them before they finished with him."

"Despite getting the discs, you think they may come after me?"

"You'd be the obvious next choice," said Wolf.

"I guess we have to assume Kurskov gave me up."

"Everyone has their breaking point. Not to worry. I have an idea."

"Do I want to hear this?"

"Just listen." Wolf rubbed his chin, his eyes on the ground. "Go to the cops. Ask them to keep a squad car on duty. You need protection. Send Reggie to her mother until this is over. Get the Santa Barbara cops to offer security if she goes up there."

McFadden got up, began circling the fire pit at Wolf's side. "How does that solve my problem?"

Wolf faced McFadden. "It gets Reggie out of harm's way. She's your number-one priority. Meanwhile, the San Diego PD is looking for these guys."

"But what about your plans to make the book public?"

"That's a work in progress. Nash can't write it overnight. His piece will shed a lot of light in some dark corners here and overseas. It'll have a shelf life of course, but it might prove a game changer. Bring a little heat on the bad boys, you know."

"Okay, I'm good with that. I can call the cops."

"Right. And there's something you can do for me."

"Name it, Wolfman."

"I need a car and the name and address of that professor."

"What are you thinking of doing?"

"Trust me."

# Chapter 56

Ivanov tossed two discs on Shurkov's desk.

"What is this you bring me?"

"Look at them. Be prepared to be amazed."

Shurkov's driver stood immobile off to one side, his face blank.

"I don't understand," growled Shurkov. "I ask for a book, you bring me these."

Ivanov planted clenched fists on Shurkov's overflowing desk. "What century do you live in? Insert the discs. Tell me what you see."

The mobster grumbled. He quit one program, ejected a disc, and replaced it with one of the two Ivanov had given him. A few strokes on the keyboard to open the folder's icon on the screen and a laundry list of pages appeared in Cyrillic and English. Shurkov stared at the screen.

Ivanov leaned over the desk and tapped an icon on the screen. "Try this one. Open this page."

Shurkov hit another key as instructed. The image of two facing pages floated into view. Studying the listed names and figures without saying a word, his eyes shifted rapidly from one side of the screen to the other. "You found the man, eh? And he gives you this?"

"Yes. He had these two copies in his possession. We took them both and destroyed his computer."

"And the man?"

"We destroyed him as well. He will not live through tomorrow."

"You are certain?"

"Yes."

Shurkov glowered at Ivanov. "Does it occur to you that these are scanned images from the original? I send you for a book and you bring back these? How are our friends in Moscow supposed to hold these in their hands and turn the pages? Do you know what they will say?"

"The man told us the book no longer exists!"

"And you believed him?"

Turning to the placid chauffeur, Ivanov said, "Alexi, tell him how we got the information from Kurskov. Do you think he lied?"

The bullet-headed man spoke, his voice high and halting. "I don't think he lied, no. He broke in my hands like a doll. I think Ivanov brings you what you want, Boss."

"Idiots, both of you," barked Shurkov. "The book is still out there. Do you understand? We cannot give them these discs in place of the real thing."

"I've done what I was sent to do," deadpanned Ivanov.

Alexi spoke up. "Maybe we go back. There is another man, Dimitri. The one this Kurskov mentioned to us. He said he works for him. You remember? He is in San Diego, too."

Shurkov shot a confused glance at his driver, then turned back to Ivanov. "Who is this person Alexi is speaking of? Who is this man? Maybe he is the one with the book."

"His name is McFadden. By the time Kurskov gave us this name he was willing to say anything. I don't think this is worth the risk. Besides, I'm needed in New York."

"Not yet," snarled Shurkov. "You're needed here. You have no choice. Both of you must go back. Find this McFadden person. Let Alexi talk to him in his own special way. Don't come back without the book."

"You insist we go back, eh? If I'm to return to San Diego I want at least a good night's sleep and a decent meal. I'm not going to spend one more night in that slop house. Give me money for expenses."

Shurkov riffled a desk drawer and stuffed an envelope with six folded one hundred dollar bills, all the while mumbling about spoiled youth.

"Not enough," said Ivanov.

Shurkov added more bills and curses in Russian. "You think I print money?"

"Why not, this is your business, no?" Ivanov grinned in triumph. "Finally, he sees the light. Okay, we leave in the morning, Alexi." Ivanov pocketed the cash and waved to the big man. "Let's go."

"Alexi, you stay. Dimitri, wait out front," ordered Shurkov. "And don't bother my girls. They have work to finish."

Ivanov arched an eyebrow at the rotund shop owner and shut the door behind him. He paused, his ear pressed against the hollow wooden door. His smile disappeared, replaced by a grim set of the jaw. He moved down the paneled hallway and lingered at the counter, flirting with the help despite Shurkov's warning.

Alexi lumbered by, scowling at Ivanov for defying Shurkov by bantering with the girls. He went out into the last of the day's heat with Ivanov on his heels. Following Ivanov's directions they drove until they found an upscale chain motel promising cable, a pool, and a continental breakfast.

Ivanov got out at the motel office and taunted the big man. "Hey, Alexi, you like to join me? I will buy your dinner. Shurkov is paying."

"*Nyet*. I have things to do. I pick you up at six o'clock tomorrow morning. We must go back like the boss says. This time we bring back the book, eh?"

"Of course. This time we get the book. But don't come before eight."

# Chapter 57

Wolf slowed as he passed the bookstore, circled the block, and parked in a weedy asphalt lot behind the shop. He called McFadden. "I had a chat with our loud-mouthed professor. He was very helpful."

"That was quick. I take it you were your usual direct self."

"Had to be. I'm on a tight schedule. You know how academics can be."

"Was he upright when you left him?"

"Sam, please. He was most cooperative."

"I'm sure. Okay, what's next?"

"I'm off to my next appointment."

"Where are you?"

"Right where I need to be. I have to see a man about a book. Actually, a lot of books." Changing subjects, he said, "You taking the missus to her mom's place?"

"Negative. Reggie's refused to go. I made it clear what's happened but she insists on staying."

"Not a good choice."

"Try telling her that."

"Sorry I got you into this. The local gendarmes still there?"

"The relief got here an hour ago."

"Right. Better than nothing. Don't tell them a thing. I'll call you later with a sit rep."

Wolf locked his car and stayed close to the bookstore's blank wall until he reached the front. Once

an auto parts store, the long, one-level cinderblock
building now housed used and rare books. Opening the
door, he reached up, silencing a dangling copper bell
with his hand. Stravinsky's *Firebird* was playing
throughout the store. Wolf closed the door behind him,
locked it, and flipped an "Open" sign to "Closed."

He stood in the front half of a cluttered shop lined with
floor-to-ceiling shelves groaning with books. The storefront's
dusty picture window, its sill lined with volumes and dead flies,
was covered in faded green film. Vintage Soviet posters
papered the walls. Piled high with paperbacks and stacked
hardcovers, two large tables dominated the open room. Towers
of books crowded an aisle leading to an alcove overflowing
with even more titles.

A steady tapping sound, like a prisoner breaking large
rocks into little ones, came from the book-lined bay. A
wild-haired, morbidly obese man, his broad back to Wolf,
sat hunched over a vintage computer, stabbing the
keyboard. Arming himself with a heavy sharp-edged
volume, Wolf came round the corner of the shop owner's
desk, startling him.

"Pardon me, I'm looking for a volume of Lenin's speeches."

"Ach! I did not hear you come in."

Smiling, Wolf moved closer. "So sorry. You apparently
were busy."

Bespectacled and bearded, Viktor Kirov overflowed an
inadequate chair, his fleshy bulk showing only the wheels
beneath him. Outweighed by at least two hundred–plus
pounds, Wolf was on guard.

"Lenin, you say?"

"Yes. His earliest speeches, if you have them."

"*Da*, let me check my reference file."

"Or better yet...perhaps something on the *Bratva*."

The word hovered in the air. Suddenly wary, the typist reached for a drawer at his sagging belly. He made a clumsy attempt to cover his sleight of hand. Wolf caught the move and shifted in anticipation.

"Ah, here it is," said the man, his hand in the drawer.

Wolf grabbed a fistful of hair and slammed Kirov's face into the edge of the desk. Caught off-balance, the stunned man was no match for the agile Wolf. One kick took out the chair from under the bookseller and he went down without a fight. Wolf pulled open the desk drawer and plucked a nine-millimeter Beretta hidden in a nest of paperwork.

Wolf crouched, keeping his distance from the sprawled figure. He waved the handgun. "Huh, so much for Lenin's speeches. Going for this pistol was foolish of you."

Kirov raised his bloodied forehead from the floor. "Who are you? If you want cash you come to wrong place. I keep very little on the premises."

"I don't want money, Mr. Kirov, I want a name."

Wolf brought the knife-edged hardcover down on the prone man's right hand, breaking the wrist. A howl of pain filled the store.

"One name and I am gone."

"Fuck you!"

"Tough guy, huh?" Wolf used the book to break the second wrist. More howls of pain. More defiance mixed with cursing.

"Here's what I'm going to do, Kirov. You have a lovely little shop here. Lots of beautiful books. I'm told your collection of antique maps is unique. But when I look around, what do I see? A fire marshal's worst nightmare." Wolf flicked a lighter before the fallen man's eyes. "Shame to see your livelihood go up in smoke."

"What do you want?"

"One name."

"Who?"

"You played chess with Professor Kurtzmann. He spoke of a Russian book with secrets. You talked to someone about this book. I want that name."

"I did no such thing."

Wolf started on Kirov's ankles in turn, reducing the bookseller to tears.

On one knee, out of reach, he played with the lighter, saying, "I doubt you could move fast enough to escape the fire if this place went up in flames."

Kirov whined. "Ahhh...bastard."

"Wouldn't disagree with you. But you're the one on the floor, not me. I can't see you getting to your feet given the shape you're in. A body like yours would melt like a candle in a fire."

Wolf plucked a parchment from a cabinet. He unrolled a czarist officer's commission and held the lighter to a corner. The antique parchment's corner curled in a tiny tongue of fire. He blew out the flame. "Can't you see the whole place going up like that? Poof."

Blackened ash drifted in front of Kirov's bloodied face. Wolf said, "I noticed you don't have a sprinkler system. Shame. Lot of treasured stuff here. You probably didn't want to spend the money, huh? Don't know how that got by the inspectors."

Wolf tore the singed scroll in long strips and piled them in front of the prone Kirov. One by one, he burned the pieces, dropping the twisted ash on the floor. He did the same with two more collectibles. "A name, Kirov. Give me the name."

From a flat metal file cabinet with keys in the master lock, Wolf unfolded a medieval map of Europe, Wolf pretended to study it while flicking the lighter back and forth at the margins. Kirov broke.

"Shurkov."

"Who?"

"Leonid Shurkov."

"Is he *vory*?"

A thumping sound. Kirov was nodding, his bloodied brow bumping the floor in defeat.

"Where is Shurkov to be found?" Silence. Wolf repeated the question.

"Van Nuys."

"You expect me to stand on a street corner and shout his name?"

"A print shop. He has print shop there."

"Do better than that, Kirov. There could be a hundred, a thousand print shops in Van Nuys."

"Odessa Copies. On Raymer Street, near Sepulveda Boulevard."

Backing away, Wolf squatted on a step stool and used his cellphone to confirm what he had been told. "See. That wasn't so hard was it?"

"He will kill you for this."

"He'll have to get in line."

Kirov fell silent, his immobilized bulk where Wolf had felled him.

Wolf pocketed the Beretta and two cell phones he found, one on Kirov, another buried on the bookseller's desk. "I'd love to stay and help you to your feet," he said, "But I can't lift heavy things. Besides, I have places to go and appointments to keep."

"Shurkov will come after you."

Wolf paused. "He'll try, of course." Heading for the shop's service door in back, he said, "But first, he will kill you for talking to me, I think." On the threshold he looked back at Kirov. "You've been very helpful."

From the floor. "Rot in hell!

"After you, asshole."

# Chapter 58

Wolf phoned McFadden from the shaded patio of a coffee shop next to a theatrical costumes store. A snap-brim hat and a pair of black stage glasses sat on the table next to his Brazilian roast. A creased map of Southern California and greater LA sat in his lap.

"Checking in, Sam."

"Bad news. Gary Kurskov died an hour ago."

An awkward pause. Wolf waited for McFadden to say something, anything.

"Never regained consciousness. What a tragedy."

"I'm sorry, Sam. That makes eight."

"Eight?"

"The book. Kurskov was the eighth person to die because of the book."

"Way too high a price to pay, Wolfman. Maybe it's time to think seriously about calling it off and coming in."

"Can't. I'm too close, Sam. I got a name at my last stop."

"Good work. We could send the cops. And the feds might be interested."

"Let 'em do their own homework. Anything new with the cops?"

"All they know is that Kurskov was translating sensitive material."

"Hmm, do they know what it was?"

"No. Kurskov's wife...widow...told them that it was important enough to make somebody threaten him."

"How'd they take the news?"

"They got excited. They're still at her place trying to tie up loose ends."

"Question: do they know we're involved?"

"No. She told them she didn't know what he was looking at. Whoever whacked him trashed his computer as well."

"It may be splitting hairs, Sam, but what she said about not knowing what he was looking at was technically true. Are the feds sniffing around?"

"They're not players yet. But I'm sure they'll be showing up here at some point. How much time do you need?"

Wolf tossed his coffee cup in a trashcan and walked to his car. "Not sure. Four or five hours, maybe. Gonna recon my next stop."

"I hate leaving you out there on your own. I ought to be with you, man."

Wolf got behind the wheel, started the engine. "You're in a good spot for now. You can't be involved. Wouldn't look good for both of us to be gone at the same time if something went wrong. Plus, you've got Reggie to think of."

"Are you doing your usual 'scorched earth' thing?"

Wolf laughed. "Funny you should say that." He scanned his cellphone's GPS for the print shop's Van Nuys location. "Don't worry, Sam, I'm scrubbing as I go. I am the stranger with no name, an invisible man. I have a hunch this next stop may be the last one I need to make. If things turn out okay I'll come in."

"Have you considered the possibility you might meet up with the animals who killed Kurskov?"

Glancing over his shoulder, Wolf pulled from the curb. "That's on my radar." Patting his jacket's pocket with the handgun in it, he said, "I picked up a little something to even the odds in my favor. But thanks for the concern. I'll be careful, Dad."

# Chapter 59

Smashing and tossing his old phone, Wolf used a new one to call the writer Nash.

"Checking in with you," said Wolf. "First of all, I just got off the phone with McFadden. You should know Gary Kurskov is dead. He was tortured and killed by unknown assailants. For lack of a better diagnosis, the cops here are calling it a home invasion gone horribly bad."

"Is there any other kind?"

"Probably not."

"I'm sorry to hear that. Was it related to the data you gave me?"

"McFadden and I agree it is definitely related. Kurskov apparently went outside to corroborate what he was seeing on that camera card I gave him."

"Sorry about his death, but him asking for outside corroboration was a dumb thing to do. What was he thinking?"

"Dunno. Probably wanted to make sure he got it right."

"So what do the cops think?"

"All they know is that Kurskov was working on something sensitive."

"Have they made a connection to the Russian *Mafiya*?"

"Not yet. And as far as we know the FBI is not part of this."

"They'll be involved before too long. The locals will ask for their help at some point. Are you and McFadden in danger?"

"We have to go on that assumption. I'm out and about. McFadden's staying close to home." Wolf heard ice rattling in a glass. "And you? How's your research going?"

"I've shaken a few trees," said Nash. "Made some contacts here and back east. I'm heading to New York next week to talk to some of the Old Guard *Mafiya* types. You want to come along, see how the other half lives?"

"Thanks for asking, but for the time being I think I need to stay close to Sam and follow this to its conclusion."

"Okay. Let me know if you change your mind."

"I do have one question for you, though."

"Shoot...figuratively speaking, of course."

The two laughed. Wolf said, "What can you tell me about a Russian guy named Leonid Shurkov? He runs a printing shop in Van Nuys."

"Ah, yes, Leonid Shurkov. He was part of that second wave of immigrants. He's Georgian. Did a lap in the gulag prior to arrival. Ran a Russian tabloid out here years ago when he first showed. He had his fingers into everything. He's mobbed up. Rumored to still run crews in the Los Angeles area. Has to be in his late sixties."

"A bad actor?"

"Oh, yeah. Shurkov's the real deal. He was involved in suspect shipping at the Long Beach port—drugs, arms, and illegals. He got tangled up in bringing in girls from Eastern Europe. Couple of them suffocated on the way over. You could talk to the feds about him. They came to the table late, of course, but they probably have a file on this guy."

"So Shurkov's someone to take seriously."

"Yeah, he's a bad dude. Top of the food chain out here on the coast before he got some competition. Sometimes it's hard to tell with these guys. They're like gamecocks, bright plumage, puffed up, strutting and noisy. But they're lethal, every one of them. Never trust them; never turn your back on them."

Wolf said, "Thanks for the info and the warning, Sean."

"Should I be asking why you're calling about Shurkov?"

"Uh, probably not."

# Chapter 60

After a leisurely breakfast, Ivanov gathered his meager belongings and paid his bill in cash. Outside the motel office he spotted the frowning Alexi leaning from the window of the white van they had used the day before.

Ivanov opened the passenger side door and stared at Alexi. "You really think it's smart to return to San Diego in the same vehicle?"

"Why not? We were not stopped last time."

Ivanov slid into the passenger seat. "Yes, but Kurskov was alive the last time we were there. We may have been seen. The police will be vigilant."

Seemingly unconcerned about the risk, the big man shrugged.

"Fine. Let us be off," said Ivanov. "I am tiring of this back and forth. I miss New York."

"You will miss it here when you are up to your neck in snow. You will remember your time in California and wish you were here. You watch. I will be right."

"Just drive."

Alexi's ragged laugh echoed in the van as they pulled into morning traffic.

*Ivanov glanced at his watch.* To make this work I have to get him to stop somewhere before we get on the highway.

They drove five blocks, leaving a livelier strip clogged with traffic for an anonymous industrial neighborhood of warehouses, auto repair shops, scrap yards, wholesale hardware depots and fenced car lots. Another series of traffic lights and they would join the interstate. Ivanov made his move.

"Pull over," he said pointing to a vacant lot between two buildings. "I have to piss."

"What? Why now?"

"Pull over! You want me to make water in the van?"

"Okay, okay. I pull over. Make it quick, eh?"

Alexi turned into a vacant square of cracked asphalt between two stuccoed cubes. "Hurry!"

Ivanov waved him into silence, got out, and made a show of relieving himself against a nearby wall. When he climbed back in the van he was pointing a Walther PPK at Alexi.

"Fool, what are you doing?"

"It's simple. I am not going with you to San Diego, Alexi."

"You crazy? Shurkov told us to go back, to find that book."

"The police will be waiting for us."

"We follow orders, Dimitri."

"And which orders would those be?"

His eyes on the gun, Alexi said, "To go back as Shurkov told us to do."

"I see. And once we have the book, will you do as he commanded you— kill me and leave my body behind for the police to find?"

"What are you talking about?"

"I overheard Shurkov telling you to kill me once we were done."

Alexi lunged at Ivanov, came up short because of the seat belt.

Ivanov fired wide, hitting the driver in the left shoulder.

Despite the seat belt, Alexi threw himself at Ivanov. With little room in the cab, the two struggled. The pistol went off, hitting Ivanov's left foot. Screaming in rage, he elbowed Alexi in the face, breaking his nose. Freeing the pistol, Ivanov jammed it against the driver's ribcage and fired three times, ending it.

Alexi slumped against Ivanov, filling the space between the seats. Ivanov squirmed free of the dead man. Despite the fire consuming his left foot, he dragged, shoved, pushed Alexi's corpse into the cargo space behind the seats. Exhausted by the effort, a grimacing Ivanov propped his foot on the driver's seat to examine his wound.

His toes were shattered. Not a fatal injury but still an unexpected turn, the bullet had exited the top of his foot, mangling the flesh. Blood seeped from a ragged hole in his shoe. In shock, but more determined than ever, Ivanov gritted his teeth, his jaw clenched in agony. He worked the bloodied shoe free, then peeled a soaked crimson sock from his foot.

*Have to work fast. No time to lose.*

Ivanov crouched in the cab, using the bloodied sock as a primitive bandage for his wound. He settled behind the wheel, started the engine, and inched toward the street. When traffic slackened he pulled into the closest lane. Every small bump and jolt of the pavement sent pain shooting through his foot. Blood pooled beneath the brake pedal. He drove for blocks, found a chain drugstore, and pulled to the curb. Ivanov wiped bloodied hands on a rag from the glove compartment and heaved himself into the passenger seat.

He lowered the window and hailed a skinny black adolescent pushing a bike. "Hey, I need a favor." The youth halted but kept his distance.

Ivanov waved two fifty-dollar bills at the teen. "Hurt my foot. Can drive but I can't walk. Would you be willing to buy me some bandages so I can fix things until I can get myself to a doctor?"

The curious youngster eyed the bills and approached the passenger side window. Ivanov wiggled the cash. "Here's money for some medical supplies, okay?" The kid inched closer. Ivanov showed a hundred dollar bill in his left hand. "Take the fifties, buy the stuff I need, and when you bring it back, the hundred is yours. Deal?"

"What you need, man?"

Ivanov scribbled what he wanted on a scrap of paper. "Here, take this list. They'll have everything I want. You keep the change *AND* the hundred dollars, okay?"

The teen snatched the notepaper. "That's all you want me to do? Buy all this shit? Medical stuff, bleach wipes, new socks? What's up with that? Slippers? Man, this a lot of stuff. You sure?"

"That's it. See, I can't walk. Can't do it myself. Deal?"

"Might need more money, man."

"One hundred is plenty. You get the bonus when I get the stuff."

The young cyclist came closer, peering in the window at Ivanov's foot propped on the driver's seat. "Man, that's fucked up," he said, wrinkling his nose at the sight. "You need a doctor, you know."

Ivanov nodded. "Yeah. It looks worse than it is. Okay, you do this for me? Take the money and get me what I need. Come back and the hundred is yours."

The grinning kid snatched the fifties. "Okay, man. Don't go no place."

Ivanov laughed to disarm the boy. "I don't think I'm going anywhere, do you?"

"Hell no. Okay then. I be back."

He leaned the bike against the passenger door and disappeared in the drugstore. Twenty agonizing minutes later he returned, his arms cradling paper bags. The teenager passed the bags through the open window. "I got that cleaning stuff you wanted too, man. What you need that for?"

Ivanov ignored the question and inventoried the supplies, his mood lightening. "Okay, you did good. Here's that hundred I promised you." He passed the bill to his impromptu Samaritan.

"You crazy, man. But I take it."

"Thanks, kid." Ivanov wormed his way behind the wheel, fighting the pulsing pain. He got back in traffic and drove until he found a deserted school parking lot next to a vacant playground. It took him a tedious, agonizing hour to clean his wounded foot, bandage it, and wrap it in surgical gauze. Ivanov slipped on a pair of clean dark socks and new slippers. He regained his confidence. He splashed bleach over the seats and dashboard in a cursory effort at cleaning the van's cab. Ivanov stripped, changing into clothes from his carry-on luggage, then bagged bloody towels and clothing. He hobbled to a trashcan and dumped the bag. After tossing the Glock in a storm drain, he got back in the van, gobbled a handful of pain relievers, and got back on the highway. He found a long-term lot near the LA airport and parked. Ivanov wiped every surface he had touched, took the lot's shuttle to the main terminal, and bought a one-way ticket on a New York flight.

*Fuck Shurkov and his book. I'm going back to New York. Verlov is going to pay. The man in San Diego is not my problem.*

# Chapter 61

*Van Nuys*

A beaming Wolf, wearing the hat and stage glasses, rapped the counter to get the attention of the girl on duty. "Hello, there, young lady. I have an appointment with Mr. Shurkov. Is he in?" The rattling machines nearly drowned out his words.

An anorexic pig-tailed blonde looked up from a monitor behind the chest-high counter. She dutifully rose from her desk. "I keep his calendar but I don't remember an appointment listed for today. You are?"

Wolf said, "Pastor Diffley. Fifth Presbyterian over Anaheim way. Well, that's odd, my secretary said she called yesterday to arrange a meeting."

"No sir, there is no note of a call," she said over the machinery noise.

Wolf charmed the dull girl. "No problem. These things happen. I can see that you are not only pretty but also very efficient. I'm sure it's my secretary's fault. My apologies. Our church has a large order to place with your shop. Mr. Shurkov will appreciate the business, I'm sure."

"Any other staff here?" he said. "Perhaps they may have taken the call."

"No sir, there is no one else today. Just me and Mr. Shurkov. I'm sorry, sir, but he is on the phone right now with another customer."

"You've been so sweet. I'll just pop in and place the order with Leonid myself. His office still in the back?"

"Yes. But truly, I can help you, sir."

Wolf waved away the suggestion. "Don't trouble yourself. You have so much work to do. I'll just say hello to Leonid. We've done business before."

Palming his cellphone, Wolf hit the shop's number. When the girl reached to answer the phone, he grinned, signaling he would show himself down the hall. He heard her answer, "Hello, Odessa Copies. How may I help you? Hello, Hello."

Wolf drew the nine-millimeter Beretta and went down a narrow hallway of cheap paneling. A door on his right opened to a storeroom, a second door, to a bathroom. He passed an open door on his left—a room of loud copiers turning out broadsides, perfect cover for his footfalls on peeling linoleum. The last door would be Shurkov. Wolf hit the print shop number again, heard the distracted girl answer and killed the call. Ear to the door, he heard a gruff voice—Shurkov arguing with another.

*No turning back.*

Wolf twisted the knob with gloved hand and rushed in, the pistol gripped in his right hand. He kicked the door shut behind him. Stunned, Shurkov's eyes focused on the

Beretta in Wolf's hands. A tinny voice babbled from a speakerphone on the Russian's cluttered desk.

"Say goodbye," mouthed Wolf.

"Myer, I must go...no time to talk."

Shurkov ended the call. Glaring at Wolf he raised both hands and started to rise. "Whoever you are, you make a big mistake. Do you know who I am?"

Poised an arm's length from Shurkov, Wolf said, "Sit down. You are Leonid Shurkov, the man I came to see."

Defiant despite the gun, the Russian said, "So, what do you want?"

"Viktor Kirov sent me."

"Who? I don't know this name."

"I think you do. Your friendly book collector. He certainly knows you, Leonid. He says you sent two men to kill Gary Kurskov in San Diego."

"Lies. I don't know this Kirov. I know nothing about someone being killed in San Diego. I run a print shop, as you see. You are mistaken."

"Why kill Kurskov? He was only a messenger. He didn't have the book you wanted."

At the mention of the book a flash of recognition came and was just as quickly gone. Gambling, Wolf said, "The man I work for sends me to sell you the book on one condition."

"What book is this you talk about?"

Wolf kept the pistol centered on Kurskov. "Don't play games, Leonid. The book is worth ten thousand dollars to my boss. We both know it's worth one hundred times that. You have one chance to bid."

"I refuse to play your stupid game."

"Really? You have one last chance." Snagging a jogging suit jacket hanging on a chair, Wolf wrapped it around the Beretta's muzzle as a primitive silencer. The gesture unnerved Shurkov.

"I will give you a number to call," said Wolf. "It may be the most important call in your life. My boss is waiting. If you want to live you will agree to the terms of sale."

"And if I refuse?"

"Then I will kill you. It doesn't matter to me either way. I do as told. You call my boss and agree to buy the book for ten thousand. If you tell him no, I kill you. Someone else will then be offered the book."

A moment passed. The Russian was sweating despite the air conditioning—a good sign. Confident he had struck a nerve, Wolf didn't take his eyes off Shurkov. "What's it going to be, Leonid?"

"Bastard. Give me the number."

Wolf recited the numerals.

"I am curious. Before you call, tell me why you had Kurskov killed. Not that I care one way or the other. He didn't possess the book, my boss did."

"Kurskov played a dangerous game…and lost. It was only business."

"We thought as much. Make your call. Put the phone on speaker so I can hear my boss. When you connect, say only, 'I will buy the book.' He will understand."

"Fool. You think I have that kind of money here?"

"Of course not. But you will make a transfer once you agree to meet the price my boss set."

Kurskov dialed. Wolf pointed the Beretta at the speakerphone. Frowning, Kurskov hit a button and the first of two rings echoed in the room. Feeling the cellphone in his pocket buzz against his thigh, Wolf tapped the unseen screen, making the connection.

"I will buy the book," said Shurkov. "Ah…Hello?"

Wolf fired, tapping the Russian twice in the forehead.

# Chapter 62

Ivanov paid cash for a one-way ticket to Newark. Pale and light-headed, he signaled for a wheelchair and breezed through security with his escort. At the gate he tipped his handler and sent a text to Sergei Helinski, alerting him to his return. Boarding early, thanks to the wheelchair, Ivanov limped to his seat.

*I am going to make it back. By the time they discover Alexi's body in the van I will be across the country. I only hope I am not too late.*

Ivanov began to relax by degrees. Only when the plane filled and backed from the gate, with the droning ritual of safety tips from flight attendants, did he let go of his fear

of being discovered. Even then, the thought of being pulled off the plane at the last minute kept him on edge until he felt the airplane leave the ground. Airborne, with California falling behind him, Ivanov ordered two mini-bottles of vodka during the attendant's liquor run and downed them both. He gobbled more pain relievers. Fighting fatigue and the throbbing in his left foot, he finally surrendered to a restless sleep.

When he reached Newark, he welcomed another wheelchair arranged by the gate attendant. Ivanov asked to be parked curbside to make a call. He sent another text to Helinski and got a response, then a call a few minutes later.

"You are back?"

"I am back, Sergei. Where are you?"

"My cousin's place. I've been staying here since he went to Florida. You remember it?"

"Yes. Are you alone?"

"Igor is with me."

"The others?"

"Dead or disappeared."

"All of them?"

"Petor disappeared yesterday. We're the only two left, Dimitri."

"Stay put. I am taking a car. I will be there soon."

"Call when you are close. I will come down to meet you."

"Where is Verlov?"

"Likely with Levich. He never leaves his side these days."

Ivanov fought a sudden wave of hopelessness. "That will be a problem. Okay. I am coming. We will turn this around. Do you believe me?"

"Yes, of course. With you back things will be like they were before."

"No, Sergei, things will be better than they were before. Much better."

"Things couldn't be worse than they are now."

"I will need a weapon," said Ivanov.

Helinski said, "I have one for you. We have been waiting for this."

"Not much longer. Look for me soon, little brother."

Helinski put down the phone and faced the man with the gun, who said, "Good. You were very convincing."

Sitting opposite a battered, defeated Helinski, Verlov waved a Glock at Ivanov's lieutenant. "Because you did as told I spare you." He smiled. "Don't take it so personally, Sergei. This was bound to happen. Your world changes and you must change with it."

"He trusts me."

"I know. Lucky for you. That keeps you alive. Unlike your foolish friend, Mintov."

Attempting to flee when Verlov and his two byki broke through the door, Igor Mintov was halfway out a window to the fire escape when one of Verlov's guard dogs caught his feet. Dragged back inside screaming and kicking, he had been knocked out and tossed next to a groggy Helinski. Grabbing Mintov's hair, Verlov's goon pulled, exposing the boy's pale neck to his curving blade. One swift cut and it was over in a spray of blood, unhinging Helinski.

Helinski held his throbbing head and eyed Mintov's pale corpse propped beside him on the blood-soaked couch. Mintov's head was nearly severed.

Helinski groaned. "You didn't have to kill him. He was just a kid."

"Oh, but I did. He was old enough to hold a gun, eh? What if he had run away and warned Ivanov? That would have been most annoying."

"So, now we wait," said Verlov.

# Chapter 63

"Looks like we caught a break." Nodding to McFadden, San Diego Police Detective Mike McManus pocketed his cell phone and said, "We should talk, Sam."

"Okay. Out back. I'll tell Reggie we're outside."

McManus poked his head outside the front door, said something to the duty cop, and went out back by the pool. Joining him moments later, McFadden asked, "Good news?"

"Maybe. One of our squads found a witness in Kurskov's neighborhood who remembers seeing a white van the night of the murder."

"That is good news, Mike."

McManus said, "Probably only a million or so white vans. But the guy did jot down a partial number. We're checking."

"Did this witness see anyone in the van?"

"Negative. But it's all we've got so far. No prints in the house. All the blood belonged to Gary Kurskov."

"Well, it's something."

"Pretty damn slim so far. Say, where's your friend?"

McFadden had expected the question. He said, "The beach."

"He's gone to the beach? Isn't that risky?"

"Wolf is a former Navy SEAL. He knows how to take care of himself. Besides, he's been cooped up here ever since the assault on Gary Kurskov went down. He'll call in at some point."

That satisfied the cop. "I'd like to be at the beach myself but I'm on the people's dime. Not doing any good here. Besides, you've got a uniform outside. We'll keep someone here until we get past this. I'll head back to the shop to see what else I can turn up."

McFadden walked him to the door. Reggie heard the front door, came out of the bedroom, and threw her arms around McFadden. "I just got off the phone with Mother. She's worried, Sam."

"Me too, Reggie. But we've got a cop outside. I'm thinking of checking in with work. Seems like years since I was last down there."

"They can do without you a little longer. I need you here."

"Maybe I'll get hold of the Wolfman and get him to spell me."

"Where is he?"

"The beach. He wanted to check out the waves. You know him. He gets restless. Say, why don't you go for a swim? Work off some of the stress."

"Only if you come with me."

"Okay. One hour max. I'll tell Deputy Fife we'll be out back."

McFadden headed for the front door, stopped, and said, "By the way, McManus said they have a lead on a white van that was seen in the neighborhood that night."

"That's a good thing, right?"

"It's all they have right now. But yes, it's a good thing."

"I'll change into my suit."

Grinning, McFadden said, "Don't bother, it'll just get wet."

"You're unbelievable, Sam. We're in the middle of a murder case, no suspects, and you're thinking about–"

"A great stress reliever."

"See you out back. And I'm wearing a suit."

"One can always hope."

# Chapter 64

Wolf disassembled the Beretta, tossed the pieces in different storm drains miles from Shurkov's shop. Likewise with the hat, sliced into shreds, and the glasses and cellphone, shattered and thrown in trashcans and Dumpsters on the way back to San Diego. He drove south, racing the clock among highway lemmings. One hundred fifty miles and three hours later, he left I-5, heading into Imperial Beach. He found the public pier, parked, and called McFadden from his perch halfway down the wooden planks.

"Checking in, Sam. What's happening?"

"Some progress. Cops have a witness who saw a white van the night Kurskov was killed. They have a partial number for the plate."

"Good luck with that. I've seen a lot of white vans today."

"Granted it's a long shot, but it's all they have right now. Care to tell me where you are?"

"At the beach like we agreed."

"That covers a lot of ground, Wolfman."

"Imperial Beach. Been watching the boys in the water. Crowded as usual. Lousy waves not worth paddling for in my humble opinion."

"That's a sign of age," McFadden said. "You treating my car kindly?"

"Running like a top. I'm at the pier, Sam. Gonna call Agent Smathers and see if he'd like to meet for dinner at the Tin Fish. Whadaya think?"

"I think that's a good idea. If we didn't have our babysitter, Reggie and I would love to join you."

"Okay, I'm halfway down the pier as we speak. Give Reggie my best. I'll be home late. Be sure to tell the duty cop I'm coming in."

"Anything else to share?"

"I'm still operating under the 'Don't ask, don't tell' rule."

"Okay. I can live with that. Later."

Wolf found the card FBI Agent Smathers had given him. Reaching the end of the pier, he called. "Hello, my name's Tom Wolf. May I speak to Agent William Smathers, please?"

"I'm sorry, sir. Agent Smathers is not available at this time. Would you like me to connect you with his voicemail?"

"Thank you."

Smathers's robotic voice apologized for, "not being able to take your call. Please leave your name, phone number, and brief message, and I will return your call as soon as possible."

Wolf waited for the recorded beep. "Agent Smathers, this is Tom Wolf, houseguest at Sam McFadden's. I'm in Imperial Beach. Thought I'd grab a bite to eat at the Tin Fish on the city pier. If you get this message within the next hour and have your evening free, perhaps we could meet. Please return my call." He recited the cellphone number and said goodbye.

To back up his story, Wolf walked to the restaurant, stopped at the bar, nursed two beers for an hour, then ordered fish tacos and another beer. He paid with a credit card. No call from Smathers. *Just as well.*

He pocketed one of the restaurant's cardboard coasters and a souvenir plastic beer cup. Wolf closed down the place and retraced his steps along the pier. The surf wasn't half bad. The wind had died, replacing the ragged chop with glassy green, waist-high walls. He watched surfers scrap for the waves until dusk, then drove north along Seacoast Drive to Elm. From there it was a straight shot back to I-5. An hour later, he turned into McFadden's driveway after being waved ahead by the duty cop. It had been a long, productive day.

# Chapter 65

*Brighton Beach, Brooklyn*

Ivanov had the town car stop mid-block from the Caspian Nights club. He gave the driver a hundred dollar bill and sent him on his way. Ivanov shuffled to a darkened storefront adjacent to the club and kept to the shadows. Couples came and went. He watched a strutting pack of alpha males enter the club followed by a preening covey of girls. Each time the door opened, vague disco-like music floated across the sidewalk.

Ivanov's injury was giving him fits, as if his foot was in a vise. Walking had opened the wound, leaking blood in his shoe. He steadied himself against the brick wall, willing away his pain.

After an interminable wait, the familiar figure of Anton, the Azerbaijani took up his usual station as the club's greeter-bouncer. Breathing a sigh of relief, Ivanov headed to the club's entrance. Whistling, he caught Anton's attention and waved. Like a bear rising on its hind legs, the burly man lumbered toward Ivanov and embraced him. "Dimitri. You appear like a ghost. Where have you been?"

"California. Levich sent me on an impossible errand."

"Does he know you have returned?"

"Not yet. I arrived only hours ago. I haven't had the time to see him."

Looking down at Ivanov's leaking shoe, he said, "You are hurt, eh?"

"A scratch. It's nothing. I need to see Levich."

Anton's eyes narrowed. Glancing about, he said, "To speak to Levich you will need to see Verlov first. I think maybe you have been replaced, Dimitri."

Ivanov scowled. "Verlov, eh? I've been gone two weeks and this is what I find when I return?"

"Things have changed. You should be careful."

"So I've heard. I want your help, Anton."

"Of course, Dimitri. What can I do for you?"

"I need the package."

"If Verlov finds out—"

"Anton, how long have we known each other? Tell me, have you fallen under his spell, too? I thought the man who could frighten you had not yet been born. Was I wrong?"

A sheepish grin from the bearded giant. "Forgive me."

Ivanov dismissed the apology. "Forgiven. Now, bring me the package."

"Of course. Wait here."

Ivanov dragged himself to the club's brick wall, leaned against it, and waited, anger replacing his waning strength. The pain in his foot flared, making him irritable. He didn't have to wait long. Anton returned, a shoebox under one arm. He handed it over to Ivanov without speaking.

"Flag a taxi for me, Anton."

"No problem." A gypsy cab pulled to the curb, spilling a quartet of club-crawling locals. The Azerbaijani told the driver to wait. Signaling Ivanov in the shadows that his ride was ready, Anton held the cab's door and then took up his station at the club's entrance, his eyes on Ivanov's silhouette in the car's rear window.

From the back of the cab, the shoebox on the seat next to him, Ivanov directed his driver down the street where Helinski's cousin lived.

"Slow down but don't stop," he said.

Studying the scene told him nothing. Helinski's relative lived on the top floor of a three-story, rust-colored brick building unchanged since the fifties. No one lingered in the lighted, ground-floor entrance hall with its bank of mailboxes and ancient elevator.

Ivanov said, "Keep going."

He gave the man another address three streets over and got out mid-block in front of a tiny bungalow dwarfed by neighboring apartment units. Nursing his crippled foot, Ivanov dragged himself up the sidewalk to a waist-high iron gate guarded by hedges. He rang the doorbell, then pounded on the doorframe. A porch light flicked on. A stout, robed matron peered at her visitor from the safety of her door— Lydia Simonev, Levich's housekeeper.

Throwing up her hands in recognition, she waddled to the storm door, opened it, and welcomed Ivanov with a hug. "Dimitri. What brings you to my doorstep at such an hour?"

"Ah, it's a long story, Lydia. May I come in?"

She took him by the elbow and ushered him into her crowded living room. "*Da*. Of course, come in. I have not seen you for what, almost two weeks now."

"The boss had me on a job."

"Oh, *da*, you go to California, eh? Please, sit." She showed him to an overstuffed chair.

"How did you know I was in California?"

"I am a piece of furniture with ears, Dimitri. I go about my day and no one pays attention to me. I hear everything and say nothing."

"The keeper of secrets, eh?"

"It is not my business to speak of such things. But for you..."

Ivanov sank down, his left foot stiff. Glancing down, Lydia clucked. "Ah, what is this? You are hurt, yes? You have troubles?"

"A truck ran over my foot."

"I don't think a truck does this, Dimitri."

He laughed despite the pain. "A very large truck, perhaps?"

"Never mind," she fussed. "You want me to help you?"

"Perhaps. I want to ask you a favor, okay?"

Fussing like a mother hen, she said, "Of course, Dimitri."

"I need to speak to the boss."

"So, call him. Better yet, come by his apartment in the morning."

"That's a problem for me. I have come back from California early."

Arms folded across her ample bosom, her eyes narrowed in a disapproving scowl. "I know what you are thinking, Dimitri. You worry about Verlov, true?"

"Yes. I don't think I can see the boss without seeing Verlov first."

Levich's housekeeper filled another chair, her frown intact. "Yes. You have to talk to Verlov. Everybody has to talk to Verlov these days. You have been gone two weeks and even you will have to talk to Verlov first."

"Why this change?"

"I think Boris Levich is not the same, Dimitri. Something has happened to him. Perhaps a stroke, eh? He listens to Verlov, no one else. Soon, I think I will no longer be able to fix meals for the boss. Maybe he gets a new housekeeper. Someone young, eh?"

"You're still young, Lydia."

The gray-haired woman blushed, waved away the compliment. "I want things to be the way they were. I think one day I will finish fixing dinner and Verlov will tell me not to bother coming in the next day."

"I'm not sure where I stand now either," said Ivanov.

"The boss always has a spot for you in his heart, Dimitri. You are like a son to him all these years."

"That was before Verlov, Lydia."

Throwing up her hands she said, "Yes, this is true."

"Can you get a message to the boss for me?"

"Of course. I will do this. Do you have a letter or something like this?"

"I give you a phone number for him to call me. But only when Verlov is not at his side. You understand?"

"Of course. Tomorrow when I bring him his lunch I will tell him."

Ivanov handed her a piece of paper. "No. Don't speak of this. Just give him this. My number is written there. Tell him I have to talk to him about California."

"Yes, I can do this, Dimitri. Trust me."

Taking her hands in his, Ivanov locked eyes with her. "This is very important, Lydia. My life depends on Boris Levich calling me at this number."

Pocketing the note, she said, "I will do it."

Ivanov rose unsteadily. "Now I must go. I have other errands to run."

"Have you eaten?"

Ivanov shook his head. "I knew you would ask. No, I have not eaten."

She pushed herself to her feet and hooked her arm in his, gesturing toward her cramped kitchen. "Then stay and have some potato soup. It's fresh. And I have bread, made this morning with my own hands. You'll stay to make an old lady happy."

"If you insist."

"I do indeed. Boris Levich can wait. Verlov can wait. They can all wait until tomorrow. Come, Dimitri. Let me spoil you. After you eat we must look at your foot, eh? You can't travel far in that condition. Maybe you sleep on the couch if you like, eh?"

"Maybe I should. Thank you for your hospitality."

"I think maybe you will put things right, Dimitri."

# Chapter 66

Morning arrived with a gift: a light fog blown out to sea shortly after sunrise, a clear sky, and a phone call from Detective Mike McManus. McFadden took the call in his den.

"Hey, Sam. We found the white van," said the cop.

"Great work, Mike."

"To be honest, it was pure luck. The kind of break we needed."

Reggie wandered by, wrapped in a white terrycloth robe, her hair damp. She blew a kiss to McFadden from the hall and got a wave in return.

He asked McManus, "What can you tell me about the find?"

"The plates matched that partial we had. Someone dumped it at one of those park-and-ride lots near LAX. They must have had a flight to catch. Probably thought no one would notice the van for a couple days or maybe a week."

"Who found it?"

"One of the lot guys. He was double-checking license plates on their master sheet. Spotted a big guy in the back, dead."

McFadden imagined the scene.

"The LAPD got there, confirmed the sighting, ran the plates, and called. I'm making a leap here, but if I was a betting man I'd say this guy was one of Kurskov's killers."

"How so?"

"The van, of course. The medical examiner thinks he's been dead for at least twenty-four hours. We think this fits within the timeline for Kurskov's beating."

"Any ID?"

"No details yet. I'm going up today to nose around. We should know more by the end of the day."

"Appreciate your keeping me in the loop, Mike."

"If this pans out," said McManus, "it might mean the other killer, or killers, caught a flight to parts unknown. It could also mean they're gone and you're out of the crosshairs."

"Or it could be a decoy to get us to let our guard down."

McManus said, "We won't pull the patrol from your house if that's what you're worried about."

"Glad to hear it. Reggie feels safer having your people around."

"Don't blame you. Okay, that's it," said McManus.

"Thanks for the call." McFadden put down the phone and looked out the kitchen window at Wolf doing underwater laps. *Better let him know what the cops have found. Hope he's not involved with the airport thing.* McFadden thought, *Don't ask, don't tell. Isn't that what Wolf said yesterday?*

# Chapter 67

The following day, feeling confident about the investigation's progress, McFadden, Reggie, and Wolf attended Kurskov's funeral. The slain man's family was there as well. The cops salted mourners at the church and cemetery with plainclothes officers. With nothing amiss, the next day McFadden put in a full day's work at his business. His hand had been sorely missed. In the wake of Kurskov's death employee morale had suffered. At a mid-morning meeting McFadden and his two partners rallied staff. Sharing what he could about the hunt for Kurskov's killers, McFadden answered questions. The mood began to lift noticeably.

Late in the afternoon, McManus stopped by McFadden's office to update details about the department's findings. After preliminaries, he changed gears.

"I'm going to speak candidly, Sam. Normally, we don't lay it all out there when we're in the middle of investigating a

homicide like this. You can appreciate why we can't share everything we find. It's a process. A lot of it is speculation. Some of it rabbit trails and some of it useless leads from the woodwork. We do a lot of sifting to get it right."

"I understand," said McFadden. "At this stage you're still in the exploratory mode. I get that."

McManus nodded. "That being said, I can tell you off the record what we do know."

"If you want me to reassure you of my silence, you have it."

"Good. The department appreciates what you've done for us with your facility here and we think you deserve some special consideration."

"Appreciate the sentiment, Mike."

"We ID'd the body in the van near the airport. The dead man is Alexi Budnov. Not exactly a choirboy. Guy had a record. Loan-sharking, gambling, and assault. He was a driver for the late Leonid Shurkov."

"Who's Shurkov?"

"A bad actor. Has ties to the rats' nest in Brooklyn's Brighton Beach."

McFadden said, "Sounds like you've stumbled on the Russian mob."

"No doubt. Both these guys are long known to be part of the Russian *Mafiya* according to the LAPD. Budnov was an enforcer. Not to disparage the dead, but people I talked to up there said he was a bit of a dim bulb. Originally a glorified errand boy, he rose through the ranks to provide muscle for Shurkov."

"You said, 'The late Leonid Shurkov.'"

McManus said, "I did. This is the odd part of the puzzle. Budnov worked for Shurkov. Now both are in the morgue. LA County Sheriff's deputies found Shurkov dead yesterday just a few hours after Budnov was identified. Shurkov had a printing shop in Van Nuys. One of his workers called the cops when she found him. They're looking for a lone assassin."

"Maybe one of their own wanted them silenced," said McFadden.

"Hey, these assholes knock off each other all the time. Kind of a territory thing, you know. Convenient for the good citizens of the county. Thins the herd, but it's a paperwork headache for the cops."

"So the van was the connection, right? How's all this play into our situation?"

"This gets ugly. Crime scene techs working the van found pieces that didn't belong to Budnov. They're guessing whoever killed Budnov was wounded during the hit. We'll know eventually if they're right when lab results come back. Might take a while."

"Any security cameras at the parking lot?"

"They have some video. I haven't seen it yet. Shurkov had cameras as well. LAPD is checking both feeds. The feds are bound to get involved at some point because of the proximity to the airport. The terrorism angle, you know. Plus, they've been tracking the Russians. It's turning into a can of worms. Crazy right now. Wish they hadn't come this far south to ruin our day."

"And Kurskov's."

"How true."

"So you're telling me it's no longer being considered a home invasion gone bad."

"Absolutely. It's a no-brainer."

"These guys are obviously connected to Kurskov's murder because of the van," said McFadden. "But what's the common factor here?"

"We don't know how this got started. We have Budnov's body in the van and Shurkov's murder on the heels of that killing. It's come full circle for those two but that's all we have. That's why it's crucial to figure out what Kurskov was working on. Any new ideas?"

McFadden hedged. "His wife said he was looking at something on his computer. Whatever it was must be connected to these deaths."

"No way to restore his hard drive. We think his killers must have taken something with them. Any other ideas what he was doing?"

"You asked that before. My answer is the same: Gary Kurskov was a contract employee. He had lots of outside projects. Was pretty secretive, you know. This had to have something to do with the Russian mob. Why else would they target him?"

"Okay. Just thought I'd ask. The mob's interest is a given but the question remains: why?" McManus got to his feet, held out a hand to McFadden. "If you think of anything that rings a bell, call me."

"Will do. Thanks again for sharing this with me."

"Keep it to yourself, Sam."

From behind the indoor range's tinted, soundproofed glass walls, Wolf watched the detective say goodbye to McFadden in the lobby. With the policeman gone, he resumed firing. McFadden entered the outer sound lock, donned a pair of earmuffs, and went into the range to stand behind Wolf. The SEAL fired the Beretta's remaining five rounds at a silhouette fifteen yards away. Wolf lowered the pistol, dropped the earmuffs around his neck, and pushed a button on the partition's wall to his left. The hanging paper target flew to him along an overhead track—the silhouette's shredded center testimony to his marksmanship.

McFadden removed the earmuffs. "Nice tight group," he said.

Wolf smiled. "Practice makes perfect, Sam."

"McManus just left."

"Caught your goodbye. Did he leave in a good mood?"

"I think so."

With just the two of them in the range, Wolf took the Beretta to a long bench at the rear of the room to disassemble and clean it. McFadden pulled up a stool next to him and watched.

"Mike's a good guy, though I never really know what he's thinking."

"Cops are always fishing," said Wolf.

"Maybe. He brought me up to speed on their investigation."

"Care to share?"

Wolf ran a cleaning rod through the Beretta's barrel as McFadden replayed the detective's report, complete with warnings about possible video recordings of Shurkov's killing. Unconcerned, Wolf rubbed oil on the pistol's machined parts and floated an idea. "Maybe it's time to pay a visit to Agent Smathers and his disagreeable partner. See if I can smoke them out about what the feds are thinking."

"The less said, the better, Wolfman."

"True. But it's good to know what your enemy is thinking."

"They're not the enemy."

Wolf reassembled the Beretta. "Figure of speech."

"Right."

"Seriously, I think I should drop in to calm our friends before I go east."

McFadden said, "This is the first I've heard about your going back east. What gives?"

"Nash thinks it would be an education to go with him on his rounds. He's arranging interviews in New York. At first, I told him I'd pass, but the more I think about it..."

"You'd be in harm's way, Wolfman. Urban warfare."

"Been there before, Sam. Remember Najaf, Falluja?"

"Not the same and you know it."

"Two reasons to go. One: I'd have Nash's back. His editor is interested. He's got the scent of a good story. And two: I want to see this tale published. I want to head off this proxy war if possible. Who knows, maybe between the two of us we could flush Kurskov's other killer who seems to have slipped the net."

"Wishful thinking. Even the cops don't know for certain the person who shot the guy in the van was part of the team that killed Kurskov."

"I admit that's a leap of faith but it makes sense. They might have had a falling out. Or maybe one of them was killed to keep him quiet. Who knows how these guys operate?"

"Leave it to the FBI."

"Hey, we've both dealt with evil people before, Sam. We know how they think, how they act. I'm not going there with my eyes shut, you know."

"I don't like it."

"Didn't think you would. But you and Reggie need your space back."

One of McFadden's instructors poked his head in the range to say he had two clients waiting. Wolf put the Beretta in a case. The pair continued the conversation in McFadden's office, out of earshot.

"Look at the upside," said Wolf. "I'll talk to the feds before I go. That will take the spotlight off you. With

Shurkov and his watchdog dead the playing field has shifted. I'll say this…I think the action heads back east to Little Odessa. My instinct tells me that's the viper's nest."

"Where you will be at a disadvantage."

Putting a hand on McFadden's shoulder, Wolf said, "I've got a friend in New York who owes me. I'll call in the chit. Plus, I'll have a seasoned guide, an interpreter to break trail."

"Nash's a writer, Wolfman, not a fighter."

"He's a survivor, Sam. You said he held up well in the sandbox."

"Again, different setting."

"I'll find a way. If I get in over my head, I'll scoot."

"No, you won't. You'll figure out how to get in the middle of it."

"Appreciate the caution. But I've done all I can do here. Time to take it to the beast."

"You'll be dealing with animals."

"Then who better to go at it than a Wolf."

# Chapter 68

Ivanov's shoebox hid a cannon. Wrapped in a silicone-treated knit bag, the matte black .40 Glock 22 and three loaded fifteen-round magazines were worth their weight in gold under the circumstances. Firepower was needed to go after Verlov. The ruthless Ukrainian and his two praetorians were well armed, but Ivanov was beyond caring. He had hidden the shoebox behind a drape in Lydia's front room and waited for her to fall asleep.

Once he heard her rhythmic snoring, he got to his feet. Ivanov borrowed one of his host's canes and hobbled to the tiny kitchen. He left a one hundred dollar bill underneath a kitschy ceramic figurine. Back at the front door, he slipped outside in the cold air and turned up his coat's collar. Ivanov steadied himself with the wooden cane and went down the steps. The painful three-block journey to Helinski's hideaway almost proved his undoing. Spent from the effort, he arrived drenched in sweat.

In an alley opposite the car-lined street fronting the apartment building, Ivanov hugged the shadows. He shook out the last of his pain pills and pocketed the empty bottle. The three-story building across the street was dark except for the lobby and Helinski's top-floor corner apartment. Flickering blue light told him someone was awake.

*Probably Sergei and Gregor playing one of those mind-numbing shooting games they both loved*, thought Ivanov. Nearly invisible in the dark, he sent a text to his second-in-command.

*You there? Know it's late. Had trouble getting a ride last night. OK to come over? Can be there in fifteen minutes.*

He got an immediate reply. Helinski would wait in the entry.

Ivanov sent a last message. On my way. He put away the phone and limped across the street, taking up position behind a waist-high rectangular stone planter where he could see the stairs and elevator. He didn't have to wait long.

Helinski came down the steps, followed by a large man holding a pistol at his back. The man with the gun paused on the landing to unscrew a light bulb in a sconce, plunging the landing into darkness. Though Helinski stood under the lobby's small chandelier, he looked anything but calm.

Backing from the stone planter, Ivanov took two steps and froze. At the bricked corner to his left, soft footsteps headed his way.

*Verlov's second guard dog?*

Unseen, but pinned between the two gunmen, Ivanov knelt, pointing the Glock at the closest threat: the building's corner where he had heard footsteps. Not enough of the man showed to guarantee a decent shot.

*Come closer. Show yourself.*

Minutes passed. Ivanov's eye shifted to the stairwell. A faint glow from a cellphone outlined a face. He felt his cellphone vibrate.

*The fool is sending me a text.*

He let the call go. If he answered, the slightest movement would reveal his position. Ten minutes came and went. Fifteen minutes. Ivanov lost feeling in his wounded foot. Twenty minutes. His knees ached from kneeling.

*Wait. Whoever moves first, dies.*

Movement. Helinski, prodded by the man on the stairs, pushed open the door and spoke to the phantom at the corner. "It's off. Come inside."

Instead of retracing his steps to the rear of the building, the man at the corner gave himself away by heading to the entrance where Helinski waited in the open door.

Ivanov smiled, thinking, A blunder I would not have made. His back to the crouching shadow, Verlov's unwary gunman passed the concrete planter.

Ivanov raised the Glock, firing twice at the broad back.

The man dropped face-first.

Helinski threw himself across the threshold, blocking the open door. Spraying six shots at the lighted entry, Ivanov stayed in the dark behind the heavy planter.

The briefest of lulls. Crouching behind the stunned Helinski, the stairway shooter fired four times. Jamming a pistol to his prisoner's head, he yelled, "Stop firing or he dies!"

Ivanov struggled upright, propped himself with the cane, his body still protected by the concrete. Fighting pain as blood flooded his limbs, he yelled. "Let him go!"

"No way! Show yourself first!"

*Eight shots. Seven left. Time running out.*

A car alarm wailed, a casualty of a ricochet. Lights came on in the neighborhood. The foolhardy few appeared in windows high above the melee.

Fearless, Ivanov closed the distance, firing the Glock, killing both.

# Chapter 69

Ivanov reached Lydia's bungalow barely ahead of the sirens and chaos. A sound sleeper, she had yet to awaken. He headed for the home's cramped bathroom, his shoe filled with blood. Propping his bloodied foot on the toilet's rim, Ivanov cleaned his wound, wrapped it in gauze, then rinsed his shoe and sock. His crippled foot newly bandaged, he hopped to the couch, exhausted.

Hours later he heard Lydia rise, make tea, then slip out the door on her way to Boris Levich's apartment. Ivanov drifted asleep, replaying the shootout in his head again and again. He awoke, his foot aflame. The color had changed to a worrisome purple shade like spoiled fruit. The stumps of his missing two toes had ballooned.

*I need help. No public clinics. Who can I trust? Abraham Pavleski, the Polish doctor. Lydia would know how to get hold of him.*

For most of the morning, Ivanov carried his phone with him, waiting for Levich's call that never came. He fought the urge to call a cab and make a run past the scene of the shooting. Instead, he spent the time cleaning the Glock. The hours passed with no call. Waiting for the housekeeper helped take Ivanov's mind off his wounded foot. Now the color of an eggplant, his oozing stumps were getting worse. Walking was a challenge.

Lydia returned early evening after a long day. Ivanov spotted her mid-block, head down as if reading messages on the sidewalk. She carried a canvas shoulder bag bulging with groceries. He let her in the front door and locked it behind her. "Let me help you with those things."

Clutching the bag, she refused. "With that foot? I will do this."

Taking a seat in the kitchen, Ivanov asked, "I waited all day to hear from the boss. No call. What happened?"

"There was big shooting last night. Verlov came early today. He was there this morning when I arrived to make the breakfast. He never left the boss's side. What could I do? I have your note." She showed him the crumpled scrap of paper. "Perhaps I try again, tomorrow."

*There has to be a way to get word to Levich*, thought Ivanov.

"Don't try it," he said. "The last thing I want to do is put you at risk, Lydia."

"Ah, Dimitri. I am not afraid of Verlov. He doesn't have his two byki with him this morning. The shooting, you know."

"They are dead?"

"Yes. Verlov has to call new people to replace his two dogs."

"Both bodyguards are dead?"

"Yes. And I am sad to tell you this, Dimitri, but your Sergei Helinski was killed as well. God rest his soul. The other two, ahhh. They were trash."

"Do you know what Verlov will do now?"

"I listen but I don't hear a thing. It is a bad time for the boss. He needs you, Dimitri."

"I cannot do anything until my foot heals, Lydia."

"We will go to a clinic. They have doctors. They could look at your problem and fix it, eh?"

"Not safe with Verlov about. But I was thinking today. I have an idea."

"Good. Tell me this idea of yours. But first, I make some tea. Then I fix something for you. You must be hungry."

Ivanov took her small hand in his. "Dear Lydia, what would I do without your help? How would Boris Levich get along without you? Without the two of us?"

While the water boiled, she sat in the hard wooden chair and looked at Ivanov. "What is this idea you have?"

"You remember the retired doctor from the Old Country?"

"Ah, Abraham Pavleski, the Pole. I don't think he is real doctor."

Ivanov dismissed her criticism with a wave. "Perhaps. But he put stitches in Pavel that time the Gypsy came at him with the knife."

"Pavleski is, how they say, a quack. No matter what is wrong, he gives everyone the same pills. All his patients say he asks too many questions but never listens because he cannot stop talking."

*She's right*, he thought. *The old man could talk your ear off. But it just might work. Verlov must not know I am hurt.*

"Where is he? Do you know how to locate him?"

She took the teapot from the stove. "Sometimes he volunteers at the senior lunch program at the synagogue on Neptune Avenue. He has an office near there, you know."

Ivanov raised his leg, rolled down the sock, and showed her the discolored, swollen flesh. He said, "I need him, Lydia. Will you call him to come here?"

She poured tea in chipped cups trimmed in gold. "You want him to come here, to my house? A Pole under my roof?"

"Yes. I think this is something that must be done in secret."

"He will want money."

"I have some."

"His hands are unsteady."

"I will watch him closely."

"He will tell everyone about this, Dimitri."

"I will make him listen to reason about keeping quiet."

She sipped in silence, her watery blue eyes fixed on the cup, not Ivanov. "Okay, if this is what you want, I try. My cousin Helen will know how to find this doctor, as he calls himself. Verlov must not know I make the call, eh?"

"Yes. The doctor will need to come soon. I must be made whole again."

"Drink your tea, Dimitri. Leave this Dr. Abraham Pavleski to me."

"Will it be possible to reach him tomorrow?"

"Drink your tea. I will find him and bring him here."

"This is important."

"Drink your tea."

# Chapter 70

Wolf sensed a trap. Exiting the jet way, he spotted two TSA clones and a pair of uniformed Port Authority cops. Muscled and menacing, with huge arms, shaven heads, and frowns, the TSA pair were practiced intimidators, not the usual dull, pear-shaped, doughy hires. A supervisor wearing black, bald and unsmiling, stood with the cops.

*Overkill*, thought Wolf, *but no sense making a scene.*

The supervisor stepped forward. "Mr. Wolf?"

"In the flesh."

"Come with us, please."

Gawking fellow passengers parted like the Red Sea as Wolf and his phalanx marched past. The group took an elevator to a lower level. Wolf couldn't resist saying, "Reminds me of an airport in Russia I visited once." Silence.

The doors opened and the escorts led Wolf down a sterile hallway to a conference room, equally sterile. They put his carry-on bag in the middle of a long table.

"Do I have your permission to examine your luggage?" said one of the TSA uniforms as he donned blue rubber gloves.

"I would have been disappointed if you hadn't asked," Wolf said. "Examine to your heart's content."

A blur of blue gloves sifted the contents: shaving kit, news magazines, an outdated iPod Shuffle, sunglasses, a change of underwear, socks, and a folded blue shirt and tie.

"I travel light," Wolf said.

The man in black held out his hand. "Luggage tag, please."

"No checked luggage."

Shrugging, the man said, "Please empty your pockets, Mr. Wolf."

An annoyed Wolf did as told, spilling keys, cellphone, coins, and mints.

"Your wallet, please."

"I know exactly how much cash I have," he said. More silence.

*A humorless bunch*, he thought. "Care to tell me what this is all about, gentlemen?"

No answer.

"Now I remember why this reminds me of that Russian airport."

The TSA man returned Wolf's wallet and pushed his pocket's contents across the table to him. "Thank you for your cooperation, sir."

"My pleasure, comrade."

A frown. The TSA guys and the cops left the room trailed by the supervisor, who turned on the threshold and said, "Can I get you a coffee or a water?"

"No, but an explanation with a shot of hazelnut would be nice."

"In due time." The door shut.

Wolf roamed, scanning the walls, corners, and the table's underside for recording devices or cameras. His search was interrupted by a knock.

The State Department's Robert Nells entered, bow tie and tweed jacket as Wolf remembered from his interview in Washington. Without offering a hand, the stoop-shouldered Nells took a chair opposite Wolf.

"We meet again, Commander Wolf. Please, have a seat. You're due an explanation, of course."

"Damn right, I am. I fly to California for several weeks and when I return I find myself in the Balkans. What gives?"

"Your humor and sarcasm still intact, I see."

"I never leave home without it."

Nells said, "I, on the other hand, never bring my disagreeable executive assistant with me when I leave Washington for a meeting with you."

"That's the only bright spot in the day so far. What gives?"

Nells placed a folder in front of him. "What gives indeed, Commander. You have been busy. A traveling man."

"No secret there. I went to San Diego to see friends."

Nells opened the file, his eyes on Wolf. Without looking at the paperwork, he said, "Ah, Major Sam McFadden, Army Special Forces."

"And his wife, Reggie."

"Ah, yes, Regina Rosario McFadden. An impressive lady in her own right. Their story...your story as well...is most interesting. Quite the adventure in the Philippines."

"You're not interested in the Philippines."

"No, I am not," said Nells, sifting his papers. "I am here to talk to you about the late Gary Kurskov, an employee of Sam McFadden's firm. You've had an interesting time in San Diego as well, Commander."

"You've heard the expression 'Shit happens,' I'm sure."

"Not often quoted in my circles. But I'm familiar with the slogan. So, what exactly did happen during your California visit?"

"You seem fond of the Socratic method, so I'll ask: what do you think happened in California?"

"Fair enough. And just so we don't waste time, mine or yours, let's say you went to San Diego to ask for Sam McFadden's help in understanding what was in a certain book you and the late Commander Colter were given during your trip to Russia."

Wolf parried the blunt question. "What makes you think we received a book in Russia? How did you reach that conclusion?"

"I appeal to your patriotism, Commander. We know you got this book from a contact while in Russia. We can assume Dan Colter encrypted the files and sent them stateside. Do you deny that?"

"You expect me to answer these allegations without counsel present? Since you're being so forthcoming about what you think you know, tell me how you reached that conclusion."

"We're dancing around the subject," said Nells. "Time is of the essence. The world is fragmenting around us. Yet you insist on minor points about the how and why of our knowledge of this book of secrets."

"You want to be frank? Okay. Dan Colter was murdered in Russia...yes, you heard me correctly, murdered. After his murder, I returned home to find my house violated by someone who scrubbed my computer clean of certain emails. My gut instinct tells me it was a black bag job done for that purpose. I'll bet no legal search warrant exists for that piece of work. Care to comment on that?"

Nells drummed his fingers on the table. "Not my department."

Wolf snapped at him. "Not your department? Does that mean your office didn't authorize it, or you farmed it out?"

"No comment."

"And what about Dan Colter's home? They not only screwed with his emails, they took his computer with them. I suppose you didn't know about that either. How did that happen? Same freelancers? Did you also know the Russian mob also paid a visit to Colter's place?"

Nells stayed silent.

"Did you ask those Russian scum what they were doing that night in Virginia Beach? I was there, Nells. I saw them arrested. Why would they be nosing around Colter's place?"

"No comment."

"You need a new line. The Russkis didn't bother with a warrant. Maybe your guys didn't either. This is still a country of laws. At least I thought it was. Can you produce a warrant for my place or Colter's?"

About to answer, Wolf cut Nells off. "Yeah, I know. No comment."

"Be reasonable, Commander. At least tell us what happened to the book."

"What if this book doesn't exist? Consider that possibility."

Nells blanched. "Doesn't exist? But we know Colter sent the contents."

"Don't think I don't know what you're up to, Nells. I'm telling you only what I think you need to hear, got it?"

"But you've practically admitted to having possession of the book."

"That's your interpretation. If that book existed, only two people knew what was in it and those people are dead."

"Colter and Kurskov?"

"I'm not saying another word without counsel present."

"What if I cut you loose? Would you be more amenable to help us?"

Wolf shrugged.

"What are you doing in New York?"

"I have friends everywhere."

"But specifically, New York?"

"I don't have to answer that. And how did you know I was coming to New York?"

"I don't have to answer that."

"Are you really with State? If you dropped your pants, would I find CIA tattooed on your ass?"

"Really, Commander, people think the CIA's under every rock."

"With good reason. You'd like me to think the prohibition against operating at home doesn't apply to the CIA since we're dealing with an international question."

"I'm thinking no such thing."

"Bullshit. Why are you so interested in this book anyway?"

"We think it might be a key to dismantling the Russian *Mafiya*. Our hope is it might give us a look at the nexus between terrorist networks, cartels, arms smuggling and global drug markets. "

"That's expecting a lot from a little book."

"That's part of what we do in Threat Finance, Commander. We have to be at our best every day. The enemy is constantly changing, very fluid. We need all the help we can get to keep our country safe."

"And you set the Constitution aside when it suits you?"

"Of course not."

"Maybe you and your Threat Finance buddies should start with the banks who operate with blinders on."

"That's a problem, I agree."

"Are we done here? I do have a life, you know."

"For now."

"I don't want to find myself being hauled off an airplane in front of an audience again."

"Then keep in mind what we've talked about. We need your help."

"Talk to my lawyers."

"I'm sure we'll meet again. Always a pleasure," said Nells. This time he held out his hand. Wolf ignored the gesture and walked out.

Alone in the wake of Wolf's release, a reluctant Nells took a cellphone from his pocket and tapped a contact's number.

"We agreed you were never to call me."

"I realize that, but we have a problem," said Nells.

"Define the problem."

"Wolf continues defiant. Denies having the book. Seems particularly upset about losing his emails from Kazakhstan and the trashing of Colter's townhouse."

"Your diplomatic approach failed?"

"It's a work in progress."

"Huh, Wolf is proving to be a thorn in your side."

Nells nodded as he listened. "Increasingly so."

"Well, he's your problem. Doing things your way is not getting us what we need. Perhaps stronger measures ought to be taken."

"I reluctantly agree."

"Well, then, get to it."

"Very well. I'll arrange a meeting when I return to Washington."

"Why wait? Make the call today. Get the ball rolling."

Eyes closed, Nells pinched the bridge of his nose. "I'd still prefer to find out what Wolf is doing in New York."

"A waste of time. You don't have the manpower on site to do that. I can't authorize that kind of expenditure without raising eyebrows here."

"Given time perhaps another run at him would prove fruitful."

"I doubt it. You've failed to settle this situation. I'm not the least bit enthusiastic about a third go. You know what needs to be done. Do it."

"We'll lose our chance at getting the book."

"Face it. You've lost whatever leverage you thought you had with Wolf. Put an end to it...or I'll find someone else willing to do it."

Sighing, Nells agreed, saying, "I'll make the call."

"Good choice. Don't contact me again unless it's to report that Wolf is no longer a threat. Do we understand each other?"

"Completely."

# Chapter 71

Figuring he could shake any airport tails Nells may have assigned to him, Wolf bought an AirTrain ticket on the Long Island Railroad. Forty-five minutes later he arrived at Penn Station. Confident he wasn't being shadowed, he walked a few blocks, found a storefront on west Thirtieth Street selling prepaid phones, and bought two. He crushed his old phone under a heel and kicked the guts into a storm drain outside the store. Using a new phone, he called Nash. Told to take a taxi to a mid-Manhattan boutique hotel, Wolf was instructed to meet the journalist in the inn's bar. Thirty minutes later, Wolf walked in the hotel's Art Deco watering hole and spotted Nash in a red leather booth. He slid across from him and told of his airport encounter.

"You seem pretty mellow about it," said Nash. "I would have called my lawyer."

"I didn't want to stare at four walls for hours while they argued about my release."

"Assholes. Sounds like FBI or CIA has a hand in this."

"They might be working with State on the Threat Finance angle," said Wolf. "I checked my sources about Nells. He is definitely assigned to that slot. My friend Colter worked under their roof for a while. I'd be willing to bet Nells at least knew who Colter was."

"Maybe one of those strange bedfellows arrangements."

"I don't want to sound paranoid," said Wolf, "but I dumped my phone after I bought a couple new ones. Didn't want to take the chance there might have been some sleight of hand going on when those guys were going through my stuff at JFK."

"Probably not a bad idea. You'd be more sophisticated than me when it comes to spotting a tracer or tracking device. Go through a lot of phones, do you?"

"An ounce of prevention..."

"Is worth a pound of tossed cell phones, apparently," said Nash. "If they bugged it they probably have your last location anyway."

"That would put them on the doorstep of Penn Station. Let 'em chase the trains for a couple days.

"So, anyway," Wolf said, "where did you set us up?"

"I have a place in Brooklyn, a loft I've been renovating. My wife and I bought it when I was working for the *Times*. It was an investment. When she was killed I lost motivation. Moved to the opposite coast. I've been back occasionally to put in some hours on it, but my heart's not in it. Still, it's a good location for us. Union Avenue and Second Street. Neighborhood's turning kinda artsy. Lots of charm."

"You don't have to sell me, Nash. All I need is running water and a place to lay my head."

"A real monk, huh? Maybe you need to get married, man."

"You're not the first person to tell me that."

Nash rattled on. "The loft has plenty of space, three-story brick, good security. Wi-Fi, the works. The bottom two floors are gutted, a work-in-progress, but we have the top floor. It's not finished but it will do for what we need. It comes with a car if we need it."

"Might come in handy instead of using public transportation."

"Yeah, it would give us flexibility. I don't think we'll be here long. Get in, get the goods, and get out."

"I like that," said Wolf. "My kind of mission."

"How did the situation end in San Diego?"

"I think things have run their course in California. That's why I'm here."

"Glad you made it. We'll check in with McFadden while we're here. He's pretty tight with the San Diego cops. They'd tell him more than the average guy. As for now, allow me to buy you a drink, Commander."

Nash called for a second Manhattan. "Hey, we're in the Big Apple."

Wolf ordered a Guinness and sipped while Nash outlined their visit to Brighton Beach—Little Odessa. "Plus, there's a rogue banker who was a good source in the past until the feds busted him on an old insider trading rap. He said he had some info on people I might be interested in."

"I'm up for whatever you have in mind. As long as you get the word out about what's going on in Ukraine, I'll be happy." Wolf also told Nash about Royce, his contact in Queens. A former Army Ranger and retired cop, Royce would add an extra level of security to what they were doing. Pleasantly surprised when Nash didn't object, Wolf assured him his friend was "a good man to have watching your back in a fight."

An hour later, the two hailed a cab and headed for Nash's Brooklyn hideaway. Halfway there, Wolf insisted on getting out and catching a second taxi. Nash went one way, Wolf another. Stopping mid-block, Wolf paid his tab and circled back to the loft's entrance on foot. Nash let him in.

They rode the building's rattling freight elevator to the top floor.

"Was that thing with the cabs really necessary?"

"If we were being tailed and lost the guy by changing taxis, we're good. But if we were being followed and didn't shake him, at least we didn't make it easy for them. Doesn't hurt to vary your routine."

A skeptical Nash said, "What if it was just your paranoia and there was nobody there? Would we still be good?"

"Laugh if you want, but you're never good in this game. Stay unpredictable. It keeps you alive. You of all people should know that."

"My apologies, you are absolutely correct." Brightening, Nash changed topics. "Pick one of the three available bedrooms. There are two bathrooms as well."

"Heads," corrected Wolf.

"Touché. There are two heads. And twelve-foot ceilings throughout."

Wolf took the center room. He dumped the contents of his carry-on luggage on a bed and examined each piece. "Clean," he announced.

"No bugs then," said Nash.

Nash hooked up his laptop and tacked a large map of Brighton Beach to a cloth-covered wall panel. Backing up to admire his work, he turned to Wolf and said, "Shall we begin?"

# Chapter 72

*San Diego*

Spanglish rap boomed from the takeout window of a Mexican restaurant where detectives Mike McManus and Bob Mathis were eating lunch on the outdoor patio. McManus already had a spot of salsa on a new tie. A cellphone buzzed. Balancing a half-eaten chicken burrito in one hand, cell in the other, he growled, "McManus. Go ahead."

His partner looked up, expectant. "LA," mouthed McManus. He listened, his response ranging from frowns to surprise. He thanked his caller and he put away the phone.

"Good news? Bad news? What'd they tell you?"

"We have a palm print and a face to go with the van. No ID yet. LA says the parking lot time stamp on the van's arrival was 1:45. The camera angle was poor but they did get a guy on film parking the van. And the shuttle driver says he thinks the guy who parked the van was definitely limping. He remembers dropping him at terminal four. That serves American, Quantas, and Cathay Pacific."

"Can't see our bad boy running to Australia or Asia."

McManus rubbed the salsa stain on his tie with a wet napkin. "See, that's why you made detective, Mathis."

"Did they ask the airlines for video?"

"Nope. The airport has security cameras at checkpoints. Our boy showed up in an American Airlines wheelchair. The guys are trying to locate the chair valet to see which gate he used. We get the gate, we get the flight."

Mathis said, "Piece of cake so far."

"Why would a guy use a wheelchair unless he needed it?" said McManus. "Doesn't make sense. Unless he thought he could clear the security checkpoint quicker."

"Yeah, but doing it by wheelchair would just attract attention. People might remember you. Plus, you're at a disadvantage in a chair. Nah, I think the chair means our gimp is hurting."

"Sheer genius," said McManus. "You keep this up and I'll be working for you."

"I'm just saying—"

"No, you're right. Our suspect is hurting. Those pieces in the van might belong to him."

"You gonna call your buddy Sam McFadden with this info?"
McManus bristled. "Who says I'm phoning McFadden?"
"It's no secret, Mike. Sort of a courtesy thing, right?"
"Geez, a guy can't brief a citizen without everyone knowing."
"So, you gonna call him?"
"Soon as I finish cleaning my tie."
"Are you gonna finish the rest of your burrito?"
McManus pushed the uneaten half to Mathis. "You got a hollow leg, you know that?"
"C'mon, I skipped breakfast." Mathis shoved a good portion in his mouth.
"Coulda fooled me. C'mon, let's make a run to McFadden's office and deliver the news in person. Maybe we could get in some range time."
"Soon's I finish the burrito."

# Chapter 73

Nash recited the day's itinerary to Wolf over coffee. "First guy we want to see is Anatoly Feldman. Interesting character. Dual American-Israeli citizenship like a lot of these folks. He's done time for arms smuggling. Knows all the players. A bit of a Judas goat I've used before."

"Can he be trusted?"

"Only when dishing out dirt about others. Absolutely untrustworthy when it comes to questions about his own involvement in various schemes."

"And you've used him before?"

"We go back to my first days stringing for the Times."

"Okay, after him what do we do?"

"The banker."

"Then?"

"Gets a little trickier from that point on. We'll need your Ranger buddy along once the word on the street gets out about my asking questions."

"My advice is to keep moving. Don't stay too long in one place."

"Good idea."

"Any way to gauge how long we'll be out?"

"No. But we'll want to drop in on the crowd at the Caspian Nights club. It's *THE* spot to be seen these days. Always good for picking up gossip from some of the wannabes. They love to feel important. They're not all made men but they'll act like it. I'll appeal to their vanity. It works most of the time."

"What do you want our role to be?"

"Cover my six, as you guys like to say."

"Are we going to find out about those missing funds being used for the proxy war?"

"I'm going to try."

"Just so you know, Royce is going to fix me up. Both of us are going to be armed."

"Why not, everybody else will be. These guys do love their guns."

"I'll call Royce and tell him where to meet. He's ready to rock and roll."

"Okay, let's do this."

# Chapter 74

Ivanov tucked the pistol at the small of his back, threw on his coat, then scribbled a note for Lydia. He phoned for a taxi. When the car arrived he locked the house and shuffled to the idling cab.

Smelling of garlic and tobacco, the gruff bearded driver took Ivanov to a newsstand for a paper, then drove to a bakery and liquor store. The cab went down Lancaster, turned south on East Seventh and dropped him at a peeling clapboard house nestled between aging homes. Ivanov labored up the wooden steps and rang the bell. An overweight blonde in a loose red silk kimono and little else

cracked open the door. A cigarette bobbed in painted lips. Nodding for him to come in, she bellowed up the stairs in a whiskey voice, "Toba, your long-lost lover boy is here!"

A shrill girlish echo from the second floor. "Who?"

"The wandering Dimitri Ivanov favors us with his presence. Get your ass down here!"

Planting a foot on the threshold, he said, "How you been, Esther?"

Glancing at the cane and his pained expression, she said, "A helluva lot better than you, apparently."

"Dropped a crate on my foot at the warehouse."

She uttered a disbelieving, "Uh-huh" and let him pass. "You should get it looked at."

"Got Dr. Pavleski to fix me up."

"That drunk? That was a mistake. You should have gone to a real doctor or one of those street clinics. Pavleski doesn't even know which end of the needle to use when he sews you up."

"He was willing and affordable."

"You'll be sorry, Dimitri."

"I don't think so."

When footsteps sounded on the stairs, the blonde sauntered into a smoky back room where a TV game show was in progress. She shut a pair of French doors behind her. A plump pale brunette wearing leotards and a plum-colored top baring cleavage bounded down the stairs.

She kissed Ivanov's cheek. "Hey, Dimitri."

"Long time, no see, Toba. How you doing?"

She spotted the cane. "What's with the walking stick?"

"Accident. Crate got away from me. It's healing. You got some time?"

"I guess. What's in the bags?"

Ivanov pulled out the vodka, followed by *bulochki s makom*.

"Russian poppy seed rolls, my favorite. You remembered."

Rewarded with a kiss, Ivanov stroked her cheek. Clapping her hands, she said, "I'll make some tea. We can share the rolls and catch up with each other. Where have you been, Dimitri? We don't see you anymore."

"Business. The boss keeps me busy, you know."

"You still working for Boris Levich?"

"Of course."

"You ought to quit doing those things."

"What things?"

Frowning, the girl said, "You know what I mean, Dimitri."

"I don't want to spoil my visit talking about that."

"Stuff like that big shooting two nights ago, huh?"

"Really? What shooting?"

"Esther said it was some apartment building not far from the boardwalk. Sirens. Cops. Ambulances. We both heard it. I couldn't sleep after that."

"Oh?" He acted surprised. "Is it on the news?"

"Good luck getting Esther to give up her game shows to see the news."

Waiting for the water to boil, he put aside the cane and sat at the kitchen table in a square of sunlight pouring through the window. "I wish it was summer already."

Toba bubbled. "Oh, me too. I love to sit by the ocean. If we were rich I'd buy a huge mansion on Long Island and have parties all night long."

"A nice dream to have."

The kettle screamed for attention. She poured boiling water in a glazed pot and dropped in a silver tea ball. She chatted non-stop while arranging a set of cups and saucers at the small table. Her chirping reminded Ivanov why he had fled her company from time to time. Pleasant enough, and a compliant lover, Toba was a talker, even under the sheets.

"I'll take Esther some tea and one of the poppy seed rolls. Don't go away." She put a cup of tea and a roll on a tray and took it to her aunt.

Ivanov closed his eyes against the stabbing pain from the Pole's botched stitches the days before. He hoped he wouldn't have to ask Esther to drive him to a clinic in Brooklyn after all.

The sun poured through the kitchen window, warming him and taking his mind off the pulsing foot. He sipped the tea, devoured one of the rolls, and was starting on a second one when Toba returned, her dark eyes fixed on him. She put down the empty tray and sank into a chair opposite Ivanov, continuing to stare at him.

Esther wandered in from her television, silent and wary.

Squinting at the women, he sat up. "What? You both look like you've seen a ghost."

"Maybe we have."

"The TV," said the older woman.

"What about it?"

"Dimitri. You're on television."

# Chapter 75

"It's not me."

Esther was having none of it. She and Toba stared at the TV news. "It looks like you."

"Doesn't even come close," Ivanov growled from the couch.

"It's you."

The artist's police sketch on the noon news bore a striking resemblance to him. Esther and her niece Toba kept glancing at the television, then back to Ivanov, then back to the television. Finally, the newsreaders moved on to something else. Esther muted the talking heads' blather.

"They say you're involved in two killings in California. Is it true?" Toba stood apart from Ivanov as though he were diseased. Her aunt threw both arms around her, certain they had a madman in their house.

"You can't stay," Esther insisted. "If they find you here we'll be arrested for hiding you."

"I'm not hiding," said Ivanov, rising from the couch. "I'm visiting. And that's not me on the screen. This is probably more of Verlov's bullshit. He's thrown me to the cops for some reason."

"Like maybe being involved in a certain shooting the other night?"

"More bullshit." Ivanov's face hardened. "Hey, Esther, do not believe everything you hear. They've got me mixed up with someone else who looks like me."

"So you're innocent," she said. "You still have to leave, Dimitri."

"Okay, I'll go…"

The women sighed as one.

"When it gets dark," he said. "I'm not going out in broad daylight. It's too risky. Verlov probably has guys looking for me."

"It's a shame," said Esther, dripping sarcasm, "especially since you're not involved in either of those two crimes, eh?"

"Shut up!"

"Why should I? You're the one who came barging in here. You're the one they're after."

"Esther, you got a big mouth. I'm telling you to shut the fuck up. I'll leave when I'm ready, not before." Glancing at a wall clock, he said, "I've got five hours to kill—"

Esther, defiant, taunted. "I hope that's all you kill."

Shouting, "Enough!" Ivanov struck her with an open hand.

Falling to the floor, Esther cowered at the foot of the sofa, a hand at her mouth, the kimono riding up over doughy thighs. Stunned, Toba knelt to comfort her aunt. Blood trickled from Esther's lips and both women glared at him. Taking a stuffed chair opposite the couch, Ivanov pulled out his Glock 22, resting it in his lap. "I'm not going anywhere."

"You didn't have to do that, Dimitri."

Unmoved Ivanov said, "Clean her up, Toba. She opens her mouth again and—"

"And what? You didn't have to hit her, bastard."

"I didn't hit her, I slapped her. There's a difference."

Ignoring Toba, his charade of an impromptu social visit exposed, Ivanov thought about his situation—hobbled, identified on TV, no wheels, no mates, and running out of options. Unless he got to Levich, help from that quarter was out of reach. Verlov was the key. He had to be dealt with, and fast.

A seething Toba went to the kitchen, returning with a glass of water for her shaken aunt. Huddling together on the couch, the two women stared at Ivanov with undisguised fury. Despite their palpable anger he remembered something Sergei had once said about Verlov's weak spot. The outline of a plan took shape. Alone, he would have to take the fight to the Ukrainian usurper. No other way. There was no choice. It would have to be tonight.

# Chapter 76

When it got dark Ivanov commandeered Esther's car along with her as driver. He had her cruise past Dagmar Danilev's modest house. Verlov's newly hired byki were sitting in a parked town car. The glowing red tips of cigarettes belonging to the two lookouts betrayed them.

*Verlov was likely inside, bedding Dagmar for the night.*

"Go around back," ordered Ivanov. "Make a slow pass through the alley but don't stop." She did as told. The back of Dagmar's house was unguarded.

Ivanov crowed to his reluctant chauffeur. "Cocky sonofabitch. He leaves the rear of the house open."

White-knuckled, Esther clung to the wheel. "Maybe a trap," she said.

"You don't understand men like Verlov," said Ivanov. "He thinks it's smart to have those two wolves on duty out front. They might as well be wearing a big neon sign. Then he leaves the back porch unguarded. What kind of fool does that?"

"Stop at the mouth of the alley," he ordered, "and let me out."

"That's it? You're not going to hurt me?"

"Wait here. Keep the car running. I won't be long. You'd better be here when I get back. If you're not here then I will hurt you. Understand?"

Wide-eyed and nodding, she did as told. Stopping at the alley's entry, she let Ivanov out and put the car in park. Gambling on his cobbled-together plan, Ivanov worked his way along the alley, hugging shadows of backyard fences, garages, and the occasional hedge. Feral cats perched on garbage cans fled his approach. He reached the chest-high chain-link fence surrounding the Danilev house. The excitement of what he was about to do overpowered any pain he might have felt. Whatever humiliation he had suffered at Verlov's hand was about to be erased forever. He slipped through the gate and gained the back porch without being heard. It had been deceptively easy.

*What if Esther is right?* he wondered. *What if it is a trap?*

The weight of the Glock 22 in his hand dispelled any fear. *Caution was for cowards.*

Ivanov crept toward the back door, silently cursing his throbbing foot, the sutures loosening with each step he took. Another score yet to settle.

He stuffed the pistol in his waistband and used a plastic credit card to force the door's lock. It yielded on his second try. He stepped inside a dimly lighted back hallway with ancient linoleum flooring, hideous flora wallpaper, and tin ceiling. Standing like a statue, Ivanov slowed his breathing and pounding heart.

Muted moans, cries, and grunting escaped from the master bedroom to his right. He imagined a writhing Dagmar pinned beneath a sweating Verlov just feet away.

Ivanov eased along the narrow back hall, feeling for the bedroom's doorknob with a gloved hand. He pushed open the door, the sounds of hurried rutting masking his footsteps. Pointing his pistol at a tangled mound of heaving sheets, Ivanov barked, "VERLOV!"

He fired four times. White flashes. Screams.

It was over in seconds.

Ivanov backpedaled from the room, retracing his footsteps to the kitchen, then the porch. He stumbled down the steps, heading for the alley.

No waiting car. No Esther.

*Bitch. You'll pay.*

Ivanov fled the alley for a gap between two houses opposite. He ignored his leaden foot in flight and emerged on a parallel street, euphoric at what he had done.

Two blocks from the scene, Ivanov hailed a gypsy cab amid the sirens. He directed the driver to Lydia's street and got out mid-block. Paid and dismissed, the taxi headed back to Brighton Beach Boulevard to troll for night owls. Inside the bungalow's iron gate, Ivanov found the front door key beneath the stone urn. He limped inside, placed the Glock inside his shoebox safe, and sank down on the couch in Lydia's front room.

# Chapter 77

At ten o'clock the next morning, Nash and Wolf met Royce in a hookah bar in Brooklyn's Sheepshead Bay. Despite the mid-morning hour, the café's interior was dimly lit. Furnishings were limited to small round tables in the front room and pillows piled on thick carpet in a semi-private alcove in the back. Nash's informer, Anatoly Feldman, had picked the spot and was due in thirty minutes. Royce had claimed a back room corner where he fashioned a perch out of embroidered cushions piled on the floor. Contentedly puffing a silver hookah, Royce hailed the two. Lean, with close-cropped salt-and-pepper hair, Royce wore two day's worth of stubble, baggy fatigue pants, black high-tops, and a gray hoodie in which he hid his handgun.

Wolf introduced the two. "Nash, meet Royce, former Army Ranger and cop. He doesn't suffer fools lightly but he makes the occasional exception...me, for example."

Royce blew a perfect smoke ring, flashed a Cheshire grin, and shook Nash's hand. "Writer, huh?"

"I am," said Nash. "We're meeting one of my sources, Anatoly Feldman. He suggested this spot. Not my first choice."

Royce laughed, a good sign.

"Obviously he didn't want to chance a meeting in Brighton Beach," said Nash. "Probably didn't want the wrong people to see us together."

"Feldman's Armenian," added Wolf. "Has family ties to the Russian mob. We're here to watch Nash's back while he pumps this guy."

"We sitting in?" said Royce.

Nash said, "No offense, but he'd never go for that."

"We're strictly security," said Wolf.

"If Feldman makes you guys I'll be sure to tell him you're with me," said Nash. "He's more likely to talk if it's just the two of us."

Drawing deep on the hookah, Royce nodded, sending a pair of smoke rings to the ceiling. Nash looked at Wolf and gestured to a low table along the wall. "I'll take a spot over there," he said.

"We've got you covered. Make sure you stay in sight. If Feldman wants you to go somewhere with him, say no. Got it?"

Nash pushed an ottoman against the wall, then signaled a server and ordered a pot of black tea and pastries for his expected guest.

Glancing down at Royce, Wolf asked, "What are you smoking?"

"Coffee and vanilla. Smooth. Try it." He offered the mouthpiece to Wolf, who declined.

"Don't know what you're missing, man."

"Yes, I do. I'll cover the entry," he told Nash and took a seat in the front room where he could see the other two. *Royce looks the part*, thought Wolf, smiling. *He might be a Ranger and an ex-cop, but he's perfect for this job. A dangerous chameleon.*

If Feldman sought anonymity in his meeting with Nash, he didn't show it. He arrived in a lime green jogging suit, turning heads despite the café's dim interior. Rotund, hawk-nosed, with hooded eyes and an unruly head of graying hair, Feldman sported a nervous facial tic and an attitude.

Plopping down on a pyramid of pillows, the Armenian said, "Why I agreed to meet with you I'll never know. Didn't you learn your lesson the last time? You nearly got us both killed. After this we're done."

"Consider me curious, Anatoly. Curious about rumors I've heard of a special book your fellow gangsters want. What's so important about it, anyway?"

Feldman eyed the pastries and teapot. Snapping his fingers for a server's attention, he ordered vodka instead.

"Little early for that, isn't it?"

"I need it. About this book, eh? Pay attention, I'm only going to say this once. Go ahead, make notes." Feldman rattled on, pausing only when the delinquent server arrived with the vodka. He dismissed her with a scolding frown. Feldman spoke in low, rapid whispers, answering Nash's patient questions. The vodka helped. Forty minutes later, he got to his feet and slithered away.

Wolf waited ten minutes before joining Nash. "Get everything you needed?"

Nash put away his notebook. "And then some. You can't make this stuff up. Well, I suppose you could but who would believe it?"

"Care to explain?"

"Later."

"Now what?" said Wolf.

Already on his cellphone, Nash held a finger to his lips. Wolf wandered to Royce in his corner. "I'd say we're done here."

Royce uncoiled. "That was one nervous dude."

"That's what happens when you play both sides."

"Got something for you in my car, Wolfman."

"Good. Felt naked in here. This could get dicey before we're done."

"Be prepared. That's my motto."

"Works for me." Wolf glanced at Nash who had ended his call. "Let's pack up. I think he's on to somewhere else."

"Good. This place is too dark, too confined, and too expensive."

Nash overheard the remark. "Then you'll like the next spot. We'll meet my banker friend in the open, a cemetery."

"Love the symbolism," said Royce.

"Being in the open has its own particular set of risks," said Wolf.

"Not a problem," said Royce. "I'm good to go."

The three went out into sunshine, Royce in the lead to check the street.

# Chapter 78

*Green-Wood Cemetery, Brooklyn*

Wolf and Nash drove north on Ocean Parkway, Royce following. They left the parkway, heading west along the wooded margins of the cemetery's 478 acres. Entering the main gate's Gothic Revival arches, they followed a serpentine road to their rendezvous point—the graveyard's iconic Pierrepont family tomb, an arched edifice crowning a leafy man-made rise.

A tour group had abandoned the tomb and was descending the knoll. Following a backpedaling guide lecturing among the headstones, one dozen people made their way to the road. As the group filed past Wolf noticed a single car parked fifty feet ahead of them, its driver nowhere in sight.

"Your banker friend is here."

Wolf and Nash got out of the car as the last of the gawkers hurried to catch up with the group.

"Do you know who is buried here?" said Nash.

"No clue."

Royce came up behind them, humorless. "Lots of dead people."

The writer spread his arms. "Boss Tweed, Louis Tiffany, and Leonard Bernstein, among the many famous and infamous."

Royce eyed the retreating tour and the surrounding crypts. Splitting to keep his distance from the other two, he headed up the hill. Circling right, he flanked the Pierrepont tomb to his left. Nash approached the ostentatious sarcophagus.

"Royce always like this?"

Wolf, his eyes on the rows of headstones and statues, answered without looking at Nash. "Always. He's got us covered. Good man to have on the job. You'll see."

At the crest, a lone figure in a tan raincoat stepped from behind entwined stone angels. "Over here."

Wolf drifted past the family monument, hand in his jacket.

"The banker. It's okay," said Nash. "Stay behind."

Melting into the graves, Royce disappeared. From his position next to a gnarled tree, Wolf kept Nash and the raincoat in sight. A decent shot from this range, he thought. Certainly makeable if they stay where they are.

They did. Nash scribbled notes, took an envelope, and wrote some more. The other man talked with his hands and, at one point, made a call on a cellphone, which he offered, to Nash. A movement caught Wolf's eye. Royce, barely visible, had changed positions.

A black car passed on the road below, drawing Wolf's attention. Two men got out, one carrying a bouquet. The pair paused behind Nash's car, then walked to a headstone steps from the road. A silent moment at the stone to lay flowers on the grave, a return to their car, and then the men were gone, to Wolf's relief. An hour passed. The meeting broke up. Wandering down the hill like a bereaved mourner, the raincoat got in his car and left. Nash lingered at the Pierrepont's elaborate tomb, Wolf close behind. As a precaution, Royce stayed out.

"Another fruitful meeting, I hope," said Wolf.

"Interesting," said Nash. "Two years ago my source helped shepherd the charter for a boutique bank—New Amsterdam Global Bank and Trust. Says once they were up and running he was given a title, a desk, and not much to do. They handled mostly commercial accounts from European banks and the occasional private client. They were moving a lot of money from day one. But he didn't think what they were doing passed the smell test. He asked too many questions. Last year he was let go with a nice severance package."

Wolf said, "This is the guy who got busted for insider trading, right?"

"The same. He was advising the bank on an unofficial basis. Took the job to make a living."

"Guy's gotta eat," said Wolf. "Does he think the bank's in bed with the Russian mob?"

"Something like that. He gave me names, dates, and a list of clients. He said he talked to the feds but didn't think they were interested."

"I think I know the end of this story," said Wolf. "The bank's a Laundromat for the mob. Part of your story right there. Now what?"

"And now," said Nash, "we go back to our hide. I need to wrap my brain around everything these two sources have told me. It's almost too much information to digest. I want to see what gold I've panned so far."

"And later?"

"Later, we go into the lion's mouth."

"The nightclub?"

"Caspian Nights," said Nash. "It'll shake things up."

"Bearding the lion in his den, as they say. When do
we go?"

"Give me one day to put my notes in order. Say,
where's Royce?"

Wolf turned in a circle, his eyes on the tombs. "Oh,
he's out there somewhere playing ghost."

"Interesting character."

"That," said Wolf, "is an understatement."

# Chapter 79

Arriving at seven as usual, Lydia bustled about in Levich's
kitchen as she had for every day of the past ten years. For the
first time in months, Konstantin Verlov's brooding face was
nowhere in sight. With no time to dwell on his absence, she
delivered a breakfast of tea, fruit, and fresh rolls to Levich's
dining room. She brushed past a pair of nameless byki who had
replaced Verlov's men and carried the tray to the table she had
set with linen and silver the night before. She placed Levich's
breakfast at a place set for one and poured steaming tea in a
porcelain cup. The morning's papers, one in Russian, one in
English, were arranged to the right of the tray, a large
magnifying glass on top.

Precisely at nine, Boris Levich, white shirt and tie
underneath a red silk smoking jacket, crossed the entry hall.
He sat at the head of the table and tested the tea. It had
cooled to his taste. Perfect, as usual. This morning, however,
Lydia closed the room's double doors behind her and timidly
approached Levich.

The old man looked at the small woman over the cup's
brim. "Yes, what is it, Lydia?"

She fished in her apron and placed Ivanov's note next to
the tray without saying a word.

Levich held the slip of paper under the polished lens. "Dimitri? You have this from Dimitri? Where is he? Have you seen him?"

"Yes. He has returned from California. He asked me to give this to you. He requests you to please call him if you wish to do so."

"Why has he not contacted me before?"

"No chance," she said. "He was afraid you would be angry with him for not calling you as soon as he returned. He thought Verlov would not let him talk to you directly. That, plus he was hurt in California, you know."

"Dimitri hurt? Tell me what you know, Lydia."

"I am not certain of all that has happened. He made me call a doctor to the house to look at his foot. He's not so good to walk, you know."

Levich let the scrap of paper fall to the tray. "Of course I will call. He must come here immediately to be by my side. This is no time to be absent."

He waved at the sideboard. "Bring me the phone."

She plucked a phone from its cradle and placed it before him. "Do you wish me to remain?"

Levich dismissed her. "No, go about your duties, Lydia." She bowed and slipped through the doors.

When Ivanov answered, Levich raised his voice. "Dimitri! What is this? I have this note in my hands. Yes, Lydia gives me this just moments ago. What has happened? Why have you not returned to see me? What? Never mind the details. You must come to me immediately."

Levich listened to Ivanov, his brow furrowed. "Not to worry. I take care of everything. I must have you back with me, my boy. I send one of Anton Sheveski's boys for you. Where are you? Lydia's place. Yes, I know. I send her with Sheveski's man, okay?"

Leaning back in his chair, Levich was relieved. "We will get you to a proper doctor. Yes, I know Verlov has been involved in many things. We can talk of this when you are here. Do not stay away one more moment, Dimitri. You have been missed, my boy."

# Chapter 80

Dimitri came in from the cold to Levich's warm welcome.

Ivanov, greeted with open arms, remained grateful but cautious. "Thank you for sending for me."

"And why not? You have been like a son to me, Dimitri. I thought you had disappeared in California, never to return."

"Things changed. We had problems out there from the beginning."

"Apparently. You trouble me, my boy. Why this game?"

"May I sit, Boss?"

Levich gestured to a gilded chair. "Of course. Rest. Lydia tells me your foot needs attention. I will have Sheveski's man take you to my physician. He is discreet, Dimitri. No one need know."

"About Verlov..." began Ivanov.

Levich threw up his hands. "I understand. There was bad blood between the two of you from the start. I ignored it. Believe me, Dimitri, I do know how these things happen. Always regrettable to have it come to the attention of the police, but Sheveski believes you had no choice."

Ivanov relaxed for the first time in weeks. "With Verlov in the way I could not reach you. He came after me, Boss."

"So I've been told. These things are bad for business. It brings unwanted attention at a time we don't need such notice."

"I didn't mean to cause you trouble, Boss."

Levich waved away the apology. "Perhaps unavoidable, eh?"

The old man stood, hands clasped behind his back. Mumbling, Levich walked back and forth in front of Ivanov, in dialog with himself. Seating himself in front of his suffering acolyte, he said, "Tell me everything about California. Leave out nothing. And I want to hear about this book."

Ivanov buried his pain and replayed the debacle in Los Angeles, altering details to put himself in better light. Levich asked few questions. When Ivanov was done, the old mobster gave him the news of Shurkov's death, shaking his confidence. Levich was well known as one who did not tolerate failure. Ivanov thought of the fate of Sasha Mikoyan and others who had disappointed the Boss. He would depend on Levich's affection for him.

"Can you walk?"

"It is painful," said Ivanov, "but I can do it, yes."

"That will be taken care of. Then we must find a place for you, Dimitri. Perhaps our friends in Miami or Chicago."

"I will go wherever you think best."

Levich smiled paternally. "Of course you will, my boy. I will have Sheveski to make arrangements. You cannot stay here, of course. The police will be certain to show on my doorstep looking for you. But first, your wounds, eh?"

Levich placed a bony hand on Ivanov's shoulder. "We will put this behind us. You will see." He threw open the double doors and called for Sheveski.

# Chapter 81

"Before I go waltzing in to some Russki nightclub," said Wolf, "I want to know what I'm putting my ass on the line for."

Royce nodded in agreement.

Nash said, "Here's what I know for sure."

The three had returned to the loft on Union and Second after spending most of the day chasing down the writer's sources. Royce had agreed to spend the night after the trio's visit to a Brighton Beach nightclub. In the hopes of uncovering more leads, Nash expected to bait club goers. He updated Wolf and Royce about what they faced if they made a night of it.

"Feldman says we'll be walking into a turf battle."

"The players?" said Royce.

"Two factions going after each other and a third or fourth waiting to see which one to back, based on the outcome."

"Smart," said Wolf. "Hotheads and pragmatists. Maybe they won't notice us."

Royce spoke up. "Not a chance, Wolfman. We'll draw their attention."

"The enemy of my enemy is my friend?"

"Something like that."

Nash said, "It might be an opportunity. One of the factions might want to throw a little gossip our way."

"Risky," said Wolf.

"I didn't come this far to back down just because some Russian scumbags can't get their act together," said Nash. "I say we risk it."

Wolf and Royce exchanged wary glances.

"I'm going," said Nash. "With or without you guys."

"Okay. We're going with you," said Wolf. "But if Royce or I see something funny we're pulling the plug. Either one of us gets a bad feeling, we're out of there."

"And I will be right there with you."

"Our call," said Wolf. "You with me on that, Royce?"

"Absolutely."

Nash went to his bulletin board with its diagram. "As I was saying…we have this turf battle going on. One of the Old Guard is trying to hold on to his spot in the food chain. The third wave is pushing him out before he's ready to go."

"Typical," said Wolf to Nash. "So how are you going to play it?"

"I'm going to ask a few questions and listen to the new breed for starters. They'll have an ax to grind and they're always willing to talk. It's good for their egos."

"Dangerous game," said Royce.

"Gotta play if I want to get something to write about."

"Your call," said Wolf. "But don't forget about running down the reasons for Colter's death and Kurskov's murder."

"I know, the damn book. That's part of the equation. Always has been."

"It's the reason I agreed to join you. That's the purpose of having Royce along. He wants justice for those guys. Don't you, Royce?"

"Roger that."

Wolf stooped at a cooler and fished in the ice for a beer. He glanced at Royce. "Want one?"

"Sure."

He handed a sweating bottle to Royce. Wolf sipped his beer and studied passing traffic in the street below the arched window. His eyes drifted across the street, settling on the building opposite. Something about the second floor.

He froze. "Don't move," said Wolf, backing from the glass. "Stay away from the windows."

"What are you seeing?" said Royce.

"Maybe nothing."

"Talk to me, Wolfman."

"Storefront across the street. Second level. Middle window. Bottom pane's broken. A reflection...maybe."

"I'll check it out."

"No. Stay put, Royce. I'll go. Taking my phone. Keep an open line."

Wolf backed from the window, threw on his hooded jacket, and picked up his Sig-Sauer, jacking a round. He went down the back stairs, avoiding the freight elevator. He slipped into the alley unseen and followed it for one block. Hood up, hands in his pockets, Wolf crossed Union Street, just another anonymous pedestrian. In the alley, he worked his way down the rear of the buildings lining Union. He found a cable company's beige van parked at the rear of the storefront opposite the loft. A prop: the vehicle was empty.

Whispering in his phone, he said, "Got an empty van in back."

"No movement since you left," said Royce.

"Watch the stairs. They won't use the elevator."

"Got it covered."

A check of the building's first floor confirmed what Wolf expected to find: deserted retail space. Sawhorses, scrap lumber, and naked studs told of a remodeling project interrupted. Wolf forced the rear entry to the empty ground floor. His eyes adjusted to the dim interior. Scurrying sounds in the walls. Shadows flitted across the floor, keeping to the margins. Rats. Big ones, fleeing at his approach.

A single set of footprints in the dust led to a narrow set of stairs climbing to the second floor. Wolf studied the fresh signs. *One shooter? Two? The second one walking in the footsteps of the first? Probably not. Too confident. It would be one.*

Ears cocked to pick up the slightest sound, Wolf waited for five long minutes. A faint cough. Shifting weight.

*Second floor. Whoever was up there will be sitting back from the broken window with his weapon resting on a sandbag or a stack of boxes. At this range an easy shot for a pro.*

He followed the footprints to the stairs, his breathing slowed. Wolf steadied his pistol with both hands. A rat, bold, curious, sat on the first step, watching him, finally yielding at his approach.

*Wait here at the bottom of the stairs? Gamble and go up?*

The decision was made for him. In the distance, a siren wailed, growing louder, coming his way. A klaxon blared. Not cops. A fire engine.

*Perfect. Wolf, you lucky bastard.*

The growing sound filled the street, covering every step he took. The roar of a big diesel rig, all blasting horn and screaming siren, flooded the building.

*NOW! Go now!*

Wolf burst through the sagging doorframe.

# Chapter 82

He caught the shooter by surprise. Two shots hit the man's upper right shoulder as the assassin turned, rifle in hand. The sniper went down, scattering a stack of empty wooden crates as he fell. Wolf kicked the scoped rifle aside, drove his other foot into the gunman's groin. Despite his pain the gunman struggled to his knees, drawing a tactical knife from a hidden sheath. He slashed at Wolf and missed. Wolf delivered another well-aimed kick, catching the wounded man in his bloodied right shoulder, sending the knife flying across the floor. The fight was over. The loser curled in pain, clutching his arm and cursing. Wolf, his pistol covering the would-be assassin, picked up the discarded rifle.

He released the box magazine, pulled back on the bolt, ejecting the live 7.62mm round. Wolf circled the injured shooter and slammed the rifle's wooden butt on the man's left hand, shattering bones. He did the same with the right. The shooter collapsed, screaming in rage, all resistance gone.

Wolf pocketed the cartridge and magazine. He called Royce. "Our shooter's down. WIA. Van out back. If you're clear, I could use a hand."

"We're good. Be right over. Stay where I can see you."

"Door at the back. Don't bother to knock. Stairs. I'm at the top."

"On my way."

His adrenaline ebbing, Wolf pulled one of the crates to him and sat at the stairs, his pistol trained on his suffering prisoner. Royce arrived, spotted Wolf, and leaped up the stairs, pistol in hand. He glanced at the evidence of the struggle and the sullen shooter.

Covered in plaster dust from the floor, the prisoner glared at both men. Dark-complexioned, curly-haired, and almond-eyed, the muscled shooter was just under six-foot. He wore black fatigue pants, black T-shirt, and black crepe-soled tennis shoes.

"Outstanding," said Royce.

"All in a day's work. Search him."

"Roger that." Royce retrieved the knife, folded the blade, and pocketed it. He dragged the wounded man into the center of the room and rolled him despite protests. He duct-taped the man's hands behind him, provoking curses and threats.

"Shut up, you pussy. You're lucky my friend here treated you with the utmost kindness. I would have skinned your sorry ass."

Royce patted the man down, finding keys and a cellphone. He found another tactical knife in an ankle sheath but no wallet or identification. Royce kept the cellphone and tossed the keys to Wolf. He pinned the shooter's hands behind him and propped him against a crumbling plaster wall.

Using his cellphone, Wolf took pictures of their prisoner.

"You have a name?"

"Go to hell, mother—"

Royce hit the man with an open hand. "Show some respect, asshole."

Snarling "Fuck you!" earned another blow from Royce and a strip of duct tape across his mouth.

"So much for playing hard-core, huh."

"A real ninja wannabe," said Royce, playing with the confiscated knives. "Whadaya think? Latino? Maybe Central America?"

"Possibly. Not Russian, that's for sure." Wolf picked up the familiar Soviet long gun. "Though our man was using a Dragunov. Interesting."

Eyeing the weapon, Royce said, "Spoils of war. I'd like to have that."

"Be my guest."

"We could drag his sorry ass downstairs and toss him in the van," said Royce. "Might find some clues inside."

"My guess is it's clean. Nothing to tie this guy to whoever sent him. He's obviously not in the mood to talk. We'll need to stop the bleeding."

"A waste of good bandages if you ask me."

"We'll need him alive to talk."

"I have a better idea," said Royce. "Keep an eye on our little buddy. I'll be right back."

Wolf stood. "Where you going?"

"Trust me. When I get back he'll sing like the proverbial canary."

"Hey, I came up here to wing the guy if I could, not kill him."

Smiling, Royce put a hand on Wolf's shoulder, whispering, "And you did a good job. Now it's my turn. I'll have this guy telling you everything you need to know in no time."

# Chapter 83

Royce was back in thirty minutes, grocery bag in hand. He dumped the contents on a piece of newsprint. Handing Wolf a sterile bandage and tape, he said, "Being a fine humanitarian, you patch him. After that, he's mine."

Wolf cut the shirt from the bleeding man and cleaned the bullet hole. He taped a gauze pad over the entry wound.

"No exit wound. I think his shoulder's shattered."

"He's lucky you didn't put one between his running lights."

"Well, he was turning at the time."

Royce knelt, flipped open one of the knives, and cut away the prisoner's trousers. With one clean stroke he severed the shoelaces and stripped the bound man's tennis shoes and socks. He bagged the clothing. Naked except for his briefs, the shooter was passive.

Putting away the knife, Royce caught Wolf's eyes. "This might be a good time to see if you can find anything in the van."

"What are you up to?"

Sitting back on his haunches, Royce said, "This is where I have a productive chat with our friend."

"Dead men don't talk. Remember that."

"Trust me. He'll talk."

"I'll give you thirty minutes alone with him."

Royce grinned. "Make it forty, but I probably won't need that."

Wolf grabbed the Dragunov and went down the stairs.

Royce asked the wounded man, "Your name?"

A shake of the head, the black eyes defiant.

Royce removed a large jar of peanut butter from the bag and placed it on the newspaper. He unscrewed the lid.

"Give me your name."

No response. Royce dipped the kitchen tool in the peanut butter and crouched alongside the prisoner. "Your name."

Silence. He spread a thick smear of peanut butter on both thighs, smoothing the pungent paste over the man's quadriceps as if decorating a cake. Royce put away his supplies and stood up, a long heavy stick in hand. He went to a wall opposite and waited.

A moment passed before they both heard faint scratching in the walls and floorboards. Drawn by the scent of the peanut butter, the first rat shot across the threshold and took refuge in a corner. The animal's yellow eyes flitted from the statue-like Royce to the sweating human just feet away. Rising on its hind legs, the rodent sniffed the air then dropped down and made its way to the aroma's source. Keeping the rat at bay with the stick, Royce toyed with the ravenous animal.

"Name," said Royce softly to the man. "What is your name?"

Wide-eyed, the gagged shooter moved his feet, startling the rat. Lifting his legs, he slammed his heels against the floor. Retreating, the animal ran to the corner and studied its antagonist.

Two more rats came through the open door. The size of small cats, they circled Royce's prisoner. Unimpressed with Royce's feints with the stick, the larger of the two leaped at the closest leg and slashed with its incisors, taking a small chunk of bloodied flesh covered in peanut butter. Pursued by the other rats, it ran past Royce with its prize. Six more of the creatures slithered from gaps in exposed lathe and sniffed the air, thick with its hint of blood. The rodents circled, coming closer.

Another muffled scream from the taped mouth. Wielding his stick, Royce scattered the rats, driving them back into hiding.

"Name."

A panicked nodding and Royce ripped the tape from the man's mouth.

Babbling, he choked out the words, "Jorge Iberra."

"And who do you work for, Jorge Iberra?"

"I...can't. I'd be...a dead man."

"What, you prefer to be alone with your little friends?"

A vigorous shaking of the head. "You...don't understand."

"Oh, but I do."

Royce replaced the tape and used the knife to cut away the man's underwear. He came back with a gob of peanut butter on the spatula. Straining, the cords in his neck standing out, his eyes bulging, the doomed assassin looked down, watching Royce coat his groin in peanut butter. The man writhed against his bonds.

Backing into his corner, Royce asked, "Who do you work for, Jorge?"

Without interference to scatter them, the rats came back, more of them this time. Pleading with his eyes, the prisoner jerked his body, shaking bolder rodents from his lower torso. Smothered screams for mercy. Royce dispersed the rats with sweeps of his stick. The tape came off once more.

"My...cellphone...a single number...I am to call."

Holding up the man's phone, Royce finished the sentence. "When you've eliminated your targets."

An angry nod. Royce had won. He put away the phone.

"As one professional to another, you understand that I have more to ask you, Jorge. As long as you keep talking, you stay alive. Lie to me and I *WILL* leave you with the wildlife. Understood?"

A resigned nod. Using the captured cellphone, Royce called the lone number. He got a robotic voice recording and said, "Phone me back in one hour." He killed the call and asked more questions. Jorge Iberra babbled for fifteen minutes while Royce kept the rats at bay.

Satisfied he had learned all he could, Royce wrapped a towel around his handgun and shot Iberra in the head.

Royce ripped bandages from the dead man's wounds and stripped duct tape from the body's ankles, wrists, and arms. He uncapped the jar and emptied the container, smearing peanut butter over the wounds, the corpse's face, and the hands. Bagging the tape and his tools, he headed for the stairs.

Behind him, the floor and walls came alive in squealing, feral, cannibalistic warfare. Batting away solitary trailing rats, Royce went down the stairs to the empty ground floor.

He called Wolf. "I think we finally have something we can use."

"I'm sitting in the van. Nothing's happening out here."

"Jorge won't be coming with us."

Wolf's voice. "Jorge? How the hell…?"

"It's a long story," said Royce. "Jorge told me all about it."

"I have to say, Royce, you still have it."

"Never lost it, Wolfman."

# Chapter 84

Levich was as good as his word. One of Sheveski's pit bulls took Ivanov to the Old Man's doctor after hours. Peeling off a bloodied sock, the physician, a bearded little man with soft hands, examined Ivanov's foot, cleaned the wound, and delivered grim news.

"Ah, you might lose your leg below the knee."

"No! You can't do that. I can't go about crippled. Fix it."

Wrinkling his nose, the doctor said, "If you had come to see me sooner, I might have been able to do something for you. Have you no sense of smell? You have signs of gangrene, my boy. This infection means at the very least you'll lose the foot."

"Give me medicine. I can't live without my foot."

The doctor peeled off his gloves. "Too late for just medicine. You need to go to hospital. I cannot do what needs to be done here in my office."

Despondent, Ivanov slumped forward. "I'd rather die," he whispered.

The doctor said, "You will certainly do that if you do not follow my advice."

"Give me something for the pain. At least you can do that."

"Maybe a few pills to get you through the week. I will write you a prescription you can get tomorrow. I will inject antibiotic. But remember, you have a decision to make... and soon."

Shaking his head, the doctor went to the examining room sink and began washing his hands. He spoke to the driver in low tones. "He needs to go to hospital as soon as possible. You will tell Levich this, yes?"

"Of course."

The physician wagged a finger. "No delays. If we are to save your friend's life, we must act immediately. Understand?"

"Of course."

"Good. I will have my nurse call to make arrangements once you have spoken to your boss."

Leaving Ivanov alone in the examining room, the doctor excused himself. Sheveski's man went outside to call Levich with the news, then returned, got Ivanov, and helped him to the car.

The ordeal had taken a toll on Ivanov. Leaning against the seat he asked, "What now?"

"I am to take you to a safe place, a room at the rear of a store. The husband and wife will look after you until things quiet down. You heard the doctor, Dimitri. You have no time to lose. You must go to hospital."

"But my leg," he wailed. "What good will I be to Levich with one leg?"

"You will be like a soldier from the war. Many of them have lost limbs."

Ivanov wasn't listening. "Who are the people you are taking me to?"

"Just a couple. They will do as told. They will ask no questions. Your face is on the news. You need to hide until things become quieter. Do not worry, you will be made comfortable."

"I have an idea. Why not take me back to Lydia's home. She will watch over me."

"No. The boss told me to take you to this apartment. It is safer."

Ivanov frowned. "I would prefer Lydia's place."

"Talk to the Boss. Leave me out of this argument of yours."

"I will call him."

"Think about the hospital, Dimitri."

"I'm not going to give up my leg."

"The doctor says it is rotting. Don't be a fool about this."

"It's my leg. I need it for a bit longer."

"What are you thinking?"

"I'm not sure. But I'm not going to give up my leg."

The driver pulled to the curb and pointed to a lighting store nestled between a Russian video outlet and a pawnshop. "There. They are expecting you." He put his hand in a pocket and Ivanov froze.

"Here, from the Boss. Take it," said Sheveski's man, handing him a roll of bills. "To keep you for a while."

Caught off-guard by the gesture, Ivanov hesitated. "Take it," repeated the man. "Tomorrow I come back with more pain medicine."

Ivanov pocketed the cash and stared at the storefront. Sensing a trap, he said, "I don't like it."

"It's not forever, Dimitri." A push on the shoulder. "Get out."

Ivanov pushed open the car door and hobbled across the sidewalk without looking back. Expecting a bullet in his back at any moment, he tensed, certain he would hear a shot. Nothing. He reached the shop's door and turned. The car was gone. Except for a drab shuffling babushka he was alone on the sidewalk. Putting aside any thoughts of flight for now, Ivanov pushed open the door and limped inside.

# Chapter 85

Nash inspected the table with its maps and notebooks, and now the Russian rifle, which Wolf uncovered.

"What happened?"

Neither man would answer.

"I see. Do I need to ask what you are doing with this gun?"

"The previous owner was on a mission."

"That mission being...?"

Royce tossed the gun's loaded magazine on the table. "You and Wolf were his mission."

Nash asked, "Did he talk?"

"Yes."

"And?"

Royce said, "And he was very helpful. Had a great deal to say."

Wolf sighted through the Draganov's scope at a window. "Royce got a name, Jorge Ibarra. He also got a contact number. We think it's the shooter's handler. I'll call an old friend who has a lot of contacts and see if he can confirm that. My guess is the rifle was probably going to be left behind once we were dead."

Puzzled, Nash looked at Wolf. "What would be the point of that?"

"Perhaps to make it look like a Russian hit," said Wolf, lowering the rifle. "Makes sense. I'm here to follow the book story and you..." Glancing at Nash, he said, "You're here because you know the Russian mob."

Wolf handed the long gun to Royce. "Guy takes us out, end of story. Leaves the rifle behind for the cops to find. The Russian mafia gets the blame. Kinda simple, don't you think?"

Royce said, "Only it wasn't the mob."

"Who then?" said Nash.

Wolf sank down in a chair, his eyes on Royce. "Tell him your theory."

"Our shooter was a contract killer. Wolf and I think he works for our side. Or rather, worked for our side."

Nash stared at Wolf. "Our side?"

Royce rolled the gun in a blanket. "Wolfman thinks this guy was here to target him. The information in the book is embarrassing to our government. Being the stubborn sort, he wouldn't cooperate and give up what he knew. They figured out he wasn't going to keep quiet. I think your helping him put you in the crosshairs, too."

"I need a drink," said Nash, heading for the cooler.

"You'll need something stronger than beer," Wolf said.

"It'll do for now. How did they find us?"

"Tell him, Wolfman."

"My name triggered a trip wire when I flew here from San Diego. When I got to Kennedy they were waiting, remember? Nells wanted to take another run at me. They palmed a locator beacon among my keys and change. I dumped it when I got to that hotel bar in mid-Manhattan."

Nash flared. "You didn't say a word."

Shrugging, Wolf said, "Didn't matter by then. I dropped it in our server's pocket when she took our drink order. That bought us a couple days at least."

"So, how did they follow us here?"

"The cemetery."

"No one knew about that," said Nash.

Arms folded, Royce leaned against the brick wall. "Only the three of us and your banker buddy. Had to be him. Maybe the feds had turned him."

"Damn." Nash dropped in a chair. "Of course, the sonofabitch."

"Don't be too hard on him," said Wolf. "The feds probably squeezed him over his involvement with that dirty bank. Your call to meet set him up."

"Two guys stopped to lay flowers on a grave while we were there," said Royce. "Did you see them?" Nash shook his head.

"They were good, but it had to be them. Planted a tracking beacon on one of our cars."

"We should check."

"Already did when we got back from across the street. Found two."

"Did you get rid of them?" said Nash.

"Not yet. They might come in handy to have feds as backup when we visit Little Odessa."

Nash threw up his arms. "You can't be serious. We can't go there after all that's happened."

"Why not?" said Wolf. "It's worth a try, isn't it? Besides, we're on the fed's radar now."

"Are you crazy? You have some sort of death wish?"

Royce put a hand on Nash's shoulder. "Nah, Wolfman's right. We'll take the feds with us even if they don't know we're on to them. If it hits the fan they'll be right there. Plus, you two need to beat the bushes at that nightclub to find out what's going on with the book thing and the mob."

"How do we know the feds will step in if we get in trouble?"

Wolf faced Nash. "We don't. But it's worth a gamble. You have to talk to these Russians. Right now you don't have everything you need. This could finish it for you. I want to see you get the story out there."

"Yeah, I know—for Colter's sake. But things have changed."

Wolf said, "Really? We know our side is worried enough to sanction a hit contract. The Russians are looking for the same thing. We go to the source to see if we can solve the puzzle. We need to see this to the end."

"But the risk," said Nash. "That's why I'm thinking it's crazy to go."

Royce smiled. "It's the perfect storm. All we have to do is make sure you both get in, talk to some people, stir things up, and get out in one piece."

"And how do we do that?" said Nash. "The 'getting out' part."

"That's why I'm here," said Royce.

Nash looked skeptical. "Oh, sure, great odds."

"We're in good hands," said Wolf.

"But what about the shooter? Won't he talk?"

Royce sounded certain. "I don't think that will be a problem."

"Well, what if they find him?"

"I don't think that's going to be a problem."

"The van," said Wolf. "We'll need to get rid of it."

Royce said, "Wait until dark. Follow me in my car. We'll find a spot near the river, dump it, and burn it. No prints, no DNA. Let his bosses deal with it."

# Chapter 86

After Wolf and Royce returned from abandoning the van, and prior to leaving for Little Odessa, Wolf called Gunny Lindgren in Virginia Beach for help in unraveling the mystery of the shooter's hiring.

"We have a phone number, Keith. Our boy was here to take us out using a Dragunov. I find that interesting, don't you? I'm not in the mood to take kindly to having my own kind set me up like that."

"Agreed. A shameful thing. I'll do what I can, Wolfman."

"That's all I'm asking. This is all off the grid, Gunny."

"Of course, I don't need to know all the details about what happened."

"Correct. But I want to know the 'why' and 'who' of this action."

"You're putting me in a tough spot."

"Hey, I'm just grateful to be upright and able to call you."

"Okay, give me a day or so."

Confident Lindgren would do his best, Wolf ended the call.

Late that night, the three left their compromised location and drove to Brighton Beach, Royce following in his car. Though their tails remained undetected, Wolf was sure they were being followed. Splitting from Wolf and Nash, Royce doubled back and found a residential street spot two blocks from the nightclub. He locked his car and headed to the Caspian Nights. Flashing a phony NYPD detective's badge pinned to his belt, an armed Royce nodded to the big

Azerbaijani gatekeeper and went inside, carrying a second pistol for Wolf in case he needed it.

Looming over Mintov, the club's manager, an officious Royce loudly announced he was there as one of New York's finest to make sure no harm came to Nash and Wolf. His ersatz detective ruse worked. Royce made a show of shaking their hands and then retreated to the end of the long bar where he stood with his back against the wall.

From his vantage point, Royce watched Nash leave his table to work the room, Wolf in tow. Only once did Royce have to leave his post to play his part. A belligerent drunk followed Nash and Wolf, berating them as unwelcome outliers. A discreet nod from Royce to the manager sent two bouncers into action. The braying gangster wannabe was ejected. Nash and Wolf resumed trolling.

They struck gold when word reached a Levich lieutenant. The bullet-headed Russian, short, broad-shouldered, cornered Nash and Wolf. The three began an animated conversation as a line of showgirls emerged to wild applause. The first of the nightclub's floorshows spilled across the dance floor to ear-splitting music and the delight of the patrons. When Royce looked again the thug had gone. Threading his way through the barely costumed dancers, he made for the table where Nash and Wolf sat.

"Are you getting anywhere?"

Nash said, "We're working our way up the food chain."

"Should I be worried about that gorilla you were talking to?"

"He's a gofer for Boris Levich, the club's owner. I think we might get a bite. I think we're about to get a visit from Anton Sheveski."

"Is that a good thing or a bad thing?" said Royce.

"Not sure yet. Sheveski's a Levich associate. And Levich is top dog in this town. He's been around since my early days."

"Does he know you?" said Royce.

"Probably. These guys have long memories."

"That could be a bad thing. Say the word and we'll pull the plug."

"Not yet, Royce," Wolf said. "I'm gonna give Sheveski one of the pages from the book. Nash thinks that oughta get some attention."

"Maybe not the kind of attention you need."

"We're not over our heads yet. Just cover our six."

Ignoring the prancing dancers, Royce returned to his post at the bar.

During the floorshow, Sheveski appeared, scowling and menacing. He was accompanied by a muscled bull-necked byki, who circled behind Wolf and Nash.

Signaling the nervous manager, Royce quizzed him. "Who's the man at the table with my friends?"

"Sorry, I do not recognize the gentleman, Detective."

"Your eyesight is as bad as your honesty, Mintoff. For your information, he is Anton Sheveski. One of Boris Levich's cronies."

The little man shrugged. "Really? I do not know him."

"You're such a poor liar."

Pretending insult, the club's manager said, "Truly, I don't know him."

"Really? It's well known that Boris Levich owns this dump and that you serve at his pleasure. Don't insult my intelligence."

"Certainly not my intent."

"Bullshit," scoffed Royce. "Can't understand the game if you don't know the players."

"If you say so."

"I do say so. Don't you have some tables to clear?" Royce shooed him away and switched locations. He shifted his eyes between the crowd, the dancers, and Sheveski. The gangster was talking with Nash and Wolf. As Royce watched, the slippery Mintoff drifted by the table and bent to whisper in

Sheveski's ear. The gangster shot a stony look in Royce's direction. Royce, showing his best neutral face, propped his right hand at the hip in an obvious display of his detective's shield. He got a contemptuous scowl in return for the gesture. Turning back to the business at hand, Sheveski took a sheet of paper from Wolf and scanned it.

*A taste of the book. Take the bait*, thought the watching Royce.

His expression unchanged, Sheveski handed it to his bodyguard and sent him away. Followed by spotlights, sequined, feathered performers worked their way among the tables, pausing to toy with men and women alike. Reforming on the dance floor with military precision, they finished their number to whistles and applause. Forming a new line, they locked arms, obscuring Royce's line of sight. Cued by a statuesque blonde, they twirled and parted in pairs, revealing an empty table where Nash, Wolf, and Sheveski had been moments before.

# Chapter 87

In a secluded, soundproofed retreat, Nash and Wolf sat on a red leather banquette across from Anton Sheveski. The back room was one of several set aside for special guests. Wolf could only guess at what went on in its confines. Lined in red velvet, with brass wall lamps and crystal chandeliers, the private chamber was a tasteless exercise in excess. Producing a single page from the sought-after book had gained them an audience with Boris Levich.

A rap at the brass-studded leather door and Sheveski stood. Nash nudged Wolf to his feet as well. The door opened and Boris Levich appeared, imperious and grim. Sheveski held a chair for the Brighton Beach godfather and stood at a respectful distance behind the old man. Levich did not extend a greeting. Instead, he held the single book page in front of him. Perching a pair of reading glasses on his hooked nose, he studied the scribbled notes of tidy Cyrillic. No one spoke. Levich removed his glasses.

"So, which of you is Wolf and which of you is Nash?"

The two identified themselves.

"Ah. So we meet again, Mr. Nash. I know your work. Lies, all of it."

Nash refused the challenge.

"And you, Mr. Wolf, seem to have caused a great deal of trouble during your stay in California." Levich held up a spotted, palsied hand. "Don't bore me with denials or details. We know you were there."

"And we know your man was there as well," said Wolf.

Looking down at the page, Levich shook his head. "The toll of business is sometimes high, no? It does not matter what the business is. There is always a cost. The point before us is this: why do you come here and present this piece of worthless paper at this late hour?"

Wolf leaned forward. "The paper is not worthless and the hour is not late. I believe you have more than a passing interest in what a page like this contains. And there are more of them where that came from."

Levich laced his fingers together. "It means nothing to me."

"Ah, but they mean something to your friends in Moscow. True?"

"Let us suppose they do. This is one page. Where are the rest? Where is this book people talk about? Do you have it?"

Careful with his words, Wolf said, "I have access to it, yes."

"And you want something in return, I suppose."

"Not money, if that's what you're suggesting."

"Not money? It's always about money."

"I want the man who came to California and killed my friend."

"If such a man existed, and if I knew of such a man, why would I give him over to you?"

"I will trade this book for such a man. I think you have the power to make this happen. You get the book. I get the man."

Ignoring Wolf's proposal for the moment, Levich turned his attention to Nash. "And what is your part in this ridiculous extortion? Why are you here? Are you not ashamed of the way you maligned our people with your book?" Grimacing malevolently, Levich shook a finger at Nash. "I hold you responsible for this slander you wrote. You made accusations that were not true. Like others, I come here to start a new life and you write lies."

"I am a journalist. I write the truth, not lies."

Levich unleashed a string of curses in Russian and Yiddish. "Oh, yes, journalists. They sometimes suffer for their efforts. I have heard of journalists being killed."

"In the Old Country," said Nash, "Not here in America."

"Well, one can never tell what may happen…even in America."

Wolf nudged Nash's knee. "Consider my offer, Mr. Levich."

"The book for this man?"

"If such a man exists," parroted Sheveski.

"Both of us know he exists," said Wolf. "I am here because the trail led here. The police in California have evidence. They are closing in. Soon, the FBI will become involved. I cannot be responsible for what will happen once the government investigates."

"Such talk bores me," said Levich. "I am just a businessman who looks after his people, nothing more. Strictly as a kindness to a guest of this club, I will have my associates ask about this 'man' you say you are looking for. But I don't think you should expect much to come of it."

Wolf said, "And I will talk to the people who have access to this book you want. If they don't hear from me, they may do something else with it."

Levich rose. Without a backward glance at Nash and Wolf, the mob boss and Sheveski abandoned the private room. In the hallway, two unsmiling byki fell in with them, one in front, one behind. Levich and his retinue left through a rear door. Nash and Wolf emerged to find a much-relieved Royce pacing the carpeted hall outside the party room.

"I was about to call nine-one-one. One moment you're sitting at a table talking with Sheveski, the next time I look, you're gone."

Wolf said, "You were watching the dancers."

"The hell I was. You guys could have been headed for a landfill for all I knew. I had your back, but we should have figured on something like this."

"Kind of hard to anticipate this kind of encounter," said Nash. "We got to see the top dog. Can't do better than that."

Royce said, "Was that old guy Levich?"

"You saw him?" said Nash.

"Yeah, that weasel of a manager, Mintoff, told me you two were in conference with the big man. I threatened to tear him a new one if you didn't turn up."

"Well, so what gives?" said Wolf. "Are we done here?"

Nash looked at him. "I picked up enough to work with. I think we'd better leave while we can."

"Works for me. We have some decisions to make."

Royce said, "Want me to scrap the tracking beacons?"

"Sure. Even though the feds know where we are, we can stick the GPS trackers on someone else's car," said Wolf. "Let them chase those people for a while. C'mon, let's blow this joint."

Royce said, "You know, that has a certain appeal to it."

"He didn't meant that literally," said Nash.

For the first time that night Royce smiled. "You don't know Wolfman well enough to make that assumption."

They left the tracking beacons and the nightclub behind.

# Chapter 88

"I think we ought to move to higher ground before it hits the fan." Cradling the Draganov rifle in his lap, Royce rubbed the oiled barrel and receiver with a clean rag and repeated his warning. "Did you hear me? I said we ought to—"

Wolf, lounging in a hammock strung between two floor-to-ceiling pillars, said, "Heard you the first time. And go where exactly?"

"Upstate. New Jersey. Florida. Anywhere but here for starters."

Nash interrupted his typing. "I'm a day from wrapping up this article. We can stay for at least another week if we need to."

Royce slipped the sniper rifle in a gun sock and tightened the drawstring. "Don't you get it? We've got targets pinned on our backs."

Nash studied his notes without looking at Royce. "If they were going to do something, don't you think they would have made a move by now?"

"Not necessarily. We don't know who's got us in their sights: old Boris and his borscht-eaters or our friends in Washington."

Wolf climbed from the hammock and took his cellphone up on the roof. The spot gave him two things: good reception and a respite from the other two. Wolf selected one of the stored numbers and initiated the call.

Gunny Lindgren's recorded voice boomed from the phone. Wolf left a detailed message and number. He didn't have to wait long for the return call.

"Hey, Wolfman, you have ESP. I was planning to call you today."

"Warms my heart to hear you say that."

A long sigh. "I don't know what you're up to now, but you, my friend, have stepped in it big time. Not the words you wanted to hear, I'm sure."

Wolf paused. "I always count on you to give it to me straight."

"Okay. Here's what little I've been able to find out so far. Your man in State, Nells, was told by his boss to take off the gloves. Guess he wasn't making much headway with you about giving up the book."

"I figured as much."

"Your playing hardball with him at Kennedy Airport didn't leave him much wiggle room, Wolfman."

"I was tired of being hassled, Gunny."

"I feel your pain. But his supervisor put the screws to him. They brought in the big guns. Sorry, bad choice of words. The contractor tailing you was a freelancer. Ex-army guy from Puerto Rico. You had the name right, Jorge Iberra. Don't know how you got him to tell you that. My source said he's never blown a mission before. He must have gotten careless."

"Not careless, just a second too slow."

"Guess there's a first time for everybody."

"Ain't that the truth," Wolf said. "What about the number on the guy's phone? Royce left a message but never got a call back."

"It's a mailbox."

"No way to trace it?"

Lindgren laughed. "You think I'm a miracle worker?"

"Damn near close to one. Got any advice, Gunny?"

"I'd say vamoose. Get out of town. Find that hole I told you about."

Wolf stayed in the shadows on the roof. "What if I contacted Nells, worked something out to get him off my back?"

Lindgren's sigh filled Wolf's ears. "Probably too late for that. If he let that dog loose on you, do you really think he'll want to talk?"

"Probably not. I'll call with a report in a few days. Thanks for the help, Gunny."

"Go find that hole, Wolfman."

# Chapter 89

Sheveski lumbered into Levich's dining room. "A word, Boss."

Levich glanced at Lydia fussing over his teapot. "Leave us."

She went through the French doors, closing them behind her.

"Sit, Anton. What news today?"

"I have confirmed that it was Dimitri who killed Verlov."

Levich said, "I suspected Dimitri might be involved. They did not get on with each other from the first. Verlov presumed too much, too quickly. Dimitri resented him, of course. It was Verlov who suggested Dimitri be sent to California to find that accursed book. He wanted him gone."

Sheveski nodded in agreement. "Undoubtedly. No one, including me, mourns the loss of Verlov, Boss. But you did not order his death as was your right. Such an affront cannot stand. Dimitri must be held accountable."

His voice flat, Levich said, "You think to advise me on this, Anton?"

Sheveski offered a tepid apology. "Of course not. I was only thinking of your reputation. This will be spoken of in the streets if we do not immediately act."

A habit of his under pressure, Levich smoothed his thinning hair. "Yes, I agree. But I think we can accomplish two things with one stroke." He pushed away from the table. Sheveski got to his feet in a show of respect and waited.

Levich wandered to the curtained window overlooking the street. The old man cradled his chin, his brow furrowed. Only the ticking of the mantel clock broke the silence. Hands clasped behind, he returned to the table, steadied himself by grasping the back of a chair, and looked at Sheveski.

As if waving away the awful truth of what he must do, he said, "Go to Dimitri. Tell him all is forgiven. Say to him that the doctor was mistaken about his leg. That he can save it after all. I pay all expenses."

"I doubt he will believe me."

"Not at first. You must disarm him. The key is not to force him to go with you. Tell Dimitri you think it was a good thing he did by removing Verlov. Convince him I, too, am relieved he is gone. Then have him to call me. I will talk to him and tell him I want to see him, that I have forgiven him."

"Boss, he won't believe me. I should just kill him and save you this trouble."

Taking Sheveski by the elbow, Levich smiled. "We need him alive. There is this man, Wolf, who wants him, remember? In exchange for Dimitri I will get the book our friends in Moscow want."

"If he refuses, may I kill him?"

Levich patted the big man's arm. "Do not be so eager, Anton. You'll have your chance. No, do not kill him. If he hesitates, say I will meet him at Lydia's house if he so wishes. Tell him he can stay there to recuperate from his wound. He trusts her. For now, we need Dimitri alive."

"At least until this Wolf gives up the book."

Levich nodded. "Yes. Once that is done, get rid of them all."

"All of them?"

For Levich, ordering the deaths was akin to brushing lint from his lapel. Arching an eyebrow, he said, "Yes, a clean sweep. Dimitri, Wolf, the writer Nash, and their friend. These four have caused me a great deal of grief, each in their own way. I mourn over Dimitri in particular. I practically raised him as my own son."

"These things happen."

"It doesn't ease the pain one feels, Anton."

The big man shrugged. Emotion, real or imagined, was not for him.

Drawn again to the window, Levich brushed aside the sheer curtain and studied the Brighton Beach skyline. "However, the death of the journalist Nash will give me great pleasure. He has been a thorn in our people's side for far too long. If only he had been in the car that long ago morning instead of his wife."

"Regrettable. Fate spared him, it seems."

"True. But that was long before your time, of course."

"These deaths will cause an uproar, Boss. It will be short-lived, but perhaps you should arrange to be away while I see to it."

"I think that would be most wise."

# Chapter 90

Levich shuffled to his den and unlocked his desk. Withdrawing a slim green notebook, he turned to a familiar spot and smoothed the pages. He made a phone call to the private line of the senior accounts manager at Manhattan's New Amsterdam Global Bank and Trust.

"Ah, Fedor, my friend," said Levich, altering his voice. "It's Marcus Pavel. I wish to transfer the bulk of my account to my bank in Zurich. I am about to invest in a rather exciting business opportunity. Time is of the essence, eh?"

"Of course, Monsieur Pavel, I understand. I am at your service."

"I know I can count on you. I wish to wire ten million five. Please make the necessary arrangements."

"Consider it done, sir. Do you wish me to send a messenger with the paperwork?"

In silky tones, Levich said, "A phone call will suffice, Fedor. The paperwork can follow in due time."

"Very good, sir. You may expect the funds to arrive within the next few minutes."

"I appreciate your thoroughness, Fedor. I show five thousand remaining in the account, correct?"

"You are correct, sir."

"I shall add to that within days." Levich leaned back, a conspiratorial smile spreading. "A pleasure doing business with you as always, Fedor."

"I assure you the pleasure was all mine, Monsieur Pavel. New Amsterdam Global Bank and Trust appreciates your business."

"Very good," said Levich. "Au revoir, Fedor."

That done, Levich went to a wall safe behind a gilded framed print of Kutuzov driving the French at Smolensk, a favorite. He withdrew a plastic bag of passports, a small black velvet bag of uncut diamonds, and two blocks of wrapped currency: American one hundred dollar bills and Euros. He packed all in the false bottom of an anonymous worn leather valise.

He went to his bedroom where he shooed Lydia from her cleaning duties. He added underwear, a pair of socks, and a fresh shirt, along with toiletries to the leather case. He tucked the valise in the back of his wardrobe where it would sit undisturbed until needed. Satisfied with his preparations, Levich returned to his study and ordered Lydia to prepare tea and a small plate of his guilty pleasure: Russian tea cakes, her specialty.

Levich opened his computer, checked the status of his Zurich account, and rejoiced silently when he saw the transfer had gone through as promised. In the morning he would transfer half of the millions to a bank in Tel Aviv. Next, Levich called a ticket broker he had used over the years and booked a one-way first class ticket to Tel Aviv for the following day on El Al. Leaving Kennedy Airport mid-morning, he would arrive at Ben Gurion International in the afternoon of the next day. Pleased with his plan, Levich waited for Sheveski's call.

# Chapter 91

Levich, who had been dozing in his favorite wing-backed chair, awoke to loud voices in the apartment's entry. Recognizing Sheveski's ragged bass, he rubbed sleep from his eyes and abandoned the chair. Summoned by repeated knocks, he opened the door to find a florid-faced Sheveski wearing out the carpet. Off to one side, a worried-looking bodyguard stood like a statue. Sheveski faced Levich.

"Dimitri is gone."

"*WHAT?* When did this happen?"

"Late this morning, if his hosts are to be believed."

"Do you doubt their honesty in telling you this?"

Sheveski shook his head.

Levich ushered the big man into his study and sat at his writing table. Drumming his fingers, his eyes bored into Sheveski. "Did your man not keep watch on him as I instructed?"

Unlike other of Levich's underlings, Sheveski was not intimidated despite the circumstances. "He brought

Dimitri his medicine last night. Everything seemed normal. The old couple had prepared dinner for him and breakfast this morning. They opened their shop as usual and went to rouse him when I called to tell them I was on my way. That's when they discovered him gone. Vanished. Perhaps it happened before dawn. Maybe sometime around midnight. Hard to know."

In a rare loss of control, Levich slammed the table, rattling his cup and saucer. Despite the outburst, Sheveski's placid expression did not change.

"I have my people out looking for him, Boss. He can't go far on his bad foot. We'll find him. Where could he go?"

Lowering his voice, Levich said, "Search Lydia's house. He has stayed there before. The foolish woman dotes on him like a grandson."

"Perhaps I should ask her."

Levich waved away the suggestion. "Not yet. Search first. If he is not found there, so be it. If he's been hiding there, take him. I will question her myself if that's so."

"We will turn the city upside down to find him, Boss."

"Well, you won't find him by standing there, Anton. Take Mikhail with you if you need another hand. Go!"

Turning on his heel, Sheveski went out the way he had come, the bodyguard in tow.

Lydia crept to the study's doorway. "Is Dimitri in trouble?"

"No. He seems to have gone out for air or some such foolishness. We are concerned for him, of course. He is being talked about on the news. The police will be looking for him as well. We need to find him first. He needs medical help."

"Poor Dimitri," she whined. "He must be in pain. A fever perhaps."

"Perhaps," groused Levich. "Who knows why he would break cover at such a time as this. Don't worry, Sheveski and his boys will find him."

"Or the police. God forbid the police. You know Dimitri. His temper."

Levich rose, put a consoling hand on her shoulder. "Yes. Wouldn't it be like our dear Dimitri to refuse to be taken by them? We must trust that Sheveski will find him first."

"I will pray that he is unharmed by day's end."

Yes, thought Levich, you pray, Lydia, though it won't do you any good. He is a dead man. Pray that we find him. My future hinges on that. Yes, pray.

# Chapter 92

Feeling cornered, Wolf called McFadden.

"Hey, Sam, checking in with you."

"So, how are things back east?"

"Tight. Pucker factor high. Caught between the proverbial rock and a hard place. Every landing zone I'm looking at is hot."

"Sorry to hear that, Wolfman. Would it help to know the feds have put a face to the name of Kurskov's killer?"

"I'm working my own angle on that but a name would help at this stage of the game."

"Your boy's name is Dimitri Ivanov. He's a bad actor. Be careful."

"How'd you find out about this guy?"

"Your favorite Hoover Suits came by on a snooping mission yesterday. They know you're back east, of course. Your buddy at State probably worked hand in glove with them to keep track of you. Anyway, this killer's face is hitting the news here as well. Apparently he works for somebody called Boris Levich in Little Odessa."

"I've met Levich."

"No kidding? You move fast, Wolfman."

"I made him an offer he couldn't refuse. I dangled a page from the book in front of him. Told him I'd give the rest of the book if he gave me Kurskov's killer."

"That was a crazy thing to do."

"Why? We knew the guy was connected somehow. It was Nash's idea to confront these scumbags in their own backyard."

McFadden's voice was laden with concern. "You guys are running a dangerous game. Maybe you should rethink where this is headed. Now I'm hearing you talking about the Russian mob and trading for a wanted man."

"We're almost there, Sam. I can feel it."

McFadden broke into nervous laughter. "Back off. Time to call in the cavalry. The feds are your best hope right now."

"Bullshit. Our own people took a run at us, Sam. Did you know that?"

McFadden sighed. "Who? Not somebody from State, I hope."

"Close. A private contractor. Haven't made the connection yet. Gunny Lindgren's looking into it for me."

"And...?"

"That's another story. I'm still standing."

"Oh, man. You have got to put an end to this. Come back out here as soon as you can. You hear me?"

"I can't. Not right now. Got to go, Sam. I'll check the news to see if this killer shows up on television again. I'm still one step ahead of the white hats...though I'm not sure if those are still the good guys. It's messed up. I'll call you."

Wolf put away his phone and looked at Nash busy with his laptop. "Are you any closer to putting this story to bed?"

Raising his hands, the writer said, "It is finished. Hallelujah!"

"You serious?"

A triumphant Nash hit the send key. "Gone! On the way to my editor."

"Can I read it?" said Wolf.

Nash offered the computer. "Be my guest. You have to realize that this is when my editor goes to work. I've put it in the best shape I could. Now it's in the hands of the editing gods."

Wolf took the laptop. "For better or for worse, huh?"

"I trust this guy. We're tight. It should knock his socks off."

Wolf stretched out in the hammock, the laptop on his chest. "You like what you've written?"

Nash grabbed a beer from the cooler, popped the top, and smiled. "I do. I think it's going to make some folks in Little Odessa and elsewhere unhappy. Might even goose the Bureau to ramp up their efforts."

"What about Washington?" said Wolf, beginning his read.

"Plenty of embarrassment and outrage to go around."

Nash plopped down on a couch near the freight elevator, beer in hand. Wolf's eyes darted across the screen as he scrolled through the story.

"Liking what you're seeing?" said Nash.

"Hmmm, so far, so good."

Royce came up the back stairs, carrying his Glock. "I'm going to say this again, guys. We ought to move while we still can."

Nash said, "I'm with you. I'm done here. We can close up the joint early as soon as Mr. Wolf finishes reading."

"Good. I have this uneasy feeling."

"Like we've pushed our luck too far?"

"Exactly."

Nash got up, wandered across the open room to Royce. "What did you have in mind for our next stop?"

"I have a cabin upstate, south of Fort Drum. Two bedrooms. Wolf's been there. Nothing fancy but it's in the woods, far from the Big Apple. I'd feel a lot better about being there while this goes down."

"What's going down?"

Royce laid the Glock on the table. "This wild plan you and Wolf dreamed up about trading the book for Gary Kurskov's killer."

Nash pointed the beer bottle at Wolf. "That's his deal. I just wanted to come along so I could take my best shot at Levich and his crew."

Royce leaned against the pillar supporting one end of the hammock, his eyes on Wolf. "What's going to happen when he finds out there is no book?"

"We'll give him printed copies from the disc and tell him the book no longer exists."

"How long before he puts a bullet between your running lights after he hears that?"

"I'll phone it in from a safe—"

Royce froze and signaled for silence. Grabbing the Glock, he crept to one of the tall windows covered in black cloth. Wolf slipped from the hammock and shut the laptop, returning it to the table. He picked up the other Glock and moved to the brick wall at the head of the stairs. Nash stood rooted to the floor, his eyes studying four camera images on the loft's security system's flat screen: two figures at the street entrance, two probing the rear of the building.

Royce caught Nash's eye, mouthing, *Where? How many?*

Pointing to the stairs, he flashed two fingers. Gesturing to the back of the building, he flashed two fingers. Wolf caught the hand signs and nodded.

Royce waved Nash to his post near the window and gave him his pistol. He slipped into his bedroom and emerged with the loaded Dragunov and a spare magazine. He crossed the room and took position near Wolf at the stairs.

The street-level intercom buzzed.

"Hello. Hello," the accent heavy, unmistakably Russian.

Looking at Royce, Wolf shrugged. *Should we answer?*

A second buzzing, longer. "Hello, Hello."

The freight elevator came to life. The pulley motor cranked, lowering the shuttered wooden cage to the ground floor. Wolf felt the platform shudder as it reached the first floor. A bad sign. Someone was operating the machinery from inside the building. Nash switched to an interior camera and confirmed it with a hand signal.

Below them the wooden gates opened, then closed. The motor hummed, spooling the cables. The cage rose. Backing from the edge of the shaft, Wolf flattened himself against a heavy vertical pillar and aimed his Glock at the shaft. Royce moved to a new position covering both elevator and stairwell. Trembling, Nash dropped on one knee behind a wooden pillar larger than himself, the unfamiliar pistol trained on the shaft.

The freight elevator rose steadily, the greased cable winding around the grinding winch. The three men tensed as the cage emerged on the top floor.

# Chapter 93

"Cover me, Royce."

Wolf inched forward, his Glock steadied in both hands. He peered through the wooden safety door's vertical slats.

"Might be a trap," whispered Nash.

Wolf grasped the cage's dangling canvas strap, pulled upwards, separating the wooden gate's top and bottom. A lumpy six-foot length of rolled carpet lay in the middle of the elevator's steel floor.

"Might be booby-trapped," hissed Royce.

Wolf nudged the carpet with a foot and got a muffled groan in response. Tucking the Glock in his belt, he dragged the bulging rug from the freight elevator, dumping it in the middle of the main room. Turning to Royce, he held out his arms. "What the hell?"

"It's him."

"Who?"

"Kurskov's killer," said Royce. "Gift-wrapped. He's not going to come out shooting."

Wolf circled the carpet, Glock in hand. Nodding to Nash, the two of them kicked with their feet, unrolling the rug. The pale, bloodied body of a naked man lay bound hand and foot. Nash stepped back, covering his nose and mouth.

"Has to be him," said Royce. "This is Levich's part of the bargain."

"Whoever he is," said Wolf, "he's barely alive."

Royce snorted. "Obviously didn't come willingly. He's your man."

A voice boomed from the bottom of the elevator shaft. "His name is Dimitri Ivanov. This is the man you want. Now, you give us the book, eh?"

"How do we know this is the right man?" yelled Wolf. "He could be anyone. Someone you picked at random."

"He is the right man. His is the face on the news. My boss keeps the bargain with you. Give us the book and we leave."

Motioning to the table, Wolf sent Nash to retrieve a thick manila envelope stuffed with printed pages from the book's scanned images. Wolf took the envelope and tossed it into the elevator cage.

"Coming down."

He closed the safety gates, tapped the buzzer to signal the unseen intruders two floors below. The cage creaked in descent. Peering over the edge of the darkened shaft, Wolf heard the gates open, footsteps, and loud voices. What sounded like a disagreement followed, angry Russian words rising from the ground floor.

"They don't buy it," whispered Royce. "Time to call the cops."

"Not yet," said Wolf.

Silence below. Then the commanding voice. "What am I supposed to tell my boss, eh? This is not book, this is just pieces of paper you make."

"Tell Levich the book no longer exists," Wolf yelled. "It was destroyed months ago in Russia. The sheet I gave him was the last remaining original page from the book. I was given the copies you now have. They are the only ones in existence."

"You cannot expect me to believe this! You lie."

"I'm not lying, asshole. Read the words and the figures. Show them to Levich. He will see they are genuine. You have the only copy I was given."

"You wait. I will call him to see what he wishes to do."

Royce crept next to Wolf. "They're playing a game. Buying time. They're up to something."

"Better make up our minds quick," Nash called from the table. He was watching the security cameras. "They're bringing in gas cans through the loading dock. Call the cops!"

Wolf and Royce gathered at the flat screen. "How will we explain these guns?" said a worried Nash, holding aloft a Glock.

Wolf focused on the scurrying images in front of him. "You think it will matter in the next few minutes? Pack your shit, Nash. Your laptop, your notes. Whatever you can't leave behind."

"But the guns," protested Nash, slipping the laptop case over his shoulder.

"Hell, if the cops get here in time, we'll just toss them in the shaft and say they belong to the Russians. Our word against theirs if we survive."

Royce gestured at the split screen. "There are four of them, three of us." "They can't see us but we can see them. I know where they are. If I take the stairs now I'll have surprise on my side. I can take them out, Wolfman. But I have to go now while they're busy getting ready to play firebug."

"What about him?" Nash pointed the Glock at the unconscious Ivanov.

"He comes with us," said Wolf. "Give Royce your pistol for backup. I'll still have mine. Royce, we go out the window to the roof next door. You take these guys out and meet in back."

Grinning, Royce hefted the Dragunov. "I like it. Here, take my car keys just in case. There's a cabin key on the ring. You know where it is."

The two shook hands and embraced.

"Give 'em hell, Royce."

"You know I will, Wolfman. See you out back."

Wolf knelt next to the unconscious Ivanov and hoisted the naked man over his shoulders. He grasped one of the Russian's hands with his left and held the Glock in his right. "Nash, open the first window overlooking the building next door."

Royce halted on the top of the stairs and waved them away. "Go now!"

Wolf heard the Dragunov firing, then an explosion. He had just lowered Ivanov's limp form to Nash on the adjacent roof when the concussion wave hit, knocking him to his knees. Covering his head with his hands, he hugged the floor as a ball of fire blossomed against the ceiling. The boiling flames rolled across the remodeled loft, the interior walls sparing him the worst of it.

Nash grabbed Wolf's arms, dragging him free of the blistered window frame belching thick black smoke. The building's sprinkler system came to life, flooding all levels but losing the battle with rivers of fire pouring down the stairs and licking at support beams.

Nash carried Ivanov to the far end of the not-yet-threatened building and returned to usher Wolf to safety as well. He shook hot cinders from Wolf's shirt and checked him for wounds. Wolf felt his head and torso, came away with bloody hands. "What the hell happened?"

Nash tore his shirtsleeve to fashion a crude compress for Wolf's bleeding scalp. "Royce must have caught those guys in the act," he said. "Never saw anything like it. A flash fire. Boom!"

"Where's Royce?"

"Haven't seen him. Hope he got out the back like he planned."

Wolf was regaining control. "What about the Russkis? What happened to them? Did they get out?"

"Hope not. They probably went up in the explosion."

"Royce. Gotta find Royce. C'mon."

"Are you sure you're in any condition to do this?"

"C'mon. Royce. My pistol," mumbled Wolf.

Nash handed him the Glock. "Saved it. If we don't need it we should toss it before the cops show."

Defiant, Wolf kept the weapon, saying, "We're gonna need it." He tucked the pistol behind him.

Nash and Wolf half-carried, half-dragged Ivanov to the fire escape and worked their way to the ground. Each breath Wolf took helped clear his head. Concentrating on what he had to do, he ran on autopilot through swirling smoke.

The sidewalks were filling with gawkers. A chorus of sirens wailed in the distance. Reluctantly, Nash lowered Ivanov to the ground and stood over him. Two women trotted up the alley through drifting embers, followed by a cyclist.

"Wait for the police, the ambulance," shouted one of the women as they neared the building. "You're hurt, mister. And this man is bleeding."

"I'll be okay," yelled Wolf. "Take care of my friends."

Feeling Royce's car keys in his pocket, Wolf stumbled along the rear of the building until he found the ash-covered Land Rover parked near the alley's mouth. Opening the passenger side door, he slid the Glock under the front seat and locked the door. He came back to the waiting Nash, who knelt in drifting smoke, Ivanov in his arms. The women and cyclist were nowhere to be seen.

"Ivanov's dead," said Nash. "There's no pulse."

Wolf said, "We should get the hell out of here while we can."

"We can't just leave him."

"The hell we can't. He killed Kurskov...and others."

"But the cops should know."

"His face is plastered all over the news. They'll know who he is."

"Besides," wailed Nash, "I can't leave. It's my building, remember? How am I going to explain a bunch of bodies once the fire's out?"

Hands on hips, Wolf looked down at Nash propping up the dead Ivanov. "Well, there's nothing here to keep me around."

"I could use your help," said Nash. "We can tell the truth. The cops will listen. You could speak to the feds. Tell them what's going on with the mob."

Wolf hesitated, moved by Nash's appeal. He agreed to stand fast until police arrived. The two went over their story while they waited. Wolf insisted their narrative be consistent. Safe from the flames for now, they rehearsed the telling. Wolf corrected the timeline Nash recited. Nash added details Wolf had forgotten. At their feet lay Ivanov.

Firefighters crawled over the roof, smashing newly installed skylights to gain access to the loft's interior. The trapped smoke, dense and dark, blossomed anew. Crews wielding soaker hoses fought to contain the flames. An ambulance rumbled up the alley through the thick smoke. Guided by a cop, it came to a stop next to Wolf and Nash. EMTs bounded from the vehicle.

Pointing to Ivanov, Nash said, "He's dead."

The paramedics knelt over Ivanov, trying to revive him without success. Waving over the policeman, Wolf pointed to Ivanov's body. "You might want to check with your supervisor, Officer. This guy is Dimitri Ivanov."

"Who's Dimitri Ivanov?" said the cop.

"He's wanted for murder in California. He's Russian mob. His face is all over the news right now. And the FBI is looking for him."

"Really? And you might be?"

"Name's Tom Wolf."

"And I'm Sean Nash, Officer. I own this building."

The cop took a step back and called on his lapel mike. He came back to Wolf. "The lieutenant's on his way over. Meantime, you guys need to check in with the EMTs. You look like shit, both of you."

While one emergency responder offered Wolf and Nash oxygen masks to clear the smoke from their lungs, his partner covered Ivanov's body with a sheet. Wolf and Nash were checked for cuts while they sat on the vehicle's bumper step breathing clean air. Offered cold water, the two downed a bottle each and asked for more. Wolf held a bottle aloft, letting the cool liquid wash over his face, rinsing soot and sweat from his eyes.

The cop's supervisor, a bull-necked lieutenant wearing a clipped mustache and a skeptical attitude, high-stepped over snaking hoses and asked Wolf to repeat his claim.

He relayed the news about Ivanov to the brass, then said, "Okay. Here's what we're gonna do. When the EMTs give you a green light, we'll get you to the precinct house and take your statements." Pausing to look them over, he added, "You guys have a place to stay?"

They shook their heads. Nash pointed to the smoldering loft. "That was it. All I have left is my laptop and what I'm wearing."

"How about you?" he said to Wolf.

"I've got my friend's car. That's it."

"Nobody to stay with? Nobody who could take you guys in?"

Wolf and Nash shrugged.

"We'll get you a city voucher for some meals, some clothes, and a couple nights in a hotel. Maybe the Red Cross will put you up. First things first."

The lieutenant nodded at the cop who had summoned him. "You guys ride with Emerson to the stationhouse and get the paperwork started." Turning to leave, he said over his shoulder, "Sorry about your loss, pal."

Nash waved in acknowledgement.

"Guess I'd better call my insurance guy."

Watching the burning building, Wolf said, "So much for your remodeling project."

The EMTs wrestled Ivanov's corpse onto a collapsible gurney and lifted it to the rear of the ambulance. They shut the rear doors and huddled with the lieutenant. He sent the crew on their way and turned to Wolf. "Emerson has a squad car at the end of the alley. He'll take you to the stationhouse."

Wolf and Nash trailed the cop down the alley, past the fire trucks, hoses, and onlookers. Glancing both ways to avoid being overheard, Nash whispered, "What about the bodies on the ground floor? What's going to happen when they find them?"

Speaking without looking at him, Wolf said, "It's going to make for some very interesting conversation for starters."

"You realize they'll find Royce, don't you?"

Wolf nodded. "I hope so. He's the only one I care about."

# Chapter 94

Sheveski's last call told Levich he had paper copies of the book's pages, nothing more. At the time, enraged at what he considered a double-cross, Levich ordered the loft torched as planned. But something had obviously gone wrong. Sheveski had not called again as promised.

Levich finished dressing and went to the television in his den. The local station had the answer. A breathless Channel Seven reporter on the scene was doing her best to describe firefighting efforts.

"We're on Brooklyn's Union Street and Second Avenue. Behind me you can see the challenge facing ladder crews. Eyewitness News has learned that several neighbors heard a huge explosion and then arrived here to see raging flames shooting from every window." Her voice continued as dramatic helicopter shots showed the conflagration being fought by three crews. "Several survivors escaped the explosion. There may be one fatality, but that is unconfirmed as of now. Stay tuned for an update."

Drawn to the screen, Levich knew instantly what had happened to Sheveski. On the street below the chopper, a tangle of hoses ended at the base of a thinning plume of black smoke. There would be no book. That much was clear to Levich.

*Sheveski might have survived, but that would prove an inconvenience if he was tied to the arson. Had all worked as expected I should have had the book in my hands by now. I cannot risk waiting one more moment.*

Levich had planned his escape well, but nagging doubts plagued him as he shut off the television. The hired car was due to arrive at any moment.

Wearing his favorite navy blue Italian suit and ivory silk tie, Levich threw on a cashmere overcoat and donned a fedora.

Picking up the leather valise, he went past the kitchen where Lydia was preparing his supper.

"Boss, you are going out? I fix your lunch for you."

"I have an errand to run, Lydia. Put it in the oven where it will keep for an hour. I'll return shortly."

"You go by yourself?"

Flashing a paternal smile, Levich said, "Am I not permitted such a privilege?"

She blushed at his mild rebuke.

"When you go home tonight, take the envelope on the table in the foyer with you."

"Do you wish me to mail it for you?"

"No, dear Lydia. The envelope is for you. *Dosvidanya*."

"*Dosvidanya*, Boss."

Levich rode to the ground floor, nodded to the doorman who held the door. A suited, unsmiling man the size of a linebacker opened the rear door of a town car. Levich sank in the backseat, the precious leather valise on his lap. The big car pulled away, bound for Kennedy Airport. Knowing he would not return, Levich gazed at Little Odessa's familiar skyline, the distant beach, the sea.

*Did the book still exist? Would my plotting be discovered? In twelve hours I will be in Israel, beyond the reach of American authorities. And if the Brotherhood in Moscow remains ignorant, I have nothing to fear.*

# Chapter 95

Questioned separately, Nash and Wolf endured four hours of interrogation by detectives. The one thing they had agreed not to divulge was the existence of the much-sought-after book.

"And this guy Ivanov," said a beefy Italian detective, "he was the reason for this bizarre arson?"

Wolf said, "I believe so. They brought him to us and dumped him. They thought that would buy Nash's silence about the Russian mob."

In a nearby interviewing room, Nash was telling his team of questioners the same thing. "I was finishing my article. Their giving up Ivanov was their version of a quid pro quo. Frankly, I don't think they were going to honor their part of the bargain."

"Our guys on the scene tell me they found five bodies on the first floor."

"That make sense," said Nash. "We counted four intruders on the security camera...and then, Royce."

"But you and Wolf made it out with Dimitri Ivanov. How did that work?"

"We wanted to turn over Ivanov to the cops. We knew he was wanted for murder in California. He was barely alive when they tossed him our way. It's obvious they were planning to torch the place anyway. It blew up in their faces prematurely."

"And your friend, Royce. How come he didn't make it out with you and Wolf?"

"We headed for a window on the top floor. There was a short drop to the roof next door. Royce must have taken a wrong turn in the smoke. It was dark. That's about the time the explosion happened."

Not completely convinced, the detective said, "Okay. A few more questions. I'll be right back."

The cop went next door where his colleagues were running Wolf through the same drill. He knocked, let himself in, and took a seat in the corner. Wolf had just finished answering a string of questions put to him by a lanky, sour-faced detective named Willis.

Willis said, "So, Royce doesn't make it out alive. How come you get away with Nash and the Russian guy and Royce gets left behind?"

"It all happened the same time the place went up in a fireball. I was handing Ivanov out a window when the place exploded."

"We don't have IDs on any of the five bodies we found on the ground floor."

"One of them will be Royce, Detective. He's a former Army Ranger. The service will have his medical records if you need them."

"You're sure he didn't get out?"

"No question. He was supposed to meet us out back. I'm sure you've got the four Russians and Royce."

The detective named Willis loosened his tie and got up from the table where he had been jotting notes. "You can stop the questioning any time and ask for a lawyer. You sure you don't want a lawyer, Mr. Wolf?"

"I don't need one. I've told you guys what happened. You can check with Nash. He was there."

"So he was," conceded Willis. "Okay. You can go...for now. We might need to call you back in if we run into problems."

"You've got my number, Detective. I'll be available."

"You sure you don't want protection? I mean, the Russian mob is a nasty bunch. They won't be happy about losing four of their own."

"Four less assholes, if you ask me," said Wolf.

"Five if you count Ivanov," said Willis.

"I stand corrected. Five. Nash and I will be fine, Detective."

"Okay. We're done for now. Thanks for your cooperation."

"Royce has an ex-wife in Boston," said Wolf. "When the medical examiner releases his body, I'd be willing to contact her and make whatever arrangements are needed."

"We'll keep that in mind. I'll have an officer give you a lift."

"Appreciate it."

Wolf left the interview room and went downstairs to wait for Nash. When he showed, accompanied by a uniformed patrolman, they asked to be driven back to the burned-out loft. Dropped there, they lingered at the site until the cop left. Wrapped in yellow crime scene tape, the charred three-story building wore sooty scars like ruined mascara. Tossed outside by firefighters during the battle, piles of burned remodeling materials covered the ground.

"Sorry about this," said a somber Wolf.

"I've got insurance. I'll survive. Though right now if someone were to make me an offer, I'd grab it."

Wolf said, "Sort that out later. Let's use Royce's car to get away."

"What do you mean, 'Get away'?"

Clapping Nash on the back, Wolf said, "Get out of town for a while."

"But the cops—"

"Hey, why hang around waiting for the Russkis to come after us?"

"What about our interviews?"

Wolf smiled. "I think they went rather well, don't you? I can read people, Nash. We boxed them in. We told the truth...so maybe we left out the part about the magic book... but we told it like it happened."

"I'm surprised you agreed to stay."

They walked to Royce's abandoned car. "You were right," Wolf said. "But now we need to make ourselves scarce for a while. Oh, don't worry—we'll stay in touch with the cops. They've got a job to do in the wake of what's happened here. But so do we."

In the car, Wolf said, "Pull out the glove compartment. It'll come loose after a few tugs. You'll find a roll of cash behind it. That's Royce's mad money for just such an occasion."

Within seconds, Nash held up the cash and flipped through the bills. "There's eight hundred here."

Wolf started the engine and turned his eyes upward. "Thank you, Royce. We're heading north to the cabin."

Nash navigated out of Brooklyn, through Queens, across the George Washington Bridge, and eventually north on I-87.

"Royce's cabin is almost five hours northwest of here," said Wolf. "We might hit some tolls."

"That means cameras."

"Trust me. They have no idea where we're going."

"Someone might have copied the license number back at the scene."

"Yeah, that's a risk."

"But five hours." Nash did the math. "That's almost three hundred miles. Do we really need to do this? Besides, you could use cleaning up."

Slumping in his seat, Wolf groused, "You don't smell so good yourself."

"I meant medically. You look like you have a bad sunburn. Maybe first or second-degree. It has to bother you."

"Some."

They drove in silence for an hour. Wolf said, "We'll stop on the outskirts of Albany for gas. We can buy some clean clothes, first aid supplies, and food."

Staring out the window at passing cars, Nash said, "I'm sorry about Royce."

Wolf nodded. "Me too. With the fire it will take them several days to ID everybody. We can use the time to plan our next move."

"I'll need to check in with my editor at the Albany stop. Our run-in with the Russian mob has to be all over the news by now."

"We'll be okay. We can call the cops if you're worried. They won't be able to put the puzzle together for a while. We'll be safe. Nobody knows about Royce's cabin."

"Where we going again?"

"Past Utica. Nearest town is Florence. Maybe twelve hundred souls. Royce bought his property when he got out of the service. Pretty little place. Forty acres. Sits in the middle of the woods. Utilities off the grid. Thousands of acres of state forest around him. He loved it. I helped put on the roof when he..." Wolf's voice softened, trailed off.

Nash didn't bother him again until they came off the highway near Albany. They refueled and bought sandwiches, cartons of bottled water, and prepaid cell phones. Wolf had Nash drive to a chain store for the rest of what they needed. Nash called his editor, was told he was out, and left a message he would try again. He got them back on the road in forty minutes and finally surrendered the wheel in Rome. From there to Florence was a silent, solitary ride with no traffic except a one-eyed pickup passing them going south.

Despite the years, Wolf found the correct gravel spur. Swallowed by the dark save for headlights, he took them all the way to Royce's cabin without missing a turn on a weedy, winding track carved from the forest. Out of habit he parked the car under a thick hardwood canopy offering good cover in daylight. They carried everything inside by flashlight. Only then did he strip off his shirt and allow Nash to apply a coat of soothing gel to his bright red arms and back.

# Chapter 96

Wolf slept without moving for ten hours. Nash was up before that, trying unsuccessfully to get a signal in the tiny clearing. Nothing worked. Frustrated, he gave up, came inside, and found a bare-chested Wolf shaving over a washbasin.

"How'd you sleep?" said Nash.

"Feel like a folding chair left out in the rain for two days."

"Your back still looks like a lobster's. Not worse, not better."

"Looks are deceiving. It feels better."

"Coffee?"

"I prefer tea. But, yeah, I'll settle for a cup of java."

Nash rummaged in the knotty pine cupboards for another mug. He poured from an enameled pot warming on the cabin's cast iron stove and set it on the counter beside Wolf.

"Can't get a decent signal. Back in Albany, I left a message on my editor's voice mail saying I'd call again. Maybe I'll go into town to see if that works."

Wolf shook his razor in the basin and toweled shaving cream from his chin. "Take the car all the way into Rome. That way you won't draw as much attention like you would in Florence. Just a precaution."

"You're right. Shoulda thought of that."

"You'll get back in the habit."

"You want anything else in town? Maybe you want to come along."

Arching his back, Wolf said, "Nah, I've put in enough car travel for a while. I'll hold down the fort while you're gone. Come to think of it, you could do me a favor."

"Name it."

"Call Sam McFadden. Bring him up to speed. He'll be worried."

"Just the thought of California makes me wish I was sitting on my deck in Santa Barbara right about now."

Wolf flashed a faint smile. "Hell, Nash, I'd like to be sitting on your deck in Santa Barbara right about now. No, belay that. Actually, I'd like to be in Santa Barbara ordering pancakes and trading quips and phone numbers with Edie, the waitress."

"Well, make that your goal then."

"I intend to when this is done. There is the little matter of the Agency's hired man. That's unfinished business as far as I'm concerned."

"Someone's bound to find the guy if they go poking around the neighborhood after the fire. Could that come back to haunt us?"

"According to Royce, they won't find much. Don't forget, the guy was going to kill us. Don't shed any tears. It was him or us."

Nash threw on his jacket. "That's a reassuring thought. On that note, I'm off to Rome to make some calls."

Wolf gave him a hand-drawn map of the area and the road to Royce's cabin. "Keep it handy." Coffee mug in hand, Wolf, shirtless, walked him to the cabin's porch. "Be back before dark. Remember, you're my only ride out of here."

# Chapter 97

After treating himself to a latte and a scone at a coffee shop, Nash called Sam McFadden in San Diego as instructed. Elated to hear from Nash, the former Green Beret kept his end of the conversation short.

"You never know who's listening these days. Sorry to hear about the loss. Tell our friend I'm following up on things from my end. Keep your heads down and keep the faith. Call home when you can."

Buoyed by McFadden's response, Nash next called his editor.

"Great to hear from you, Sean. I heard the news about the shootout at the O.K. Corral. Geez, you had me worried. Everyone here thought it was a case of déjà vu. Oh, by the way, got your stuff."

"So, what did you think?"

"Some of your strongest writing. You did a job on the Russian mob. You haven't been this tough since..."

"Since Danae's death. I know. I hope you can find the space, Roger." An unsettling pause. "Roger, you do have room for it, don't you?"

"Well, space isn't the problem with the piece."

"Talk to me. What's going on?"

"It's the suits, Sean. The boys in legal think the piece is too long on opinion and short on facts."

Nash finished his coffee and crushed the cup in anger. "Don't do this to me, Roger. Do you know what I've been through? Do you realize how I put my neck on the block for this story?"

"Of course I do. Look, I think it's a dynamite piece, Sean. It's just that legal is not going to let it fly. At least not the way it's written. I can't run it without them signing off on it. And right now they won't touch it."

"Tell me their objections. Maybe I can tweak it. Tone it down."

"No good, Sean. They got up on their hind legs about it. You know how they are. They want me to spike it."

Stunned, Nash got up from the coffee shop and walked outside, the phone to his ear. "That's it. You're telling me you're not going to go to the mat on this one."

"I can't, Sean. They won't budge."

"I practically wrote this piece in my own blood."

"Don't be so dramatic, Sean."

Yelling, "Fuck the lawyers!" Nash killed the call. He got back in the car, his head against the steering wheel, tears in his eyes. For fifteen minutes, Nash sat there without moving. Finally, he started the engine and drove away.

Nash found his way back to the cabin and parked under the thick umbrella of leaves as Wolf had done. He got out of the car and climbed the stairs with leaden legs. Wolf was as he left him—shirtless. He was studying a framed topographic wall map of Oneida County when Nash came through the door. "I got your tea," said the writer, handing him a small tin.

"Outstanding. Appreciate it. Hey, you look like you just learned your puppy died. What's going on? Did you get hold of McFadden?"

Slumping in a chair, Nash nodded. Wolf put away the tea and sat opposite him. "So, what's the skinny from San Diego?"

"Sam says he'll do what he can on his end. He'll make some calls. You're to keep the faith, watch your back. Call when you can."

"Something's eating you. What is it?"

Slamming a fist on the table, Nash snarled, "Fucking lawyers!"

Wolf stiffened. "Your editor, huh? Let me guess. You called your editor and he passed on your piece, didn't he?"

In a dark mood, his eyes on the floor, Nash nodded without speaking.

"Don't tell me. The magazine's lawyers think your piece is libelous."

"All he told me was that the legal department said it was too long on opinion and too short on facts."

"Bullshit. It's a solid piece of reporting and we both know it."

Finally looking Wolf in the eye, Nash threw up his hands, saying, "On one hand he tells me it's some of my best writing. On the other hand...it doesn't matter. It's not going to see the light of day."

"They got to them," murmured Wolf.

"Who?"

"The Agency, the White House, State. Somebody in one of those outfits got to the magazine's publisher. They got the lawyers involved."

"How can you prove that?"

"I can't. That's the beauty of what they've done. Can't trace it." Wolf got up from the table, agitated. "I've seen this before. In our case it's kill the messenger. Since they didn't kill the messenger, kill the message."

Whirling on Nash, he said, "You know, we should have expected this. Should have seen it coming. Hard to anticipate something like this, but you have to give it to them. They're playing hardball."

"You sound so sure about this."

Wolf came back to the table. "Oh, I am. I'm certain. That guy at State I told you about had to have a hand in this."

"Nells?"

"That's the sneaky bastard. I'll bet his fingerprints are all over this."

"No one will touch my copy with a ten-foot pole," groaned Nash.

"You could take this to the *Times*. You can post it online, leak it to Fox, CNN, Public Radio, or the BBC. Any one of those outlets would love a scoop like this. One of them is bound to run with it."

"They, whoever 'They' might be, are probably already closing those avenues while we sit here in the middle of nowhere," said Nash.

"What about a shotgun mailing to every news outlet you can think of?"

"They'd eventually come after you and they'd ruin me."

"You willing to risk it?" said Wolf. "This would be so public they couldn't afford to touch you."

"But they'd know you were involved. We go public with this and you'd be on their short list."

"Hell, I'm already on a dozen short lists."

Wolf's rapid-fire delivery was like a locker room halftime speech. Nash caught the fire. "Okay, let's start with the *Times*.

If the Gray Lady goes for it we're halfway home. After that, we could post my version anonymously."

Slapping him on the back, Wolf said, "Now you're back in the fight."

"Let's drive to Rome," said Nash. "I'll call some people at the *Times* and run this past them. If they go for it, I'll send the file. They can have the byline."

"They'll go for it," claimed Wolf. "This is their kind of story. Tell them they have first shot at it. If they hesitate, say you're ready to go online with it. They'll smell blood in the water."

Nash took a long look at Wolf's healing back and arms. "You good enough to go to town?"

Throwing on a shirt, Wolf said, "Be hard to keep me from a fight."

# Chapter 98

*Renaissance Hotel, Tel Aviv*

Boris Levich, his mind foggy from the twelve-hour flight from New York, didn't register the ringing phone. He rolled over, irritated at the interruption of a half-formed dream. Levich propped himself on bony elbows when the ringing finally stopped, replaced by a blinking red message button. He rubbed sleep from puffy eyes, stretched, and yawned like an aging lion. Levich threw off the sheets and pushed himself into a sitting position on the edge of the king-sized bed.

He shuffled to the suite's balcony and opened the doors to the sound of waves on breakwaters far below. The Mediterranean stretched to the horizon like shimmering blue silk. From his fourteenth-floor aerie, ant-like beachgoers dotted the brilliant white sand beyond the tiled promenade. To his right, a crowded forest of masts filled the Tel Aviv Marina. To his left, more high-rises and beach. A gentle breeze parted the gossamer curtains. Levich gripped the balcony railing, closed his eyes, and leaned back, inhaling the sea air. Israel, an oft thought-of destination, was a reality at last.

His life's journey—begun in Kiev, forged in the Gulag's brutality, shaped by the Brotherhood's internecine cannibalism, tempered by his immigrant's struggle to survive and eventual triumph in Little Odessa's criminal netherworld—ended here among his fellow Jews.

*No one can touch me here*, he told himself. *I have arrived. I am not some penniless Ukrainian Jew washing ashore, seeking the favor of those in authority. It will be those in authority who will soon be seeking my favor. I may have fled my adopted country in the eleventh hour but I am still a man to be reckoned with. And if I believed in God I would say he had blessed me but that would be superstitious nonsense. I have made my own way as before. Tel Aviv suits me. There is an energy here I can tap into. My journey ends here.*

Later, Levich checked his messages. As expected, his Brotherhood contact, Viktor Askov, had been delegated to call and welcome him. He was to phone again this evening.

*Good*, thought Levich. *Viktor will be useful. He will introduce me to others who have gone before me. I will have to be careful to study the structure here and move only when I am guaranteed success. One must be cunning.* Levich smiled at his image in the bathroom mirror. *I am certainly that.* He showered, shaved, and dressed in the one set of clothes he had carried in the valise. As he expected, the slothful TSA drones had not done a thorough search of the case.

Refreshed, Levich went downstairs to the hotel's Africa Restaurant. At a table overlooking the beach, he asked for a pot of coffee and a carafe of orange juice. While waiting for those to arrive, he prowled a groaning buffet piled high with fresh fruit, pastries, cheeses, and breads. Feeling strangely liberated in his temporary anonymity, Levich piled his plate and stopped to order a vegetarian omelet. He ate a leisurely breakfast as he watched the beach parade. In the afternoon, he did some shopping to begin replacing the wardrobe he had abandoned in his flight.

When Viktor called again, Levich was ready to receive him. They agreed to meet in the hotel's Renaissance Club Lounge with its spectacular views of the ancient Jaffa seashore. Claiming a private corner window with two facing couches and a table laid with Russian pastries and a silver coffee service, Levich played the role of a lord about to entertain a petitioner.

He rose to greet Viktor Askov with a smile and a genuine embrace. "How good it is to see you, my friend. You are looking well. Israel agrees with you, eh?"

"Israel agrees with all of us," growled his guest. A burly peasant thug with wide-spaced eyes and a flattened nose earned in bar brawls, Askov looked as if he still belonged on some master's estate in czarist Russia. Wearing a sport coat and open-necked white shirt, the Spetsnaz veteran was ill at ease in the palatial surroundings.

"You pick a good spot, Boris Levich. This is expensive, you know."

Levich smiled conspiratorially. "Yes, I think it will cost me three hundred dollars a day, Viktor."

"How long do you expect to stay here?"

"Ten days, I think."

Levich watched his guest run the numbers in his head. Glancing about the lounge, Askov shook his head, impressed at the cost.

"So, Viktor, what can you tell me about our friends? I'm glad you came to see me. I don't forget your courtesy."

Waving away the flattery, Askov sipped his sweetened coffee. "Ah, we are anxious to hear what things have changed in America for you, what brings you to our shores. These are tough times for us, Boris Levich."

Levich wagged a bony finger. "Not good to hear that. I was told this is the land of opportunity. What news from the Brotherhood?"

Lowering his voice, Viktor said, "You must realize the Americans are busy here. Their FBI works with the government. There has been talk of shutting down some of our operations just to make things easier for a while."

"Did I choose the wrong time to arrive?"

"No, of course not. It's just that with the situation between our enemies and us, we cannot afford to be so high profile, you know?"

Nodding sagely, Levich made his pitch. "Which of the bosses should I call on? I need to hear what they advise for a man like me who arrives not knowing all the players, you know."

"You want to know where you can fit in, eh?"

"Yes, something like that. I don't come to be idle, Viktor Askov. There is always room for one more at the table, eh?"

Askov pondered Levich's remark. "Okay, I understand what you are asking. Let me report to them that you have arrived safely and that you are telling me you wish to be accepted into the circles. True?"

"It would be an honor, Viktor. I wish to settle here. It's a dream come true for me. I have always longed to return. I've thought of little else all these years."

"Okay. I will do what I can to arrange this."

"Please convey my best wishes to the council. When you have news, call me. I will be here for the next ten days."

Askov grinned. "In that case, I'd better make arrangements quickly before you run out of money, eh?"

"I'll manage for a while, Viktor. Perhaps they will let me wash dishes to pay my bill."

Askov finished his coffee and got to his feet. "Somehow I don't think you are going to have to do such a thing."

Levich walked his guest to the elevator. In the lobby, the two parted with a hug and Levich returned to his room to make two calls.

# Chapter 99

*Brooklyn*

Nash yelled down the charred stairwell. "Who's there?"

Footfalls on the steps, then a face appeared on the soot-filled landing. "Jerry Little, your insurance adjustor, Mr. Nash. You think it's safe?"

"The top floor seems sound enough," said Nash.

It had been a week since the fire. Wolf and Nash had returned to the blackened loft to meet with Nash's insurance company representative. They waited on the top floor.

Wearing a bright yellow vest and a hardhat plastered with the company logo, Little, a cherubic chatterbox ventured upstairs, camera and digital tablet in hand. After introductions, he did a cautious walk-through with Nash. Snapping pictures and typing notes, Little explored the damage and a gaping hole in the roof made by fire crews.

Wolf's attention was drawn to the gutted storefront across the street. Two patrol cars had arrived and parked. Wolf glanced out a charred window frame at two uniforms peering in the smudged windows. As he watched, the second pair of patrolmen headed to the rear of the building.

"Uh, oh," said Wolf. "We got visitors."

Nash deserted the adjustor and came up behind Wolf. "Oh, shit. What are they doing here?"

"Probably got a call."

Nash stepped back from the window. "What are we gonna do?"

Putting a hand on Nash's shoulder, Wolf's blue eyes bored into him. "We're going to remain calm. We don't know anything about that building, do we?"

"Right. We don't know a thing," said Nash. "We're just here to meet with my insurance agent about the fire."

"Good. Take a deep breath and finish the walk-through with Mr. Little."

"But if the cops come up here—"

Wolf said, "Then I'll do most of the talking. Take your cues from me."

Nash caught up with the agent and Wolf continued his vigil at the window. Imagining the scene on the second floor of the building opposite, Wolf remembered Royce's assurance to Nash when the journalist had asked about the sniper. *"I don't think that will be a problem." Wasn't that what Royce had said?*

As Wolf watched, a van joined the parked squads. Two crime scene techs with kits got out and followed a waiting officer inside.

*This is going to be interesting.*

# Chapter 100

"Not a good sign," murmured Wolf softly, as a medical examiner's van arrived across the street from Nash's ruin. As Wolf watched, an unmarked sedan arrived and two plainclothes detectives got out. One of the officers spoke with the uniformed cops. The other detective eyed the burned loft and crossed the street to intercept the insurance adjustor, who was leaving. The two chatted on the sidewalk as Nash and Wolf watched from the top floor.

"I know this guy," whispered Wolf. "Name's Willis. He interviewed me the day of the fire. He's a Columbo wannabe."

The detective sent the agent on his way and spotted Wolf in the charred window above.

"HELLO!"

Wolf gave Nash a reassuring squeeze on his arm and peered out the window. "Up here."

"I'm Detective Willis, Seventy-third Precinct."

"I recognized you, Detective. C'mon up, but be careful."

At the top of the stairs, Nash deadpanned to Willis, "We had a fire."

Willis said, "Do tell." Testing the floorboards with his foot, he said, "This structure might not be safe. You thought of that?"

Wolf greeted the cop. "Ah, Detective Willis. What can we do for you?"

"For starters, you can explain where the hell you two have been for the last three days." Red-faced from the climb, Willis, short and round-faced, said, "My lieutenant's been chewing my ass about getting hold of you. He's got the press climbing all over him for details about this fire and the five victims found here."

"Sorry about being out of touch," said a convincingly contrite Wolf. "There's lousy phone reception where we're staying."

"Where's that, Canada?"

"Just about. A friend's cabin north of Albany."

"Geez, why didn't you say something? We made arrangements for you to stay in the city, you know."

Wolf said, "We didn't think it was safe."

"My lieutenant will be happy to know his wandering witnesses are back in town."

Willis brushed ashes from his shoes. "One of the neighbors called to say someone was rooting around in the place. We gambled it might be you guys."

"Nice to know the place is being watched," said Nash.

Willis shrugged. "Good neighbors. What can I say?" Glancing across the street, he said, "Actually, that's not the reason I'm here."

Nash stiffened. Wolf waited for the next question.

Willis nodded at the blackened brick walls. "You gonna rebuild?"

"If the city doesn't condemn it."

"Do yourself a favor, don't bother rebuilding. Better yet, take the settlement money and run." Stooping to pick up a cracked brick, Willis said, "Old bricks like these get baked and they may turn to dust sooner than you think. I'd bet this wasn't the first fire."

Nash played the innocent. "It was for me. I'll see what they offer before I make up my mind. So, what can we do for you?"

Willis tossed the brick and rubbed the dust from his hands. "I read the report on what happened. The arson investigator says it was deliberate. No question about it." Sniffing the stale air, he said, "You can still smell the gasoline. That never goes away. We haven't ID'd the bodies yet."

"No surprise," said Wolf. "But we know one of them was our guy."

"So I heard. Sorry about that."

Wolf gambled. "What's going on across the street?"

"Oh, that," said Willis. "Some building inspector found a body on the second floor. Looks like he might have been there a while."

"That must have been a shock," said Wolf.

"Yeah, I bet it was."

"A homeless guy?"

"Who knows?" Willis wandered to the nearest window and looked across the street, his back to Wolf and Nash. "Did you happen to notice any activity over there? I mean, while you were using this loft? Anything out of the ordinary?"

"Not that I recall," said Wolf. "We were preoccupied."

"You, Mr. Nash?"

Shrugging, Nash repeated Wolf's words. "Like he said, 'We were preoccupied,' Detective."

Willis said, "If you notice anything funny once we pack up, let us know. People coming and going. Drifters. That sort of thing."

He studied the remnants of the loft. "Hope you come out okay on the insurance, Mr. Nash."

"Thanks."

Pausing on the top step, Willis said, "We'll try to get you closure as soon as we can."

"Not an easy job," said Wolf. "Any timetable on when our friend's body will be released, Detective?"

"That'll have to come from the medical examiner's office. Give them a call by week's end. Ah, one more thought," said Willis, poised to leave. "You ought to keep an eye open. The Russkis are still out there."

"Will do," said Wolf. "As soon as we're done here we're going to ground again."

"Good plan. Remember, they have long memories and they don't look kindly on losing four of their own."

"Royce was worth one hundred of them, Detective."

# Chapter 101

The Russians did not come that day.

The insurance agent handling the destroyed loft called Nash when he and Wolf were back on the road, heading north to Royce's cabin. The building and its contents had been declared a total loss. The company proposed a generous settlement. Wolf and Nash spent the evening discussing the offer while feeding kindling to the cabin's cast iron stove.

"Take it," counseled Wolf. "You can rebuild or go abroad, or go back to Santa Barbara and write that novel you said you always wanted to."

"Maybe later. I want to hang around and see how people react to next month's *Times Sunday Magazine* cover story on the Russian mob." Nash had found a receptive audience at the magazine after prolonged discussions.

Wolf shook his head. "You can do that from the comfort of your beach condo. You don't need to make yourself a target by staying here."

"I'm anonymous. I'm not getting the byline," grumbled Nash. "I only turned over my first draft because they agreed to run it after reworking it."

"You knew that was the price for getting it into print."

A moody Nash threw another piece of bone-dry maple in the fire and shut the iron door with a poker. "I know. A guy's got a right to bitch about it if he wants to."

"Let it go," said Wolf. "The point was to get the story out there."

"Okay, it's going to be out there, then what?"

Wolf warmed his hands at the stove. "The last time we went into town I checked train timetables using the coffee shop's Wi-Fi. I plan on going back to Washington a few days ahead of your piece running in the *Times*. I want to make a house call on an old acquaintance. Keep Royce's car as long as you need it. You're welcome to stay here in the meantime."

"You're coming back then?"

"Affirmative. Once the medical examiner releases Royce's body I'll head back to make arrangements for his funeral with his ex-wife. He wanted his ashes scattered here. She never liked being in the woods, but I'm going to make damned sure he gets his wish."

They sat in silence. Wolf fed another foot-long piece to the flames in the stove's belly. The fire licked at the wood, popping sparks in the mound of glowing embers. He shut the stove's door. "Take the money, Nash."

"I'm thinking about it. Don't want to make a decision I might regret."

"Take your time. How about we head back to Albany in a couple days? You can drop me at the train station so I can catch a shuttle to Penn Station and from there, Union Station in Washington. Keep the Glock," said Wolf. "It's frowned upon to pack a weapon on board a train. No need to attract attention. Hopefully you won't need it, but you never know."

"That leaves you unarmed."

Wolf said, "Don't worry about me. I'm sure I can find a sharp stick or a rock somewhere. I'll be okay."

"If I know anything about you, you'll be looking for trouble once you get to Washington."

"Me? I wouldn't hurt a fly."

# Chapter 102

Levich didn't waste time. Constantly on the phone, he made dozens of contacts in Tel Aviv and Jerusalem from a list he had compiled over the years. Courting the influential, he met for lunch in the hotel's Club Lounge, seducing the impressionable with first-class meals served with a view of the aquamarine sea. Writing checks on his newly opened account, Levich seeded charities run by rabbis, a support-starved Jewish antiquities museum, a private girls' school, a struggling health clinic, and an ultra-orthodox yeshiva desperate for funds.

Collecting praise, goodwill, and grass roots connections in the first eight days, Levich extended his stay at the Renaissance Hotel by an additional week. During that time the exiled godfather hooked the first of his politicians. A conservative member of the Knesset took the bait through word of mouth. A confidant of one of the rabbis running a charity, the greedy politico walked away with an envelope stuffed with five thousand of Levich's dollars. It was a start. The money, like Levich's other largesse, was an investment.

Viktor brought Realtor Ari Berezov to Levich's suite. Seeking a home where he could entertain in privacy, Levich was prepared to spend well to permanently anchor his roots in Israel.

Over tea, Berezov showed a portfolio of secluded, tasteful homes in southwest Tel Aviv's Neve Tzedek neighborhood. "You will love this district," he promised. "Many influential people reside here. A former prime minister, several cabinet members, successful artists, and highly decorated IDF generals make their homes here."

"In America," said Levich disingenuously, "I was just another ordinary businessman in New York. I lived in a modest five-room apartment. I valued my privacy and my security. Crime can sometimes be a problem in New York, you know. Given human nature I assume the same is true here, yes?"

"So I've heard," said Berezov. Winking, he said, "Rumor has it several Mossad veterans live quiet lives along these shaded streets, so rest assured your security concerns will be of no concern."

"I take you at your word. Any suggestions as to a particular home?"

"Ah, for a client with your tastes and requirements, I have several choices in mind," he beamed. "With your permission I will arrange some showings, should you wish me to do so."

"I would like that. Viktor, you will come with us, of course."

"Of course. My pleasure."

As Berezov discreetly busied himself with brochures and city maps, Viktor leaned close to Levich's ear, whispering, "We really should meet with Uri Koronsky first. He has been waiting to see you."

"Of course, Viktor. First, let's see what Mr. Berezov has for us."

"Koronsky is not used to waiting. Those seeking his favor are the ones who usually do the waiting."

"Well, let us send a message, Viktor. I am not seeking his favor. When we do meet it will be as equals. We'll meet when the time is right, not before. And I will pick the time."

"I do not think he will take kindly to such an affront."

"Maybe a little affront goes a long way, eh? Trust me, Viktor, Koronsky can wait."

All smiles, Levich rose and ushered Berezov to his suite's door with the understanding they would begin their search on the morrow.

The next day, Levich looked at homes in the city's Neve Tzedek quarter. Like all enterprising realtors, Berezov showed his client a house exceeding the budget they had agreed upon. Aside from the price, the house proved too extravagant for Levich's needs. A second home too small, a third too modern, a fourth in need of nagging repairs.

On the second day, the first house they toured again topped the budget. But the fourth place, on the district's Kfar Saba Street, met Levich's expectations. Berezov offered up a whitewashed, walled, two-story garden villa built in faux Moroccan style with a central courtyard, fountain, and rooftop area for entertaining—furnished.

"This will do," declared a pleased Levich.

Within three days, his offer was accepted.

A week after taking possession, and with Viktor at his elbow, Levich spread his wings. A cook-cum-housekeeper was hired, as was a gardener. Moving ahead, Levich offered his trough to a member of a cabinet sub-committee. Next, a Likud firebrand bellied up to Levich's banquet table and left with a hefty sum he promised to add to the party's coffers. Whether the money ended up where it was pledged was not Levich's concern. Two more members of the Knesset—noisy anti-government troublemakers with small armies of admirers—took his money and spread the word of his generosity. By then, Levich was ready to meet key players in Israel's organized crime world—the affronted Uri Koronsky among them.

# Chapter 103

Wolf caught the Empire Service's 1:10 p.m. train and arrived at Penn Station without mishap. Ninety minutes later, he was aboard the Acela Express, heading to Washington's Union Station. Wolf arrived in the capital, flagged a taxi, and rode in silence, his mind on Nash, Royce, and the man he had come to confront.

At his condo's doorstep, Wolf gave the placid Tunisian driver thirty dollars and hurried inside. He made a sweep of his place, found nothing amiss, and spent an hour on the computer, checking emails.

*Still no word about Colter's family.* Odd. The effort to flesh out Colter was beginning to look like a permanent dead end. Abandoning his search, he next scoured the net's White Pages for information on the State Department's Nells. Amazing what's out there, he thought, making notes. There were five

Nells listed, none named Robert. There was, however, a C. Nells on a fashionable Georgetown street Wolf recognized. He copied the address.

He slept four hours, rose before dawn, and slipped unseen into the lower-level garage. He drove away in his BMW, his goal: to confirm the Georgetown address as Nells's.

Leaving Alexandria, Wolf took the George Washington Memorial Parkway northwest along the dark Potomac, eventually passing an awakening Reagan National Airport. He crossed the Arlington Memorial Bridge, circled the Lincoln Memorial, and headed north past the familiar State Department complex. Wolf made good time in the nearly deserted streets. On P Street NW, he bypassed an idling delivery truck and turned right on Twenty-sixth Street NW where he parked mid-block.

*Piece of cake.*

Wolf killed his lights and engine, his BMW now one of twenty-some cars lining both sides of the street. The trip from his house to Georgetown's East Village district had taken just twenty minutes. But then, that was done in pre-dawn traffic. A daylight run would not be as easy. But a first try to fix the location was a precautionary reconnaissance.

The coveted neighborhood, less than ten miles from his Alexandria townhouse, might as well have been on another planet. Nells had done well for a career diplomat—his home a wide, two-story Federal-style brick house. Painted a tasteful cream, with a trio of tall windows and black shutters on both levels, it was trimmed with white stone details. Lining sidewalks on both sides of the street, mature trees added leafy charm. Wolf imagined the professional ranks on this street living in cloistered comfort.

He strolled to the end of the block, to his right, a tiny coffee shop. He ordered an espresso and pastry from the moon-faced Asian woman, bought a paper, and went back to his car, his eyes taking in every detail. A few lighted windows winked on in upper floors of homes in the pre-dawn darkness, the street's residents stirring.

Wolf sipped in silence, one eye on Nells's home in his rearview and side mirrors. A light went on upstairs behind gauzy curtains. Forty-five minutes later, Robert Nells, his signature bow tie and tweeds peeking from under a gray Burberry wool cashmere topcoat, came out the front door, newspaper and briefcase in one hand, ceramic travel mug in the other.

*Gotcha*, Wolf said to himself, smiling.

Nells got into a late-model, dark blue Lexus and pulled from the curb. After noting the time and jotting down the license plate for future reference, Wolf got out and did a recon on foot, this time studying Nells's house. A sturdy wooden ramp with a railing led to a side door. A taxi stopped in front of the Nells residence. A small brown woman got out and walked around the side of the house, using the ramp, a bulging bag in her right hand.

*Maid? Home health care worker? Interesting.*

Wolf sat for thirty minutes until a light shone in the far right, second-floor window. Two shadows, one taller than the other, shuffled past filmy curtains.

*So much for privacy*, he thought. *So, an invalid. A complication? Maybe.*

Having seen enough, Wolf drove away, retracing his route to Alexandria. Later that day, he called the Nells residence, got someone with a thick Hispanic accent.

"Good afternoon. Is this Maria?"

"No, señor, this is Consuela."

"Of course, Consuela. May I speak to Mr. Nells, please?"

"Señor Nells will not return until six this evening. Do you perhaps wish to leave message?"

Wolf declined. "No. Just an old school friend calling. Nothing important. I shall try again later. Gracias, Consuela."

Wolf drove back that evening to confirm his observations. A man of habits, Nells returned home between 6:00 and 6:05 as he would on the following two days. The maid, or personal care attendant, had been there both days, giving Wolf a fix on her routine as well. She always stayed fifteen minutes past Nells's arrival before a taxi fetched her at 6:20. Wolf had been there both times, timing the unsuspecting pair to make sure. That interval between Nells arriving home and the attendant leaving would be crucial. Give or take a minute or two, the behavior of both was predictable. Nells would likely be upstairs, the maid downstairs, anxious to leave, maybe watching for her ride. Playing the "old friend" Wolf would time it just right, arriving just as the taxi showed.

*This is too easy.*

# Chapter 104

*Georgetown, Washington, DC*

The next day, Nells showed at 6:05. Parking the Lexus three cars back from Wolf, he carried the same briefcase up the front steps and went inside. Fifteen minutes later, Wolf spotted the approaching taxi and got out of his car. Crossing the street, he timed his arrival perfectly—rapping the heavy brass knocker at the exact moment Consuelo opened the varnished black door. Startled by the stranger in front of her, she opened her mouth to say something but Wolf spoke first. Disarming her with a smile, he said, "Ah, Consuelo. Buenos noches."

Hesitating, she looked beyond him at the waiting taxi, unsure.

"We meet again," said a cordial Wolf. "Is Señor Nells home?"

As if cued, the taxi driver tapped his horn impatiently.

"Sí. Uh, yes, he is just home. And you?"

Wolf gently pushed past her, saying, "Colonel Forester. We're old friends. Classmates. He must be upstairs, right? It's okay."

The taxi's horn sounded. Behind his smile, Wolf blessed the driver.

Just inside the entry, Wolf gestured to the cab. "Don't let me hold you up, Consuelo. I'll wait downstairs for Robert... Señor Nells."

Winking at her, he said, "Go on. I'll be fine."

Shrugging, the perplexed brown woman left Wolf standing in the doorway and charged down the sidewalk to her ride. At the cab, she paused, looking back. Waving to her, Wolf shut the door and locked it in case she changed her mind.

In front of him, a curving staircase topped with mahogany and a wall-mounted chair lift track for an invalid. Voices murmured above.

Hearing footsteps crossing the second level, Wolf moved into a sitting room, where matching white silk love seats faced each other across a glass coffee table piled with oversized picture books. Two towering bookcases flanked a marble fireplace. Beyond the sitting room, a living room with a second fireplace. Filled with couches and wing-backed chairs, the room was four walls covered in oil paintings framed in gilded wood—dour New Englanders, small children on a seashore, packet ships, and garish floral arrangements side by side. Two mirrored end tables flanked the couch. Each table held an exquisite slender multi-colored glass lamp with delicate cobweb designs.

*Tiffany's handiwork. Probably the real thing*, mused Wolf.

Yet another room, a formal dining room, with polished dark wood table and eight chairs beneath a crystal chandelier, looked out at a formal garden at the rear of the house. Clipped hedges, the work of a gardener, surrounded wicker patio furniture on flagstones. Treading softly, Wolf wandered into a kitchen off the dining room. A single sweating Manhattan sat on a granite island in a sea of white oak cabinets. Nells had obviously made himself a drink before relieving the Hispanic helper. Footsteps, and then Nells was there in the kitchen door.

"What the hell...What are you doing here?"

Enjoying the surprise, Wolf said, "I'm pleased to see you again, too."

Stunned, Nells was at a loss for words.

"Consuelo and I were chatting just before her ride came. Nice lady."

Fumbling for words, an agitated Nells sputtered, "I could have you arrested for breaking and entering."

"Really? Seems to me I was invited in by your help."

"How dare you violate my household!"

"Can the dramatics, Robert. You don't mind me calling you Robert, do you?" Wolf moved, keeping the granite island between Nells and him. "And you've got a lot of nerve talking about violating a household."

"What do you want, Wolf?"

"Let's talk about violating a household. What do you call sending an assassin after someone? I'd call that downright inhospitable. I'd call that contracting for murder, wouldn't you?"

"I don't know what you're talking about."

Wolf slammed a fist on the granite. "Bullshit! You had two of your goons tag my car in a New York cemetery in order to track my friends and me. Then, you sent a hit man to kill us."

"I did no such thing."

"You are a piece of work, Robert."

"What do you want, Wolf?"

"I want you to call off your dogs, for starters."

Hearing a sound upstairs, Nells looked away. "My wife..."

"Wonder if she knows what you've been up to."

"She's not part of this. She's ill."

Wolf didn't soften. Ordering him into the living room, he said, "Sit down. We've got some things to talk about."

"And if I refuse?"

"You won't. You're not the type."

Nells reached for his drink. "Do you mind?"

"Not at all. You might need it."

Wolf followed Nells to the living room with the paintings. He stood apart, his eyes fixed on the sulking diplomat on the couch. Wolf picked up one of the beautiful lamps and held it aloft against the ceiling light.

Nells wavered. "Please don't handle them."

Wolf ignored him. "Tiffany pieces, aren't they? Turn of the century."

"1901, to be exact. There are only seven of these lamps known to exist."

"They ought to be in a museum."

"My wife is fond of beautiful things, Mr. Wolf."

Lamp in hand, Wolf said, "Does she know about your dark side?"

"I don't follow."

"Mark Twain said, 'Every man is like the moon. He has a dark side.'"

Nells hissed, "People in your profession would certainly know about man's dark side."

Waving the lamp, Wolf said, "I'm curious. What are these worth?"

"They're priceless," said Nells. "Gifts from my wife's parents."

Shifting gears, Wolf set down the lamp. "Why did you send this shooter after us? Was it your idea, or somebody higher in the food chain?"

Nells finished his drink without answering.

Wolf produced a cell phone, said, "All I have to do is call my friends waiting outside. They'd love to give you a taste of your own medicine."

Someone coughed upstairs. Wolf pointed to the ceiling with his cellphone. "Maybe they'd like to pay a visit to your wife."

Eyes blazing, Nells stared at Wolf. "You're not capable of doing something like that. I know that much."

"You're right," said Wolf. "That's not my thing. But my friends aren't bound by the same code. They like to hurt people, Robert. It's strange, but they seem to enjoy it."

"I don't believe you."

"Really? Did you know I've got an arrangement going with some people I met in Little Odessa? Brutal guys. Normally, I don't mix with this scum. But what do you know, it turns out they have a score to settle with you as well." Nells put down his glass, his eyes following Wolf. "Seems your department had something to do with missing money they say belongs to them."

Sensing he was making headway, Wolf continued. "They killed people in California to make their point. I know you heard about it. And I know you're aware of what happened in Brooklyn. Your guy didn't succeed in killing us."

"He's not my guy," said Nells. "I didn't send him after you. You've got to believe me. I had nothing to do with that."

"Ah, but you know who did send him. One call and these animals are going to come in here and go upstairs." Wolf raised the phone.

"Wait a minute! It wasn't my idea. I tried to talk to you. You wouldn't listen. At the airport—"

"What was that all about?"

His eyes pleading, Nells was visibly weakening. "I appealed to your patriotism. I wanted you to help us. You wouldn't listen."

Wolf towered over him, raising his voice. "Blame the victim, huh? You were trying to fuck me over, Robert. I take that personally."

"Not me! Not me!"

Waving the phone, Wolf shouted, "Who then? If not you, who?"

Head in hands, Nells said, "Someone else made the call."

"A name, Robert! Give me a name!"

"Preston Jacobs!"

"Is this guy at State?"

Nells shook his head. "No, he's with the Agency."

"CIA?"

A nod, a shaking of the head. A mumbled, "Yes."

"Why?"

Wringing his hands, Nells blurted, "You were going to blow the cover on the operation we had going in Ukraine."

"You mean that half-assed idea about funding a proxy war against pro-Russian militias in the eastern part of Ukraine?"

Another nodding, another mumbled, "Yes."

"For that you were willing to kill my friends and me?"

A resigned shrug.

"How high does this go?"

"Don't know. I only know what Jacobs told me. That's all I know, really."

Wolf nodded at the ceiling. "If you're lying to me, she won't stand a chance with those Russian scum."

"I give you my word."

Wolf laughed. "As if that's worth anything at this point."

"But it's the truth."

Wolf picked up the slender Tiffany lamp, drawing Nells's eyes.

Eyes wide, Nells held his breath. "No."

Wolf hurled the heirloom against the hearth. Sobbing, Nells fell to his knees at the foot of the couch, the carpet covered in thousands of tiny colored glass shards. Trembling, he shrieked, "Do you know what you've done?"

Leaning close to Nells's ear, Wolf bellowed, "That's your wife if what you've told me turns out not to be true."

He lifted the second lamp from the other end table, turned it in his hands. "Shame to lose this one as well."

Panic in his voice, Nells begged, "Please, no. It can't be replaced. I've told you what I know."

"It's just a material thing, Robert."

Nells raised himself on one knee, arm outstretched. "Don't."

"You'd be next once the Russians were through with her."

Nells folded, sobbing, "I won't...please...let me have it. Please."

Wolf returned the decorative lamp to its place. "It's up to you, Robert."

Then Wolf was gone.

# Chapter 105

Levich set a table for smugglers, arms dealers, counterfeiters, pimps, and drug dealers. They flocked to his house along with their women, tawdry tarts in revealing dress. Making a dramatic entrance after lesser peers had gathered, Uri Koronsky worked the room, two muscled pets in tow. He and Levich, both alpha males, faced off using rapier wits as weapons.

Koronsky, built like a wrestler whose tanned scarred face had kissed the canvas once too often, wore the requisite open-collared shirt, revealing a hairy chest draped in a gold chain from which dangled a mezuzah. Tel Aviv's reigning crime prince made an elaborate speech welcoming Levich. With a stunning blonde on his arm, Koronsky toasted the new arrival and future competitor.

"Though he comes to us late in life, the Brotherhood greets Boris Levich and wishes him well. We who prosper in Israel extend a hand. Watch and learn, my American friend." Though he meant not one word of it, the raucous crowd cheered both men.

Beaming, Levich raised a glass in Koronsky's direction. "Ah, yes. My heart is warmed by the welcome extended to me, brothers. May all prosper."

Interrupting each other with repeated toasts of "L'Chaim, L'Chaim," hangers-on lower in the pecking order curried favor with the big dogs in the room while cleaning Levich's platters. Warned that undercover police had arrived to monitor the gathering, Koronsky slipped out the rear garden gate, his brief attendance purely for show. Nothing had been settled between Levich and him. Still, Viktor was impressed a major player like Koronsky had shown, Levich less so.

"May the police lose their way when they search for your door," chimed in a voice from the back of the crowded room. Laughter swept the room.

"L'Chaim," rang out again. After four hours of eating, drinking, toasting, and verbal jousting, the group thinned, and then dwindled to a handful that Viktor eventually shooed out the door. Even the cops had grown bored, save for two patrol cars with uniformed officers left behind.

While Viktor supervised the cook and her helpers cleaning and restoring order to the mansion, Levich took to the roof garden with a chilled bottle of Stolichnaya vodka. The night air revived him. Reflecting off the underside of low-hanging clouds, Tel Aviv's skyline glowed in the distance. Levich peered over the low parapet to the street below. The police had gone. Levich headed for an open-sided tent shelter erected in the middle of the roof and settled against a small mountain of silk pillows piled on a couch. He poured a tumbler of Stoli and toasted himself.

"L'Chaim."

*So that was Uri Koronsky, the big man, eh? The proverbial big fish among a school of little ones. Tiny fish kissing the big fish's behind. A Sabra without the blood of the Gulag in his veins. Dangerous and arrogant, a bad combination. He bears watching.*

Footsteps. Viktor wandered up the stairs to the roof, a bottle in his hand. The old soldier was a marvel in how much liquor he could hold. He stood in the shadows, the bottle to his lips.

"Good party," he said between swallows. "A good beginning, Boss."

He had begun calling Levich that shortly after being hired. Verlov had done that, Ivanov as well. Even Lydia in a lifetime ago. Now Viktor.

*Yes, I am the boss*, thought Levich, smiling. *I've earned the title. Maybe I have come to the table late in the game as Koronsky says. But I have faced more formidable odds and triumphed. I will brush aside this irritating upstart. The town is not big enough to hold us both. It will take time. He will never see it coming.*

"How did Koronsky appear to you, Viktor? Was he genuine?"

"You cannot trust the man, Boss. He would as soon cut your throat as look at you." Sinking at a corner of the couch, the Spetsnaz veteran took a long pull on his bottle and wiped his mouth with the back of his hand.

"You surprise me, Viktor. I thought you an admirer of the man."

A snort. "Koronsky? No! I wanted you to know him face to face. When you held off meeting him I confess I thought it foolish. But it seems you have the upper hand. Yes, it goes to you—this first round in a long bout."

Nodding, Levich said, "I like this boxing image."

"Have you ever entered the ring, Boss? Ever faced another man with no place to go? A crowd chanting for blood, yours or his? I have done this."

Pouring another shot, Levich said, "I have never experienced this. Though I witnessed such sights in the Gulag. The guards loved to see us fight among ourselves. It amused them. They put men up to it and waged bets."

"Exactly. That would be Koronsky's way. Mark my words, Boss. He will throw punches at you from behind another man. He's good at it."

"You give me good advice, Viktor."

An alcoholic growl agreeing from the shadows. "Mark my...words."

Levich leaned forward, his glass full, held high in a toast. Viktor tapped the neck of his half-filled bottle against the shot glass.

"L'Chaim," they said in unison.

# Chapter 106

*Alexandria, Virginia*

Wolf slept with a Beretta under his pillow. He would have preferred a Sig-Sauer or Glock, but his source had been cleaned out two days before and had offered only the Beretta for sale. It would have to do.

The Sunday after sweating Nells for information, Wolf woke to Gunny Lindgren's ragged voice in his ear. He plucked the cellphone from a nightstand, then tried to slow Lindgren's machine-gun delivery. "At ease, Gunny. You're running over your own words. Slow down. Try again."

"Have you seen the Sunday *New York Times?*"

"I don't subscribe but I can guess what you're calling about."

"Your boy's story is on the cover," roared Lindgren.

Still groggy, Wolf sat up. "This was the weekend it was scheduled. Have you read it?"

"Just finished it. Big play. The yogurt is gonna hit the fan before this is over. Man, you have to read it, Wolfman. All of Washington is gonna scream bloody murder about this."

"Good. That's what Colter wanted."

"Well, bless his dearly departed soul. He got his wish."

Wolf put his feet on the floor. "Thanks for the wake-up, Gunny."

"I'm going to make some calls," crowed Lindgren. "You can believe the White House folks are going to need a quick change of underwear before this is done. Man, I'd love to be a fly on the wall in the Situation Room."

"I'm up. Gonna get dressed and get to the nearest drugstore for a copy."

"Okay, keep me posted on what happens next. You're full of surprises."

Lindgren rang off. Wolf showered, shaved and dressed. He drove to the nearest mini-mall and bought two copies of the

Sunday *Times*. Nash was still at the cabin and would want one. "I'll call him," he said aloud. Back in ten minutes, Wolf made tea and breakfast, read part of the piece while he ate, then sat on the couch, newsprint scattered across the carpet. The magazine cover was a gripping graphic: one-hundred dollars bills stacked in a suitcase floating in a sea of blood, silhouettes of the Kremlin and the U.S. Capitol dome in the background. Nash's original draft, rewritten by a two-person team, pulled no punches.

*No way to hide from these revelations*, thought Wolf. *Heads will roll.*

He reread the story, tried calling Nash. No answer. Remembering the poor cell reception, he gave up. He called Lindgren back and compared notes.

"This doesn't look good for the White House, Wolfman. And if I were those douchebags at State I'd be polishing up my resumé about now."

"I think the story has legs, Gunny."

"Damn right. This is gonna shake up the Agency as well. I've got my ear to the rail but so far, haven't heard a thing."

"Still think I should find that hole for myself?"

"You won't be able to find one deep enough. But it's not a bad idea. The Russkis are not known to convene congressional oversight committees to investigate screw-ups like this. They are known to just start shooting. Yeah, I'd go to ground if I was you."

"That's what you said before. I took that advice and hightailed it to San Diego. Look what happened to me out there."

"You're a big boy, sir. You can handle it."

"I've got to call Sam McFadden. Talk to you later, Gunny."

Wolf waited two hours and finally put in a call to San Diego.

"Have you seen the Sunday *Times*, Sam?"

A prolonged sigh. "Yeah. I have to hand it to you, Wolfman. You and Nash actually pulled this off. I had my doubts."

"I know. I forgive you, my son."

"Wish Kurskov had lived to see this."

"Bummer," said Wolf. "There's some comfort knowing a few of the guys who had a hand in his murder ended up dead. Doesn't make it any easier, I know, but what can I say?"

"What's next?"

Wolf got off the sofa and walked laps around his living room. "I have no idea. Nash is out of range right now. I might drive up to the cabin to check on him. He may not have gotten the byline but at least he got the story."

"He's put the spotlight back where it belongs," said McFadden.

"For the time being. You know our fellow citizens. They have a short attention span."

"So does Congress," said McFadden. "At least they have the power to subpoena people and keep this issue active with hearings."

"Won't help the next mid-terms," said McFadden. "Stand by for damage control from the White House. I can't believe they didn't have a hand in it."

"Affirmative. I'm gonna try Nash again. Say hi to Reggie."

"Roger that. Watch your six, Wolfman."

"Always, Sam."

# Chapter 107

Nash still wasn't answering. Grabbing a beer and sandwich, Wolf sat glued to the television, watching the Sunday morning talk shows. Toggling back and forth between NBC's *Meet the Press*, CBS's *Face the Nation* and

ABC's *This Week*, he listened to the usual pompous blather. Apoplectic congressmen, apologetic presidential surrogates, and turgid academics praised and dissected the *Times* story in turn. Fox News and CNN were doing their best to stoke the fires. All the shows had raided the capital's retired military aviary for hawks and doves alike. Lindgren called again, cackling with glee about some Agency colleague he was sure was due for sacking as a result of the news.

"You sound much too vindictive, Gunny. Especially for someone who claims he's no longer in the game."

"It's a case of chickens coming home to roost."

"Care to elaborate?"

"My smiling lips are sealed. But let's just say justice is being done."

"Call me when you've calmed down," said Wolf. They both laughed.

Hanging up, Wolf went online. The BBC was reporting Russian television condemning the West and hinting of darker CIA plots yet to come. In Ukraine, some of those named in the *Times* reporting went into hiding. Devoting a day of live programming, Parliament's official channel, Rada TV, showed politicians of all stripes trading insults with one another. One by one, florid-faced speakers rose to denounce Russian stations for saturating the country with distorted news reports. He was right. The story had legs.

That evening, the president interrupted a family vacation and fundraising tour in Savannah drawing rooms to make a brief appearance at a hastily called press conference at Ft. Stewart. Professing outrage at the alleged plot to use Russian *Mafiya* money in an ill-advised effort to combat pro-Russian forces in eastern Ukraine, he promised a full inquiry. Congress, he pledged, would be asked to work hand-in-hand in a bi-partisan investigation. All would come to light, he promised. Those responsible would be called to account for their actions. Delivered with his best stern expression in place, the president's remarks were brief. The press rose as one to hurl questions but he ignored them. Beating a hasty retreat, he left behind a hapless assistant press secretary as sacrificial lamb. Turning on the decoy, the press savaged him.

# Chapter 108

Nash finally called.

"I've been trying to get hold of you," scolded Wolf. "You must have been holed up at the cabin all this time."

"Yeah. Sorry. Bad reception. I'm good now."

Wolf heard traffic in the background. "Where are you, Rome?"

"Utica," said Nash. "On my way down to the city to take care of business."

"The loft?" *Had Nash taken the money after all?*

"Correct. I took the money."

"Good choice. What's next?"

"I decided not to rebuild. I'm selling. I've got a buyer."

Wolf sat down. "A buyer? That was quick."

"Yeah. It's ironic. The CEO of a small chain of coffee shops likes the spot. He's in town for meetings and asked to stop by."

Wolf laughed. "Great. Just what the planet needs, another coffee shop."

"Well, the lot's not big enough for a Walmart. Anyway, I'm meeting the buyer and his property acquisitions agent this afternoon. We'll sign the papers after they take a last look."

"And then?"

"Back to Santa Barbara."

"Wise man. You been following the uproar over the story?"

"From a distance. I went in to Florence to pick up a copy of the Sunday *Times*. Read the piece two or three times. Woulda changed a few things, but overall I was pleased with it. It's bittersweet, of course."

"Yeah, but you nailed them all, Nash. There's still a lot of fallout. And it ain't over yet. There's a long line of fat ladies waiting to sing."

Wolf heard Nash laugh. *A good sign*, he thought. *It had been a while.*

"I'll call you when I'm done with the paperwork. You can come back up here. I'd consider it an honor to help you put Royce where he belongs."

"Roger that. Thanks for calling, Nash. I'm heading out for a three-mile run to work off some stress."

"Did you get to make your house call?"

Picturing Nells on his knees, surrounded by colored glass shards, Wolf said, "I did."

"Work out the way you wanted?"

"Even better than I imagined. I'll tell you about it when I see you."

They finished the call. Wolf changed into sweats and running shoes. He went out the front door. A government-issue sedan and two Hoover suits were waiting for him at the curb.

# Chapter 109

*Neve Tzedek District, Tel Aviv*

Levich was on his roof when word came of Uri Koronsky's death.

Viktor brought the news along with a chilled unopened bottle of Gamia Brut and two long-stemmed flutes. He popped the cork and poured.

"From the Golan Heights Winery, Boss. Appropriate, no?"

Levich grinned, his eyes squinting against the dying sun. "I commend your taste in champagne and symbolism, Viktor."

"I am, as you say, Boss, 'a diamond in the rough, eh?'"

"Worth your weight in gold, old soldier." Lifting his glass, Levich proposed a toast to his fallen competitor. "To Uri Koronsky. May he find no rest in Sheol."

"L'Chaim!"

Levich moved to the shadows under the awning. "Now we move quickly before the vacuum fills. How many of Uri's men can be brought under my wing?"

Viktor downed his glass and poured another. "All of them save Teddy Nirov and his brother Ari. They fancy themselves leaders but they are spineless. They should be dealt with before they regain their senses."

"See to it, Viktor."

"I already have. They are both lying in a drainage ditch on a farm south of here. In the morning they will be found. The police will be called, of course."

"Of course," marveled Levich. "You're becoming indispensible, Viktor."

"That is my role, Boss. You give the orders, I make them good."

Arching an eyebrow, Levich said, "True. Except I don't remember ordering the death of the Nirov brothers."

Polishing off his drink, Viktor poured another. "Of course not. But you were about to, yes? This saves me the trouble to arrange it and it saves you the trouble of—"

"Ordering it done," interrupted Levich. "You are a dangerous man, Viktor."

"Only to myself and the girls down at Gina's club."

"Go, Viktor. Go enjoy yourself. You have earned it."

The Spetsnaz veteran got to his feet, his glass raised. "To the Boss!"

"And to you, Viktor Alexander Askov."

"L'Chaim!"

# Chapter 110

On the front steps of an Alexandria, Virginia condo fifty-eight hundred miles away, Wolf stared at the two dark-suited strangers coming up his walk. White, clean-shaven with short hair and serious expressions, the pair might as well have held signs reading "FBI." Wolf met them halfway. His visitors reached inside their jackets for the badge ritual. He beat them to it.

"You guys proselytizing?"

They paused, hands in their inside pockets. The taller of the two said, "I beg your pardon."

"I said, 'Are you proselytizing?' Our association frowns on soliciting. Aren't you Mormons?"

The badges came out. "No sir, we're with the FBI. Agents Callahan and Drummond."

Wolf grinned. "I'm just messing with you. What can I do for you? I was about to go for my afternoon run. Care to join me?"

Callahan, the tall one, smiled. "Another time. We'd like to follow up with you about that shoot-out and arson in Brooklyn."

"I told your other agents all I knew during the interview. I lost a friend up there, you know."

"Yes, we know. His autopsy report confirms that he died from smoke inhalation and complications from three bullet wounds."

"Royce was tough, gentlemen."

"The other four, all of whom were ID'd, were naturalized citizens living in Brighton Beach."

"I know that. I told your guys we were being targeted by the Russian mob from Little Odessa. It should all be in the report."

"It was. But we're here about another matter."

"Is this going to take long? I'd really hate to miss my run."

Drummond, the shorter, athletic-looking one, moved closer. "Would you prefer to accompany us to the field office?"

Wolf faced him. "What is this? Good cop, bad cop? You guys want to talk, fine. Let's talk right here. But make it quick. And lighten up, Agent."

Smiling, Callahan shrugged. "Sure. We can talk here. We're looking into an odd coincidence that happened several days after the fire and shootings."

Wolf was silent, his expression neutral. The tag team kept at it.

"What can you tell us about a body found across the street only three days after the loft battle?" said Callahan.

"You mean the homeless guy they found?"

Drummond again. "Who said it was a homeless guy?"

Staying cool, Wolf rubbed his jaw. "I believe it was Detective Willis. Yes, I remember now. Willis was with the Seventy-third Precinct. That's the local cop shop where the loft was located."

Callahan said, "Remarkable memory, Mr. Wolf."

"Training. I was in the Navy Special Ops for twenty years. We're taught to be observant. It was a memorable event, gentlemen. I mean, coming on the heels of the arson and my friend's death."

"Nothing else you remember about this body being found?"

"What can I say? I didn't visit the scene. Detective Willis asked if we had seen anything out of the ordinary in the building across the street. I said none of us had noticed any activity prior to our fire."

"The dead man was ex-army. Did the detective mention that?"

"He did not. Lot of homeless veterans in our cities. It's a shame."

"This guy was apparently not homeless," volunteered Drummond.

Locking eyes with the agent, Wolf said nothing.

"We're still looking into the circumstances of the victim's cause of death. By the way, will you be staying in the city?" said Callahan.

"Hard to say. I do a little contracting here and there. If it's important you can always get hold of me through my lawyer."

Drummond sniffed. "We know where to find you."

Wolf couldn't help himself. "You know, Agent Drummond, you seem to be trying hard not to be a likeable guy. And you're succeeding. For a public servant, and an FBI agent at that, you're kind of an asshole. I thought you guys had better manners."

Callahan, the peacekeeper, stepped in. "Okay, I think we're done here. Thanks for your time, Mr. Wolf. We'll be in touch."

Wolf bent down, pretending to tighten his laces. "Anytime, Agent Callahan. Have a nice day. Next time bring a different partner."

With the agents back in their car, Wolf trotted to the street and broke into a steady pace, taking out his anger on the pavement.

# Chapter 111

Nash's potential buyer and another man were waiting when the writer arrived at the site of his abandoned loft. The two were craning their necks and pointing at the charred upper levels. Pulling to the curb behind a town car, Nash hurried to the sidewalk. Apologetic, he held out his hand.

"Mr. Rothstein, sorry to keep you waiting. Traffic was a bitch."

The building's purchaser shook hands. "Ah, Mr. Nash, Stewart Rothstein. We finally meet." Bundled in a silk scarf and black lamb's wool coat, the gray-haired Rothstein smiled at Nash. Gesturing to his companion, who stood apart in a dark trench coat, he said, "Phil Sergon, my company's accountant. The man who watches the money. He has the final say when it comes to buying potential sites."

Turning to his balding finance advisor, Rothstein waved. "This is Mr. Nash, Phil. Let's take a final look before we sign the papers, okay?"

Nash warned, "There are some unsafe spots, Mr. Rothstein."

Gripping Nash's arm, Rothstein winked, said, "Not to worry. I've seen worse. In a year, you won't recognize the place." Glancing upwards, he said, "Before you got here Phil and I were discussing my options."

"Which are...?"

"It might have to come down. All of it, Mr. Nash."

"I suppose."

Rubbing his hands in anticipation, Rothstein said, "The property is prime, of course. But all this brick and stone will have to go. I mean, look at the guts of the building."

Ushering Nash to the door, he said, "Just from a cursory glance I'm afraid I can't salvage any of it. I mean, the walls, the floors, the beams. All weakened. Wouldn't you agree?"

"You're right. The building's integrity has been compromised."

They went through the door, the accountant close behind them.

Sniffing the air, Rothstein wrinkled his nose. "Must have been quite the thing to experience."

"It was intense," agreed Nash.

"Is the elevator machinery a total loss? Might we take a look?"

Nash followed Rothstein to the lift's crumpled wire cage. "You can see the cables were severed by the explosion when—"

Feeling the hard steel barrel at the base of his skull, Nash froze.

"Do you know who I am?" Rothstein, his face twisted in a sneer, backed from the lip of the shaft where his companion had pinned Nash with a pistol against his neck.

Swallowing hard, Nash felt sweat trickling down his back, soaking his shirt. Shaking, he managed a weak, "No."

"I am the devil," said Rothstein, "here to see you sent to hell."

About to speak, Nash felt his head explode.

# Chapter 112

"Sam, it's me."

McFadden blew a kiss to Reggie and walked to the far side of the patio, out of earshot. "You're down, Wolfman. I can tell."

"It's Nash. He's dead. Cops called ten minutes ago."

A long pause.

"You still there, Sam?"

"Yeah. Please tell me its not one of our own involved."

"No. The lead detective thinks it was a Russian mob hit. Payback."

"I'm sorry to hear about Nash. He was a terrific journalist, an honest reporter. A risk-taker."

"That he was, Sam. I hate to call you with such terrible news."

McFadden said, "Retaliation for those four byki in the shootout?"

"Likely. To lose four of their soldiers in one fight was humiliating. My gut tells me Boris Levich put out the hit."

Phone to his ear, McFadden retraced his path along the patio. "The last time we talked you said the feds told you he's in Israel. Their government will never give him up. He's untouchable."

A long pause. "Nobody's untouchable, Sam. Even in Israel."

Switching topics, Wolf said, "Got the final results from the autopsy. Off the record, the doc says he thinks Royce took out all the bad guys before he died, even though it was a toss-up between smoke inhalation and fatal wounds. Either one would have killed him. But I know he didn't miss. He never missed. Shoulda been me, Sam."

"That's not what Royce would say if he were still here."

"I know. Seems like everyone I'm close to ends up dead."

"It's in the job description, Wolfman. I, for one, am glad you're still alive and kicking ass. Reggie would say the same."

"I feel bad about getting you and Reggie involved, Sam. There's no way to know what the mob will do...now, or in the future."

"We both know life's uncertain. But I don't want you looking back. It's counter-productive. We'll take it one day at a time, agreed?"

"Roger that. You and Reggie are too good to me, Sam."

McFadden circled the pool. "Don't wait too long before you come see us again. Welcome mat's always out for you."

"Good to know. I've got all kinds of details to pull together out here before I can seriously think about moving on."

"What about Nash? He has no family, right?"

"On his side, no. But his wife's family still lives in Pennsylvania. I've been in touch. They said they'd have the funeral. His wife is buried in the family plot. That's probably where he belongs. Don't know what will happen to the Brooklyn loft or the Santa Barbara condo and the contents."

"And Royce?"

"I'm taking his ashes up to Florence, New York. His ex-wife is okay with it. He wanted to be buried in the forest near the cabin. I have the spot picked out."

"I can hop a plane if you need me. Say the word."

"Stay with Reggie, Sam. I'll call you when this stage of the game is done. After that…"

"Understood, sailor. Watch your six."

"Always, Sam."

# Chapter 113

"Tell me again why I am visiting this dig?"

Levich and Viktor sat in the middle seat of a white van, its tinted windows keeping out the sun's glare, the air conditioning washing cool air over them. They had left the pavement of Highway 4, the old Haifa–Tel Aviv road, for a rough gravel track with little traffic. Somewhere farther west was Ashkelon and the sea. Leading deeper into scarred scrubland, the rutted route was testing Levich's patience.

Viktor said, "We visit because you support this small archeological project. The director's brother is a high-ranking national police official. Your goodwill gesture will eventually pay dividends. For you it is five thousand dollars, a pittance. Without your support and the volunteers who do the work, this excavation would not happen. For the group making this dig, your money is the difference between continuing to search for ancient clues or folding up their tents and returning empty-handed."

Despite the air conditioning, Levich mopped his brow. "So now you have turned me into a patron of archeologists? Besides this gratitude what else do we gain?"

"Not only for the cultural heritage, Boss." Lowering his voice, Viktor said, "This dig is the perfect cover for moving the product. Who would suspect such a use of a heritage site? Our Bedouin contacts bring in the merchandise under cover of darkness. When we have stored enough, we ship it to Tel Aviv. Foolproof, Boss."

"And for this I am a respected man, eh?"

"And a rich one. And getting richer, Boss."

"I don't like being this far out of the city. I don't want to come this far again, Viktor. You can handle this from now on."

"No problem. We should be there soon. Not far." Leaning over the front seat, Viktor tapped the driver's shoulder, asking about the distance to the dig site. Turning to Levich, he said, "Ten minutes and we are there."

Fanning himself with a straw hat, Levich said, "Keep in mind I'm not in the mood to hear a lecture from some scholar on pottery fragments no bigger than a fingernail."

"You won't suffer a word, Boss. The scholars are gone. In their absence we have Saul, ex-paratrooper from the IDF. He mans the site for us. You'll see how it is possible to hide so much product with so little effort in the desert."

The van rattled on, earning the driver a frown and warning from Levich about his recklessness. Trailing a rising tail of dust, the van slowed.

"We're close," said Viktor.

Negotiating the last hundred yards in low gear, the van's driver crept up a steep, rock-strewn slope and came to a stop just short of two sprawling tents overlooking a parched, twisting wadi. The camp was deserted. Clouds of dust swirled around the van, eventually dying to reveal wheelbarrows, rows of shovels, and large wooden-framed screening tables set on sawhorses.

The smaller of the two tents shaded a large plank filled with potsherds and plastic bags full of what appeared to be small white stones. Empty cots with sleeping bags lined one side of the shelter. In the middle sat a mess table. A sweating canvas water bag hung from a tripod.

Their driver got out and called to a figure leaning over a table in the second, larger tent. The man looked up, acknowledging the visitors with a wave. Thin, deeply tanned, and bearded, he spoke to the driver, then ambled to the van. Viktor got out, shielding his eyes from the afternoon sun.

Levich did not move, preferring instead to stay in the van. "This is our welcoming committee?" he said.

The bearded man in khakis shook hands with Viktor and then hailed Levich. "Ah, Boris Levich, welcome. I'm Saul. So, you come to pay us a visit, eh? Pity the academics are not here to welcome their financial angel. But that would have been inconvenient, eh? Let me show you where your money is going. We have a surprise for you."

Urged by Viktor, a reluctant Levich climbed from the van. Shaking hands with the paratrooper, he donned the straw hat and said, "Where is the security I'm paying for?"

"My Bedouins, you mean? They're bringing in a shipment tonight."

"And the police?"

"They'll stay away as long as they are paid."

"More of my money, eh, Viktor?"

"Money well spent, Boss."

Saul waved Levich forward. "Come, I show you the surprise we have prepared for you."

With Viktor and their driver behind him, Levich followed Saul through a narrow cleft in ochre-colored rocks. Halting at a dark, nearly perfect rectangular opening chiseled from the rocky soil, the little column crowded next to a heavy stone slab leaning against a rock wall above the opening.

"What do you think?" said Saul. "My crew just finished excavating this space today. It is perfect for our purposes. I think you will find that it suits you."

"I suppose it is quite useable," said Levich, "for our purposes."

"We can store one hundred kilos in here with ease. By tomorrow night this will be completely filled."

Levich said, "Can you guarantee that the volunteers who work on this dig will not stumble on your handiwork?"

"This vault is a recent creation. They don't know it exists."

"Excellent," said Levich, peering in the cavity. "Is this the surprise you spoke of?"

Hit from behind, Levich lost his footing and tumbled into the deep pit.

Stunned, he groped the ground under him, his entire body aching from the impact. Rising to his knees, he steadied himself against the wall.

"What...happened?"

Eight feet above him, Viktor's face floated into focus. "You fell."

"I don't remember," mumbled Levich. He stood, raising both arms. "Don't just stand there, Viktor. Fetch a ladder. Help me up."

"I can't do that."

"What? Are you crazy? Enough of this nonsense. Help me."

The paratrooper joined Viktor at the chiseled rim. "No one can help you, Boris Levich. This is the end for you."

Color drained from Levich's face. Staring up at a gloating Viktor on the edge of the pit, he understood. "If it's money you want, I can arrange that. But first you must draw me up from this hole."

"That we cannot do."

Levich bargained. "I have money, Viktor. A lot of money."

A chilling reply. "I know. I've watched you for months. I know your account passwords, your secret codes. I know how to access your accounts. You thought I was some drunken, simple ex-soldier you could use and toss away some day, eh? I was who you wanted me to be."

"But why, Viktor, old comrade? You don't have to do this. Think clearly."

Tossing pebbles at Levich's feet, Viktor said, "Oh, but I am thinking clearly. I do have to do this. How else am I to return the money you took from the Brotherhood?"

"Is that what this is about, the money?" Levich leaned against the stone walls towering above him. "We don't have to return it, Viktor. We can share it. On my word. That would be some five million for you alone. Give me your hand, old friend."

"Take a long look at the light, Boris Levich. Fix your eyes on what little sky you can see. This is to be your tomb."

Signaling to the van's driver and Saul, Viktor ordered the two to help put their shoulders to the leaning slab. A waterfall of loose stone fell into the pit.

"Then shoot me! Be merciful! Kill me!" screamed Levich.

"NO!" yelled Viktor. "Suffer in the dark."

Spewing curses, Levich leaped at the corners and fell back. He clawed at the walls of his grave. The big stone above him moved, showering him with dirt and rock. Straining with great effort, Viktor and the other two stood the huge slab on edge, then leaped back, letting it drop into place, sealing Levich in his tomb. Using shovels and picks, they tossed rubble over the hewn block, obscuring it. After thirty minutes, the ground looked like the debris field of a hundred other digs.

Muffled screams sounded for a few minutes, ceased, then started again.

The intermittent wailing lasted for hours but there was no one to hear it.

Eventually, there was only silence.

# Chapter 114

Nash's story did indeed, as Wolf predicted, have legs. Certain Nells's role in the Ukraine debacle was given a pass, Wolf made an anonymous phone call to a congressional aide serving with a House subcommittee investigating the plan's origins. His second clandestine call went to both counsels serving their respective partisan masters on the Senate Judiciary Committee. The Beltway buzzed with gossip. Subpoenas were threatened and then issued when lawyers for potential witnesses

stonewalled. Capitalizing on the issue, House and Senate members paraded in high dudgeon for the evening news. Ghost-written opinion pieces glutted the *Times* and *Washington Post* op-ed pages. Carnivorous cable talk show hosts, fed a diet of leaked CIA briefings given Congress, ate guests alive. Disgusted with the usual screaming matches between talking heads, Wolf turned off the TV and called McFadden.

"It's a circus, Sam. Every day we get something new to digest."

"It's not just the media's fault," said McFadden. "You had a hand in it."

"I feel like Doctor Frankenstein's assistant."

McFadden said, "I'm curious. The White House trotted out the vice president as apologist-in-residence. How'd he get tagged?"

Wolf was unsympathetic. "I have it on good authority that his national security advisor played godfather to the whole hair-brained scheme."

"Any proof?"

"Some of Nash's notes that didn't make the final cut."

"Maybe you should feed some of that to your media contacts."

Groaning, Wolf said, "Nash was it."

"Sorry, Wolfman, that was a cheap shot."

"Nah, you're right. I can't manage this thing. It has a life of its own. I should let it go."

"The cops here think the case is wrapped up."

Wolf dared a question. "Did they ever track down the killers who took out Shurkov?"

"They're saying it was kept in the family. Russian mobsters whacking one another." McFadden paused. "That should ease your mind, Wolfman."

"Don't know why that would."

"I'm just saying..." McFadden added, "You had me worried the last time we talked."

"Meaning?"

"Meaning we talked about Boris Levich fleeing to Israel. I said he was untouchable and you said, 'Nobody's untouchable. Even in Israel.'"

"I do remember saying something like that."

"Don't go to Israel, Wolfman."

"I have no plans to do that."

"Good. I'll hold you to that."

"I'm not promising that I won't make a few phone calls."

"You're incorrigible."

"Funny you should say that, Sam. That was Colter's line."

"He was right. So...no Israel?"

"Phone calls, yes. Israel, no."

# Chapter 115

*Epilogue*

Robert Nells did not survive the notoriety of the Ukraine plot. He and his supervisor, along with their CIA contact, were found guilty of violating numerous federal statutes, perjury, and lying to Congress under oath. Turning on each other in court, their defense crumbled and they were sentenced to three, five, and eighteen months respectively.

In Nells's case, the price of his legal defense cost him reputation, career, family, and future. Both the home on Twenty-sixth Street NW and its contents were sold to pay his mounting legal bills. The elegant Federal-style home sat vacant for 120 days, finally selling for $1.5 million—a "steal" according to the realtor. Among the heirlooms auctioned in an estate sale was the surviving Louis Tiffany Cobweb lamp. It fetched seven figures, money Nells never saw. He is housed at the federal correctional facility in Morgantown, West Virginia. His invalid wife is in an assisted living manor in Prince Georges County, Maryland. Lawyers gobbled most of the proceeds; the assisted living facility took what was left.

Agreeing to turn state's evidence in return for a lighter sentence, the vice-president's national security advisor served twenty months at Pensacola's federal security camp. The vice-president steadfastly denied any knowledge of his senior aide's role in the Ukraine proxy war fiasco. A presidential pardon is rumored to be in the works.

New Amsterdam Global Bank and Trust, another casualty, was locked down by regulators and its assets seized. Bank officers not quick enough to flee were fed to the courts piecemeal.

The family of Sean Nash's wife buried him next to their daughter. Using proceeds from the insurance settlement on the Brooklyn property and the sale of the Santa Barbara condo, they established a journalism scholarship named for Sean and Danae Nash.

McFadden's business prospered. With personal security a growth industry, it turned a profit for the third consecutive year. McFadden and Reggie recently hosted a party for the San Diego Police officers who protected them during the search for Kurskov's killers.

True to his promise, Wolf buried Royce's ashes in a quiet glade deep in the forest behind the cabin. The Ranger's former wife, who lives in Boston, sold the cabin and four acres surrounding it, then deeded the remaining land to the state of New York.

Wolf made his calls to Israel. A friend, who served with Shin Bet, reported Boris Levich's disappearance. A former Spetsnaz soldier and cashiered IDF paratrooper had run the missing Brighton Beach godfather's crew in his absence. Both were gunned down in a daylight gun battle with a rival gang outside a Tel Aviv club.

Six months later, volunteer archeologists unearthed human remains during a dig south of Tel Aviv. News reports said the dig team's initial excitement about finding what they supposed an ancient tomb turned to horror once it was determined the remains were those of a male victim who had apparently been buried alive. A tailor's embroidered label and custom-made shoes confirmed the bones were those of Boris Levich.

Thirteen months to the day after Wolf first returned from Russia, he received a plain brown envelope containing a glossy five-by-seven snapshot. The photograph was a close-up of a familiar marble surface—the north wall of the CIA's lobby in the agency's original headquarters building. Centered in the picture was a black five-pointed star newly carved one half-inch deep in the polished stone. Turning the photo in his hands, Wolf read the message scrawled on the back.

*This is Colter's star. You deserved to know. With all my love, Yana.*

www.ingramcontent.com/pod-product-compliance
Lightning Source LLC
Chambersburg PA
CBHW060149260626
47160CB00001B/193